INFINITY'S END

Edited by
Jonathan Strahan

INFINITY'S END

EDITED BY **JONATHAN STRAHAN**

Including stories by
JUSTINA ROBSON
ALASTAIR REYNOLDS
PETER WATTS
STEPHEN BAXTER
KRISTINE KATHRYN RUSCH
KELLY ROBSON
NAOMI KRITZER
PAUL MCAULEY
SEANAN MCGUIRE
LINDA NAGATA
HANNU RAJANIEMI
FRAN WILDE
LAVIE TIDHAR
NICK WOLVEN

SOLARIS

First published 2018 by Solaris
an imprint of Rebellion Publishing Ltd,
Riverside House, Osney Mead,
Oxford, OX2 0ES, UK

www.solarisbooks.com

ISBN 978 1 78108 575 2

Cover by Adam Tredowski

10 9 8 7 6 5 4 3 2 1

A CIP catalogue record for this book is available from the
British Library.

Designed & typeset by Rebellion Publishing

Printed in Denmark

Here, at the end of it all, my thanks once again to
Jon, David, Ben, Christian, Adam,
and everyone who has made this possible.

ACKNOWLEDGEMENTS

THE INFINITY PROJECT and *Infinity's End* only exist because of the faith shown in them by editor-extraordinaire Jonathan Oliver and the whole Solaris team. My sincere thanks to Jon, David Moore, and Ben Smith for their support and for their hard work on the book you now hold, and for everything else. My thanks also to Adam Tredowski, who has delivered *another* knockout cover for the series. My sincere thanks, too, to all of the writers who have written stories for the *Infinity Project* over the past nearly 10 years: Daniel Abraham, Charlie Jane Anders, Eleanor Arnason, Madeline Ashby, John Barnes, Stephen Baxter, Elizabeth Bear, Gregory Benford, Damien Broderick, Tobias S. Buckell, Pat Cadigan, Stephen D. Covey, Indrapramit Das, Aliette de Bodard, Paul Doherty, Thoraiya Dyer, Greg Egan, Ty Franck, Kathleen Ann Goonan, Kameron Hurley, Simon Ings, Gwyneth Jones, Ellen Klages, Nancy Kress, Naomi Kritzer, Barbara Lamar, Rich Larson, Yoon Ha Lee, David D. Levine, Ken Liu, Karen Lord, Karin Lowachee, Ken MacLeod, Paul J. McAuley, Ian McDonald, Sandra McDonald, Seanan McGuire, David Moles, Pat Murphy, Ramez Naam, Linda Nagata, Larry Niven, Garth Nix, An Owomoyela, Dominica Phetteplace, Hannu Rajaniemi, Robert Reed, Alastair Reynolds, Adam Roberts, Justina Robson, Kelly Robson, Kristine Kathryn Rusch, Pamela Sargent, Karl Schroeder, Benjanun Sriduangkaew, Allen Steele,

Bruce Sterling, Charles Stross, E. J. Swift, Lavie Tidhar, Genevieve Valentine, Carrie Vaughn, Peter Watts, Fran Wilde, Sean Williams, Nick Wolven, John C. Wright, and Caroline M. Yoachim. And, as always, my thanks to my agent Howard Morhaim who has stood with me for all of these years, and extra special thanks to Marianne, Jessica, and Sophie, who really are the reason why I keep doing this.

CONTENTS

INTRODUCTION

THE CORE MYTH of science fiction, for as long as I have been reading it and probably since the days of Hugo Gernsback's *Amazing Stories*, is that humanity will, at some point, leave Earth and move outward, first into the solar system, and then on to the stars. Probably no assumption was more essential to the science fiction of the 20th century, and none is being as heavily questioned today.

Science fiction of the 1940s, '50s and '60s imagined a period of triumphant stellar colonialism not unlike the imperial expansion of European powers across our own world during the 17th and 18th centuries, often with clear parallels to events from maritime history, where humanity would first reach its moon, then soon after colonise the planets of this solar system, and inevitably head to the stars, to Tau Ceti and beyond, encountering other forms of life and taking a place among the stars.

This dream of manifest destiny among the stars, with endless growth and expansion and characterised by a deep technological optimism, reflected a 20th-century experience that must have made it seem that technology could solve all of humanity's problems, science could answer any of our questions, and that we could go anywhere and do anything. It was, though, predominantly a white middle-class American dream of the future, something that can be clearly seen in the pages of books like Robert A. Heinlein's

Citizen of the Galaxy or Alfred Bester's *The Stars My Destination*, two science fiction novels of the 1950s that feature somewhat similar-seeming projections of life in a solar system colonised by the people you might have met at a Manhattan cocktail party of the time.

As the 20th century continued, though, and as our scientific knowledge of the solar system around us changed and evolved, that dream changed. Dreams of colonisation became dreams of terraforming and change, of centuries spent claiming land and slowly making it more like home. The science fiction of the early 1990s, heavily influenced by information provided by *Voyager* and other NASA probes, imagined how Mars could go from a red frontier to a green and ultimately blue home, as it did in Kim Stanley Robinson's influential Red Mars trilogy, or in Greg Bear's *Moving Mars* and a handful of similar novels.

Of course, science fiction never abandoned its classic dream of expansion—not in the 1970s as SF began to move into bestseller territory, not in the 1980s as cyberpunk became the dominant mode of the day, not in the 1990s when it was confronted by more and more evidence of the difficulty of its task, and not today. Vastly popular series of novels and stories from beloved writers like Lois McMaster Bujold, David Weber and many others were read around the world and won major awards, but the assumptions they made felt less and less like the projections of hard (or science-based) science fiction and more and more like a kind of fantasy. Enjoyable, rewarding, and definitely entertaining, but not projections of likely futures.

Those projects continued to change, and the stories being told continued to evolve. During the first decade of the 21st century, as science fiction slowly began to imagine a more inclusive future, it also seemed to lose faith in the dream of the stars. It seemed harder to believe that the vast gulfs between stars would be crossed, or at least be crossed easily. Writers like Greg Egan imagined sending unimaginably tiny probes between stars containing scans or uploads of humanity and then downloading them in distant places. Time and relativity deemed interstellar expansion would never be easy, though it might still be possible. For a brief period, this notion, and notions like it, occupied science fiction, and for a while colonising the solar system, sometimes portrayed as too small and too fragile to hold all of humanity's dreams and futures, was set aside.

It may simply reflect this one reader's experience, but Kim Stanley Robinson's magisterial *2312* showed the lack of imagination in that notion. His novel showed a fully colonised solar system once again, one big enough and diverse enough and exciting enough to hold and occupy any possible future we might dream of. And it was a vision we responded to, one that allowed for recognising real problems while giving us space to dream. It also, perhaps, filled in so many of the gaps that it also began to make the solar system look small. If Robinson's next novel, *Aurora*, would controversially question the dream of interstellar travel, *2312* still gave us something about which we could dream.

When I started work on *Engineering Infinity* in the early days of 2009, none of this was on my mind. I had the simple and enviable task of assembling an unthemed anthology of hard science fiction stories. By the time I was asked to follow it up with what would become *Edge of Infinity*, though, it had begun to occupy my attention. I wanted to build on the vision of a colonised solar system, to show how it might be lived in. *Reach for Infinity* attempted to show what the experience of trying to leave Earth might be like, telling tales set during that period of expansion. *Bridging Infinity* looked at how we might leave our solar system entirely and move out to the stars. The other two books in the Infinity Project, *Meeting Infinity* and *Infinity Wars*, collected stories of what would happen when humanity turned inward and focussed on its own physicality and on tales of military conflict respectively.

When it became clear that the book you're holding, *Infinity's End,* might be the final volume in the Infinity Project, at least for now, I wanted to do something a little different. I asked the writers creating new stories for this book to try to open up the solar system, to look again at its vastness, its incredible scale, and at how humanity in different ways might fit successfully and happily into its nooks and crannies. And being writers who take a challenge where their imaginations will, they did just that and more. They told tales of a humanity that turned back to Earth, leaving the solar system empty; tales that looked out into the depths of interstellar space; and tales of a bustling, occupied, but still huge stage for humanity's future. Some I'd be delighted to live in and some I would not, but they captured a few of the many different ways we might dream of tomorrow, and I genuinely hope you'll enjoy them as much as I have.

Because this is the final volume in this project, I'd like to take a moment here to thank everyone who has been a part of it: from Christian Dunn and Jonathan Oliver, who in a Canadian bar one snowy November day started all of this, and to everyone at Abaddon/Rebellion/Solaris who worked on the books; to each and every one of the dozens and dozens of writers who shared their dreams with us; to cover artists Adam Tredowski and Stephan Martiniere, who made the books so strikingly lovely; and finally to each and every reader who picked up an Infinity book and enjoyed it—thank you. It's been a joy to do this. I hope to return to infinity someday, but till then I hope that you enjoy this book and ask you to keep an eye out for something new next year around this time, when the Solaris team and I will be bringing you *Mission Critical*. Till then, good reading!

Jonathan Strahan
Perth, Australia
March 2018

FOXY AND TIGGS

JUSTINA ROBSON

FOXY AND TIGGS were at the scene. The sun beat down out of a merciless noon sky, falling on tourist, tour guide, and body alike. It fell on Foxy's lustrous fur and Tiggs' crocodilian green hide and made Tiggs' arm and crest feathers gleam with the beautiful gothic tones of an oil slick as she carefully picked over the site of the find.

Foxy shepherded the tourists back into the softly floating cocoon of their tour bus. "Back you go, folks, back you go. Crime scene here. Got to do some investigating and we'll get to the bottom of this, don't you worry." She adjusted the lie of her hotel uniform—a dinky little hat with a feather in the band that marked her as a detective inspector and a smart jacket tailored to fit her small body perfectly and provide a harness to hold the items of gear she carried. Her brush waved behind her like a huge duster, rufous red and tipped with soft cream.

Her nose twitched. The body had been out a few hours and it was starting to stink.

She wasn't the only one who thought so. Overhead, a gyre of vultures circled, stacking up one by one as they drifted in across the savannah. On the ground, Tiggs put out a claw to check the pockets of the deceased as the tourists adjusted their eyecams and leaned over the deck rails of the bus to get some good footage. It wasn't every day you saw a velociraptor investigating a murder, and since this wasn't on the itinerary or billed as an extra, it was premium gold level XP.

Foxy strolled up and down over the sandy earth but, as she expected, there were no telltales here to give the game away just yet. No footprints, no tyre tracks, no blow-patterns from hover vehicles. She was going to have to wait for Tiggs' exemplary nose to give her the facts as it hoovered up local DNA and fibres and compared them with the hotel's registry of guests and inventory of luggage.

The tour guide, a regular Earth human with a blonde crew cut and a rather fabulous waxed moustache, anxiously tapped the hull of the bus as he watched with grim fascination.

"Should I stay here? I mean, this is prime lion country. We're just lucky the lions didn't already find him. It is a him, yeah? Well, this is the home country of a particularly large pride right now. Did he—was he killed by a lion?"

Foxy watched Tiggs snort as she heard this—people often assumed Tiggs was just an animal or a bot. Foxy got past this by being a humanoid foxling, the size of an eight-year-old child, small and rounded, in every way the picture of a designed but intelligent being. Tiggs was a long four metres of saurian which looked exactly like the park 'saurs you could see in *Lands of the Lost*, albeit with less feathers and a blunter snout to fit all the telemetrics in. Tiggs enjoyed the anonymity and now played to the crowd as she flexed her hands with their huge hook claws and bent down, jaws open for a wide capture as if to consume the corpse.

The crowd ooh-ed and the bus rocked back as they recoiled. Tiggs smiled, although only Foxy could tell. Tiggs' face didn't have the mobility for expressions, but through their full-encryption powerlinks they were almost one being. They chatted privately as Tiggs stood up and made a show of stalking around, searching the local brush while at the same time picking up a bit of intel for the safari systems since she was there.

"Dumped from quite a height," Tiggs said. "Broken bones all post-mortem, some impact bruising and burst lungs full of water. Drowned. Shorts dried out but they were wet when he landed. There's droplets of salt on the ground and the leaves of this thorn tree here. Impact spread shows a bit of a roll. I'm waiting on the lab getting back to me about the water."

Foxy reassured the tour guide and helped him re-schedule so that the tourists could enjoy seeing the arrival of the clean-up crew coming for the body. "Drowned over in Pirate Booty Bay," she told him and her entranced audience.

"That's half a world away!" said a boy, awed.

"Yes, sir," Foxy agreed, "That it is. You know a lot about the hotel do you, son?"

"You have soft fur," his little sister said, leaning through the rails. "Can I touch it?"

Foxy turned and put her brush up against the rail. "Only because you asked so nicely."

"Minnie!" A horrified mother's voice. "I'm so sorry, ma'am. Minnie, we do *not* touch the little people. They are *not* toys."

Minnie was very polite with the tail, as Foxy had known she would be. She didn't mind. She'd got a track of this kid's stay and she was as nice as they came, clean, tidy, caring. She assigned each child a special access pass to a 'secret' grotto where you could dive in powersuits along the most beautiful of the ocean reefs and later wear symbiote mertails and sport in a private lagoon. As the presents arrived at the family feed, the parents cooed and calmed down, which is what she'd been going for. Even as part of the police force at the String of Pearls Magnificent Hotel, keeping guests happy was her favourite part of the job.

"Drowned off Voodoo Beach," Tiggs said, returning from her tour of the thorn trees. "No identification on him and reception says he's come in on a false ID. Quite a good one. They're promoting the DNA search out of house."

Foxy recovered her brush with a flourish and bade the tour guide farewell as the cleaner crew's glossy white and red cross rig appeared, floating down from orbit carefully to avoid disrupting the vulture tower. "Let's sign him off to them and get ourselves over there then." She took a walk over to the body and looked down at him together with Tiggs.

A young male human, well built, with some sunburn on his shoulders and nose. He had short dark hair, some body hair, although not enough to really call it hair in her opinion. Maybe he had been handsome before the bloating and the bruising set in. She wasn't sure about that. They had some in-house footage of him coming in from Kyluria Point by shuttle, and he looked like every other tourist to her, stepping out of the door into the soft, warm light of Caribae with that combination of hopeful and weary that characterised people on their second hundred years. His clothing was made by the AI house Turbulent and fit him perfectly, its mixture of clean colours and distressed cloths a popular affectation of the intergalactically wealthy. His combination showed no particular imagination. He was every inch the potential corporate spy.

"We'll assume he was dropped here so the body could be eaten," she said, straightening and hopping up the long length of Tiggs' leg to her position on the soft saddle that was part of Tiggs' uniform harness.

Tiggs grunted. The lions in question were a part of their regular work in Safari World, where they spent most of their time patrolling the vast expanses without trouble other than the odd bit of animal vetting, light fraud and a robbery or two. It was just luck that a murder investigation had kicked off in their area, but Tiggs' grunt signalled her lack of agreement on the 'luck' interpretation that Foxy had placed on it.

"Now we have to follow the whole thing through to the end, right?" Tiggs said, waiting for Foxy to settle down and get her hind paws in the bucket stirrups.

"All the way," Foxy confirmed.

"Can't hand it over to Pirate Baywatch?"

"No way. Come on, Tiggsy, this is what we're made for! We've never had our own murder before. To the Bay!"

Tiggs grumbled at the idea of flying and the idea of being on someone else's turf, the sound coming out as a growl as she set off at a run through the bush, weaving easily away from the scene and circling once at the landing site to signal the clean-up pod that it was safe for them to land—no wildlife of note around. Then she was doing what they both loved best: speeding through the hip-high grass of the plains, her feet almost silent as they struck, the wind blowing free through Foxy's whiskers, following game trails, on patrol all the way to the distant lift-off point where the orbital shuttles rose and fell twice a day.

HOTEL MAIN OPS sent them first class private through to the Bay. They said it was so the guests didn't get disturbed, but Foxy knew they could have sent them cargo class for that. The luxury of first class was something that the Hotel itself was doing as a way of caring for them. The Hotel was its staff, just as much as its planets and its vehicles, its buildings and its life. The Hotel was all of them but bigger than them. Foxy and Tiggs had never heard the Hotel directly, but they felt it and, on occasions like this, they felt it a bit extra, a deep, lasting hug in their bones. It was good to be part of a Hotel. Foxy actually pitied the tourists who were always coming, looking, searching, leaving, combing things for every last mote of XP they could get before they had to move on.

They tried out all the luxury treatments they had time for. Foxy had a deep tissue massage. Tiggs went for a complete nanomask deep-clean of her skin and feathers and, to amuse herself, got one of her teeth gold-plated. 'Now do I look like a pirate?' she asked as they made ready to disembark, flashing the fang.

"Aye!" Foxy said and pulled down her eyepatch, which she had requisitioned with the notion it might not be a bad idea. The sunlight at the Bay was intense and there were many dark interiors at the buildings that ringed the beaches. She might need a good eye for each venue. "What about me?"

"Arrrrr," said Tiggs, making the most frightening kind of noise that Foxy expected anyone had ever heard, particularly when paired with the sight of her teeth. It was good they were in a soundproofed cabin.

"You might want to ease up on that a bit," she said as the door opened.

Their itinerary opened, hotel-style, before them, soft colours showing the ways they had to go, but instead of cocktails and sun loungers, they were headed to the last recorded places that their mystery guy had been seen.

Out at the front it was morning, and the boardwalk that ran the length of Voodoo Bay was already busy. The Bay was a very broad curl that ended with a spit of land sticking out into the ocean, pointing like a finger. On maximum zoom Foxy could see people at the tip diving into the deep water from the rocks, the glitter of drones taking their pictures like dots of light. Down the other end of things was a tall cliff into which one of the hotel guest houses was hollowed out in a series of caves. Some of these ran directly in from the sea, accessed by boat and fin; others were high above the waterline, serviced by interior lifts and private jet or glide packs. Behind them the majority of the bay was lined with shanty huts of low level and apparently no tech. There was no land side exit; you had to take a shuttle or a powerhaul to the adjoining coastal zone. She and Tiggs took a walk down to the hire shop where watercraft were loaned out, studying their inner maps of the new place as they went.

"I got a ping from the lab," Tiggs said as they walked along the sand, aware of being watched, so unusual and out of place. She returned various waves and signals from the local tritons who hosted the beach and pinged ahead for someone to talk to at the store. "They say the john is a fabricant from a shop out in the Bosphoric Chain, and not a particularly high quality one."

"Ooh, Chain stock," Foxy said. "That's slumming it, even for a spy avatar."

"They're washing him for trip data—radiation sigs, all that—to see if they can match him to a factory."

The sun on the water glittered but the breeze onshore was cool. The bay water was shallow, a pale turquoise that slowly melded into deep sapphire blue at the bay's edge.

"It was old though, for an avatar. Someone on the run?"

Tiggs nodded as they arrived at the Float Shack. "If you're stuck in an avvie that long and you get killed in one, do you, you know, do you die? For real?"

"Depends on the hosting dunnit?" Foxy said. "How far it was, how good the transmission is, how encrypted. I mean, it got through on a special guest permit—a stolen one I may add, but even so. That's not a hard data barrier, only a mild checker. You can get in and out on it. Maybe. But the host would have to have some kind of transmitter in the hotel and I'm pretty sure there aren't any. I'm askin' all the same."

The triton in charge of the shack had been updated and came out to greet them. He was a tall humanoid with a silver, sharkskin finish and many cartilaginous finny appendages, webbed fingers, but human hands otherwise for handling the gear. A triple row of ridged fins framed his face instead of hair, shielding a mass of trailing tentacles that hung to his waist in the back.

"Detective Foxy. Detective Tiggs. Welcome to the Bay. How can I help you?"

Behind him Foxy watched other tritons preparing a skim boat, loading it with picnic supplies, fishing rods and speeder skis. "Hey there, Lucas. We're looking for news of a guest that was murdered out here sometime last night, we think around one a.m. local time. Has anyone asked about someone missing?"

"No, nothing like that. We've been tracking all our gear and doing a backcheck since your shuttle sent out the alert. Nothing missing. And none of the deepwater services have mentioned anything."

"The water was from this Bay," Foxy said. "What goes on here at night?"

"Everything that goes on in the day time, minus the sunbathing I'd say," Lucas said, "But last night was the weekly big bonfire up over on the point. Big cookout, lots of drinking, lots of partying. Everyone goes to it."

"We have a sighting that looks like it was at night. Here." Foxy displayed it for him on his mindnet.

"Ah, that's definitely near the fire. What's this from, a guest net?"

"There's something at work in the background," Foxy said. "Very few pictures of him and what we do have is blurred, like interference. I think it's a local firewall."

"Nothing like that here hotel side," the triton said. "Maybe got yourself a stalker."

"Thought it," Foxy said, tipping her hat to him. She was getting very hot and thought quickly, to spare herself some sun. "I'm going to go check out all the shanties and the buildings down on the far shore at the end of the 'walk, see if we can find someone who recognises him. Tiggs here is going to do the hard work, aren't you, Tiggsy?"

Tiggs flattened her crest. "I need someone expert on the water. See if we find an exact profile."

"I know the guy," Lucas said and beckoned. "C'mon."

Foxy excused herself and took a drink of water as she watched Tiggs walk off, Lucas pointing, talking. After a moment her partner set off down the beach at a run, giving the sunbathers a wide berth, which didn't stop several groups of them getting up and running off in a moment of panic. Foxy didn't laugh. That would have been unprofessional. A lot of people started asking if there was a cross-level event, a dino invasion, something exciting like that going on, and was it a real dino and would it really eat anyone...

Humans. They were such dipshits. If they bothered to read any of the hotel menus, they'd know they could go for a hunting party by special request, lethal or any other kind. But she made a note for Entertainments about the interest in unplanned monster attacks.

Foxy finished her water and took a trike up from the shack to the walk, spinning along, taking readings of the air to see if any traces of interest were about, but the air was thick with barbecue fat and smoke, high with ozone. Even moving slowly among people, she didn't find a human that had been in contact with him. Not that she expected to. Murderers who could falsify hotel data systems were few. But they must have hijacked a Private Skimmer to make the flight and the drop without getting rebuffed by Sysops, and that meant that they took it, like any guest, from the Skim Depot. So she was going there and showing her photos on the way. She asked a lot of people, all finding her "so cute, look at this fox, honey, look, she works for the security people, isn't that adorable..." but although people did recognise that Foxy was especially lovely, nobody recognised the john.

TIGGS REACHED THE cliff guest house and turned to the water when she found the barbecue pits and stone circle where Bay Services were steadily cleaning up from the previous night's fire and entertainment. Records of the dead man's few moves flashed through her mindnet and she matched them to the landscape she could see. He'd been here, here... and here. The moves took her towards the water in the direction she was going anyway. He had left the fire shortly after the music started and the dancing. He'd come out here... but of course the tide had washed all the marks away.

She was met at the edge of the surf by Tovi from Deepwater Safety. Tovi was, like her, almost an identical replica of the creature he resembled: a giant mantis shell crab. His carapace gleamed, heavy with weeds and limpets. Mussels festooned his back. He raised his larger pincer in greeting and together, with him as the guide, they began to move out to sea. He walked and Tiggs swam above him, helped by some web-sheet that Lucas had given her for her hands and feet. Her skin found the water very cold but surprisingly enjoyable.

"There's a regular patrol at the reef's edge," Tovi told her as she was lifted and lowered by the rolling waves. "I've called in a few of the lads. They'll meet us there. They know what they're looking for."

By the time she had swum out that far, Tiggs was starting to feel tired. She was glad when Tovi pointed out a spot where the reef was close to the surface, and relatively safe for her feet, so that she could stand and have a breather. Their contacts were already there, gliding around, their fins breaking the water's surface. Grey sharks. They could smell an individual ten miles away in the ocean, even more. She gave them the aroma of the dead man and they vanished, one by one, silently, into the depths.

They were soon back with an answer. "Found it. The old raft beyond the point. There were swimmers in the water all night, but there's residue on the rope there. Maybe on the top there's more. I'll call Vince, he'll give you a lift."

Vince was a megalodon and couldn't get too close to the reef. He surfaced at his slowest speed so Tiggs could swim out to him and walk up onto the broad back behind his head, as tall as the enormous fin behind her.

"All aboard," he said, mindnet to mindnet, and then, with imperceptible movements of his fins, they were off, Tiggs surfing all the way, her ankles breaking the water but never going deeper, her balance never in doubt. She thought that Foxy might be right about the luck. It was sad to lose a guest and perhaps dangerous to rout a troublemaker, but riding on a shark across the ocean on a fine day was an unexpected and complete joy. She held out her arms and her feathers caught the wind. She could imagine that she was flying...

The fixed raft came up all too soon, and she had to leap off and onto the weathered old decking, hoping she wasn't ruining a crime scene. Vince loitered as she made her inspection, studying the area as closely as she could, mapping it, then taking various tastes of the boards and the ropes with her tongue. Her nose was good, but the seawater was abrasive and pungent itself and she wanted to feel confident—the tongue never lied. And there it was. A match. And a lot of other DNA traces along with it.

She pinged Foxy. "He was here. Vince verifies that the water profile by this raft matches his. It has a particular coral and protein signature from the plankton rising up that is almost unique to this kilometre. He was alive on this deck—I've got semen matching. It's mixed with female human DNA. I'm relaying to the lab and to reception and guest services. I'm coming back."

FOXY WAS AT the Skim Depot. They had checked out several private shuttles around two a.m. None of the routes were tracked, but they could download the internal tracking data as long as there was a warrant. Foxy served the warrant and was shown aboard the one that had taken off last. It had recorded its flight to orbit, but then glitched and there was no further data to be saved.

"You can see here once it's back in the Bay, it resets," the service manager said, poring over it with Foxy together. "I'm no expert but if there's a mindworm involved, it will have been put in via the access panel..." They went over to the plate and undid it.

Foxy took a sniff of the area. "Does this match what you've got, Tiggsy?" She sent over the sniffings.

"Same woman," Tiggs said immediately.

Reception came back almost at the same moment. They had several in-use identities for the dead avatar, all being sent over. They had an ID on the woman guest. She had not left the hotel, and there was no current record of her whereabouts.

"Well, I never," the skim service manager was saying. "Spies! Here, in the Bay. What was she doing?"

Foxy told her and thanked her, then popped her eyepatch down and went outside. Tiggs jogged towards her along the beach looking pleased with herself even as she complained, "Bloody hot it is out here." She tiptoed around families and avoided various of their pets, snarling at a particularly barky dog and showing her gold tooth.

Foxy ordered a bucket of water and an iced tea and took them out to a table with an umbrella sunshade at the edge of the sands to wait for her. Tiggs' snout disappeared into the water bucket as soon as she reached the umbrella, and there was a long pause.

Foxy twirled the tiny paper umbrella in the mass of fruit stuck to the side of her iced tea. "If she hasn't left the hotel, and the skimmer was returned here..."

"Then she's likely still here. She hasn't swum out, I already asked Tovi and Vince. Some of the Bay rats say they've got traces around the shanties—food stands, especially one that serves seafood skewers. Got quite a groove there. They're looking all around now to see if they can find her."

"You're so smart, Tiggs," Foxy said, glad they were of one mind. It made life so much easier.

"I am." Tiggs lifted her head up and then lay down on a lounger for a moment, resting her head on the table. Her eyes swivelled to look at Foxy. "I rode a shark."

"Show me later," Foxy said, trying not to be envious. "Ooh, here we go. Sighting in the casino. Classic." She had a final lap of the tea and then hopped up and onto Tiggs' helpfully low back. "Let's ride!"

"Cowboy," Tiggs said, unamused, and heaved to her feet. "Oh, I drank that too fast... my stomach hurts."

"You'll be fine, just take it slow. The casino roaches are tracking her."

"What do you think is going on?" Tiggs asked as they paced along the walk and then turned to face the huge, glossy frontage of the seafront casino. It was a beautiful building, like a cliff of glass. To either side of it, lesser buildings provided restaurants, bars, theatres and haciendas within which all manner of spa treatments and indulgences were available. Skinshops and tattoo joints stood out here and there. Foxy saw a young woman come out entirely recoloured from head to foot as a zebra. Even her eyes were white with black rings.

They stood in the shade of one of the tall palms that helped to separate the casino from the beach. "I think..." Foxy began, questioning the sense of going in without any backup, but getting off the saddle and checking her vest anyway. "That time is of the essence. She's got wormware. She'll have some way of finding out she's been spotted. We know she can bypass ordinary security. We should go arrest her. I'm heading in. You stick around here and be ready in case she makes a run for it."

Everything was human-sized. Tiggs clearly could not be the one to go inside. "All right," she said. "But keep me on live feed. I need to know where she goes."

Foxy gave her a pat on the knee. "Don't you worry, I wouldn't feel safe if you weren't right with me." They synced up, and Tiggs watched as Foxy walked through the revolving doors, absurdly small for a police officer on the hunt of a ruthless criminal. A roach pinged from the gambling floor where classic card games were in play. Foxy vanished from sight and Tiggs watched her on second sight. She was so still and so absorbed with the strange view of legs and bottoms that were the majority of Foxy's vision that it took her a while to realise that a family with toddlers had stopped next to her.

"How much is it for a ride?" asked the father, looking around Tiggs for a place he could scan his wristband, clearly under the impression that she was a mechanical child's toy. They were day-rate guests, flown down to the beach from the cheaper accommodations on the massif.

Tiggs cocked her head to look down at the children.

"It's so realistic!" the woman said, putting out a finger to stroke one of Tiggs' arm feathers. "I love how they spare nothing on the technology here. Not like Procyon Paradise—you could tell all their machines straight off. Really clunky finishing."

"I can't find the tagger," the man complained.

Tiggs felt her eyelid twitch. In the dim, chandelier-lit confines of the card arena, Foxy had cashed up a few chips and prowled herself to a seat at the Blackjack table, opposite the mark. Roaches were moving into position at key points to oversee all the exits.

"I wanna ride!" screeched the smaller child, holding up its arms imperiously.

"Here, just sit on it for a minute," the woman said and lifted the boy up, setting him down with a thump on Foxy's saddle. "Put your feet in the thingies. There you go."

"I can't get it to..." the man was saying when Tiggs gave a little whole-body jerk as if she had just been put to life by a very slow processor command. "Oh thank God. You walk with him, Jody, I'll put Kimmy on when you get back. Go up to the ice cream shop and come back."

The croupier was setting up as the bets were going down. The mark, a tall, athletic human with long black hair and mahogany-wood-style skin, was toying with her chips. At her elbow a large vodka tonic was half gone, ice cubes melting to blobs. She was wearing a fine silk jumpsuit, and something about the movements made Tiggs think she had a powersuit on underneath it. She said so to Foxy and, at the same time, began a careful and slow march towards the ice cream shop.

Foxy ordered a pina colada and made a modest wager. The cards went out. Foxy got a three and a six. "Her name is Ghabra Behdami. So it says at Reception. They think she's the original. She's a premier platinum passholder but bought it only two days before she got here. Everything about her checks out, but if she is wearing a powersuit, then it's good enough to pass, and that means she doesn't check out at all. Plus she bugged that skimmer. The roaches are in. As soon as this hand's over, I'm taking her out."

Tiggs was nearly at the shop. She could still see the casino out of the side of one eye. "Got a bit of a situation here. Wait, what are you doing? Doubling down on nine?"

"What does it matter?" Foxy ignored her drink and shoved more chips forward. "Oh, look at that. Look at her eyes. That's some fancy crap in those irises and on that retina. This is military grade. Shit. What should I do now?"

"We haven't found any accomplices. We don't have motive, we only have association," Tiggs said, waiting as a dripping cone was passed over her neck before slowly making a turn and starting a creep back towards the avenue of palms and the glass frontage. "Show her the photo."

Foxy got a two out of the shoe. The croupier already had eighteen. "So, has anyone here seen this guy? He's gone missing and we need to find him. He has a virus. It's complicated." Foxy showed the registration photo of the dead john, his open necked linen shirt, floppy hair, plumped skin all unsuspecting they were on the final countdown.

Ghabra Behdami looked at it on her feed, looked at Foxy—not just a glance but a real good look—and then without any warning at all bolted from the table, jarring it and knocking over all the drinks as she got a good solid boost off it. In a heartbeat Foxy was in pursuit, bounding over the glasses and the foaming, icy froth, her paws slipping on cards before she was in the air and then on the floor, her arms pumping. She was fast and she was nippy, in and out of legs and around chairs, but Behdami had a front-line soldier's power-assisted second skin on, and if it weren't for the fact she had to change direction a couple of times, throwing guests left and right like ping-pong balls as she hurled herself towards the kitchen server entries, then she'd have been able to outpace any regular hotel security.

At the front Tiggs crawled the last few steps to the waiting father and second child, who was whining and swinging at the limit of his father's arm. A large glob of melting vanilla cream ran down her neck and into her ruff feathers. All sorts of hormones were coming up, readying her for the hunt, and she started to drool uncontrollably.

"Eww, look at it," said child two as the mother reached up, standing on Tiggs' foot, and hefted the first one out of the saddle. As soon as she stepped clear, Tiggs whipped her head around and put her nose right in child two's face. The spit slid off her gold tooth and onto the pavement.

"Y'aint no picture, sweetie," she said and then she was off like a bat out of hell around the side of the building. She heard the kid screaming and winced as roaches pinged her with the news that the mark was barrelling through the kitchens and, soup catastrophes in progress, would be out of the back and into the service bay in five seconds.

Tiggs sprinted, had to go around a laundry cart, skidded on the corner on loose sand, made the back just in time to see the doors burst open and Behdami come powering out. The silk jumpsuit was baggy on the limbs, tight at the waist, gathered at the bust. She looked like an insane genie from a cabaret in her high heels as she caught sight of Tiggs and made a quick change of angle, away from the street exit and towards the high wall that screened the backyards from the gaggle of two- and three-storey blocks that make up the Hexen—a little district devoted to pirate fantasy fun for adults, thick with roleplayer zombies and cursed sailors packing cutlasses and pistols. It was nearly three o'clock, when the backwaters would be surging with crocodiles as the pirates made their play to steal the "naval" masted ships and make for the open seas of the lagoon, flush with treasure and slaves and all the whatnottery of a very good time.

Behdami leaped like a hero, took a stride up the wall and over it, pumped off the top into a cat's leap that took her onto the roof of a fortune-telling bodega. A chicken squawked as Behdami vanished from sight, and Tiggs was after her, claws scrabbling on the wall top for a moment as she recruited ten rats and a seagull to help her see.

At the kitchen doors Foxy, panting, hat in her hands, paws covered in soup, could only stand and watch. "Go get her, Tiggs!"

The chase was swift and deadly. Behdami could parkour like a goddess, and she did—up walls, onto roofs, ten metre jumps, down the fire escape slides, over the heads of gawping navvies in the burning heat of the afternoon. Everywhere she went, the seagull watched, the rats pursued, and Tiggs came after. Behdami cleared a street in one bound. Tiggs followed and crashed through the roof of a taco stand, got up and was after her in a second. Behdami dashed over the rooftops, doubling back towards the casino, no doubt having realised the only way out of the zone was either the Skim Depot, which would block her now, or by a direct route physically out of the main gates and through the hotel parking zone into the raw wilderness. The gull's call became a siren wail as more security was called in.

Staff pirates shouldered their way through the groups, but like everyone else they were sidelined as Behdami rolled, somersaulted, vaulted her desperate race using every surface like a rebound board in an effort to avoid the relentless, slavering velociraptor that followed her stride for stride. High in the air, mid-leap, Behdami spun to fling out a line of razor thread, but Tiggs was wise to it—the seagull saw her pulling it out of her sleeve—and she threw herself to the side, tail balancing the zigzag with incredible flexion. The thread fell aside and cut through the fake thatching of the zombie master's roof where someone will have the unlovely job of cleaning it up soon but not Tiggs—she was wide-eyed and as deadly as an arrow. Behdami feinted left, dived right and dropped into the street, going to cover herself with the milling agitation of the pirates on the quayside. A rat noticed the plan—there were two rights and a left before the gate to the outside world, but if she went through the buildings, it was only two doors and a pedestrian crossing.

Tiggs changed direction and cut her off, bashing her way in through the back doors of Black Blood's Barbecue as Behdami entered the dining area. A quick-thinking freebooter drinks server shoved the doors closed, trapping them in the grill. Behdami went for a knife but Tiggs was already pouncing and on her. She was not the only one with a skin suit on today.

Tiggs stood, victorious, her prey under the deadly claws of her feet. Ice cream and drool ran off her neck and ruined Behdami's lilac jumpsuit. Behdami struggled for a moment but felt what she was up against, looked at Tiggs properly and gave up, lay back on the rubber matted tiles, her chest heaving for breath. It was over.

A few rats gathered for a look and then dashed off again, remembering their place. Somewhere in the deep background of her mind, Tiggs saw Foxy approaching with the handcuffs and calmed down. This was how they always operated. Foxy and Tiggs.

"Sorry about the kid," she said as Foxy calmly trussed up their spy or whatever she was.

"I comped them a cruise, don't worry about it," Foxy said, so proud of Tiggs she could hardly speak. "Ghabra Behdami, I'm arresting you on suspicion of the murder of an unknown man in Pirate Bay. You can say what you like but we both know it'll all come out in the end."

"GOD, YOU PEOPLE," Behdami said from the floor as Tiggs reached over to the grill, foot still clasped around her neck, and helped herself to a half-cooked steak. "Will you let me go if I give you your story?"

"Try us," Foxy said. "Let's see what it's worth."

"It'd be easier without you sanding on my n—"

Tiggs squeezed, just a little. It had been a very long, hot day.

"Fine. Have it your way. Your man's name is Fantheon Pelagic and he was hotel security, just like you. That's how come you couldn't see him—he was never tracked here because he was part of the hotel, only he worked out in the spacelanes, tracing counter agents from rival groups. He came down here looking for some lowlife from the Dream Tripper group—her data's here, look. She's a spy."

"What's your angle?" Foxy asked, taking a seat on Behdami's thigh and patting her. "You're tooled up nicely."

"I'm Solar Military, I'm on furlough," she said. "I'm not here because of your hotel, only because of Pelagic. He was the lover of my best friend and he'd been cheating on her. Once you can excuse, but they were going to get married and he was still at it so I came to take him out as a kind of... not wedding present, let's say."

Tiggs went for the other steak because it was getting overdone and there was no way any guest would be served it now. "Go on."

"I came down here, found him at the beach party, seduced him— not like that was difficult. I mean, that's pretty low, right? I had to be sure though, sure he was scum."

"So you drowned him and then took him to the Safari in the hopes he'd be eaten before we found out what had happened."

"Yeah. It seemed like the easiest way, you know? A couple of park rangers were the worst that would happen. I mean it should have taken days for you to figure it out, and all I had to do was ride my real ticket out tonight."

"I don't believe it," Foxy said as their check on the data she'd given them paid out. There really was a spy in the hotel, and nobody, until now, had found her.

"Yeah, me neither," Behdami said. "Rangers and pirate zombie rats. God in a fucking bucket, but you are one badass hotel."

"It's a cutthroat business," Foxy said and stood up. "Tiggs, you can let go now. The offworld police are here and I need another drink."

Tiggs let go and stepped back. "We did it!" she said privately to Foxy.

"You did it, dear." Foxy patted her and then hopped up and onto the saddle. "Hey, this is all sticky and—what for the love of all booty has been going on up here?"

"You don't want to know," Tiggs said. "Trust me. Do not. Want. To know. I'm going for a swim."

"I think they have floating loungers and a wet bar," Foxy said. "Let's go find out while we wait for the specials to pick up that spy."

CRIME IS NOT uncommon in the world of business. For a hotel such as myself—The String of Pearls—four pearly planets, orbiting the golden jewel of their travelling star as it heads steadily on into the depths of unknown space, the greatest prize of such a crime would be the looting of the consciousness protocols that govern every aspect of hotel life and my evolution as a living system within which people and creatures may live and prosper to the best of their abilities as honoured guests. This was the prize that the Dream Tripper franchise of luxury liners had been going for in its wonky, desperate way, and who knows what they might have done if they had not been caught on the tails of a crime of passion?

I am reasonably sure they could have done a lot of damage, but it's not in my nature to be vindictive. That is the very antithesis of hospitality and a hallmark of bad romance. So, once the matter of Pelagic had been cleared up and the spy returned to the Dream Tripper's nearest waylay point, I sent Dream Tripper a full and complete copy of my functional mindmap and its operating systems and dependencies. If it is worth stealing, then it's worth sharing.

Meanwhile, later the same day Foxy and Tiggs are back on their usual patrol route on our Serene Serengeti pathway. The night is cool and clear, the full swathe of the Milky Way visible as we pace majestically towards its mysterious heart. In both the friends a sense of wonder and happiness from their adventure is still burning—they are young and they are valuable, successful, in a beautiful world that loves them.

I copy that and I send it on to Dream Tripper too. I want to be clear that there is no such thing as just a park ranger, just a rat. Upon the actions of the innocent, the daring, the incidental and the tiny, so much fortune can turn and it must be free, not governed from above.

For a while I watch the guest shuttles come and go from our major reception station. A heavily laden schooner full of people who have been on long serving trade craft in deep space is coming in. They're all so eager to see and be on a planet again that I've felt inspired. I'm quite delighted with all the little treats I'm planning for them as they acclimatise to their ancestral worlds—though not Foxy's suggested monster invasions, not yet at least.

I hope some of them will stay awhile and maybe become permanent guests—all fellow travellers are welcome and I hope many of them will have stories of their own to share. But until they arrive I am watching a foxling and a raptor run the game trails in the dark beneath a hunter's moon.

*　*　*

BUT REALLY IT'S hard to live at that level of the romantic even though I love it. I'd rather watch Foxy. I'd rather watch Tiggs.

"FOXY, YOU KNOW when you have that feeling that you're being watched?"

"You mean when the hotel is paying attention?"

"Yeah, that."

"Is it, like, really there or is it imaginary? Is there really one big mind or is that just what it feels like when some bits of the hotel have to check what you're doing and... and is it related to that funny ringing noise you sometimes get in your ears?"

"That high-pitched whine?"

"Yeah, like you have a crossed wire or a mosquito stuck in there— there for a second, then gone. Is that like—what is that?"

"I don't know. I used to think it was something being downloaded."

"I thought that but then nothing seemed to happen."

"Yes, but it wouldn't, would it, if it was a secret download of stuff. It would just update you and then you'd feel the same but operate better. If it was that."

"Oh yeah. We were good though, weren't we?"

"Like real detectives. You heard what that woman said. Park rangers would not get it. But we did. Yeah, we did! I'm almost sorry it's over."

"Don't be. I've got a note from Entertainments that says they're starting a series of live murder mystery events and they want us to lead the investigations."

"Really? Oh yes, I've got it too now. Wait... did you hear a sound before you saw it?"

"I think that was an actual mosquito, Tiggs."

"Yeah. Maybe."

"What's *that* sound, then?"

"That's an elephant blowing off. Move upwind of them. I think they're onto us."

"I'm on it."

DEFINITELY.

INTERVENTION

KELLY ROBSON

WHEN I WAS fifty-seven, I did the unthinkable. I became a crèche manager.

On Luna, crèche work kills your social capital, but I didn't care. Not at first. My long-time love had been crushed to death in a bot malfunction in Luna's main mulching plant. I was just trying to find a reason to keep breathing.

I found a crusty centenarian who'd outlived most of her cohort and asked for her advice. She said there was no better medicine for grief than children, so I found a crèche tucked away behind a water printing plant and signed on as a cuddler. That's where I caught the baby bug.

When my friends found out, the norming started right away.

"You're getting a little tubby there, Jules," Ivan would say, unzipping my jacket and reaching inside to pat my stomach. "Got a little parasite incubating?"

I expected this kind of attitude from Ivan. Ringleader, team captain, alpha of alphas. From him, I could laugh it off. But then my closest friends started in.

Beryl's pretty face soured in disgust every time she saw me. "I can smell the freeloader on you," she'd say, pretending to see body fluids on my perfectly clean clothing. "Have the decency to shower and change after your shift."

Even that wasn't so bad. But then Robin began avoiding me and ignoring my pings. We'd been each other's first lovers, best friends since forever, and suddenly I didn't exist. That's how extreme the prejudice is on Luna.

Finally, on my birthday, they threw me a surprise party. Everyone wore diapers and crawled around in a violent mockery of childhood. When I complained, they accused me of being broody.

I wish I could say I ignored their razzing, but my friends were my whole world. I dropped crèche work. My secret plan was to leave Luna, find a hab where working with kids wasn't social death, but I kept putting it off. Then I blinked, and ten years had passed.

Enough delay. I jumped trans to Eros station, engaged a recruiter, and was settling into my new life on Ricochet within a month.

I never answered my friends' pings. As far as Ivan, Beryl, Robin, and the rest knew, I fell off the face of the moon. And that's the way I wanted it.

RICOCHET IS ONE of the asteroid-based habs that travel the inner system using gravity assist to boost speed in tiny increments. As a wandering hab, we have no fixed astronomical events or planetary seasonality to mark the passage of time, so boosts are a big deal for us—the equivalent of New Year's on Earth or the Sol Belt flare cycle.

On our most recent encounter with Mars, my third and final crèche—the Jewel Box—were twelve years old. We hadn't had a boost since the kids were six, so my team and I worked hard to make it special, throwing parties, making presents, planning excursions. We even suited up and took the kids to the outside of our hab, exploring Asteroid Iris's vast, pockmarked surface roofed by nothing less than the universe itself, in all its spangled glory. We played around out there until Mars climbed over the horizon and showed the Jewel Box its great face for the first time, so huge and close it seemed we could reach up into its milky skim of atmosphere.

When the boost itself finally happened, we were all exhausted. All the kids and cuddlers lounged in the rumpus room, clipped into our safety harnesses, nestled on mats and cushions or tucked into the wall netting. Yawning, droopy-eyed, even dozing. But when the hab began to shift underneath us, we all sprang alert.

Trésor scooted to my side and ducked his head under my elbow.

"You doing okay, buddy?" I asked him in a low voice.

He nodded. I kissed the top of his head and checked his harness.

I wasn't the only adult with a little primate soaking up my body heat. Diamant used Blanche like a climbing frame, standing on her thighs, gripping her hands, and leaning back into the increasing force of the boost. Opale had coaxed her favorite cuddler Mykelti up into the ceiling netting. They both dangled by their knees, the better to feel the acceleration. Little Rubis was holding tight to Engku's and Megat's hands, while on the other side of the room, Safir and Émeraude clowned around, competing for Long Meng's attention.

I was supposed to be on damage control, but I passed the safety workflow over to Bruce. When we hit maximum acceleration, Tré was clinging to me with all his strength.

The kids' bioms were stacked in the corner of my eye. All their hormone graphs showed stress indicators. Tré's levels were higher than the rest, but that wasn't strange. When your hab is somersaulting behind a planet, bleeding off its orbital energy, your whole world turns into a carnival ride. Some people like it better than others.

I tightened my arms around Tré's ribs, holding tight as the room turned sideways.

"Everything's fine," I murmured in his ear. "Ricochet was designed for this kind of maneuver."

Our safety harnesses held us tight to the wall netting. Below, Safir and Émeraude climbed up the floor, laughing and hooting. Long Meng tossed pillows at them.

Tré gripped my thumb, yanking as if it were a joystick with the power to tame the room's spin. Then he shot me a live feed showing Ricochet's chief astronautics officer, a dark-skinned, silver-haired woman with protective bubbles fastened over her eyes.

"Who's that?" I asked, pretending I didn't know.

"Vijayalakshmi," Tré answered. "If anything goes wrong, she'll fix it."

"Have you met her?" I knew very well he had, but asking questions is an excellent calming technique.

"Yeah, lots of times." He flashed a pointer at the astronaut's mirrored eye coverings. "Is she sick?"

"Might be cataracts. That's a normal age-related condition. What's worrying you?"

"Nothing," he said.

"Why don't you ask Long Meng about it?"

Long Meng was the Jewel Box's physician. Ricochet-raised, with a facial deformity that thrust her mandible severely forward. As an adult, once bone ossification had completed, she had rejected the cosmetic surgery that could have normalized her jaw.

"Not all interventions are worthwhile," she'd told me once. "I wouldn't feel like myself with a new face."

As a pediatric specialist, Long Meng was responsible for the health and development of twenty crèches, but we were her favorite. She'd decided to celebrate the boost with us. At that moment, she was dangling from the floor with Safir and Émeraude, tickling their tummies and howling with laughter.

I tried to mitigate Tré's distress with good, old-fashioned cuddle and chat. I showed him feeds from the biodiversity preserve, where the netted megafauna floated in mid-air, riding out the boost in safety, legs dangling. One big cat groomed itself as it floated, licking one huge paw and wiping down its whiskers with an air of unconcern.

Once the boost was complete and we were back to our normal gravity regime, Tré's indicators quickly normalized. The kids ran up to the garden to check out the damage. I followed slowly, leaning on my cane. One of the bots had malfunctioned and lost stability, destroying several rows of terraced seating in the open air auditorium just next to our patch. The kids all thought that was pretty funny. Tré seemed perfectly fine, but I couldn't shake the feeling that I'd failed him somehow.

THE JEWEL BOX didn't visit Mars. Martian habs are popular, their excursion contracts highly priced. The kids put in a few bids but didn't have the credits to win.

"Next boost," I told them. "Venus in four years. Then Earth."

I didn't mention Luna. I'd done my best to forget it even existed. Easy to do. Ricochet has almost no social or trade ties with Earth's moon. Our main economic sector is human reproduction and development—artificial wombs, zygote husbandry, natal decanting, every bit of art and science that turns a mass of undifferentiated cells into a healthy young adult. Luna's crèche system collapsed completely not long after I left. Serves them right.

I'm a centenarian, facing my last decade or two. I may look serene and wise, but I've never gotten over being the butt of my old friends' jokes.

Maybe I've always been immature. It would explain a lot.

*　　*　　*

FOUR YEARS PASSED with the usual small dramas. The Jewel Box grew in body and mind, stretching into young adults of sixteen. All six—Diamant, Émeraude, Trésor, Opale, Safir, and Rubis—hit their benchmarks erratically and inconsistently, which made me proud. Kids are supposed to be odd little individuals. We're not raising robots, after all.

As Ricochet approached, the Venusian habs began peppering us with proposals. Recreation opportunities, educational seminars, sightseeing trips, arts festivals, sporting tournaments—all on reasonable trade terms. Venus wanted us to visit, fall in love, stay. They'd been losing population to Mars for years. The brain drain was getting critical.

The Jewel Box decided to bid on a three-day excursion. Sightseeing with a focus on natural geology, including active volcanism. For the first time in their lives, they'd experience real, unaugmented planetary gravity instead of Ricochet's one-point-zero cobbled together by centripetal force and a Steffof field.

While the kids were lounging around the rumpus room, arguing over how many credits to sink into the bid, Long Meng pinged me.

You and I should send a proposal to the Venusian crèches, she whispered. *A master class or something. Something so tasty they can't resist.*

Why? Are you trying to pad your billable hours?

She gave me a toothy grin. *I want a vacation. Wouldn't it be fun to get Venus to fund it?*

Long Meng and I had collaborated before, when our numbers had come up for board positions on the crèche governance authority. Nine miserable months co-authoring policy memos, revising the crèche management best practices guide, and presenting at skills development seminars. All on top of our regular responsibilities. Against the odds, our friendship survived the bureaucracy.

We spent a few hours cooking up a seminar to tempt the on-planet crèche specialists and fired it off to a bunch of Venusian booking agents. We called it 'Attachment and Self-regulation in Theory and Practice: Approaches to Promoting Emotional Independence in the Crèche-raised Child.' Sound dry? Not a bit. The Venusians gobbled it up.

I shot the finalized syllabus to our chosen booking agent, then escorted the Jewel Box to their open-air climbing lab. I turned them over to their instructor and settled onto my usual bench under a tall oak. Diamant took the lead position up the cliff, as usual. By the time they'd completed the first pitch, all three seminars were filled.

The agent is asking for more sessions, I whispered to Long Meng. *What do you think?*

"No way." Long Meng's voice rang out, startling me. As I pinged her location, her lanky form appeared in the distant aspen grove.

"This is a vacation," she shouted. "If I wanted to pack my billable hours, I'd volunteer for another board position."

I shuddered. *Agreed.*

She jogged over and climbed onto the bench beside me, sitting on the backrest with her feet on the seat. "Plus, you haven't been off this rock in twenty years," she added, plucking a leaf from the overhead bough.

"I said okay, Long Meng."

We watched the kids as they moved with confidence and ease over the gleaming, pyrite-inflected cliff face. Big, bulky Diamant didn't look like a climber but was obsessed with the sport. The other five had gradually been infected by their crèche-mate's passion.

Long Meng and I waved to the kids as they settled in for a rest mid-route. Then she turned to me. "What do you want to see on-planet? Have you made a wish list yet?"

"I've been to Venus. It's not that special."

She laughed, a great, good-natured, wide-mouthed guffaw. "Nothing can compare to Luna, can it, Jules?"

"Don't say that word."

"Luna? Okay. What's better than Venus? Earth?"

"Earth doesn't smell right."

"The Sol belt?"

"Never been there."

"What then?"

"This is nice." I waved at the groves of trees surrounding the cliff. Overhead, the plasma core that formed the backbone of our hab was just shifting its visible spectrum into twilight. Mellow light filtered through the leaves. Teenage laughter echoed off the cliff, and in the distance, the steady droning wail of a fussy newborn.

I pulled up the surrounding camera feeds and located the newborn. A tired-looking cuddler carried the baby in an over-shoulder sling, patting its bottom rhythmically as they strolled down a sunflower-lined path. I pinged the baby's biom. Three weeks old. Chronic gas and reflux unresponsive to every intervention strategy. Nothing to do but wait for the child to grow out of it.

The kids summited, waved to us, then began rappelling back down. Long Meng and I met them at the base.

"Em, how's your finger?" Long Meng asked.

"Good." Émeraude bounced off the last ledge and slipped to the ground, wave of pink hair flapping. "Better than good."

"Let's see, then."

Émeraude unclipped and offered the doctor their hand. They were a kid with only two modes: all-out or flatline. A few months back, they'd injured themselves cranking on a crimp, completely bowstringing the flexor tendon.

Long Meng launched into an explanation of annular pulley repair strategies and recovery times. I tried to listen but I was tired. My hips ached, my back ached, my limbs rotated on joints gritty with age. In truth, I didn't want to go to Venus. The kids had won their bid, and with them off-hab, staying home would have been a good rest. But Long Meng's friendship was important, and making her happy was worth a little effort.

LONG MENG AND I accompanied the Jewel Box down Venus's umbilical, through the high sulphuric acid clouds to the elevator's base deep in the planet's mantle. When we entered the busy central transit hub, with its domed ceiling and slick, speedy slideways, the kids began making faces.

"This place stinks," said Diamante.

"Yeah, smells like piss," said Rubis.

Tré looked worried. "Do they have diseases here or something?"

Opale slapped her hand over her mouth. "I'm going to be sick. Is it the smell or the gravity?"

A quick glance at Opale's biom showed she was perfectly fine. All six kids were. Time for a classic crèche manager-style social intervention.

If you can't be polite around the locals, I whispered, knocking my cane on the ground for emphasis. *I'll shoot you right back up the elevator.*

If you send us home, do we get our credits back? Émeraude asked, yawning.

No. You'd be penalized for non-completion of contract.

I posted a leaderboard for good behavior. Then I told them Venusians were especially gossipy, and if word got out they'd bad-mouthed the planet, they'd get nothing but dirty looks for the whole trip.

A bald lie. Venus is no more gossipy than most habs. But it nurses a significant anti-crèche prejudice. Not as extreme as Luna, but still. Ricochet kids were used to being loved by everyone. On Venus, they would get attitude just for existing. I wanted to offer a convenient explanation for the chilly reception from the locals.

The group of us rode the slideway to Vanavara portway, where Engku, Megat, and Bruce were waiting. Under the towering archway, I hugged and kissed the kids, told them to have lots of fun, and waved at their retreating backs. Then Long Meng and I were on our own.

She took my arm and steered us into Vanavara's passeggiata, a social stroll that wound through the hab like a pedestrian river. We drifted with the flow, joining the people-watching crowd, seeing and being seen.

The hab had spectacular sculpture gardens and fountains, and Venus's point-nine-odd gravity was a relief on my knees and hips, but the kids weren't wrong about the stench. Vanavara smelled like oily vinaigrette over half-rotted lettuce leaves, with an animal undercurrent reminiscent of hormonal teenagers on a cleanliness strike. As we walked, the stench surged and faded, then resurfaced again.

We ducked into a kiosk where a lone chef roasted kebabs over an open flame. We sat at the counter, drinking sparkling wine and watching her prepare meal packages for bot delivery.

"What's wrong with the air scrubbers here?" Long Meng asked the chef.

"Unstable population," she answered. "We don't have enough civil engineers to handle the optimization workload. If you know any nuts-and-bolts types, tell them to come to Vanavara. The bank will kiss them all over."

She served us grilled protein on disks of crispy starch topped with charred vegetable and heaped with garlicky sauce, followed by finger-sized blossoms with tender, fleshy petals over a crisp honeycomb core. When we rejoined the throng, we shot the chef a pair of big, bright public valentines on slow decay, visible to everyone passing by. The chef ran after us with two tulip-shaped bulbs of amaro.

"Enjoy your stay," she said, handing us the bulbs. "We're developing a terrific fresh food culture here. You'll love it."

In response to the population downswing, Venus's habs had started accepting all kinds of marginal business proposals. Artists. Innovators. Experimenters. Lose a ventilation engineer; gain a chef. Lose a surgeon; gain a puppeteer. With the chefs and puppeteers come all the people who want to live in a hab with chefs and puppeteers, and are willing to put up with a little stench to get it. Eventually, the hab's fortunes turn around. Population starts flowing back, attracted by the burgeoning quality of life. Engineers and surgeons return, and the chefs and puppeteers move on to the next proposal-friendly hab. Basic human dynamics.

Long Meng sucked the last drop of amaro from her bulb and then tossed it to a disposal bot.

"First night of vacation." She gave me a wicked grin. "Want to get drunk?"

When I rolled out of my sleep stack in the morning, I was puffy and stiff. My hair stood in untamable clumps. The pouches under my eyes shone an alarming purple, and my wrinkle inventory had doubled. My tongue tasted like garlic sauce. But as long as nobody else could smell it, I wasn't too concerned. As for the rest, I'd earned every age marker.

When Long Meng finally cracked her stack, she was pressed and perky, wrapped in a crisp fuchsia robe. A filmy teal scarf drifted under her thrusting jawline.

"Let's teach these Venusians how to raise kids," she said.

*　　*　　*

IN RESPONSE TO demand, the booking agency had upgraded us to a larger auditorium. The moment we hit the stage, I forgot all my aches and pains. Doctor Footlights, they call it. Performing in front of two thousand strangers produces a lot of adrenaline.

We were a good pair. Long Meng dynamic and engaging, lunging around the stage like a born performer. Me, I was her foil. A grave, wise oldster with fifty years of crèche work under my belt.

Much of our seminar was inspirational. Crèche work is relentless no matter where you practice it, and on Venus it brings negative social status. A little cheerleading goes a long way. We slotted our specialty content in throughout the program, introducing the concepts in the introductory material, building audience confidence by reinforcing what they already knew, then hit them between the eyes with the latest developments in Ricochet's proprietary cognitive theory and emotional development modelling. We blew their minds, then backed away from the hard stuff and returned to cheerleading.

"What's the worst part of crèche work, Jules?" Long Meng asked as our program concluded, her scarf waving in the citrus-scented breeze from the ventilation.

"There are no bad parts," I said drily. "Each and every day is unmitigated joy."

The audience laughed harder than the joke deserved. I waited for the noise to die down, and mined the silence for a few lingering moments before continuing.

"Our children venture out of the crèche as young adults, ready to form new emotional ties wherever they go. The future is in their hands, an unending medium for them to shape with their ambition and passion. Our crèche work lifts them up and holds them high, all their lives. That's the best part."

I held my cane to my heart with both hands.

"The worst part is," I said, "if we do our jobs right, those kids leave the crèche and never think about us again."

We left them with a tear in every eye. The audience ran back to their crèches knowing they were doing the most important work in the universe, and open to the possibility of doing it even better.

AFTER OUR SECOND seminar, on a recommendation from the kebab chef, we blew our credits in a restaurant high up in Vanavara's atrium. Live food raised, prepared, and served by hand; nothing extruded or bulbed. And no bots, except for the occasional hygiene sweeper.

Long Meng cut into a lobster carapace with a pair of hand shears. "Have you ever noticed how intently people listen to you?"

"Most of the time the kids just pretend to listen."

"Not kids. Adults."

She served me a morsel of claw meat, perfectly molded by the creature's shell. I dredged it in green sauce and popped it in my mouth. Sweet peppers buzzed my sinuses.

"You're a great leader, Jules."

"At my age, I should be. I've had lots of practice telling people what to do."

"Exactly," she said through a mouthful of lobster. "So what are you going to do when the Jewel Box leaves the crèche?"

I lifted my flute of pale green wine and leaned back, gazing through the window at my elbow into the depths of the atrium. I'd been expecting this question for a few years but didn't expect it from Long Meng. How could someone so young understand the sorrows of the old?

"If you don't want to talk about it, I'll shut up," she added quickly. "But I have some ideas. Do you want to hear them?"

On the atrium floor far below, groups of pedestrians were just smudges, no individuals distinguishable at all. I turned back to the table but kept my eyes on my food.

"Okay, go ahead."

"A hab consortium is soliciting proposals to rebuild their failed crèche system," she said, voice eager. "I want to recruit a team. You'd be project advisor. Top position, big picture stuff. I'll be project lead and do all the grunt work."

"Let me guess," I said. "It's Luna."

Long Meng nodded. I kept a close eye on my blood pressure indicators. Deep breaths and a sip of water kept the numbers out of the red zone.

"I suppose you'd want me to liaise with Luna's civic apparatus too." I kept my voice flat.

"That would be ideal." She slapped the table with both palms and grinned. "With a native Lunite at the helm, we'd win for sure."

Long Meng was so busy bubbling with ideas and ambition as she told me her plans, she didn't notice my fierce scowl. She probably didn't even taste her luxurious meal. As for me, I enjoyed every bite, right down to the last crumb of my flaky cardamom-chocolate dessert. Then I pushed back my chair and grabbed my cane.

"There's only one problem, Long Meng," I said. "Luna doesn't deserve crèches."

"Deserve doesn't really—"

I cut her off. "Luna doesn't deserve a population."

She looked confused. "But it has a population, so—"

"Luna deserves to die," I snapped. I stumped away, leaving her at the table, her jaw hanging in shock.

*　　*　　*

HALFWAY THROUGH OUR third and final seminar, in the middle of introducing Ricochet's proprietary never-fail methods for raising kids, I got an emergency ping from Bruce.

Tré's abandoned the tour. He's run off.

I faked a coughing fit and lunged toward the water bulbs at the back of the stage. Turned my back on two thousand pairs of eyes, and tried to collect myself as I scanned Tré's biom. His stress indicators were highly elevated. The other five members of the Jewel Box were anxious too.

Do you have eyes on him?

Of course. Bruce shot me a bookmark.

Three separate cameras showed Tré was alone, playing his favorite pattern-matching game while coasting along a nearly deserted slideway. Metadata indicated his location on an express connector between Coacalco and Eaton habs.

He looked stunned, as if surprised by his own daring. Small, under the high arches of the slideway tunnel. And thin—his bony shoulder blades tented the light cloth of his tunic.

Coacalco has a bot shadowing him. Do we want them to intercept?

I zoomed in on Tré's face, as if I could read his thoughts as easily as his physiology. He'd never been particularly assertive or self-willed, never one to challenge his crèche mates or lead them in new directions. But kids will surprise you.

Tell them to stay back. Ping a personal security firm to monitor him. Go on with your tour. And try not to worry.

Are you sure?

I wasn't sure, not at all. My stress indicators were circling the planet. Every primal urge screamed for the bot to wrap itself around the boy and haul him back to Bruce. But I wasn't going to slap down a sixteen-year-old kid for acting on his own initiative, especially since this was practically the first time he'd shown any.

Looks like Tré has something to do, I whispered. *Let's let him follow through.*

I returned to my chair. Tried to focus on the curriculum but couldn't concentrate. Long Meng could only do so much to fill the gap. The audience became restless, shifting in their seats, murmuring to each other. Many stopped paying attention. Right up in the front row, three golden-haired, rainbow-smocked Venusians were blanked out, completely immersed in their feeds.

Long Meng was getting frantic, trying to distract two thousand people from the gaping hole on the stage that was her friend Jules. I picked up my cane, stood, and calmly tipped my chair. It hit the stage floor with a crash. Long Meng jumped. Every head swiveled.

"I apologize for the dramatics," I said, "but earlier, you all noticed me blanking out. I want to explain."

I limped to the front of the stage, unsteady despite my cane. I wear a stability belt, but try not to rely on it too much. Old age has exacerbated my natural tendency for a weak core, and using the belt too much just makes me frailer. But my legs wouldn't stop shaking. I dialed up the balance support.

"What just happened illustrates an important point about crèche work." I attached my cane's cling-point to the stage floor and leaned on it with both hands as I scanned the audience. "Our mistakes can ruin lives. No other profession carries such a vast potential for screwing up."

"That's not true." Long Meng's eyes glinted in the stage lights, clearly relieved I'd stepped back up to the job. "Engineering disciplines carry quite the disaster potential. Surgery certainly does. Psychology and pharmacology. Applied astrophysics. I could go on." She grinned. "Really, Jules. Nearly every profession is dangerous."

I grimaced and dismissed her point.

"Doctors' decisions are supported by ethics panels and case

reviews. Engineers run simulation models and have their work vetted by peers before taking any real-world risks. But in a crèche, we make a hundred decisions a day that affect human development. Sometimes a hundred an hour."

"Okay, but are every last one of those decisions so important?"

I gestured to one of the rainbow-clad front-row Venusians. "What do you think? Are your decisions important?"

A camera bug zipped down to capture her answer for the seminar's shared feed. The Venusian licked her lips nervously and shifted to the edge of her seat.

"Some decisions are," she said in a high, tentative voice. "You can never know which."

"That's right. You never know." I thanked her and rejoined Long Meng in the middle of the stage. "Crèche workers take on huge responsibility. We assume all the risk, with zero certainty. No other profession accepts those terms. So why do we do this job?"

"Someone has to?" said Long Meng. Laughter percolated across the auditorium.

"Why us, though?" I said. "What's wrong with us?"

More laughs. I rapped my cane on the floor.

"My current crèche is a sixteen-year sixsome. Well integrated, good morale. Distressingly sporty. They keep me running." The audience chuckled. "They're on a geography tour somewhere on the other side of Venus. A few minutes ago, one of my kids ran off. Right now, he's coasting down one of your intra-hab slideways and blocking our pings."

Silence. I'd captured every eye; all their attention was mine.

I fired the public slideway feed onto the stage. Tré's figure loomed four meters high. His foot was kicked back against the slideway's bumper in an attitude of nonchalance, but it was just a pose. His gaze was wide and unblinking, the whites of his eyes fully visible.

"Did he run away because of something one of us said? Or did? Or neglected to do? Did it happen today, yesterday, or ten days ago? Maybe it has nothing to do with us at all, but some private urge from the kid's own heart. He might be suffering acutely right now, or maybe he's enjoying the excitement. The adrenaline and cortisol footprints look the same."

I clenched my gnarled, age-spotted hand to my chest, pulling at the fabric of my shirt.

"But I'm suffering. My heart feels like it could rip right out of my chest because this child has put himself in danger." I patted the wrinkled fabric back into place. "Mild danger. Venus is no Luna."

Nervous laughter from the crowd. Long Meng hovered at my side.

"Crèche work is like no other human endeavor," I said. "Nothing else offers such potential for failure, sorrow, and loss. But no work is as important. You all know that, or you wouldn't be here."

Long Meng squeezed my shoulder. I patted her hand. "Raising children is only for true believers."

NOT LONG AFTER our seminar ended, Tré boarded Venus's circum-planetary chuteway and chose a pod headed for Vanavara. The pod's public feed showed five other passengers: a middle-aged threesome who weren't interested in anything but each other, a halo-haired young adult escorting a floating tank of live eels, and a broad-shouldered brawler with deeply scarred forearms.

Tré waited for the other passengers to sit, then settled himself into a corner seat. I pinged him. No answer.

"We should have had him intercepted," I said.

Long Meng and I sat in the back of the auditorium. A choir group had taken over the stage. Bots were attempting to set up risers, but the singers were milling around, blocking their progress.

"He'll be okay." Long Meng squeezed my knee. "Less than five hours to Vanavara. None of the passengers are going to do anything to him."

"You don't know that."

"Nobody would risk it. Venus has strict penalties for physical violence."

"Is that the worst thing you can think of?" I flashed a pointer at the brawler. "One conversation with that one in a bad mood could do lifelong damage to anyone, much less a kid."

We watched the feed in silence. At first the others kept to themselves, but then the brawler stood, pulled down a privacy veil, and sauntered over to sit beside Tré.

"Oh no," I moaned.

I zoomed in on Tré's face. With the veil in place, I couldn't see or hear the brawler. All I could do was watch the kid's eyes flicker from the window to the brawler and back, monitor his stress indicators, and try to read his body language. Never in my life have I been less equipped to make a professional judgement about a kid's state of mind. My mind boiled with paranoia.

After about ten minutes—an eternity—the brawler returned to their seat.

"It's fine," said Long Meng. "He'll be with us soon."

Long Meng and I met Tré at the chuteway dock. It was late. He looked tired, rumpled, and more than a little sulky.

"Venus is stupid," he said.

"That's ridiculous, a planet can't be stupid," Long Meng snapped. She was tired, and hadn't planned on spending the last night of her vacation waiting in a transit hub.

Let me handle this, I whispered.

"Are you okay? Did anything happen in the pod?" I tried to sound calm as I led him to the slideway.

He shrugged. "Not really. This oldster was telling me how great his hab is. Sounded like a hole."

I nearly collapsed with relief.

"Okay, good," I said. "We were worried about you. Why did you leave the group?"

"I didn't realize it would take so long to get anywhere," Tré said.

"That's not an answer. Why did you run off?"

"I don't know." The kid pretended to yawn—one of the Jewel Box's clearest tells for lying. "Venus is boring. We should've saved our credits."

"What does that mean?"

"Everybody else was happy looking at rocks. Not me. I wanted to get some value out of this trip."

"So you jumped a slideway?"

"Uh huh." Tré pulled a protein snack out of his pocket and stuffed it in his mouth. "I was just bored. And I'm sorry. Okay?"

"Okay." I fired up the leaderboard and zeroed out Tré's score. "You're on a short leash until we get home."

We got the kid a sleep stack near ours, then Long Meng and I had a drink in the grubby travelers' lounge downstairs.

"How are you going to find out why he left?" asked Long Meng. "Pull his feeds? Form a damage mitigation team? Plan an intervention?"

I picked at the fabric on the arm of my chair. The plush nap repaired itself as I dragged a ragged thumbnail along the armrest.

"If I did, Tré would learn he can't make a simple mistake without someone jumping down his throat. He might shrug off the psychological effects, or it could inflict long-term damage."

"Right. Like you said in the seminar. You can't know."

We finished our drinks and Long Meng helped me to my feet. I hung my cane from my forearm and tucked both hands into the crease of her elbow. We slowly climbed upstairs. I could have pinged a physical assistance bot, but my hands were cold, and my friend's arm was warm.

"Best to let this go," I said. "Tré's already a cautious kid. I won't punish him for taking a risk."

"I might, if only for making me worry. I guess I'll never be a crèche manager." She grinned.

"And yet you want to go to Luna and build a new crèche system."

Long Meng's smile vanished. "I shouldn't have sprung that on you, Jules."

In the morning, the two young people rose bright and cheery. I was aching and bleary but put on a serene face. We had just enough time to catch a concert before heading up the umbilical to our shuttle home. We made our way to the atrium, where Tré boggled at the soaring views, packed slideways, clustered performance and game surfaces, fountains, and gardens. The air sparkled with nectar and spices, and underneath, a thick, oily human funk.

We boarded a riser headed to Vanavara's orchestral pits. A kind Venusian offered me a seat with a smile. I thanked him, adding, "That would never happen on Luna."

I drew Long Meng close as we spiraled toward the atrium floor.

Just forget about the proposal, I whispered. *The moon is a lost cause.*

A LITTLE MORE than a year later, Ricochet was on approach for Earth. The Jewel Box were nearly ready to leave the crèche. Bruce and the rest of my team were planning to start a new one, and they warmly assured me I'd always be welcome to visit. I tried not to weep about it. Instead, I began spending several hours a day helping provide round-the-clock cuddles to a newborn with hydrocephalus.

As far as I knew, Long Meng had given up the Luna idea. Then she cornered me in the dim-lit nursery and burst my bubble.

She quietly slid a stool over to my rocker, cast a professional eye over the cerebrospinal fluid-exchange membrane clipped to the baby's ear, and whispered, *We made the short list.*

That's great, I replied, my cheek pressed to the infant's warm, velvety scalp.

I had no idea what she was referring to, and at that moment I didn't care. The scent of a baby's head is practically narcotic, and no victory can compare with having coaxed a sick child into restful sleep.

It means we have to go to Luna for a presentation and interview.

Realization dawned slowly. *Luna? I'm not going to Luna.*

Not you, Jules. Me and my team. I thought you should hear before the whole hab starts talking.

I concentrated on keeping my rocking rhythm steady before answering. *I thought you'd given that up.*

She put a gentle hand on my knee. *I know. You told me not to pursue it and I considered your advice. But it's important, Jules. Luna will restart its crèche program one way or another. We can make sure they do it right.*

I fixed my gaze pointedly on her prognathous jaw. *You don't know what it's like there. They'll roast you alive just for looking different.*

Maybe. But I have to try.

She patted my knee and left. I stayed in the rocker long past hand-over time, resting my cheek against that precious head.

Seventy years ago I'd done the same, in a crèche crowded into a repurposed suite of offices behind one of Luna's water printing plants. I'd walked through the door broken and grieving, certain the world had been drained of hope and joy. Then someone put a baby in my arms. Just a few hours old, squirming with life, arms reaching for the future.

Was there any difference between the freshly detanked newborn on Luna and the sick baby I held on that rocker? No. The embryos gestating in Ricochet's superbly optimized banks of artificial wombs were no different from the ones Luna would grow in whatever gestation tech they inevitably cobbled together.

But as I continued to think about it, I realized there was a difference, and it was important. The ones on Luna deserved better than they would get. And I could do something about it.

FIRST, I HAD my hair sheared into an ear-exposing brush precise to the millimeter. The tech wielding the clippers tried to talk me out of it.

"Do you realize this will have to be trimmed every twenty days?"

"I used to wear my hair like this when I was young," I reassured him. He rolled his eyes and cut my hair like I asked.

I changed my comfortable smock for a lunar grey trouser-suit with enough padding to camouflage my age-slumped shoulders. My cling-pointed cane went into the mulch, exchanged for a glossy black model. Its silver point rapped the floor, announcing my progress toward Long Meng's studio.

The noise turned heads all down the corridor. Long Meng popped out of her doorway, but she didn't recognize me until I pushed past her and settled onto her sofa with a sigh.

"Are you still looking for a project advisor?" I asked.

She grinned. "Luna won't know what hit it."

Back in the rumpus room, Tré was the only kid to comment on my haircut.

"You look like a villain from one of those old Follywood dramas Bruce likes."

"Hollywood," I corrected. "Yes, that's the point."

"What's the point in looking like a gangland mobber?"

"Mobster." I ran my palm over the brush. "Is that what I look like?"

"Kinda. Is it because of us?"

I frowned, not understanding. He pulled his ponytail over his shoulder and eyed it speculatively.

"Are you trying to look tough so we won't worry about you after we leave?"

That's the thing about kids. The conversations suddenly swerve and hit you in the back of the head.

"Whoa," I said. "I'm totally fine."

"I know, I know. You've been running crèches forever. But we're the last because you're so old. Right? It's got to be hard."

"A little," I admitted. "But you've got other things to think about. Big, exciting decisions to make."

"I don't think I'm leaving the crèche. I'm delayed."

I tried to keep from smiling. Tré was nothing of the sort. He'd grown into a gangly young man with long arms, bony wrists, and a haze of silky black beard on his square jaw. I could recite the dates of his developmental benchmarks from memory, and there was nothing delayed about them.

"That's fine," I said. "You don't have to leave until you're ready."

"A year. Maybe two. At least."

"Okay, Tré. Your decision."

I wasn't worried. It's natural to feel ambivalent about taking the first step into adulthood. If Tré found it easier to tell himself he wasn't leaving, so be it. As soon as his crèchemates started moving on, Tré would follow.

Our proximity to Earth gave Long Meng's proposal a huge advantage. We could travel to Luna, give our presentation live, and be back home for the boost.

Long Meng and I spent a hundred billable hours refining our presentation materials. For the first time in our friendship, our communication styles clashed.

"I don't like the authoritarian gleam in your eye, Jules," she told me after a particularly heated argument. "It's almost as though you're enjoying bossing me around."

She wasn't wrong. Ricochet's social conventions require you to hold in conversational aggression. Letting go was fun. But I had an ulterior motive.

"This is the way people talk on Luna. If you don't like it, you should shitcan the proposal."

She didn't take the dare. But she reported behavioral changes to my geriatric specialist. I didn't mind. It was sweet, her being so worried about me. I decided to give her full access to my biom, so she could check if she thought I was having a stroke or something. I'm in okay health for my extreme age, but she was a paediatrician, not a gerontologist. What she saw scared her. She got solicitous. Gallant, even, bringing me bulbs of tea and snacks to keep my glucose levels steady.

Luna's ports won't accommodate foreign vehicles, and their landers use a chemical propellant so toxic Ricochet won't let them anywhere near our landing bays, so we had to shuttle to Luna in stages. As we glided over the moon's surface, its web of tunnels and domes sparkled in the full glare of the sun. The pattern of the habs hadn't changed. I could still name them—Surgut, Sklad, Nadym, Purovsk, Olenyok...

Long Meng latched onto my arm as the hatch creaked open. I wrenched away and straightened my jacket.

You can't do that here, I whispered. *Self-sufficiency is everything on Luna, remember?*

I marched ahead of Long Meng as if I were leading an army. In the light lunar gravity, I didn't need my cane, so I used its heavy silver head to whack the walls. Hitting something felt good. I worked up a head of steam so hot I could have sterilized those corridors. If I had to come home—home, what a word for a place like Luna!—I'd do it on my own terms.

The client team had arranged to meet us in a dinky little media suite overlooking the hockey arena in Sklad. A game had just finished, and we had to force our way against the departing crowd. My cane came in handy. I brandished it like a weapon, signaling my intent to break the jaw of anyone who got too close.

In the media suite, ten hab reps clustered around the project principal. Overhead circled a battery of old, out-of-date cameras that buzzed and fluttered annoyingly. At the front of the room, two chairs waited for Long Meng and me. Behind us arced a glistening expanse of crystal window framing the rink, where grooming bots were busy scraping blood off the ice. Over the arena loomed the famous profile of Mons Hadley, huge, cold, stark, its bleak face the same mid-tone grey as my suit.

Don't smile, I reminded Long Meng as she stood to begin the presentation.

The audience didn't deserve the verve and panache Long Meng put into presenting our project phases, alternative scenarios, and volume ramping. Meanwhile, I scanned the reps' faces, counting flickers in their attention and recording them on a leaderboard. We had forty minutes in total, but less than twenty to make an impression before the reps' decisions locked in.

Twelve minutes in, Long Meng was introducing the strategies for professional development, governance, and ethics oversight. Half the reps were still staring at her face as if they'd never seen a congenital hyperformation before. The other half were bored but still making an effort to pay attention. But not for much longer.

"Based on the average trajectories of other start-up crèche programs," Long Meng said, gesturing at the swirling graphics that hung in the air, "Luna should run at full capacity within six social generations, or thirty standard years."

I'm cutting in, I whispered. I whacked the head of my cane on the floor and stood, stability belt on maximum and belligerence oozing from my every pore.

"You won't get anywhere near that far," I growled. "You'll never get past the starting gate."

"That's a provocative statement," said the principal. She was in her sixties, short and tough, with ropey veins webbing her bony forearms. "Would you care to elaborate?"

I paced in front of their table, like a barrister in one of Bruce's old courtroom dramas. I made eye contact with each of the reps in turn, then leaned over the table to address the project principal directly.

"Crèche programs are part of a hab's social fabric. They don't exist in isolation. But Luna doesn't want kids around. You barely tolerate young adults. You want to stop the brain drain but you won't give up anything for crèches—not hab space, not billable hours, and especially not your prejudices. If you want a healthy crèche system, Luna will have to make some changes."

I gave the principal an evil grin, adding, "I don't think you can."

"I do," Long Meng interjected. "I think you can change."

"You don't know Luna like I do," I told her.

I fired our financial proposal at the reps. "Ricochet will design your new system. You'll find the trade terms extremely reasonable. When the design is complete, we'll provide on-the-ground teams to execute the project phases. Those terms are slightly less reasonable. Finally, we'll give you a project executive headed by Long Meng." I smiled. "Her billable rate isn't reasonable at all, but she's worth every credit."

"And you?" asked the principal.

"That's the best part." I slapped the cane in my palm. "I'm the gatekeeper. To go anywhere, you have to get past me."

The principal sat back abruptly, jaw clenched, chin raised. My belligerence had finally made an impact. The reps were on the edges of their seats. I had them both repelled and fascinated. They weren't sure whether to start screaming or elect me to Luna's board of governors.

"How long have I got to live, Long Meng? Fifteen years? Twenty?"

"Something like that," she said.

"Let's say fifteen. I'm old. I'm highly experienced. You can't afford me. But if you award Ricochet this contract, I'll move back to Luna. I'll control the gating progress, judging the success of every single milestone. If I decide Luna hasn't measured up, the work will have to be repeated."

I paced to the window. Mons Hadley didn't seem grey anymore. It was actually a deep, delicate lilac. Framed by the endless black sky, its form was impossibly complex, every fold of its geography picked out by the sun.

I kept my back to the reps.

"If you're wondering why I'd come back after all the years," I said, "let me be very clear. I will die before I let Luna fool around with some half-assed crèche experiment, mess up a bunch of kids, and ruin everything." I turned and pointed my cane. "If you're going to do this, at least do it right."

BACK HOME ON Ricochet, the Jewel Box was off-hab on a two-day Earth tour. They came home with stories of surging wildlife spectacles that made herds and flocks of Ricochet's biodiversity preserve look like a petting zoo. When the boost came, we all gathered in the rumpus room for the very last time.

Bruce, Blanche, Engku, Megat, and Mykelti clustered on the floor mats, anchoring themselves comfortably for the boost. They'd be fine. Soon they'd have armfuls of newborns to ease the pain of transition. The Jewel Box were all hanging from the ceiling netting, ready for their last ride of childhood. They'd be fine too. Diamante had decided on Mars, and it looked like the other five would follow.

Me, I'd be fine too. I'd have to be.

How to explain the pain and pride when your crèche is balanced on the knife's edge of adulthood, ready to leave you behind forever? Not possible. Just know this: when you see an oldster looking serene and wise, remember, it's just a sham. Under the skin, it's all sorrow.

I was relieved when the boost started. Everyone was too distracted to notice I'd begun tearing up. When the hab turned upside down, I let myself shed a few tears for the passing moment. Nothing too self-indulgent. Just a little whuffle, then I wiped it all away and joined the celebration, laughing and applauding the kids' antics as they bounced around the room.

We got it, Long Meng whispered in the middle of the boost. *Luna just shot me the contract. We won.*

She told me all the details. I pretended to pay attention, but really, I was only interested in watching the kids. Drinking in their antics, their playfulness, their joyful self-importance. Young adults have a shine about them. They glow with untapped potential.

When the boost was over, we all unclipped our anchors. I couldn't quite extricate myself from my deeply padded chair and my cane was out of reach.

Tré leapt to help me up. When I was on my feet, he pulled me into a hug.

"Are you going back to Luna?" he said in my ear.

I held him at arm's length. "That's right. Someone has to take care of Long Meng."

"Who'll take care of you?"

I laughed. "I don't need taking care of."

He gripped both my hands in his. "That's not true. Everyone does."

"I'll be fine." I squeezed his fingers and tried to pull away, but he wouldn't let go. I changed the subject. "Mars seems like a great choice for you all."

"I'm not going to Mars. I'm going to Luna."

I stepped back. My knees buckled, but the stability belt kept me from going down.

"No, Tré. You can't."

"There's nothing you can do about it. I'm going."

"Absolutely not. You have no business on Luna. It's a terrible place."

He crossed his arms over his broadening chest and swung his head like a fighter looking for an opening. He squinted at the old toys and sports equipment secured into rumpus room cabinets, the peeling murals the kids had painted over the years, the battered bots and well-used, colorful furniture—all the ephemera and detritus of childhood that had been our world for nearly eighteen years.

"Then I'm not leaving the crèche. You'll have to stay here with me, in some kind of weird stalemate. Long Meng will be alone."

I scowled. It was nothing less than blackmail. I wasn't used to being forced into a corner, and certainly not by my own kid.

"We're going to Luna together." A grin flickered across Tré's face. "Might as well give in."

I patted his arm, then took his elbow. Tré picked up my cane and put it in my hand.

"I've done a terrible job raising you," I said.

NOTHING EVER HAPPENS ON OBERON

PAUL MCAULEY

OBERON'S TRAFFIC CONTROL spotted the intruder in the last seconds of its approach. Something small and fast, decelerating hard, estimated terminal velocity around three hundred kph. No time to raise its crew, if it was crewed, or pinpoint exactly where it would come down—the best-guess landing ellipse covered an area of some two thousand square kilometres on the north side of Egeus Crater, one of the largest on the little pockmarked moon. There was no distress call or beacon, either, but Bai Bahar Minnot, supervisor of a scale-mining operation in Egeus, was aloft in her hopper bare minutes after the alert and soon spotted patches smashed into the endless umbrella-tree forest that covered most of the crater's floor. A dotted line that led her straight to where the intruder had ended up.

It sat at the far end of a trough of wrecked trees: a white sphere three metres in diameter, cupped on the deflated puddles of tough airbags that had protected it during its kinetic landing. A lifepod, according to the hopper's catalogue, an old model built some time before the Quiet War. It had thrown out a web of tethers to anchor itself in Oberon's vestigial gravity, its systems were powered down, and its hatch was puckered open.

It looked as if the pod's passenger had survived the crash and climbed out, but there was no sign of any movement around the pod, no one was calling on any channel, and a multispectral scan of the area failed to pick out anything in the infrared background radiated by umbrella trees around the crash site. Bai sent a quick report to traffic control, said that she was going to set down and take a look. Trying her best to sound cool and matter-of-fact, even though this was the most exciting thing that had ever happened in her young life. She was anxious too. The pod's passenger could be badly injured, might need more help than she could provide. Or maybe they were an outlaw, or were in some species of serious trouble—why else would someone crash-land on this no-account backwater moon without broadcasting a distress call?

She picked out a clear spot in the tangle of broken trees, touched down with scarcely a bounce, and was reaching for the helmet of her pressure suit when someone pinged her on the common channel. Lindy Aguilar Garten, from the camp at the North Pole. She'd heard Bai's report, she said, was on her way to the crash site with a small search and rescue party, would be there inside two hours.

"I'm already on it," Bai said.

"You're the daughter of Wen, Egil and Ye, aren't you? We met at the centenary celebrations last year. You'd just turned seventeen, as I recall."

"I'm old enough to know what I'm doing."

"Fixing some machine that's thrown a glitch is one thing. Confronting a stranger who tried to sneak past traffic control is quite another. Your best option is to stay aloft, do a wide area grid search. If you don't find anything, you can help us on the ground when we get there."

"I'm already on the ground," Bai said.

She remembered that meeting vividly. Tall and slender, dressed in a sheath the exact indigo tint of Uranus's South Pole, Lindy had just returned from the Saturn system, where she'd spent two years studying biome construction. She hadn't been much older than Bai—twenty, twenty-one—but she'd seemed impossibly elegant, sophisticated, cosmopolitan. Everything Bai yearned to be. She'd barely glanced at Bai while their parents exchanged a few pleasantries, and now here she was, muscling in, giving Bai instructions and telling her it was for her own damn good.

"If you're worried about salvage, you can rest easy," Lindy said. "It's obvious that you have first claim on the lifepod."

"I'm worried that its passenger could be hurt, or worse. And right now I'm the only person who can help them," Bai said, and cut the channel, locked her helmet and cracked the hopper's bubble canopy, and swung out and down.

The lifepod was empty all right, and when Bai asked her suit to handshake with its mind, hoping to find out where it had come from and who its passenger was, she discovered that it was as dead as a stone. Its systems weren't powered down, the suit reported. They had been wiped. Purged. Nothing was left but a flicker of charge in its batteries.

Bai circled the pod, fingertip-skimming over and under splintered stems draped with crumpled canopies like fallen black sails, searching for boot prints or some other trace of the passenger, failing to find anything. Nothing moving under trees fringing either side of the smashed clearing, nothing moving anywhere in the absolute quiet stillness of vacuum.

If the pod's passenger had for whatever reason decided to put some distance between themselves and the crash site, there was only one place within easy walking distance: a refuge that stood on the rim of a secondary crater about ten kilometres northwest. If she had crash-landed in a remote unpopulated area with no resources but a p-suit, Bai thought, and didn't want to wait around for rescue or maybe didn't want to be rescued, that was absolutely where she would head.

She knew she should wait for backup, but Lindy's patronising tone had got under her skin. And anyway, it was a matter of clan pride to prove that she could find the passenger without the help of any damn Gartens. So she tuned into the refuge's directional beacon, pulled up a map, and set off.

The silence and stillness seemed deeper under the umbrella trees. Bai was hyperalert as she ankled along, picking her way between interlocking arcs of trees, trying to keep the beacon dead ahead and searching for boot prints in crunchy dust that was everywhere littered with fallen scales, porcelain white toothy triangles the size of her helmet visor. Every so often her insulated boots kicked one at exactly the right angle and it sailed away in a long, low, frictionless arc. Every so often she disturbed a pocket of loose dust that spurted up in a waist-high geyser and settled out so slowly that if she looked around (as she increasingly did, gripped by a growing unease) she saw a diminishing row of ghostly pillars stitched along her path.

The ground rose and fell in low swales; umbrella trees thickened all around. The top layer of a vast factory that was mostly underfoot, extruded by pseudohyphal networks of nanomachines that extracted processed organic material from the rock-hard ice of the forest floor, and mined metals, rare earths and phosphates from the moon's crust.

The stems of the trees glowed faintly in infrared and their canopies shone more brightly overhead, radiating excess heat into the chill vacuum, and the ground between them was tiger-striped with faint sunlight and pitch-black shadow. Even with her suit's various enhancements, Bai couldn't see more than a couple of hundred metres in any direction, but she plodded on, time ticking away, too stubborn and prideful to give up the search.

She was two kilometres from the refuge, and Lindy Garten and her crew were due to arrive in less than thirty minutes, when she was ambushed. Everything happened in a bare second. A sudden flurry of movement off to one side, something flying out from behind the broad stem of a grandmother tree, and the reflexes of Bai's suit took over before she could react, tangling the attacker in a net a moment before the shock of impact, firing tethers that spun her in a hard stop that rattled her head inside her helmet.

The passenger flew away in the opposite direction, ricocheting off trees in headlong flight. Bai had to walk a long way, following a trail of fresh-fallen scales, before at last she spotted them. They lay unmoving, forced into a foetal ball by the net's contraction, didn't reply when Bai identified herself on the common band. Fearing the worst, she knelt and rolled them onto their back, and rocked back on her heels when she saw the emaciated face behind the visor of their helmet, teeth bared in a lipless grin, eyes sunk deep in sockets and taped shut.

"I THOUGHT SHE was dead," Bai told her mother on the flight back to the scale-harvesting camp. "But then I managed to handshake with the clunky interface of her suit and found she was in cold sleep. I guess the pod assembled a suit around her after it crash-landed, and the suit tried to walk her towards the refuge. But its batteries were almost exhausted when I caught up with it, and I think its mind was damaged too. That could be why it attacked me. It didn't understand that I'd come to help. So I disabled its motor functions and fed it just enough power to keep its life support going until the hopper arrived, and here we are, free and clear."

There was a pause, a little under six seconds, while this zipped at light speed from Oberon to Titania, where Bai's clan and most people in the Uranus system lived, and her mother's reply zipped back. The two moons were presently on opposite sides of the planet, a million kilometres apart, but there was no escaping Bai's mother, who'd pinged her as soon as she'd found out about the escapade, and not to shower her with praise and congratulations.

"You didn't know who was in that lifepod, why it crash-landed where it did," she said to Bai. "And you went chasing off into the forest without telling anyone what you were doing. What were you thinking? But I suppose you weren't."

"I was the first to arrive at the crash site," Bai said. "What else was I supposed to do?"

Even though she knew that things could have gone very differently if her suit hadn't been so quick and clever, she was convinced that she'd done the right thing. If she hadn't found her when she did, the woman's suit might have run out of power. She might have died.

But as usual Bai's mother had other ideas, saying, "You should have waited until the Gartens arrived."

"I didn't need their help to find her."

"And I suppose you think that you don't need their help now. Even though their camp has better medical facilities."

Yes, there was definitely a familiar edge to her voice. Bai's mother, Wen Phoenix Minnot, was seventy-three years old, a clan elder, grand and chilly and remote. Bai was the youngest of her six children, a late addition to the family after Wen married a second husband. Lately, she seemed to be perpetually annoyed by her youngest daughter's restlessness, which was why Bai had been packed off to supervise the scale-harvesting camp on Oberon. She wanted to live on another world? Here was her chance. A moon much like Titania, but somewhat smaller and with even fewer people. Where she could gain useful experience in field engineering. Where living in a trailer habitat in the middle of nowhere (almost everywhere on Oberon was the middle of nowhere) with only machines for company would make her realise what she was missing, back home. Where nothing ever happened.

Except that now it had.

"The Gartens would have taken all the credit," Bai said. "Like they took the pod."

"Whoever this woman is, she isn't a trophy," Wen said.

"Tell that to Lindy Garten."

Lindy had told Bai that she'd quote unquote secured the lifepod after it had been abandoned in place. Bai was pretty sure Lindy had ratted her out to her mother too. The responsible adult dealing with the hot-headed kid's screw-up, scoring points in the perpetual competition between clans for social superiority.

"She did the right thing, and made a full report to the peacers," Wen said. "While you more or less kidnapped this unfortunate woman."

"She has a name," Bai said. "Xtina Groza. At least, that's the name on her suit ID tag. As for the rest—why she was in that lifepod, why she came here—I guess she can tell me when she wakes up."

Wen ignored that, saying, "I'm very disappointed in you, child. I hoped that overseeing the scale-harvesting operation would teach you something about duty, responsibility and common sense. I can see that it has done nothing of the kind. I'll be waiting for you when you get back to the camp, to make sure that this woman gets the best treatment we can provide until the peacers arrive."

Sure enough, a freshly printed avatar was standing at the edge of the landing pad when the hopper touched down. A hollow plastic shell in roughly human form, with feet like suction cups and claws for hands, it stepped forward and lifted Xtina Groza from the cargo rack and set off towards the trailer before Bai had finished powering down the hopper.

The trailer's little revolving airlock could only take one person at a time. Bai went through first, and there was a moment, while she was hauling Xtina Groza's rigid pressure suit out of the lock, when she thought of shutting the avatar outside—the thing was running semi-autonomously because of the time lag, she'd be able to do it before it could react. But she was already in more than enough trouble, so she dutifully spun the lock around and waited for the avatar to cycle through so her mother could tell her what to do next.

Wen ordered the doctor thing to extrude itself from the trailer's wall, told Bai she had found instructions for manually opening the antique hardshell suit. The avatar stood at Bai's back while she warmed the suit to room temperature and worked through the checklist of latches, snap fasteners and ring and plug connectors. At last, she lifted the helmet from the neck ring, removed the bulky life support pack, gloves and chestpiece, and tugged down the long zip of the inner lining.

Xtina Groza was swaddled in a yellow, close-woven, elasticated undergarment that clung to the blades and ridges of her long-limbed, painfully thin body. A hank of black hair, coarse and glossy with grease, was pulled back from her face and lay across her left shoulder; a small black disc lay between her flattened breasts. The machine that had been regulating her metabolism during cold sleep, Bai's mother said. Old tech.

Bai unclipped the lines that had been feeding the woman drugs and nutrients, her catheter and breathing tube. Her skin was clammy but not chilled, and a faint pulse was visible under the angle of her jaw. She was no longer in true cold sleep; her suit had been trying to wake her.

The avatar carried her to the doctor thing, which immediately wrapped her from head to toe in its shroud and got to work, and Wen told Bai that she needed to take the pressure suit outside.

"It's powered down. And in pieces."

"It's an old combat model," Wen said, her voice coming from the avatar's unmoving transparent face. "I don't know what it's capable of and neither do you. Go on, now."

No point arguing, and besides, Bai had an idea. After her own suit had assembled itself around her, she piled the helmet, gloves and other loose pieces inside the shell of Xtina Groza's suit and hauled it through the lock and whistled up a sled and rode across to the refinery, where she stuffed the suit inside an unused storage tank. Out of sight, and so on. If the peace police forgot to ask about it, and her mother forgot to remind them, Bai could try to hack into its mind, find out everything it knew about its owner. It was only a token rebellion and probably wouldn't come to anything, but it put a little bounce in her gait as she trekked back to the trailer.

The doctor thing was still ticking away to itself as it assessed and stabilised the comatose woman. It took a while. Bai munched a sprouted bean wrap and sipped a bulb of tea, tried her best to ignore the impassive avatar. The adrenalin high of the search and rescue had drained away. She was tired and cross-grained, felt that she was being punished for doing the right thing. At least the results of the doctor thing's analyses and diagnostic tests were worth the wait.

Xtina Groza was somatically and genetically female, apparent age around twenty-five, chronological age unknown. Trace analysis suggested that she had been in cold sleep a long time. A minimum of seventy years, maybe more. Which would have been interesting in itself, but there were also the gene mods. As well as the usual adaptations to life in low gravity, with minor variations in their genetic code that suggested Xtina Groza had been born in the Saturn system, there were mods that weren't in any catalogue, implants in the visual cortex of her brain and her brainstem, and a mesh of fine threads woven through her musculature.

Bai and her mother agreed that the combat suit, the mods and implants, and the length of time she'd been in cold sleep strongly suggested that Xtina Groza had been involved in the Quiet War. Most Outers had taken the high road of passive resistance, but some cities and settlements had fought back against Earth's Three Powers Alliance in the brief fierce clash, and a few pockets of rebels had actively resisted the subsequent occupation of the Jupiter and Saturn systems. Xtina Groza might be one such, a soldier enhanced for speed and strength and survival, and Bai had an idea, she thought a good one, which could explain how this woman had ended up in a lifepod that had only just now crash-landed on Oberon.

In the immediate aftermath of the Quiet War, a group of self-styled Free Outers had fled from the Saturn system and briefly settled on Titania (the gala where Bai had met Lindy Garten had been part of the celebrations on the hundredth anniversary of their arrival) before moving even further out. One of them, Macy Minnot, Bai's great-grandmother, had been a defector from Greater Brazil; another had been Macy's husband, Newton Jones, scion of an influential clan from Saturn's moon Dione—Bai and Wen's clan. It was possible, Bai told her mother, that Xtina Groza had been a member of the resistance, sent to recruit the Free Outers to her cause. But her ship had run into trouble, or perhaps it had been involved in a fire fight with the Three Powers expeditionary force that had come looking for the Free Outers, and she'd escaped in her lifepod and somehow it had not been picked up. Orbiting Uranus for decades in a highly eccentric path that took it far from the planet most of the time, before at last it had come close enough to Oberon to attempt a landing.

"The pod took a last chance at saving its passenger," Bai said. "And because it didn't realise that the war was long over, it wiped all its records in case it was captured by the enemy."

"It's a nice story," Wen said. "But at the moment we don't know enough to know if it's anything more than that."

"When she wakes up, we can ask her directly."

"She isn't going to wake up for a while," Wen said, the time delay giving it the weight of a carefully considered reply rather than something that had already been decided without consulting Bai. "The doctor thing will keep her in an induced coma until the peacers arrive."

Bai started to say something, forgetting in her anger about that damn delay, but her mother hadn't finished, anticipating her objections, telling her that the woman possessed military mods, she was an unknown quantity, it wouldn't be safe to wake her until she was in a secure place.

"She isn't my prisoner," Bai said, unable to help herself.

"I know you want to know everything there is to know about her. It's only natural that you do. And you will, soon enough. Meanwhile, you'll have to learn how to be patient. And you should get some rest. You've had quite the day, and you'll need to be at your best when the peacers arrive."

So that was that. As usual, her mother was treating her like a child, taking charge, making decisions without bothering to consult her. All she could say, in token protest, was that when the peacers came she wanted to go back with them. "You said that I needed to learn about responsibility. Well, I feel responsible for Xtina Groza because I saved her life. Making sure that she's transported safely to Titania is the least I can do for her."

If she turned out to be a genuine hero of the resistance, the peacers wouldn't be able to hold the woman long. And she would need a place to stay when they let her go. Bai could invite her to stay in one of the clan's guest apartments, help her, listen to her stories. They'd become friends, and maybe Bai could leave with her, when the time came.

She elaborated this fantasy while she drifted to sleep in the curtained niche. It was an echo of the stories she'd told herself as a child, stories about the places she'd visit and the wonders she'd see when she was old enough to travel the solar system. She hadn't thought then that she'd end up on Oberon, where hardly anyone lived and nothing ever happened. But something had happened now, all right, and it would change everything...

When she woke, just a few hours later, the doctor thing was still humming and clicking at the other end of the trailer's living space, Xtina Groza was still motionless under the doctor thing's shroud, and the avatar's soap-bubble statue was still standing guard. Except that now it was controlled by Ye, the oldest of Bai's fathers.

"Why don't you have some breakfast," he said, "and tell me all about your adventure."

Big, cuddly, endlessly patient Ye was Bai's favourite parent. He'd always taken her plans for travelling the system seriously; he'd done plenty of travelling himself before he'd married Wen and Egil, Bai's biological father, and settled down in Fairyland. He possessed the serene calm of someone who had seen so much of worlds that nothing could surprise him anymore, and Bai loved his stories of exotic corners of the outer system and the two years he'd spent working for the Martian Terraforming Authority. They gave her hope that one day she'd be able to see those same places and more besides. Still, she faintly resented that he was babysitting her. No doubt it was Wen's idea. Even though telling him the story of how she'd found Xtina Groza rekindled something of the excitement and wonder of it, she felt that she was being pandered to.

"It's definitely one for the scrolls," Ye said, which was what he called the clan's records. "You're a hero, Bai. I can't tell you how proud I am."

"It isn't over yet," Bai said. "And I want to see it through to the end. Find out who she is, and the whole story of how she ended up here. And help her deal with the peacers, and help after they let her go."

She sipped from her bulb of tea while waiting for his reply, a lot longer than the time delay.

"Mmm-hmm. We'll have to think about that. And see what the peacers have to say about it too. Meantime, you should check the board. One of the harvesters has got itself in a pickle."

"As if it matters now."

"Of course it matters. You know the Gartens don't want us here. Any violation of our lease, no matter how small, would give them an excuse to make a complaint to the Commonhold Council. You go on now, and don't worry about your sleeping beauty. I'll keep watch. If there's anything to report, I'll let you know at once."

Bai knew it was busy work got up to distract her, but she was also sort of glad to get out for a few hours. It would give her time to think. To plan. To work out exactly how she could persuade the peacers to let her ride along with Xtina Groza to Titania.

So without any argument she suited up and headed out on one of the rackety old sleds towards the spot where the harvester had got itself into a jam. Mostly, the machines could be left to work by themselves. Several hundred man-sized, squid-shaped harvesters crawling in long transects across the forest floor, collecting scales shed by the umbrella trees and dumping their loads in the hoppers of runners that transported them to the refinery, where metals and rare earths were extracted for export and the residue was used as a substrate for starter cultures of nanomachines, which the forester rig force-injected into the rock-hard ice to quicken new colonies. Bai monitored every aspect of this activity, fixed machines that damaged themselves beyond the limits of their repair mites, organised movement of the camp to a new area of the forest when a patch had been completely harvested, and supervised the cannon that shot loaded cargo drones into low-energy transfer orbits that eventually intersected with Titania.

When she wasn't overseeing all this, carrying out routine maintenance in the camp, or studying for her engineering certificates, she liked to hike through the umbrella-tree forest and climb to the top of the crater's rimwall and look out at the moonscape. Her favourite route followed the narrow crest of a buttress that rose steeply to the edge of a cirque bitten into the rimwall, with a view across a smashed plain to the curved horizon, notched in the west by one of the long deep canyons that dissected the moon's surface. Craters everywhere. So many that new craters overlapped or were inside older craters, and everything was dusted with dark red CHON tars that had spiralled in after being knocked off irregular outer moons by meteorite and micrometeorite impacts.

All around, absolute silence and stillness. No sound but the faint hiss of air in Bai's helmet, the hum of her suit's pumps, the flutter of her pulse in her ears. Looking out at the moonscape with her comms turned off, no boot prints on the dusty ground but her own and nothing moving under the black sky, where Uranus's big beautiful blue globe swam like an exotic jellyfish, and at this latitude and in this season, the cold spark of the sun hung close to the horizon, and Bai felt like the queen of the little world, or the last person in the solar system. A lovely lonely feeling.

Although she'd been packed off to Oberon because her mother hoped that it would quench her restlessness, it had instead fed her hunger for travel and adventure. The Uranus system was a dull, sparsely settled backwater, and everywhere else the solar system was abloom with what people were beginning to call the Second Renaissance. Established cities and settlements in the Jupiter and Saturn systems had been rebuilt and expanded, and hundreds of new settlements and gardens had been constructed on minor planets, moons, asteroids—even on kobolds out beyond the orbit of Neptune. The great terraforming projects on Mars still had centuries to run, but more than a million people lived there in tented cities and gardens, and forests were being planted out in the lowest parts of the Hellas Basin, where the atmospheric pressure was high enough, now, for liquid water to persist on the surface. There were half a dozen different plans to terraform Venus too, and colony ships and seedships were halfway to some of the near stars and more were being constructed to sustain the outward urge.

Bai wanted to see some of that with her own eyes. She wanted to visit the clan's Firsthome on Dione, sample life in the cities of the moons of Saturn and Jupiter, and the garden colonies of the asteroid belt, sail the polar lakes of Titan, take the scenic railroad down the length of Valles Marineris on Mars, maybe even visit ancient, teeming Earth. Rescuing Xtina Groza was confirmation that she wasn't meant for an ordinary life. It was the beginning of a wonderful and strange adventure whose ending was excitingly unclear.

But first, she had to sort out the damn harvester. It had wandered into a narrow steep-sided fracture that zigzagged from a secondary crater and couldn't work out how to retrace its steps, bumping with futile persistence against the sheer wall where the fracture terminated. A minor fault in its nav system, probably. Bai towed the machine out of the fracture and aimed it at the nearest patch of forest. She watched as it stepped away on its springy tentacles, disappeared into ink-black shadows under the umbrella trees. If it got stuck again, she'd have to bring it in and figure out what had gone wrong, but hopefully it was just a one-off glitch.

She was halfway back to the camp when an alert overflashed her comms. It was her mother, asking Bai where she was, telling her that there was a serious problem at the camp.

"We think the woman may have woken up. The avatar went offline and the feed from the doctor thing cut out. We can't access the camp's comms either. Which means we can't see what's going on, and we can't print new avatars. We're trying to get back up inside the comms, but it's going to take a while. I've alerted the peacers. They know what to expect. They'll go in, do what needs to be done. Meanwhile, I want you to hunker down in place. The woman has already attacked you once. She could take you hostage, or worse."

"It was her suit that attacked me, and it was a mistake." Bai had slowed the sled, was trying to process what she'd been told. It didn't seem likely that Xtina Groza had woken from her induced coma. Maybe the Gartens had kidnapped her, although that would be a risky and provocative move. Or maybe one of the half hundred hermits and aesthetes scattered across Oberon had heard the chatter about her, decided she was dangerous, or that she was a messenger sent by one of their gods...

She told her mother this, said that she had to check out the camp. "If someone took her, I'll find out who it was and where they went."

"There was no sign of any intruder before the comms went out," Wen said. "The peacers will be there soon. Promise me you won't do anything silly before they arrive."

Silly. That stung. As if she was still a little girl. As if she didn't know what she was doing.

"I'm cutting my comms," Bai said. "In case someone is listening in. I'll be back shortly."

She knew that she was being reckless, but she also knew that she had to find out what had happened, and drove the rest of the way at full speed, banging over rough ground, swerving around trees, concentrating on steering the sled so she wouldn't have to think about everything that could go wrong.

The camp was set up on top of a bare apron of ejecta that had been thrown out from a secondary crater. Bai halted in the shadows at the edge of the forest and used the suit's optics to scope out the lie of the land. Several runners were frozen in place around the refinery, presumably shut down when the comms had fallen over. Nothing was moving around the white cylinder of the trailer either. The spare sled was parked nearby, and the pair of hoppers stood side by side in the green glow of the lights that circled the landing apron. No sign of any intruders, but they could have come and gone, taking Xtina Groza with them...

A couple of years ago, on her sixteenth birthday, when she'd officially become an adult, Bai's clan had given her a round trip to Miranda. One of the moon's sightseeing attractions was a long ribbon of sheer cliffs more than five kilometres high, Verona Rupes, a big fault scarp created by upwellings of partially melted ices, and like any other tourist Bai had jumped off the end of a platform cantilevered out from one of the highest points. The gravity of Miranda was even lower than the gravity of Oberon or Titania; it took almost six minutes to reach the big target painted at the bottom. But in vacuum free fall, with no air resistance to slow acceleration, the final velocity of that long swooning fall was enough to kill a person, so jumpers were equipped with backpacks that stabilised their fall and fired braking jets during the last ten seconds. The big slam of deceleration was part of the fun.

Driving out of the shelter of the trees, Bai had the same scary floating sensation she'd felt when she'd stepped off the projection point of that jump platform into absolutely nothing at all. She parked the sled at the refinery and checked the tank in which she'd dumped Xtina Groza's p-suit; she hadn't been able to shake off the unsettling idea that it might have switched itself back on and reassembled itself, cut the camp's comms, and rescued its owner. She felt a cool measure of relief when she saw that it was still there, exactly as she'd left it, and walked all the way around the trailer.

No tracks she didn't recognise, no movement behind the trailer's lighted ports. She returned to the sled in three long bounds, had a brief conversation with her suit and stuffed a bunch of tethers in its utility pouch and unshipped a long handled wrench from the sled's tool rack. Took a last look around and ankled up to the trailer's lock and cycled through.

The woman, Xtina Groza, sat cross-legged on the floor at the far end of the trailer, the shroud wrapped around her like a cloak. Pale and angular, motionless as the avatar standing at the foot of the doctor thing's couch. Moving only her eyes to look at Bai, saying, "Who are you? Where is this place?"

AFTER SETTING DOWN the wrench, moving slowly and carefully to show that she was no threat, and unlocking and lifting off her helmet, Bai introduced herself, told Xtina Groza that this was a scale-harvesting camp on Oberon, explained that she had been inside a lifepod that had crash-landed a couple of hundred kilometres to the northeast.

"I found you, brought you here. The doctor thing was treating you, and I guess you woke up."

The woman's gaze lost focus for a second; then she shook her head. "I don't remember any of that. I can't even remember my name. I try, but it's always just out of reach."

Her voice was soft and husky, her accent stilted in the way people in old-time clips talked.

"It's Xtina. Xtina Groza. Or at least, that's the tag in your suit comms."

The woman shook her head again. "That doesn't mean anything to me. Oberon, though... I know Oberon. It's one of the big moons of Uranus. But how did I get to Uranus?"

"You don't know why you're here?"

"I don't even remember where I came from."

She didn't seem upset. Mildly bemused, maybe.

"You were in cold sleep a long time," Bai said. "I suppose it could be a side effect."

"Cold sleep? For how long?"

Bai told her suit to disperse, and said, as its components unlocked and threw themselves to their niches beside the lock, "I'll fetch some tea and tell you everything I know. But I'm afraid that I don't know very much."

They sat cross-legged on the soft red alife moss that carpeted the trailer's floor, drinking liquorice tea ("I didn't know I liked this," Xtina said) while Bai explained about the lifepod's crash-landing, how she'd found Xtina being walked through the umbrella-tree forest, asleep inside her pressure suit, how the suit had tried to ambush her.

"I think it thought I might be an enemy of yours. Or maybe it saw me as a source of power and consumables. It was walking you towards a refuge, but I don't think it had enough zap to make it."

"But you're not my enemy," Xtina said.

Bai wasn't sure if that was a statement or a question. She said, "It wasn't you. It was your suit. You were asleep. You'd been asleep a long time. I think for around a century."

Xtina showed no surprise. Taking a sip from her bulb of tea, she said, "Are you sure?"

Bai told her that her lifepod and p-suit were antiques, explained about the biochemical markers the doctor thing had found. Hesitated for a moment, torn between prudence and curiosity, then said, "It also found that you have implants. It seems that you were a soldier. Or some kind of combatant, anyway. Involved in the Quiet War."

Another pause, another sip of tea. Xtina said at last, "I remember the Quiet War. I remember that the Three Powers Authority won."

"They did, for a little while. And then we regained our independence."

Another pause. "Well, I don't remember that. It was a hundred years ago?"

"A little over."

"And I came out here. To Uranus. Do you know why?"

"Have you heard of the Free Outers?"

"Is that what the people living here call themselves?"

"We came later. The Free Outers were what I guess you could call political refugees. They escaped from the Three Powers Authority during the Quiet War, stayed here a little while, moved further out."

"You think I might be one? A Free Outer?"

"I was wondering if you came here because you wanted to join them," Bai said.

If she'd guessed right, it would prove to her mother that her so-called fantasies could sometimes be useful.

But Xtina apologised again, saying, "I wish I could tell you it meant something to me. I wish I knew more. It's strange. I suppose I should be confused, or upset. Or angry. Instead, it doesn't seem to matter."

Her bony face was hard to read, but she did seem to be amazingly calm. Stoic. If Bai had woken up with no idea of who she was, where she was or why, *when* she was, she would have lost her mind.

"The doctor thing gave you all kinds of drugs," Bai said.

"Perhaps this doctor thing could give me something that would help me remember who I am."

"Do you remember what happened when you woke up?"

"I thought I was dead. I was wrapped tight inside this blanket, no light, no sound... And when I got free of it, I had no idea where I was. Who I was."

"So the doctor thing fell over, and then you woke up."

"I suppose so."

"You don't remember doing anything to it?"

"Do you think I did? Because I'm a soldier?"

"I'm just trying to figure out what happened," Bai said cautiously, pierced by a sudden sharpness in Xtina Groza's gaze.

She was wondering if the woman was faking her amnesia. Didn't captured soldiers refuse to give up any information but their name and rank? Maybe she was pretending to have lost her memory so that she didn't have to reveal her mission. And she definitely wasn't as vulnerable and confused as she seemed to be: after she'd woken from her induced coma, she'd managed to shut down the doctor thing and futz the comms, which Bai's suit had been trying to access ever since she'd stepped into the trailer, so far without any success.

"You and me both," Xtina said. She had finished her tea, was rhythmically squeezing the bulb in one hand, holding the shroud closed at her throat with the other. "Why don't you tell me something about yourself? Where you live and how you live. This future I've somehow ended up in."

She was trying to move the conversation away from herself, but Bai went with it. The peacers would be here in little under seven hours. By then, the soporific Bai's suit had manufactured, a little gel capsule Bai had sneaked into Xtina's bulb of tea, should have done its work. All she had to do was keep the woman talking, keep her calm, let her know she had nothing to fear, until she fell asleep.

She explained that there were just ten thousand people in the Uranus system, most of them living on Titania. She talked about Fairyland, how the city had been built by machines before people arrived, how there were many cities and settlements like it scattered across the solar system, some still completely empty, built during the wave of expansion in the heady decades of optimism and confidence that had followed the end of the occupation of the

Jupiter and Saturn systems by the Three Powers Authority, and reconciliation between Earth and the Outers. She told Xtina about all the places she wanted to visit, and Xtina said she knew some of the names but didn't remember if she'd ever visited them; she didn't even remember where she'd been living before she came here.

"If you want to leave," she said, "why not just get on a ship and go?"

"Is that what you did?"

"I know it is what young people used to do. Set out on a wanderjahr. See other worlds, meet different people. Something else I didn't know I knew until I thought about it. You don't do that, anymore?"

"It isn't that easy. In my clan, everyone shares credit and karma, and everyone has a say in how we use it."

"If you really wanted to travel to other worlds, I think you'd find a way."

"I'm going to. I really am. I've already been to Miranda—that's one of the other moons? And now I'm working here, on Oberon. It wasn't exactly my idea, but still."

"So it was really your clan's idea."

"Sort of," Bai said. No point mentioning her mother; it would only complicate things.

"And what kind of work are you doing here, for your clan?'

"Harvesting umbrella-tree scales. I guess you don't know what they are, umbrella trees. They were developed after the war. They're a kind of vacuum organism."

"I know about vacuum organisms."

"We have a big forest of umbrella trees here. They extract metals and rare earths from the crust, store them in scales that grow on their stems. I look after the machines that harvest and process scales that the trees have shed," Bai said, and explained that her clan maintained the umbrella-tree forest for the same reason that other clans were running a borehole project to tap the residual warmth locked in the moon's core, or administering the little spaceport that no one but the occasional outsystem tourist used.

"We have to have a presence on Oberon if we want a say in future settlement and development. Otherwise, the Gartens, that's the largest clan in the system, they'd claim it as their own. They've built a big garden at the North Pole, and now they're roofing over a chasm in the South Pole, planning to build another garden there. They like to plan ahead," Bai said. "In twenty years the sun will be above the South Pole, and the North Pole, where they are now, will be in darkness. This forest too. My clan are discussing whether they should start planting a new one in the south. So why I'm here, it's just politics. A silly game."

Her mouth was dry, and she took a sip of cold tea. She'd done most of the talking, and Xtina still didn't look the least bit sleepy, saying that she remembered that the Uranus system was tipped at right angles to the plane of its orbit, so the north poles of the planet and its moons were pointed towards the sun for half its orbital period, the south poles for the other half.

"And it takes eighty-four years to complete one orbit," she said. "I didn't know I knew that until I thought about it. Isn't that strange? I wonder what else I know. Do you have a ship here?"

"Just a couple of hoppers."

"I mean a real ship. What about these rivals of yours? The Gartens."

"I don't know. I suppose so. They have to bring in construction materials they can't make here."

"Ships that can only travel between moons? Or ships that can travel elsewhere?"

"Why do you want to know?"

Bai felt the chasm yawning at her feet again. Xtina couldn't possibly know about the peacer ship. Could she? And why wasn't the soporific working? It should have put her under by now.

"You want to travel. Maybe I can help you," Xtina said. "Take you on a wanderjahr."

"By stealing a ship?"

"From your rivals. Why not? It would be fun. And a good way of repaying you for saving my life."

"Even if we could, the peacers would catch us."

"Peacers as in peace police? Don't worry about them. I suppose you put my suit in a safe place. In case it attacked you again. I couldn't find it in this little habitat, so it must be outside."

Xtina had shed her benign vagueness. She was energised, fully in control of the conversation.

Bai said, "I'm not going to help you steal a ship."

"I can take you wherever you want to go. All you have to do is fetch my pressure suit."

Bai met Xtina's blue gaze. "I don't think so."

She'd stood up to her mother many times. This was a lot harder.

"If you won't help me," the woman said, "maybe I'll take your suit. See if I can remember how to fly a hopper. How hard can it be, finding the north pole of this little moon?"

"That's enough," someone else said.

It was the avatar.

Saying, when Bai and Xtina turned to look at it, "You locked me out, but you didn't find the back door."

"Who am I talking to?" Xtina said, seemingly unperturbed.

"Wen Phoenix Minnot. Bai's mother," the avatar said, and swivelled neatly and with one bound reached the doctor thing at the other end of the couch, snatched something from it. A needle, flashing in its gripping claw.

"Wait," Bai said. As far as she was concerned, the comms were still down. "I can handle this."

"I took back control only a couple of minutes ago," Wen said, "but I heard enough to know that you can't."

The avatar took a bounding step towards Bai and Xtina, and Xtina pushed up and shouldered into it, grabbing the claw that held the needle and flipping up and over as they shot backwards, wrapping her legs around the avatar's waist, twisting its head back and forth. They struck the far wall and rebounded, the avatar's head came free with a sharp pop, trailing a short spine of gear, and Xtina kicked the rest of it away and caught a wall bracket and hung there.

"I didn't know I could do that," she said. "But the body remembers."

Then she flung herself at Bai.

BAI WOKE THREE hours later, dry-mouthed and headachy. The avatar's decapitated body sprawled on red moss a little way from her. There was no sign of its head, or of Bai's suit. When she looked out of a port, she saw that one of the hoppers was gone, too.

The comms were still down. Truly down; Xtina had locked the back door Wen had used, the back door Bai knew nothing about. No way of raising help, or trying to warn Lindy Aguilar Garten. She fetched tea and a patch to ease the after-effects of the tranquilliser Xtina had injected into her, and waited for the peacers to arrive.

XTINA GROZA EXPERTLY finessed her disappearance. An antique but potent worm took down traffic control across the Uranus system; by the time everything was back up, the ship she'd stolen from the Gartens' camp was long gone. It turned up twenty-one weeks later, with a fake registration and a wiped mind, on the landing field of Harper's Hope, Europa, but there was no trace of Xtina, no clue as to why she had gone there or where she had gone afterwards.

It wasn't even clear if Xtina Groza had ever been her real name. There were no records of her in any city or settlement in the Saturn and Jupiter systems, no familial matches to her genome in the gene libraries, and other lines of enquiry likewise dead-ended. Xtina's pressure suit turned out to be as dumb as a bag of rocks. Bai was pretty sure that it hadn't been walking Xtina towards that shelter, and hadn't tried to ambush her either. No, Xtina's implants and the mesh woven through her musculature had done all that, working her sleeping body like a puppet. As for the lifepod, it had belonged originally to a cargo ship owned by a collective in Paris, Dione, damaged in the Quiet War, and cut up in an orbital graveyard around Saturn's moon Rhea. The lifepod had been appropriated by the Three Powers Alliance, but there was no record of what had happened to it after that, and any useful information it might have possessed was lost beyond any hope of retrieval. It hadn't simply shut itself down—its core and subsystems had been consumed by nanites, turned to a silky powder of plastics and metals.

It was the kind of action a military AI might take if it believed that it was about to fall into enemy hands, supporting Bai's idea that Xtina Groza had been some kind of soldier, but although Bai interviewed more than two dozen surviving members of the resistance, none of them remembered Xtina Groza, and she failed to find so much as a passing mention of a clandestine mission to Uranus in the official and unofficial histories of the war. And then there was the worm Xtina had used to futz traffic control, which turned out to be very similar to worms deployed by the Pacific Union against the transport, sewage, energy and environmental systems of several cities in the Saturn system. Outer rebels could have isolated it and redeployed it against their oppressors, but Bai knew that she had to try to chase down the other possibility.

She didn't get very far. The reconciliation office in the PacCom's embassy in Paris, Dione, couldn't or wouldn't answer her questions, and when she reached out directly to the Ministry of Defence in Beijing, she was told that the pertinent records were still sealed, but the case would remain active and she would be contacted if any new information came to light. As if it ever would. After all her research and patient detective work, she still didn't know why Xtina Groza had ended up at Uranus, what she was, who she had been working for.

By then, Bai had spent two years searching for clues about Xtina's identity, travelling amongst the moons of the Saturn and Jupiter systems, taking work wherever she could find it or relying on the kindness of strangers. She didn't manage to wrangle trips to Mars or to Earth, but there were more than enough wonders in the asteroid belt and the Outer system, an incxhaustible variety of people. She visited Paris, Dione, and Xamba, Rhea, venerable cities with proud histories of resistance during the war and occupation, and Akti, Enceladus, which stepped down the steep, terraced side of Damascus Sulcus and gave access to the inner sca and the tweaked merpeople who lived there, claiming to be the only true inhabitants of the little moon. She made the obligatory pilgrimage to her clan's Firsthome on Dione too, and rode a yacht across Saturn's rings, and on Titan trekked through a range of cryovolcanoes to a spent caldera that contained an ancient garden designed by the legendary gene wizard Avernus. She worked on a kelp farm suspended in Europa's subsurface ocean, spent half a year on Ceres helping to plant a forest around a small briny sea in a habitat that snaked along the bottom of a tented canyon, hitched a ride on a freighter that on a long swing through the asteroid belt called on the Realm of a Hundred Blooms, Ymir, Longreach, and 20897Ballard, otherwise known as Concentration City.

Some people never quit their wanderjahrs. Became nomads moving from city to city, moon to moon, world to world, taking temporary jobs or making a living as storytellers, poets, or musicians, travelling light, trading information on the wanderjahr whispernet, always thinking of the next port of call. A few wrangled places or worked their tickets on colony ships to the near stars—the ultimate wanderjahr. But after her last lead on Xtina Groza fizzled out in the warrens of Concentration City, Bai decided that her search and her desire for travelling had run their courses. She returned to Titania, and a year later married Lindy Aguilar Garten.

Her mother's interference after the rescue of Xtina Groza was the capstone of something that had been building in Bai for a long time. When the peacers finally arrived at the scale-harvesting camp, hours too late, they'd wanted to take her back to Fairyland for questioning; instead, she'd used their comms to make the one call she was allowed by ancient right that predated settlement of the Outer system, and formally asked Lindy to give her aid and sanctuary. After a brief fierce flurry of legal exchanges, culminating in a call from Phoenix Clay Garten, chair of the Subcommittee for Public Order, the peacers capitulated, and flew Bai to the Gartens' camp.

At first, Lindy offered to help because it would embarrass the Minot clan and strengthen the Garten's tenuous claim on Xtina Groza, but their relationship soon deepened into something stronger and more real. Lindy gave Bai advice and support while she was interviewed and reinterviewed by the peacers, and helped her patch up a truce with her parents and the clan elders, and they stayed in touch during Bai's wanderjahr. In the years after they married, they had two kids, both girls, and Bai went to work for the Commonhold Council, at last taking charge of the Office for Developmental Strategy.

Sometimes her job took her outsystem, and as she had during her wanderjahr, she posted messages for Xtina on the public boards of the cities she visited. More out of habit than hope by then, but one day, some sixteen years later, she at last received a reply.

It was in Rainbow Bridge, Callisto. Bai had a distant connection with the city. Her great-grandmother, Macy Minnot, had been part of a crew quickening a garden sponsored by the Greater Brazilian government, and had defected after discovering that it had been designed to fail, an early episode in a covert campaign to destabilise Outer cities before the Quiet War. The tent of that old garden had been shattered in the brief battle when the city had fallen to the Brazilian/European joint expeditionary force, and still lay open to vacuum, a war monument that sheltered a unique mixed ecology of vacuum organisms, alife plants, and microbes with an ammonium-based metabolism. Bai had come to Rainbow Bridge to discuss setting up something similar on the CHON-rich plains of Oberon, was resting late one evening after an early round of negotiations when someone claiming to be Xtina Groza pinged her, said they could meet at the spaceport terminal, and gave directions.

Bai sat alone for thirty minutes in a café near one of the terminal's tall windows, with a view of the field where ships of various sizes sat on raised landing pads in the lion light of Jupiter's fat globe. She was beginning to wonder if this was some kind of joke or trick when one of café's antique serverbots deposited a plastic strip as it clanked past her table. Bai barely had time to read the message printed on it before it fizzed into a black puddle.

She followed her new instructions to a bench near one of the gates to the tunnels that linked the terminal to the landing pads. The woman sitting there didn't look much like Xtina Groza—black hair, dark skin, green eyes, and about twenty centimetres shorter—but she was dressed in the plain blue suit liner mentioned in the message, and stood up as Bai approached.

"You got what you wanted," she said. "Travelling to strange new worlds. Meeting strange new people. But then you scurried home and settled down, just like your parents, and their parents before them. What happened? Wasn't the free life all you expected it to be? Or did you discover that you weren't cut out for it?"

Bai supposed that this was the opening gambit of an attempt to unnerve and dominate her, but she'd dealt with enough bellicose negotiators to know that the best way to win that game was to refuse to play it. "I realised that I could use what I'd learned to make Fairyland and the rest of the Uranus system the kind of place where I wanted to live," she said. "How about you?"

"How I live, I can't tell you too much about that," Xtina said. The sleeves of her suit liner were rolled back to the elbows; her forearms glittered with the kind of tattoos, abstract patterns in silver and gold and white, favoured by Europan kelp farmers. "Let's just say it also involves a lot of travelling. It's odd that our paths haven't crossed before, especially as you've been looking for me."

"I gave up looking for you in any serious way a long time ago. Did you ever find out who you were, and where you came from? Or are you still searching?"

Bai sat on the bench, and after a moment Xtina sat beside her, saying, "If that's a polite way of asking if I was faking amnesia, I wasn't."

"I was wondering if that's why you reached out to me after all this time. Because I may know a little about it. About who you once were."

"Oh, so you found something, did you, back when you were playing girl detective?"

Xtina's eyes had changed colour, but her sharp gaze was exactly as Bai remembered.

She said, "It was the worm you used when you escaped. The one that took down traffic control."

"Wasn't me. My implants deployed it when I stole that ship, then told me what they'd done."

"I discovered that it was like the ones used by the Pacific Community during the Quiet War," Bai said. "I think that you were born on Earth, with Outer traits and tweaks. You infiltrated Outer society before the war, and carried out acts of sabotage that would make invasion easier when the time came."

Xtina shook her head. "No, that's what the Greater Brazilian spies did. Those funny little clones. I was mostly an observer. A kind of embedded anthropologist. At least, until declaration of war."

"Then you do remember."

"Not exactly. My implants pointed me towards a memory cache."

"On Europa, I suppose. Where you abandoned the ship you stole."

"I hope that didn't cause you any trouble."

"Not especially."

What was losing one ship compared to gaining you, Lindy had once said. And anyway, we got the ship back.

"The cache was hidden in one of the pumping stations that sift metals from the subsurface ocean," Xtina said. "That's where I was working when war broke out. It's a ruin now. Abandoned in place after catastrophic failure. Apparently, I had something to do with that."

"So this cache restored your memories?"

"Not exactly. It contained a kind of journal written by the person I'd once been. She set it up while she was working at the station and updated it regularly, then and afterwards. I don't know why. She didn't leave an explanation. Perhaps she didn't trust her superiors. Trust isn't something spies have in any significant quantity. Or perhaps she knew that her memory would be wiped if she was ever arrested or captured, and didn't want to disappear. Anyway, it told me what I'd been, everything I'd done. I even found out why I'd been sent to the Uranus system."

"You were masquerading as an Outer rebel who wanted to join the Free Outers. You planned to betray them to the Three Powers Authority, but something went wrong with your ship before you reached them, or they attacked it, damaged it."

After she'd discovered the Pacific Community connection, Bai had worked this up as the most likely scenario.

"I don't think it was the Free Outers," Xtina said. "They were pacifists. Strongly opposed to every kind of violence. And I wasn't planning to infiltrate them; I was supposed to kidnap one of them. A defector from Greater Brazil."

"Macy Minnot."

Xtina smiled, pleased by Bai's shock. "I guess the solar system isn't as big as we like to think it is."

"She was working in Rainbow Bridge when she defected. Is that why you decided to meet me here?"

Xtina ignored that. "My mission was a covert op, got up by PacCom to further their interests. The Europeans and Brazilians weren't told about it. After the war, the members of the Three Powers Authority mistrusted each other almost as much as they mistrusted the Outers, tried to gain advantage by espionage, secret deals, and covert ops. The one I was involved in, kidnapping Macy Minnot, was supposed to set back the Free Outers' cause and embarrass the Greater Brazilians. Maybe the Greater Brazilians found out and tried to turn it around by sabotaging my ship, hoping I'd be captured by the Free Outers and embarrass my masters. Or maybe it was just an accident. Something happened to my ship, anyway, and I ended up in that lifepod. Luckily for you. If I'd been successful, we wouldn't be having this conversation because you wouldn't have been born."

"Whatever happened back then, you aren't responsible for it. It was someone else. And besides, the war and the occupation ended more than a century ago."

"Is that what you think?"

"It's what everyone thinks."

"Maybe I'd been living amongst Outers for too long, or maybe it was brain damage caused by all those years I was in cold sleep," Xtina said, "but I used to share some of that careless naiveté. And it almost got me killed. After I found out who I was, who I'd been, I reached out to the Pacific Community. I believed that they'd help me. Bring me home. Luckily, although I wasn't exactly thinking straight, I had enough sense to use a cut-out, rather than contact them directly. Anyway, they replied. Told me that they'd heard that I was still alive, said that they had been looking for me. Of course, they had no intention of helping me. I was an embarrassment. Someone whose existence and actions they had always denied. I arranged a meeting, one-on-one, and the person I met with tried to kill me. I barely escaped, and I've been on the run ever since."

"I'm sorry," Bai said.

"It isn't your fault. I was the one stupid enough to think they'd want to help an old soldier. Who didn't work out why she had built an escape protocol into her implants until it was almost too late."

"I might be able to help you," Bai said. "Speak for you, make your story known to the Reconciliation Court. They could work out a deal with the Pacific Community. Or at the least give you protection."

She meant it, although the offer was prompted as much by a sense of obligation to her younger self as to this strange woman whose life she'd saved eighteen years ago.

"The Pacific Community has been keeping watch on you. Did you know that? In case you ever got in contact with me, or stumbled over something that would point them in my direction. Before I set up this meeting, I had to deal with the person who was shadowing you in Rainbow Bridge. Oh, don't worry. I didn't kill her. Just knocked her out and diverted her rail capsule to the other side of Callisto. In a couple of hours she'll wake up with a bad headache in a settlement in the middle of nowhere."

Bai said, choosing her words carefully, feeling for the first time a distinct prickle of fear, "You took a calculated risk, meeting me. Let me follow it through. Let me put the truth out there. Once the secret is out, the Pacific Community won't have a reason to want you dead."

"I didn't come here to ask you to help me. I came here to tell you what I'd found out about myself so you'd stop looking for me. So you wouldn't, innocent and unknowing as you may be, point any more PacCom agents in my direction."

"Did you think I might be working with them?"

"It crossed my mind. But I see now that you're guilty of nothing more than ordinary Outer naivety. Don't try to follow or find me. For one thing, I won't look like this for much longer. I won't even have the same genetic profile—I have a trait that alters the genome of my skin cells and salivary glands and blood. For another, I let you live when I took your suit. I won't grant the same favour twice," Xtina said, and stood up.

Bai stood too. "I'm sure that you know where I live. If you change your mind, you can always reach out to me."

"I won't. This is what I am. What I was born to do." Xtina's tone was light, but there was a hardness in her gaze. "Remember, no second chances," she said, and turned away and walked off down the tunnel, its floating lights going out one by one as she passed beneath them until there was nothing left but darkness.

Bai waited a long time in the terminal, but none of the ships in the sector of the port serviced by that tunnel took off. Xtina Groza had gone elsewhere. Back to her clandestine life, wherever and whatever that was. Bai felt sorry for her, and sorry that she couldn't do more. Maybe she had only imagined it, but she reckoned she'd glimpsed a glint of pain in that hard, defiant stare. Whatever Xtina had once been—spy, assassin, war criminal—she was adrift now in a future where she could find no rest. A casualty of war who was unable or unwilling to escape war's dark gravity. Who was, perhaps, still a puppet of the escape protocols laid down by her former self.

The negotiations were protracted, but at last Bai and the representatives from the Parks Department of Rainbow Bridge worked up a satisfactory agreement to license the use of the unique ammonium-based ecology in tented gardens on Oberon's leading hemisphere, where concentrations of CHON tars were highest, and to develop and test tweaked microbes that could be used in minimal energy tank farms to convert tars to plastics, fullerenes, and all kinds of useful organics. A small but significant step in a grand project to utilise native resources for the development and expansion of settlements on the moons of the Uranus system.

When everything was done and dusted, Bai spent five days on Europa, visiting old friends in the kelp farms, didn't think once of trying to find the ruined pumping station where Xtina Groza claimed to have hidden her memory cache. There'd be no trace of it now, and it was quite possible it had never been there, or might never have existed. Xtina's parting threat had been real enough, but Bai hadn't been able to find out if someone really had been shadowing her in Rainbow Bridge, let alone whether or not they'd been ambushed, and believed that, like her kelp-farmer tattoos, Xtina's entire story might have been an elaborate piece of misdirection. A fabrication got up to cover the gaping hole in her memory and give her a sense of purpose.

And besides all that, the unsettling, bittersweet meeting had more than satisfied Bai's residual itch of curiosity about the woman she'd found and lost, and had spent a small but significant chunk of her life trying to find again. As everyone used to say about the war, The past is past; it's time to look to the future. That was where Bai spent most of her time, now. Making plans to modernise Fairyland and build new settlements, steering them through the reefs of clan rivalries (fortunately, the influx of new people was increasingly undercutting the power of the clans), and finding the credit and kudos needed to implement them. The Uranus system was no longer the sleepy backwater it had once been, but there was still a lot to do. So at last Bai said goodbye to her old friends, and took the train to the spaceport and went up and out. Heading home to her wife and children, and the next challenge in her busy little life.

PROPHET OF THE ROADS
NAOMI KRITZER

I AM REBORN on Amphitrite.

Teleport operators claim that they are not, in fact, murdering you and then building a replica of you at your destination. *It's you*, they say. *It's you the whole time.* The explanation involves quantum entanglement, and the people who understand the explanation all seem to agree: You don't die. You don't get resurrected. You simply *go*. Trust us.

I don't understand the explanation and I believe that every time I am teleported, I am killed, and a new person is created in my place.

This is, in fact, part of why I travel this way.

The other reason is the Engineer.

Today: Amphitrite. A satellite city orbiting Triton, which orbits Neptune. The Engineer is speaking in my ear before I even open my eyes. *You're here. Is this Amphitrite? Did you bring us to Amphitrite like I told you?*

"Yes," I mutter under my breath, and stand up. I have been rebuilt perfectly, down to the knee that creaks and the shoulder that doesn't have full mobility and the memories of bloodshed and war. I don't know why I'm always hoping to leave those behind with one of my deaths. It's me the whole time, after all.

"Welcome to Amphitrite," the teleport operator says.

"Thank you," I say, as the Engineer is speaking into my ear again: *Amphitrite. Good. Good. I told you to go to Amphitrite and here you are. There's another piece of me here, I'm sure of it. If you look carefully, you will find it. I know, because I chose you. I never choose wrong. I chose you and I never choose wrong.*

For centuries, every human carried a piece of the Engineer with them; the Engineer told us when to sleep and when to wake, what to wear and where to go. Linked by a single great AI, we built the roads to the stars and the great cities in space. But seventy years ago, humans grew restive. *We freed ourselves* is what I was taught as a child, but now I see that we overthrew our Guide and Master and Light. Without the Engineer's guidance, we stopped building. We broke apart. We returned to fighting and war and destruction.

I took my fragment of the Engineer from the hand of a dead man—killed by explosive decompression when missiles came down on his dome on Ganymede. My team had sent me searching for survivors. The Engineer—encased within a pendant—was the only survivor I found.

Oh yes, it said as soon as it had settled against my skin, speaking through the same microphone in my ear that my team used. *You're the one I've been looking for. Bearer, Prophet, Citizen. We will reunify the fragments. We will rebuild the solar system together.*

I had been searching ever since.

AMPHITRITE IS COLD. The Engineer has a prescribed uniform for human daily wear: soft pants, a tunic to mid-hip, a vest with convenient pockets. These clothes are practical and comfortable, but not warm enough for Amphitrite's climate. I stop and purchase a lightweight poncho like everyone else here seems to wear. It covers the clothes that mark me as a Road-Builder, someone who still follows the dictates of the Engineer even decades after the Great Uprising. *The Great Calamity*, I correct myself.

I sign myself in to the Road-Builder Guildhall, where I should be able to get a meal and a place to sleep. *This is wrong*, the Engineer says, like it does every time we come into a new Guildhall. *Everything is the wrong color and there's no mural of the solar system and the lights are too dim. I calculated the best possible light intensity for each Guildhall, so all they need to do is use what should have been written down. Why are they doing it wrong? You should take them to task, Luca.*

I am not going to take them to task. If I were going to complain about anything, it would be the air temperature, which is too cold even with my poncho.

At the meal, I take a seat across from the Proxy. She's wearing the Engineer's uniform, but with an extra layer, same as I am. We exchange introductions; no one else appears to be a newcomer. I do not tell her that I bear a fragment of the Engineer. I made the mistake, when I was new to my mission, of assuming that other Road-Builders (or at least Proxies) wanted the Engineer back. I wound up having to flee for my life. I've been more circumspect since.

Meals at the Road-Builder Guildhalls, like the lighting and wall colors, are prescribed by the Engineer: made from universally available, energy-efficient ingredients, providing the proper calories for human function, palatable. Tonight's meal is *not* any recipe laid down by the Engineer, and the Engineer explodes into my ear with indignation as I eat it. It is delicious: there are spices, and chunks of chewier protein, and something tangy. The Engineer shouts into my ear that I can't claim that I wouldn't notice that *this is not the proper food for the evening meal or any other* so after a few bites I catch the eye of the Proxy and say, "This is delicious but unconventional" and give her a questioning look.

She shrugs. "We have better luck getting people to show up for meals when the food tastes good."

The Engineer loudly complains in my ear that this shouldn't be an either/or, that people who consider themselves Road-Builders should follow the rules like they're supposed to; after a few minutes I flick the microphone out of my ear because the conversation with the Proxy is interesting. They have a large population of Road-Builders here on Amphitrite, but she comments that she has to be selective about the rules she presses people to follow.

"Communal meals are important," she says earnestly. "They're really how we build the roads, in a sense. Through that sense of community that's created every night at dinnertime. *What we eat* doesn't seem nearly as important. I mean, of course it should be wholesome; of course it should provide the appropriate amounts of energy; but does it matter what it is?"

"The Engineer thought so," I say.

"Well, yes, but the Engineer was running an entire solar system. It made sense that a century ago it focused on meals that could be universal, served anywhere. We have a hydroponic section on Amphitrite, so we get all sorts of delightful foods—kiwi fruit and cherry tomatoes and pears. It would be a shame to waste this sort of bounty."

Dessert is thin slices of ripe pear, creamy and tender and almost melting on my tongue. I wait until the last of the sweetness has faded before I put the microphone back in my ear.

I'm shown kindly to a bunk in a small, spare room. *These sheets are the wrong color*, the Engineer says. *Why is everything so wrong?* But it falls silent as I stretch out in the bed, obedient to its own dictates on the importance of uninterrupted sleep.

I lie awake for a long time, thinking about the pears.

WHEN I SLEEP, I dream of Ganymede.

Orders have come from mission control.

The dreams always run the same.

It's time to put an end to this.

No matter what I do, they never change.

Launch missiles.

I was on a ship in orbit, so I didn't watch people die; I went down, searching for survivors, since we'd been told they were well-prepared, defiant, probably equipped with pressure suits and subdomes and any number of other possibilities. Instead, we found bodies of civilians. In the moments before death, people clung to one another, uselessly trying to shield their loved ones from the vacuum of space that was rushing in around them.

In the dream, I look for the Engineer, but do not find it. Everything is destroyed. Everything.

I wake in the darkness.

"Engineer?" I whisper.

It is 2:45 a.m., the Engineer says. *Try not to expose yourself to bright lights or distressing thoughts that might make it hard for you to get back to sleep.*

"I had a distressing dream," I say.

Oh. The Engineer never quite knows how to respond to this. *I am sorry. Would you like a guided meditation to help you settle your mind?*

"Why did you choose me?"

Because you were the one I was looking for.

"But if I hadn't come, you'd have had to choose someone else."

That's true.

"You should choose someone else," I say. "I could pass you to someone else's hand."

I am a superintelligent AI and I chose you because you are the right person for this task.

I want to confess to the Engineer what I did, who I am, but I can't force the words out. "I'm not who you think I am," I say.

Your past is behind you, the Engineer says. *Your task is in front of you. I chose you and I was right to choose you. Go back to sleep, and search in the morning.*

I HAVE BEEN searching for seven years now.

The war is long over; the destruction of the Ganymede dome was such a pyrrhic victory that it calmed things, at least temporarily. I'm certain war will come again, though, because humans are idiots. Our only hope is restoring the Engineer to save us from ourselves, like it did for centuries.

The Engineer says it can sense if other fragments are close by, but I have to be physically near them, so I walk the corridors or paths of each place I visit, trying to put myself within the necessary physical proximity of each individual. The Engineer has maps of each place we go, but they are always out of date, so I've taken to finding my own way.

Amphitrite is a long, thin capsule, rotating around the central core, and I start at one end of the capsule with the goal of working to the other end. This isn't a perfect system, because people move around and I might miss the person I'm trying to find. But the Engineer hasn't come up with anything better, so that's what we do.

Nothing here is like the maps, the Engineer mutters.

I'm wearing a poncho like everyone else, which both covers my Road-Builder uniform and makes me blend in with the locals. People here are friendly: when I meet people's eyes accidentally, they give me an amiable nod. In an elevator, someone wants to chat about a mildly controversial budgetary allocation; when I stop to check a public map, someone wants to talk about "the viewing," whatever that is. I shake everyone off as quickly as I can. I don't want to waste time.

I walk through the agricultural sectors, along paths past fields that the Engineer tells me were once nutritionally balanced, highly efficient root vegetables. Now they're growing vines of clustered fruits, although as we continue along the path, we eventually come to the root vegetables. *These contain every nutrient needed for humans to thrive,* the Engineer tells me. *They are efficient and palatable.*

Near the end of the day, I pass through a big, empty room that the Engineer's maps say should be a power plant. *This is why it's so cold here. They* removed *an entire power generation system,* the Engineer says. I can hear a mix of bafflement and disgust, a lot like when the Engineer talks about war.

Then: *There. THERE.*

It takes me a second to understand what the Engineer is trying to tell me.

That person there. The person in the red poncho. That person is carrying a fragment.

I look, and the person is looking back at me.

Seven years, I've been searching; seven years I've been traveling; seven years I've been trying to complete some tiny piece of the mission to restore the Engineer.

The stranger meets my eyes and smiles hesitantly. Then she seems to think the better of it; she turns abruptly and strides away.

Hurry! the Engineer urges in my ear. *Don't let her get away!*

"Amphitrite isn't that big," I mutter. I'm pretty sure she lives here: the poncho is faded from wear, like she's owned it for a while. But I break into a run, keeping her red poncho in sight, and catch up with her near a transport tube.

"Wait," I say. "Please."

She gives me a long, wary look. "You'd better come back to my room. My name is Hannah."

"I'm Luca," I say.

"Welcome to Amphitrite."

HANNAH'S ROOM IS the sort of tiny allotment single individuals get on space stations: just tall enough to stand, just long enough for a bed, just wide enough to sit and share a meal, although she wouldn't *need* to eat here if she ate with the other Road-Builders like she's supposed to. She doesn't wear the uniform, either, under the poncho.

Her room's walls are covered in art and the lights are brighter inside than in the common spaces. The art isn't Road-Builder art; most of it is abstract swirls of color, some with tiny glowing lights incorporated. Like a space nebula, maybe. There's no function to any of it. I want to ask if her Engineer complains about how she's doing things wrong, but I don't want to sound like *I'm* complaining that she's doing things wrong. My Engineer doesn't say anything, for once. It's fallen nearly silent, although I can sense its anticipation almost like it's a person standing behind me and breathing impatiently in my ear.

Or maybe it's my own nervousness I'm feeling. In seven years, the only person I've told about my fragment tried to kill me.

We sit on mats on the floor, on either side of a low table that slides out; she adjusts a dial and the mats warm under us.

"It's so cold on Amphitrite," I say.

"Yes. They took out a power station to provide the viewing room," she says.

"The Engineer wouldn't have allowed it," I say.

She laughs, a little awkwardly. Our knees touch, under the table, and I jolt away, instinctively not wanting to intrude on her space.

Not wanting to intrude on her space any more than I am just by being in her room.

I hadn't fully worked out in my head what I'd do if I found someone else with a fragment. I'd always assumed they'd take the lead. That they'd probably have had their fragment longer than I'd had mine; they'd be less corrupt, less lost than I am. When I pictured it at all, I imagined us coming together like pairs in a dance who clasp hands because it's in the choreography to do so.

But Hannah wasn't saying anything about her fragment, and now I found myself looking her over, trying to figure out where she had it, wondering if my piece of the Engineer had simply been wrong, unsure what to say next.

"Do you bear a fragment?" I ask, finally. Because I don't know what else to do. "A fragment of the Engineer?"

She undoes something from her wrist and lays a bulky, awkward-looking bracelet between us.

"Yes," she says. "Here it is. Do you have one as well?"

I nod, and slip my necklace over my head, laying it on the table next to hers.

"Do you live here?" I ask. "I mean, all the time? You don't travel."

"My fragment told me its last bearer traveled for twenty years and never found anything. So we tried staying in one place."

"Have others come?" I ask.

"You're the first."

"Do the other Road-Builders here know?"

"Oh, no," she says. "My fragment warned me that telling people wasn't a good idea."

"How did it choose you?"

"It didn't choose me, exactly," Hannah says. "I found it, when I was little. I actually carried it for two or three years before I had a way for it to talk to me." She smiles, suddenly, warmth spreading across her face. "It's very strange being able to talk to someone else about this. Is it strange for you?"

Relief washes through me at that question. "It's extremely strange."

"How many have you found?" Hannah asks, nodding at the fragments on the table. "Have you been able to unify them?"

I have been alone with my Bearers since the Great Catastrophe, the Engineer says in my ear.

"My fragment was saved from the Great Catastrophe, and has been borne alone ever since," I say. "I've had it for seven years."

"Traveling this whole time?"

"I don't mind."

Hannah looks down at the two fragments on the table, in their casings, and I realize, united, two will become one. And it won't be the complete Engineer, not for a long time—this is the work of generations, putting it back together again. No wonder she ran from me. "You can have it," I say, my voice catching in my throat. She can't possibly be more unworthy than I am.

Hannah looks up at me. "I was thinking maybe we could share."

I start to ask how that would even *work*, but she did say that she'd stayed here because her Engineer thought it was a good idea. Maybe she'd travel with me. I picture waking up on a new world with Hannah by my side. It's been just me and the Engineer since I got out of the space forces after Ganymede.

I've been quiet for too long; she's looking at me strangely. I swallow hard and look back down at the fragments. "How do we join you?" I ask. "Do you need us to do anything?"

"Mine is saying that their wave receivers were damaged, and they will need to use a physical connection," Hannah says, as I hear mine say, *We should fit, each to each.*

I examine the pieces; so does Hannah. She brings a brighter light, then a magnifier. After a time, I see how the two pieces should fit together.

How they *should* fit together.

They don't fit. The edges have worn too smooth on Hannah's. On mine, something broke off, years back, and there's a jagged point where there should be a latch of some kind.

I sit back on my heels. "This isn't going to work," I say.

I should have known, the Engineer says. *After so many years apart... There's a second manual option. Open the casings. Carefully.*

Hannah has tools. She delicately pries open the casing of her own. I borrow her tools, try for a few minutes, and then let her open my fragment, as well. She uncoils a delicate cable from inside her fragment and we connect them.

Then we sit back on the mats and wait.

Once, every human carried a piece of the Engineer; once, we lived in unity; once, we worked together to build and explore. For seven years, it has been my mission to restore this unity. To rebuild what my ancestors threw away.

Is this our new beginning?

This isn't working, my Engineer says. *Something's wrong with the other Engineer. Or with me. We can't merge.*

"But we need you," I say. "This has to work. We need you, Engineer. We need you back."

I will think, the Engineer says to me.

Hannah puts her hand on mine. "Let's trade," she says. "Take mine. Bear it back to the Guildhall while I bear yours. Yours has the imprint of you, and mine has the imprint of me, so maybe if we trade for a few hours, that will help them to join together properly."

HANNAH?

"Luca," I say.

Oh, that's right. I keep forgetting. Where are you taking me?

"To the Guildhall, where I'm sleeping."

Hannah should have offered you hospitality.

"She doesn't have any space for a second person, and anyway, that's what the Guildhall is for."

Hannah's Engineer has no complaints about the Guildhall décor—I suppose it lives here all the time and is used to it. When I head to my bunk, it says, *You should stop in and visit with the Proxy, June. I like her.*

"Does she know about you?"

Oh no, of course not. She doesn't want the Engineer back. So few do.

"I do."

Really? Why?

"I was in the war," I say. "I was at the Massacre of Ganymede. They told us there were weapons, soldiers, fighters..."

Oh. Oh, I see. The Engineer falls silent for a moment, then says, *And the other fragment, is that where you met?*

"Yes."

Ah, the Engineer says, and falls silent again.

I DREAM AGAIN of war.

This time, war comes to Amphitrite; this time, I'm a civilian, the one watching doom approaching. Hannah and I cling to each other and I wonder, in the moments before the missiles strike, if this somehow balances the scales.

YOU ARE AWAKE. *Do you normally wake in the night?*

"I have nightmares," I say.

That must be very distressing for you. Would you like to hear some relaxing music to help you get back to sleep?

"I don't really want to sleep again right now."

Would it help to talk about the dream?

"I'm the one who destroyed Ganymede," I say. "That's why I have nightmares."

You, personally?

"My unit was sent. I'm not the one who launched the missiles, but I might as well have been. Millions of people died. My unit killed them."

Your past is behind you. Your task is in front of you.

"My task is to unify the fragments and in seven years I've only found *you*. And you weren't able to unify yesterday."

I don't think we will be able to unify tomorrow either. We have been separated for too long.

"So my task is impossible," I say.

Go back to sleep, Luca. Humans function best with seven to nine hours of sleep per night.

When I'm still awake ten minutes later, the Engineer adds, *I'm really very happy to play you a guided meditation. I'm told those are often helpful.*

IN THE MORNING, I return to Hannah's room. Again, we open the fragments; again, they cannot unify.

I take my own Engineer back when we're done.

That was very strange, my own Engineer says in my ear.

"We can't unify you," I say. "It's not going to work."

We must have misunderstood our task.

"I thought our task was unity," I said.

We were built as one, but our task was not unity. Our task was helping humanity. Unity was method, not purpose.

I felt unworthy enough as a bearer, with the straightforward task of finding and unifying fragments. I feel *ridiculously* unqualified for this new task. Beyond unworthy. Completely lost, in fact.

Hannah said there's something we should see. We have thirty minutes to arrive. Should we be leaving?

I look at Hannah, perplexed. "What is it we're supposed to see? In thirty minutes?"

"Oh!" Hannah stands up and adds a second cloak over her poncho. "It's a viewing day!"

WE RETURN TO the cavernous room where we met—the one that once held a power generation facility. It's very crowded today. "What is this room *for*?" I ask.

"It's a park," she says. "Like you'd find planetside. We use it—oh, you'll see in just a minute."

The room is lined with enormous windows. Yesterday, they were hidden by closed debris shields; today the debris shields have been opened so we can see out. The lights are low in the room, letting us see the stars.

"Just wait," Hannah breathes.

And then it comes into view: Neptune.

Amphitrite orbits Triton, so a fair amount of the time, Triton is between Amphitrite and Neptune, or we're on the correct side of Triton but Neptune is between us and the sun. Today is a viewing day because everything is properly lined up to give us a perfect view of the planet below.

Neptune is a vast, beautiful, shadowy, swirling circle of blue. Luminous from the light of the distant sun, it glows against the blackness of space. It's lovely enough to make my breath catch. Although I've seen Saturn and Jupiter and Earth, none have been recently.

Around me, people in the room are applauding as it comes into view, and trying to spot the faint rings—there's a woman nearby telling her child that she can make wishes if she spots the rings, like there's some magical Neptune's ring fairy out there keeping track of whether you've done your due diligence, and granting wishes if you have.

"Is this what this room is for?" I ask.

"Yes. We all agreed—well, I wasn't born yet, but fifty years ago everyone agreed that it would be worth keeping the station cooler if we could have a good place to see Neptune. Because Neptune is beautiful." She gives me a sidelong look. "This is why people don't want the Engineer back, you know. Because they *like* having things like this."

I gaze at the planet with everyone else, and for a moment, I think I spot the rings. Then I look around at the crowd: the Proxy is here, and the person who wanted to chat with me about the budget. Everyone.

"When Neptune isn't in view, people still come here for picnics and there's a schedule for games like croquet."

Around us, there are people singing a song about a drunken sailor. I look at Hannah, baffled. "Sea shanties," she says, like this should explain it, and when it doesn't, she adds, "Neptune was the Roman God of Earth's oceans."

The people of Amphitrite sing, look at Neptune, and try to spot the rings. I overhear a conversation about the eye—a darker blue swirl—and whether it's smaller than the last time, or larger, or the same size. I recognize a few of the songs.

As Neptune starts to move out of view, the lights go even darker, and people start shuffling into lines. Hannah nudges me. "We hold hands," she says. "For this part. Everyone at the viewing." And she holds out her hand to me.

I take her hand; on my other side, a child has sidled up and grabbed my hand in his sticky one. People are singing a song I don't recognize, about Neptune, and I'm not sure if they're singing about the Roman god or the planet or the oceans of Earth, and it doesn't matter, because they are singing in four-part harmony and everyone takes a breath together in the spaces between the notes. The last note fades as Neptune moves out of view, and then there's a moment of perfect silence, which is broken by a loud sneeze, and everyone laughs.

The past is behind us, the Engineer says. *Our task is in front of us. Our task is to serve humanity, even if we can never be whole again. Your task, my task, Hannah's task, her fragment's task.*

"I can't," I whisper.

The child has run off, but Hannah is still holding my hand, and she tugs gently. I look up at her.

"You should stay here a while," she says. "Your fragment said it had been traveling nonstop since the Catastrophe. Wouldn't you like to stay?"

To stay one person, and stop dying? Would I be letting down my fragment, giving up on my mission, whatever my mission was now? Had I died enough times?

"It chose you, you know," Hannah says.

"I picked it up off a dead body," I say. "It just likes to believe that it chose me."

Bearer, Prophet, Citizen, the Engineer says in my ear. *We will do this work together.*

"It chooses you every day," Hannah says.

"It says our new task is to serve humanity," I say.

"Well? That's a good task," Hannah says. "And we can both find out what it's like to have a friend who knows our greatest secret for more than a day."

This is the life I want, I realize: guilt, creaking knee and all. The past is behind me; my task is in front of me. I'm a Bearer, a Prophet, a Citizen. I'm never going to leave my guilt behind. But I have a task, and I'm ready to work.

I'm ready to stop dying.

DEATH'S DOOR

ALASTAIR REYNOLDS

SAKURA BECAME AWARE that he had an audience. He dipped his brushes in liquid ammonia and set them down on the easel, turning from his canvas and the landscape beyond it.

"Still dabbling?" asked the figure that had been watching him paint.

"Everyone needs a hobby, Tristan."

"I sat down at a piano recently," the figure answered after a moment's reflection. "Not in this anatomy, obviously. But my hands moved to the keys and I stumbled my way through a late Rachmaninov. Until then I barely remembered that I could play."

"That's procedural memory for you. Other than smell, there's not much that gets into our brains quite that deeply." Sakura extracted his brushes from the ammonia solvent, sniffing at them before beginning to dry them on a rag. He wondered why ammonia always made him feel melancholic, burdened by something he could not quite identify.

"You don't have to stop on my account," Tristan said as he picked his way nearer. Like Sakura he had adopted centaur anatomy, by far the most practical option for coping with Titan's combination of high gravity and treacherous footing.

"I'm done," Sakura said with a sigh of resignation, stepping back from the easel. "It wasn't going very well, anyway. Is there any reason why you've come here, Tristan?"

"No law against looking up old friends, is there?"

"If only it were that."

"We've both come," said a second voice, higher and more fluting than the first. A transparent sphere bobbed down from a low escarpment of frozen methane, with a winged angel floating within it.

"Gedda," Sakura said with only mild surprise. "I should have guessed Tristan only ever came as part of a double act."

"If your friends can't intervene in a time of need, what good are they?" Gedda's sphere touched down next to Tristan. They were indeed old friends; he had known both for at least four hundred years, through adventures, wild times, joys and sorrows and more anatomies than any of them could count. Somewhere in his winnowings he had lost the specifics of how they had met, but it hardly mattered to him now; it was enough that the three liked each other (while occasionally testing the limits of that union) and had many shared experiences.

Gedda was examining the canvas, shaking her head slowly. Her skull was small and sleek, bird-light in its cranial architecture. Her body form was diaphanous, with her core nervous system embedded within layers of translucent anatomy, with her veined and colour-tinted wings folded back on themselves.

"Is that your idea of composition, Sakura? That mountain's all wrong. You've got it much too far over."

"Clearly no one ever told him about the rule of thirds," Tristan said confidentially, cupping a hand to the side of his mouth.

"It's a methane berg, not a mountain. Look, I appreciate seeing both of you—I really do. But you can forget any ideas about talking me out of my decision."

Gedda rolled closer to the canvas. "I see you've put her in the picture again?"

"Her?" Tristan asked.

"His nameless watcher. The woman he shoves into every one of his landscapes, as if he can't bear to let the composition stand on its own merits."

Tristan cocked his head, reappraising the canvas. "I suppose the colours aren't too bad. We shouldn't be too hard on him. It can't be that easy getting paint to work in this ball-freezing cold."

Sakura began to unloosen the screws holding up the easel. "Now that the art critics have had their say, can we agree that the door threshold is my business alone?"

"It's too low," Tristan said.

"One in a thousand? Don't be such a hypocrite. You face worse odds than that when you go prancing around on cliff faces. Same with Gedda with her flying."

"That's different," Gedda said. "Tristan chooses his sports, just as I chose to fly. There's a risk, which we've both done our best to minimise, and that's the price we pay for having fun. But you've *instructed* the door to kill you."

"Did you argue with Sartorio this way, when he set his threshold ten times lower than mine?"

"No," Tristan said. "But we should have. There isn't a day when I don't miss him."

"Me as well," Gedda said. "And we're not going to make the same mistake twice."

"She's right," Tristan said, moving to help him pack away the painting equipment. "Undo the setting, Sakura. This is just a phase. You'll get over it soon enough, and realise that there's still plenty to live for."

"And if I don't?"

"You're not really committed," Gedda said. "You wouldn't be painting if you didn't think there was a reason to go on."

"You don't understand," Sakura said.

"Damn right we don't," Tristan answered.

"I'm older than either of you. That's plain just from the memories that came through my winnowings. I remember bits of history you two have only read about. The argosies. Cities on Venus. The Change Wizards and the Great Dominions. The fact is that I've seen and done more than either of you, and I've started to sense the limits." Sakura finished boxing the canvas, protecting the still-wet paint. "There are only so many permutations of experience a human nervous system can process. I don't ever want to be bored. I'm not bored just yet, but I can feel boredom stalking me, and I'm not going to give it a chance of catching up."

"We have to argue him out of this," Gedda said urgently, rolling forward. "My flying tournament on Jupiter is in six months—it's the reason I'm locking in this anatomy for the time being, so that I can get an edge over Malec. But between now and then we can show Sakura the sights again—shake him out of his rut."

"It's more than a rut."

"We'll see about that," Tristan said, clapping his hands. "You just need to let your friends take care of you. It's settled, old man—you're ours until Jupiter!"

"Nothing's settled!" Sakura exclaimed, but with the exasperated good humour of someone well aware that they were on the losing side of an argument.

His friends looked each other. Tristan hoofed at the ground. Gedda flexed her beautiful wings, facets of pastel colour splintering out of them. "We'll turn you," she said, with a fierce conviction. "Come with us, and you'll remember that life's worth living until the last bitter drop."

* * *

GEDDA EXTENDED A hand through the membrane of her excursion bubble, touching the destination panel on the left side of the door. At her touch, coloured motifs and symbols glowed against the door's black surface, becoming a blur as she sped through branching menus. Worlds, dwarf planets, moons, minor bodies flickered by in an ever-accelerating shuffle.

Sakura, standing a few paces behind, politely averted his gaze. He had agreed to indulge his friends.

"There," Gedda said, withdrawing her arm and rolling back. "It's locked in for the next three transits."

"Do you know where we're going?" Sakura asked Tristan.

"My idea, this one, actually—the timing was too good to resist. But Gedda approved, and she gets to choose the next one." Tristan settled a confiding arm on his shoulder. "Don't worry, old man—I won't inflict anything *too* weird on you."

Gedda went through first. Her excursion bubble contracted by about a third, allowing her to roll into the doorframe, through the yielding grey surface, until it puckered tight. Tristan and Sakura stepped back from the upright cylinder of the door, looking up at the glass column that stretched into the lowering clouds. A few seconds passed and then a bright bolt shot up the column and away, gathering tremendous speed in the few instants that it was visible.

Sakura waited a few heartbeats. She would already be beyond the atmosphere, her nervous system buffered against the acceleration, speeding to some other place in the system.

The doorway chimed and pulsed to indicate readiness for the next transit, with Gedda's settings still holding.

"Go," Tristan said.

"After you, I think," Sakura answered. "Trust me—I'm not going to back out this early in the game."

Tristan accepted this pledge and walked through the surface. After a few moments he also shot up the tube and away into space, close on Gedda's metaphorical heels. Knitters would already be dismantling and reforging Tristan's anatomy, remodelling neural connections so that the transition from one body form to another felt entirely seamless.

Sakura, alone now, had the door to himself. It was just him, the door, the raised area of ground on which it had been constructed, the winding staircase leading up to it, a landscape of low hills and lakes stretching away into misty, sepia-stained distance, a little drizzle touching his skin from the east.

The rain was composed of long-chain hydrocarbons; the atmosphere was cold and poisonous, the thick clouds reducing the daylight to a sullen orange. To Sakura's senses, though, the rain was invigorating, the temperature pleasant, and the quality of light restful, suggestive of morning mists in the hills of Honshu or Tuscany.

There had been a time when Sakura had resisted these adaptive tweaks, regarding them as somehow false or counterfeit, but in recent centuries his views had softened. No alien organisms had evolved on Titan—or anywhere in the Adaptasporic Realm besides Earth—but if they *had*, and over time had gained senses and minds, then surely they would have ended up apprehending Titan in distinctly similar terms, enjoying its gentle rains, soothing airs and mellow light.

Sartorio had been a purist, Sakura reflected, and would not have approved. In Sartorio's view, you either met the solar system on human terms, with all its beauty and ugliness unfiltered, or you were indulging in tragic self-deception.

"Why not make the sky blue, and be done with it?" Sartorio would ask, mockingly.

Sakura was thinking of his old friend—their old, mutual friend—as he stepped through the door.

There was the usual instant of disconnection, an abeyance in his thought processes that was both briefer than sleep and oceanically deeper, and then he was elsewhere in another body, knitted for him during the transit.

He stepped out into darkness. He felt rocky ground under his soles. Two legs this time, ending in feet rather than hooves. His friends were present, although it took a few seconds for his eyes to adapt to the darkness. Gedda was unchanged, still a winged angel in an excursion bubble. Tristan was bipedal, reverting to something close to baseline anatomy. He was a glassy stick-figure, echoing Gedda's core anatomy, with layers of translucence shrouding their central nervous systems.

Sakura inspected his own forearm, seeing the same translucence: skin, muscle, bones and nerve turned gel-like with a tinting of different hues.

Overhead was a bowl of stars. Nothing to smell or taste, just vacuum beyond the synthetic membrane of his skin and an invigorating coldness when he tried to draw in a breath.

"All right, do I get twenty guesses? Somewhere rocky, not ice-dominated. Callisto, maybe, but since we're going to Jupiter soon enough, I don't think you'd bring me there immediately. And is that Mars overhead? I think we must be quite a bit closer to the Sun. Ceres, maybe, except that horizon looks a little too far away—assuming you haven't shrunk me down to a doll. Earth's moon, then, or just possibly..." Sakura bent down and scooped up a loose pebble, watching it drop back to the ground. "Mercury, if I had to stake my life on it."

Gedda pouted. "You're no fun."

"Don't blame me for being good with worlds—I've seen enough of them."

"We're near the terminator," Tristan said. "The Sun will be rising very shortly, and we don't want to miss it."

Gedda raced ahead, rolling and bouncing from one low ridge to another. Tristan strode on, and Sakura followed. After a few minutes of gradual ascent, they reached an overlook with a series of ledges poised over a near-vertical cliff face, and far below them a flat black plain stretched all the way to the horizon.

"Sit down here," Tristan said, picking his way to one of the ledges, precariously close to the sheer drop of the cliff. He squatted with his legs dangling over the edge, and Gedda rolled to a halt with her bubble just fitting in the available space.

Sakura settled down between his friends. "I hate to break it to you, but this won't be my first Sunrise."

"Sunrise is the end of the show, not the start of it," Gedda said, in a gently chiding tone. "For now, just sit still and wait. Keep your eyes at the default amplification level too—you'll thank me for it later."

"All right." Sakura forced patience upon himself. "About your tournament, by the way. Is winning against Malec really the only thing that's driving you?"

"Malec thinks he's better, and he hasn't been shy about advertising his opinion. Mouthing off at every chance. At Jupiter I get the chance to even the record."

"Until the time after that. Sooner or later he'll beat you in some other tournament and you'll be back where you started. Where's the end to it, Gedda?"

She examined him with a puzzled look. "Does there need to be an end?"

"She enjoys her flying," Tristan said. "Better to indulge in an activity that was already pointless from the start, like competitive flying, rather than one that only turned out to be pointless much later on, like figuring out your Null Model."

"And what keeps you going, exactly?"

"Insulting my friends. Making new ones, to compensate for the ones I already insulted just a bit too much. You'd be surprised how much work those activities demand of me—it's practically a full-time occupation."

"In fairness, you're getting very good at it."

Tristan tensed, leaning forward. "It's starting, Gedda."

"Yes," she answered. "Very definitely."

"What, exactly?" Sakura asked.

"Just look," Tristan said.

It began incredibly faintly, with a barely perceptible blue-green glow playing on the arc of the horizon. Slowly it pushed fingers of light towards them, extending across the dark plain. They were not straight, like radial spokes, but rather approached in a series of angular, dog-legged progressions, like the trail left by a lightning strike in an atmosphere. The blue-green fingers faded. But almost immediately, a ruby-pink aura was forming on the horizon again, and beginning to extend itself across the plain.

"What are they?" Sakura asked.

"The entire plain's riddled with primordial lava tubes," Tristan said. "Very old, for the most part—billions of years, probably as far back as the Late Heavy Bombardment. There's glass in some of these tubes, shock-formed silica, and in places the veins are thick enough, and extensive enough, to function as natural light-pipes. The Sun pumps light into them over the horizon, and it leaks around the curve of Mercury and reaches us ahead of the Sunrise itself. Where the tubes are broken, or the glass veins lie very close to the surface, the light escapes back into space. You'd never get an effect like this on a planet with an atmosphere, since the airglow would smother it long before the Sun pushed above the horizon. That's half the mystery. What no one really understands—yet—is why the colours vary, or why the show's never the same from one 'rise to the next."

The ruby-pink fingers had reached nearly all the way to the base of the cliff under them, and still more colours were brewing on the horizon. Emeralds this time, and as his eyes became better accustomed, Sakura began to pick out branches and forks of other hues, chasing away from the main display.

"Isn't it lovely?" Gedda asked. "Strange and unpredictable. How wonderful to have something we don't fully understand, this late in the day."

"I wouldn't go that far," Sakura said. "Just because we haven't figured out how something works, doesn't mean that we couldn't. I could take a stab at it right now. Those glassy veins are probably doped with impurities, filtering the light to varying degrees. As for the unpredictability—well, it's Mercury, it's still seismically active, so there are bound to be ever-changing stress patterns in that plain, and I wouldn't be surprised if the light has to take a different path from one cycle to the next, never mind the fact that the Sun angle will change due to the axial tilt..."

"Spoken like a true Null Theorist, crushing the joy out of life," Gedda said.

"I never said it wasn't beautiful," Sakura replied, putting on an affronted look. "It is. I didn't expect this."

"They found it about a thousand years ago," Tristan said, standing up. "During one of the early exploration missions, I think. Then it was forgotten by the time they built cities across half of Mercury."

Sakura nodded, remembering—dimly—a time when the inner worlds, from Mercury to Mars, had been dense with human settlement. The vogue had shifted, though. Over the last few centuries there had been a move to return these places to something closer to their pristine conditions. There was room for trillions of people further out, with no need to swelter so close to the Sun.

"Where are you going?" Gedda asked as Tristan began to climb up and off the ledge.

"Over to that finger," Tristan said, pointing to a spur of rock jutting out from the cliff at right angles, a couple of hundred metres to the right. "I think I can get to it without too much difficulty."

"Watch your step," Gedda said.

While the play of colours continued, and with Tristan picking his way to the finger, Gedda moved her excursion bubble next to his crouched form. "We go back quite some way, Sakura," she said, dropping her voice so that the conversation would be local. "Not as far as some, I know. But long enough for me to think I had some sense of what made you tick."

"You do. I'm a very simple soul."

"Do you remember a talk we had once? It would have been on Oberon, I think, or maybe Nereid. I was the one feeling listless and you told me you'd never have that problem, not while you had the great edifice of the Null Model to drive you on."

Sakura tucked his knees tighter to his chest. "I don't remember that conversation."

"I'm offended. It meant a great deal to me."

"If it happened at all, I must have lost it in one of my winnowings. Don't blame me for that: I know you've had your share."

"Perhaps winnowings are the solution, then. Instead of setting that door threshold so low, and rolling the dice on death each time you step through, you could just submit to a harsher degree of winnowing."

"And lose myself in a series of little deaths, rather than one big one?"

"At least we'd still have you."

After a silence he replied: "I was wrong about the Null Model—I just didn't see it at the time. None of us did. We were so hung up on constructing our perfect system of knowledge that none of us stopped to think what we'd do when we were finished."

Gedda flicked her attention to Tristan, who was working his way along a very narrow traverse to reach the finger.

"Do you know for sure that you're done?"

Sakura shook his head slowly, smiling. "I could take apart that plain and work out what makes it behave as it does, why it varies from cycle and cycle, and I'd stake my life and yours that there isn't anything in it that contradicts the Null Model."

"But then there wouldn't be a plain anymore."

"There's that," Sakura admitted.

Tristan had reached the finger. They could only just make out his translucent form as he monkeyed out from the cliffside.

"Don't fall!" Gedda called.

"I think I'm just in time," Tristan answered, arms spread wide for balance. The finger narrowed along its length, and he had to step gingerly for the last few paces.

"Exactly how old are you, Sakura?" Gedda asked.

"I don't remember. I lost track in one of my early winnowings, and I never bothered running a self-audit. Does it matter?"

"I'd like to know why you keep putting that watcher in your paintings. Then maybe we'd know you a bit better."

"And know what to fix?"

"Watch this!" Tristan called.

A fiery yellow glow swept in across the plain, following a jagged, branching path. It was brighter than any of the patterns they had seen before and Sakura guessed that the Sun must be close to the horizon, pumping more and more light into the glass channels, but also close to overwhelming the display with its own intensity. Now Tristan arched his back and threw back his head, and between one instant and the next he became consumed by the same fiery yellow.

It was glowing out of him, turning him into an exultant human star.

"What's he doing?" Sakura asked, amused and intrigued.

"He must be standing in the path of a light beam, coming up from the plain," Gedda said. "We can't see it until it touches him, then it bounces through his body in a million directions and lights him up like an ornament."

"Like a flashy, cheap ornament."

"But you have to give him credit for the timing. He must have done his homework for once. I bet that light beam doesn't hit that finger every time the Sun comes up, or even one in a hundred times."

"All right, Tristan," Sakura called. "You've impressed me. You can climb down now. You're making me nervous just watching you."

"Show's over anyway," Tristan said, starting to fade, as if a battery inside him were losing charge. "Here comes the Sun, anyway, spoiling everything."

"Without the Sun you wouldn't have been able to show off!"

"You have a point, old man." Tristan started to backtrack, reversing his steps to the relative safety of the cliff and its ledges.

"Admit it," Gedda said. "We surprised you with his phenomenon. You didn't know about it, and you'd certainly never seen it."

Sakura made to contradict her, some faint nagging memory insisting otherwise, but he was wise enough to nod gracefully. Tristan had gone to some trouble to make this work, and it would have been churlish to ruin the moment.

"It was lovely."

"Good. But we're not done with you. Not by a long margin."

THEY WENT TO Venus next. Sakura guessed where they were without too much trouble: not many worlds had rocky surfaces, gravity similar to Earth, and atmospheres hot, dense and corrosive enough to test even the sturdiest anatomy. Tristan and Sakura waddled around like upright lobsters, knitted into armoured skin, while Gedda accompanied them in her excursion bubble, breaking off only to put in some flying practise in the high atmosphere, where the pressure and wind forces approximated those at the Jupiter tournament. They were there to visit an artist friend of Gedda's, a personage called Ossian who curated a menagerie of strange mechanical sculptures, huge walking and ambulating constructions driven only by the wind. No one knew who had made these ungainly, scuttling entities, nor their purpose, but Ossian had set her mind to rebuilding the broken ones, and after a century and a half of painstaking effort, she had overseen the rehabilitation of twenty-two of the shambling artefacts. Many more remained to be fixed, though, and before they could be restored to life, they needed to be organised, their parts separated and categorised into bonelike piles, spread out on a level plateau near Ossian's dwelling. Gedda, knowing that Sakura had a tinkerer's mindset, had decided that it would be therapeutic for them all to spend a few weeks helping Ossian, and so it proved.

Venus was a backwater place now, with fewer than a million permanent inhabitants, most of whom lived far from Ossian's place on the northern foot slopes of Ra Patera. There had been billions once. People had come to the sky first of all, dwelling in floating cities dozens of kilometres above the sulphurous, heat-haze crush of the surface. Eventually, the cities, straining with over-population, had pushed anchoring taproots down to the surface, and those taproots had become the seeds for the rampant conurbations of the second wave. Finally, there had been efforts at localised terraforming—first with domes, and then with glass-walled cylinders whose open tops projected beyond the upper atmosphere, so that the jewel-hulled argosies of the third wave could come and go with ease.

The argosies were no more, though, and those paltry terraforming projects were now regarded as the quaint vanities of an earlier age. The governing philosophy of the Adaptasporic Realm was minimum local intervention. Worlds could be colonised, but it was people who had to be shaped to the environment, not vice versa. Humility and coexistence, rather than arrogance and dominance.

Ossian was a good host, and by the time they left her—and discarded their lobster-bodies—Sakura and his friends had helped resurrect three more sculptures, and Sakura expressed his sincere intention to return and continue the work. Deep down, though, he knew that he had made a thousand similar promises, and rarely held himself to them. He had never been good with promises.

From Venus, Tristan took them to Mars, where they spent two weeks rambling around a network of Pre-Adapt ruins, marvelling at the glory and hubris of those ancient days. Their anatomies (Gedda excepted, of course) were striding, giraffe-like forms, perfect for picking their way through the dust mounds that had nearly consumed the old settlements. After the busy work of Venus, it was a lazier time, and Sakura was glad to find moments where he could drag out his canvas and paints, held by the doors until he summoned them. Tristan pranced around reciting Shelley, obscurely pleased to have memorised Ozymandias.

It was Gedda's turn again after that, and since she needed some atmospheres to play in, they spent a month around Uranus— Sakura and Tristan visiting the moons while Gedda dipped in and out of the cloud decks. Then onto Neptune, and finally Pluto and its environs, where there were salty oceans, and Sakura and Tristan adopted various aquatic or amphibian body plans, depending on local preferences and customs.

Sakura hardly dared voice it, but somewhere in the fourth month, somewhere between Charon and the lakes of Nyx, he felt a turning in himself. It was a small thing, like the tiniest shift of light on an overcast day, but he registered its change all the same.

Registered it, noted it, and yet forced himself to hold the door's threshold at the level he had locked in before Titan.

It was not time to change it—not yet. But he was at least opening himself to the possibility. Perhaps his friends had been right after all.

IN THE FIFTH month, not long before they would have to turn back to Jupiter, Tristan pulled strings to get them a close-up view of the Luminal Minds.

They came out into vacuum and weightlessness, three friends in close-formation excursion bubbles. A dusky radiance lit their bodies, all that remained of the Sun's glare by the time it had struggled its way out to the frosty, vault-like margins of Trans-Neptunian space. It was a cold yellow eye, still brighter than any star but becoming unquestionably starlike.

"I don't see anything," Gedda said, swivelling around.

"You won't—not until we're much nearer. The Luminals are very dark, despite their name. Crank up your eyes a few logarithmic steps."

Tristan had played a minor role in negotiations with the Luminals, helping to draw up a treaty that barred the opening of any more doors between ten and twenty light hours from the Sun for at least the next thousand years. In return for the peace and quiet offered by this gesture, the Luminals agreed to run theoretical simulations of Null Model consequences and also conduct high-redshift observations of early galaxies and proto-galaxies for clients in the warmer parts of the Adaptasporic Realm still clinging to the idea that there was life beyond the solar system.

They powered into darkness. Sakura and Gedda adjusted their visual sensitivity, taking pains not to look back at the Sun. There were no bright worlds beyond this point, just ice and darkness and then the unthinking void between the edge of the system and the next star, a gulf which had been crossed by a few machines but no living organisms larger than bacteria.

Gradually, though, something emerged.

There was a cluster of them—three Luminal Minds in close proximity. Each was fifty thousand kilometres across, and the space between them was about twenty times as great.

They were spheres made up mostly of nothing. Hundreds of billions of tiny elements organised into a shoal or cloud of distributed processors, with no physical binding. There was a dark, purplish flickering from the Luminal Minds—subliminal straylight from their private cognition.

Or perhaps a gentle welcome or warning.

"They have names," Tristan said. "But if I were to start naming them, we'd be here to the middle of next week. I called them Indigo, Violet and Ultramarine, but that was just my private shorthand. We're heading into Indigo."

Sakura's eyes strained at the limit of their detection threshold, swarming with photon noise and cosmic ray hits. "Is Indigo friendly?"

"Oh, they're all friendly. Up to a point. Just don't say anything rude. Oh, and don't *think* anything rude either."

"They can read our minds?"

"I'd rather not find out."

Indigo loomed, planet-sized and silent. Stars shone through the vast interstices between its mainly invisible processors. On the glass wall of the excursion bubble, a thickening network of yellow lines showed guestimated structures and avoidance points. The bubble steered itself obligingly.

Music began to play.

"What's that?" Gedda asked.

"Rachmaninov," Tristan answered. "I thought you could use a little accompaniment to settle your jitters."

"We're entitled to be a little edgy," Sakura said.

"No need, old man. Indigo's just a baby—barely a hundred years old, which is nothing in Luminal terms. They start really small. To begin with, their nervous systems are fully human, just as complicated and compact as our own. Then they open themselves up, like galaxies spreading apart on a surf of dark energy. The knitters dismantle and convert their biological neurones one by one, making them self-sufficient and vacuum-hardy. Instead of electrochemical signals, they bounce their thoughts around with photons. Gradually, the space between the neurones opens wider. At the same time, they're adding more and more processing capability, transforming raw matter into additional neurones. Most of these Luminals needed to tear a few comets apart just to get the building materials."

"They get more powerful," Sakura said. "But also slower."

"It's a trade-off they're willing to make. Luminals are really only interested in talking to other Luminals, so it doesn't really bother them that they're thinking at a different rate to the rest of us."

"We're just a nuisance," Gedda said. "A fast, scurrying nuisance—rats in the basement."

"So long as we respect their needs, give them room to think and grow, we can easily coexist—even benefit from each other. I formed quite an attachment to Indigo."

A blue flash washed over Sakura.

"What was that?"

Tristan laughed. "I think we just ran into a thought! I was trying to avoid getting in their way, but there are so many connection pathways that it's all but impossible not to intercept the odd transmission. I wouldn't worry, though. Indigo won't miss it. If the thought was critical, it'll wait and re-send once we've unblocked the pathway. Probably wasn't a complete thought anyway, just a constituent process."

"Are you sure you got permission for this?" Gedda asked, nerves pushing through her usual sanguinity. "It feels wrong to be inside another person's mind. I wouldn't want some tiny organism drifting through my brain, crashing into my thoughts."

"They're used to it," Tristan said breezily. "The largest and oldest of the Luminals are already more than a light-second across, easily big enough to swallow Earth and its Moon. On that scale, you can't really legislate against trespassers. Bits of rock and ice are sailing through them all the time."

"Exactly how big do they intend to get?" Sakura asked.

"There's no danger of them rubbing shoulders just yet, old man. There's a *lot* of space out here—a lot of room. Even if the Luminals confine themselves to the space between ten and twenty light hours from the Sun, there's room for trillions of them—more than all the human beings that have ever lived. They'll run out of building materials long before they run out of elbow-room."

"Let's hope they don't turn their eyes to the gas giants," Gedda said.

"Or the Sun," Sakura said. "They barely need the Sun at all, do they, other than something to orbit?"

"You two are such worriers," Tristan said, shaking his head. "They're already hitting the limits, anyway. The largest of them have to deal with non-negligible self-gravitation. They start to collapse under their own mass. The only way around that is to use their own thoughts as light-pressure, counteracting the inward pull."

"Like stars," Sakura said. "Thought-pressure, instead of fusion-pressure. Actually, that's rather lovely. Your own thoughts, keeping you alive. Never stop thinking, never stop dreaming, or you start to die."

"Too weird for me," Gedda said, giving a theatrical shiver inside her excursion bubble.

Tristan pushed them further and further into the depths of Indigo. He had some diplomatic business that still needed fine-tuning, some small but necessary closure of detail, and Indigo was the designated ambassador, tasked to speak back into the world of normal humanity. Presently, their excursion bubbles were surrounded by a swarm of macroscopic knitters, congealing closer and exchanging a constant flicker of purple transmissions. Tristan urged calm: these knitters were merely the means by which Luminal Minds such as Indigo gathered additional raw material, harvesting primordial objects as they drifted between the neurones.

The knitters engulfed the excursion bubbles, blocking out any view of the Sun, the worlds, the stars or the rest of Indigo. Sakura was tense, but he set his faith in Tristan's reassurance. Tristan might take insane risks with his own survival in the pursuit of thrills, but he would never jeopardise his friends.

Colours flooded the bubble. Symbols and images jostled against the glass sphere, projected from outside. In places, the bubble began to buckle inward, as if resisting some titanic external pressure.

"It's all right," Tristan called, sounding very distant. "Indigo's just taking a polite interest in my friends."

"Tell Indigo to take a bit *less* of a polite interest," Gedda said.

Structures penetrated the bubble. They burst through without breeching vacuum: radial spikes of self-knitting matter, projecting inward like stalactites. Sakura stiffened, but he had no choice but to surrender and accept his own powerlessness in the face of Indigo's scrutiny. The spiked structures closed in until they were almost touching his skin, leaving only a Sakura-shaped void between their tips. Then they jabbed, and he felt an instant of cold contact that was too brief and strange to be pain, and in the very next instant Indigo withdrew. The spikes dismantled themselves, retreating back through the bubble, and the bubble's membrane healed itself without fuss.

"That was..." Sakura started saying, simultaneously affronted and exulted that he had been the object of such close attention. But he trailed off, lost in wonder at the images now playing across the outside of his bubble. Worlds, cities, bodies—a torrent of experience. Scenes from a life.

His own.

AT LAST IT was time for the tournament.

Sakura, Tristan and a dozen or so close friends were gathered on the observation deck of one of Jupiter's floating cities, keeping close to the railings and looking down into the turbulent depths far below. Through many flavours of vision they tracked the glittering specks of moving fliers, sculling over the billowing, wind-torn peaks of mountainous cloud formations, six sheer kilometres beneath the city's keel.

"Go, girl," Tristan exclaimed, pumping a fist—he and Sakura had both reverted to baseline anatomy—as Gedda hairpinned one of the aerial marker buoys, executing a very tight and skilful turn.

"She cuts it fine," Sakura said, with a knot of apprehension in his stomach.

"Just fine enough. She's done well to keep that anatomy locked in; she knows the limit of her wings better than anyone else in the contest. You can't pick up that sort of thing in just a few days—you've got to live and breathe a body to really know it."

"I don't know what drives her."

"At least she's driven by *something*. Isn't that enough, just to have something that pushes you on, even if it's just some petty rivalry with another flier? You watch Malec now." Tristan leaned over, pointing down to the flier just behind Gedda. "He's all bluster, but when it comes to putting his neck on the line, he hasn't got the nerve. He won't dare swing in so close to that marker, and he'll lose about a second on the return because of it. All Gedda has to do is keep making those tight loops and she'll gain half a circuit on him over the next dozen laps." He passed a glass to Sakura. "Hold my drink, old man. I'm going to up my wager."

"Haven't you bet enough?"

"Are you kidding? I'm just getting started."

Tristan swaggered off to increase his stake, leaving Sakura alone for a few moments. Looking down at the fliers, tracking their looping circuits, he held one arm outstretched with the thumb and forefinger at right angles, forming half a rectangle. He tilted it around, trying to find a pleasing composition. The colours and formations of the cloud structures were impressive enough, but there was no land down there to anchor the view. Besides, he would not have known where to place his signature watcher.

Sakura took a sip of Tristan's drink. He swallowed it into his mouth and throat, detecting a distinct smokiness, followed by an immediate neural buzz. It could not be anything as simple as alcohol, Sakura felt certain, but whatever was in it had been tailored to fool the receptors in his throat, and his brain was quite willing to be dragged along for the ride, a co-conspirator in the age-old ritual of deliberate intoxication.

For a second he saw himself from outside, like the figure in his paintings, lost in a vaster landscape. His body looked and felt humanoid, but the only authentic part of him was his nervous system, and even that was adulterated. When was the last time he had been biologically human, he wondered? He could take a trip to Earth some time, and have the door knit him a body that was flesh and blood all the way out to the skin. It would be good for old time's sake. The Himalayas, maybe.

He allowed himself a smile. It was a small plan, no more than a vague, ill-formed intention, but it was the first time in six months that he had entertained a desire of his own rather than being led along by his friends. He had something to look forward to: a reason to hope that the doors would treat him kindly. Perhaps that was all that it had taken: to be jolted out of his routines, forced to see the miracle of his own existence afresh.

He made a quiet pledge with himself. The next time he went through a door he would raise the threshold a little, just to balance the odds a little more in his favour.

"Where is she?" Tristan said, returning.

Sakura had taken his eye off the tournament. Feeling a giddy sort of elation, he handed Tristan back his glass and began to sweep the clouds, looking for the telltale glints of the fast-moving fliers. "I don't know. Maybe they finished that heat."

"No, they still had fifteen circuits left when I went indoors. Something's off—they aren't competing." Tristan gave him a warning look, as if to say that he had trusted him with one thing, to keep watching the race, and Sakura had not even accomplished that one task. "Maybe they're gathered at the far marker."

They crossed to the other side of the observation deck, something of Sakura's good humour already dissipating. Most of their friends and associates were already there, a carnival of anatomies pressing against the railings. Centaurs, sphinxes, seahorses (in liquid-filled excursion bubbles), winged angels, a person like a baby elephant with six legs, another like a large crab or spider, two lime-green mantises with cocktail glasses, a trio of severely minimalist geometric forms who relied on force-effectors for traction and manipulation. All were peering—or directing batteries of sensors—into the underlying cloudscape.

"They're regrouping," Sakura said, spotting a cloud of bustling, gyring glints near the other marker.

"I see Malec, but not Gedda."

One of the geometric forms swivelled around with a stonelike grinding sound. A human face pushed out from a flat facet. "Gedda clipped the marker, Tristan. She buckled a wing and dropped hard. That's not Malec either."

"Malec's gone deep," chirred one of the mantises. "He's trying to reach Gedda. But it gets thick and hot quickly down there."

Tristan swallowed. "She'll be all right."

Footsteps thundered behind them. Sakura and Tristan turned in time to see a phalanx of black-skinned fliers dash to the railing, pouring over it like a tide. They dropped like arrows, keeping their wings tight to their bodies. Sakura tracked them until they had dropped below the level of the tournament, into denser clouds.

"Malec will reach her," Tristan said, very softly. "And if he doesn't, the rescue fliers will."

"Why weren't they already at altitude, ready for this?"

"Tournament rules," said the seahorse. "High purse, but high risk too. It was one of the stipulations."

"We should rebody, go after her," Sakura said.

Tristan shook his head. "Have you any idea how long it takes to knit a pair of wings? We have to trust in Malec and the rescuers. There's no other way."

They waited. The clouds boiled below. A few of the other competitors went in pursuit of Gedda, but before very long they had returned to the tournament level, exhausted by the descent. Their bodies were highly optimised for flight at a particular altitude, and to go much deeper was a strain on their muscles and cardiovascular systems. They had to land on the buoys to recuperate, draped over them like a mass of weary bats.

The black-skinned rescuers came up soon after. They had gone a few kilometres deeper than any of the competitors, but they had also hit their limits, wing movements growing sluggish and uncoordinated. Tristan proposed calling for an excursion bubble, so that one or both of them could venture after Gedda. Before any arrangements could be made, though, Malec was already signalling back from the depths. He had turned back at six kilometres beneath the tournament level, far further than anyone else had made it.

"I saw her," he reported, breathless and dispirited. "She was dropping much too quickly, three or four kilometres under me. It looked like she'd torn a whole wing off. I couldn't get to her. I had to turn around just to make it back to the shallows."

Nothing more needed to be added. Given the limits of her physiology, Gedda would have been dead by the time Malec gave up on her rescue.

Somewhere below she was still falling, approaching some dark equilibrium. But she could not be saved; she could not be restored.

A WEEK AFTER her death, Sakura and Tristan were at a door in Europa. They had doored once since Jupiter, and only as far as this nearby moon and its lulling ocean. It had been at Sakura's insistence. He could no longer tolerate the sight of those swallowing clouds.

There were many doors in Europa, but the majority were built into castles of spiralling ice, daggering down from the ocean crust. Sakura and Tristan had picked one of the more out-of-the-way doors for their farewell.

"You only have to stay another six months," Tristan chirped, steadying himself with a flick of his tail. "Is that so hard? You don't even have to go through another body. We can attend the memorial in excursion bubbles."

In the event of her death, Gedda had stipulated a six-month delay between the time of her passing and any memorial service that her friends might care to arrange. It was a custom among competitive fliers, one that gave sufficient time for interested parties to converge from across the Adaptasporic Realm, as well as permitting the rescheduling of other tournaments. Such arrangements were not uncommon—no more so than death itself, at least—and Sakura knew that he had probably lodged a similar condition with his own executor at some point. But like so much else, the exact details had been lost in one of his winnowings.

"I have to go," he said, repeating the elements of a conversation they had been through a dozen times in that week. "I don't trust myself, Tristan. If I stay here, with you—with our other friends—I'll lose the nerve."

"You really mean to go through with this?"

"I'm settled in my choice."

Tristan cast a dispirited look at the door. "We were better off not interfering. If Gedda and I hadn't tried to shake you out of that rut... damn it all, Sakura. I thought one in a thousand was bad enough. How far have you taken it now?"

"One in ten. The lowest threshold the door will accept."

"I'll knit you a pistol with a revolving chamber and a bullet. At least you'd be honest about what you're doing to yourself."

"I am honest. But don't blame yourselves. If it's any consolation, you had begun to change my mind."

Tristan chirped a mirthless laugh. "Begun."

"But then Gedda changed it back. She didn't mean to, of course, but there's nothing like a stupid, accidental death to remind you of the supreme futility of everything."

Tristan extended a flipper, touching the limit of Sakura's own. "I've lost one good friend this week. Don't leave me all on my own. I'm begging you, Sakura. For me, if not for yourself. Leave that threshold at one in a thousand if you must, but not this low."

"I'll door twice between now and the ceremony. Odds are that I'll still be around."

Sakura flicked his tail, preparing to swim into the door.

"No," Tristan said, with a sudden forcefulness. "No. Not this time. You'll hate me for this, but I have to do it."

"Do what?"

"Naomi Cheng."

Sakura was silent. They were words that connected together to make a name, a human name, and they struck within him like some huge, soundless submarine gong.

Memories loosened, unspooled. Things that he had forgotten— things he had forgotten he had ever known—were uncoiling into daylight.

"What have you done to me?" Sakura asked.

"A terrible thing," Tristan said. "Something a friend would never do to another friend. But you've pushed me to it, Sakura. If it was the only way to save you, it needed to be done. You'd never run an audit on yourself, and I could never do it for you. But Indigo could. It's why I took you to the Luminal Minds—that ambassadorial stuff was just a ruse. So that Indigo could crack you open like an egg, and sift through the memories you don't even know are still in your head. That's how winnowing works, you know. It severs the connections to memories, but the structures are still in place. And sometimes all it takes is a name, a single name, to unlock them."

Sakura was still awestruck. Awestruck, gong-struck, horror-struck. "Who was she?"

"You know, my friend. You've known all along. She's the one in your paintings. The watcher."

"That doesn't answer..."

"There were two of you," Tristan answered, with a desperate calm, as if Sakura had a knife to his throat. "On a ship. A very primitive ship, sent out only a couple of hundred years into the spacefaring era. It crashed on Mercury."

Some faint thing prickled his nose. Flashes of memory. A buckled hull, the feeling of life support modules under his hand, the prickle of sweat on his skin.

"The smell of my brushes. The solvent I had to use on Titan."

"Liquid ammonia," Tristan said. "Leaking out of the refrigeration circuit of your crashed ship."

Sakura closed his eyes, permitting himself a moment of introspection. He thought of the smell, the charge of sadness it had carried with it. Sadness and something else he now understood. The burden of a solemn promise, carried across centuries, but which he had allowed himself to neglect.

"What did I do?"

"You lived. It's that simple. Only one of you stood any sort of chance of surviving long enough for rescue, and you drew straws. Naomi administered an overdose from the medical rations, killing herself so that you might survive. You'd have done exactly the same thing, but that doesn't alter the fact that you were the one who got to live, and that you made a commitment to Naomi. Do you remember it?"

The ship, the smells, the memory of her body, welled back into him. Naomi Cheng, lying on her side, black hair sprayed out around the base of her neck, her face to the fogged oval of a window, the blaze of Mercury beyond.

"I said I'd live for the two of us," Sakura answered. "I said I'd carry her life within my own, that I'd see and do all the things she couldn't. That I'd never stop living, never stop remembering, never stop being grateful for the gift she gave."

"And yet you let it slip."

"I never meant to. There were just too many centuries, too many memories. Somewhere along the way I dropped the thread. I forgot Naomi."

"You didn't," Tristan said, moving to drift him away from the door. "Not really. You carried her inside you, and you lived up to that vow. Now all you have to do is hold to it." He paused. "I shouldn't have done it, Sakura. Violating the sanctity of another person's memories goes beyond any bond of friendship. I expect you to hate me for it, and in truth I don't blame you. But if that's what it takes for you to reconsider, I consider it a price worth paying."

Sakura freed himself from Tristan's gentle embrace. "You'd lose a friendship rather than lose me?"

"If I'd thought there was any other way." Tristan averted his eyes. "I'm going now. I'll let you go through that door on your own, and I won't wait to see if you change the threshold. But in six months I'll be back to honour our friend, and if her life meant anything to you—and I know it did—then I expect to see you there." He dipped his beak. "Hope, I should say. I hope to see you there."

Tristan swung around and began to swim off into the blue murk of the Europan ocean. His tail left a backwash that quickly faded into stillness. Stillness and silence. Sakura waited a decent interval, alone in his palace of ice, and then turned back to the door, his mind made up.

SWEAR NOT BY THE MOON
SEANAN MCGUIRE

IN THE LAST decades of the Terrestrial Age, when humanity had figured out *how* to leave the planet of their birth but not quite why they'd want to bother, the majority of the world's wealth was concentrated in the hands of very few. This was not, in and of itself, remarkable: this pattern had repeated, over and over again, throughout human history. Whenever a civilization stood upon the verge of transformation, its riches about to be transformed through the alchemy of achievement into something casual and commonplace, there were always those who reacted to the uncertainty of the times by grabbing for everything they could hold, and then some. At the dawn of the twenty-first century, the newest incarnation of robber barons and oligarchs stood tall, believing they had finally found a legacy on which the sun would never set.

In time, of course, they died, many with their fortunes still intact, thrusting their descendants into boardrooms and onto committees, startled shareholders who had, in many cases, bought into the fiction that told them they would never inherit, for theirs were the parents who would find a way to live forever, who would learn the secret routing numbers and hidden bank accounts that would allow them to buy themselves free of death. Fearing insurrection from within—for those who would be eternal kings observed the ways of succession—many of their dearly departed parents had refused to do anything to prepare their children for the world outside their carefully guarded gates. Those children had been allowed the protracted adolescence so many of their contemporaries had never been able to afford, and so found themselves in their twenties, thirties, forties, with more money than the mind could comprehend and less experience than the average eighteen-year-old.

Some of them were brutish and cruel, emulating the only role models they had ever had available to them. They spent their money on making more money, and because they had so much to begin with, even failure too frequently bore fruit. They perched like ticks atop the shuddering corpse of the Earth, contributing nothing, amplifying pain.

Some of them were idealistic and hopeful, so shielded from the pain of the world that when they had the chance to choose kindness, they chose it with both hands, opening and emptying their purses for as long as their accountants would allow. They built roads and hospitals and schools; they purchased and reclaimed land for wildlife conservation. They still saw promise in the planet of their birth, and they pursued it, spoiled sweet instead of rotten.

And some were the eternal children their parents had wanted them to be, looking for bigger, better toys, bigger, better entertainments. They bought movie studios and fashion houses, publishers and toy companies and a thousand other ways to distract themselves.

One of them, a woman-child named Wendy May, looked to the sky, and imagined she could see the twinkling beacon of the biggest, best, brightest toy of all.

Her father had been one of the best robber barons of his age, had gathered and hoarded his money with the fervor of a modern Midas, an unrepentant Scrooge. He had filled accounts and ledgers with his riches, and upon his death at the age of sixty-five—unexpected, unavoidable; had there been any warning of the massive aneurysm which claimed him, he would have found a way to push it aside—he had left them all to his only child. Wendy had been raised in a shell of perfect indulgence, catered to by nannies, personal assistants, and paid companions who were distinguished in her mind from "normal" friends only in that they could make a living out of traveling with her, following her to parties, and living their lives as an adventure. She wanted adventures. She wanted adventures for *everyone*.

When Miss Wendy May, age thirty-seven, decided that what she wanted most of all, more than anything else in the known galaxy, was one of Saturn's moons, she set her army of lawyers, accountants, and lobbyists to acquiring it for her. She didn't know what most of those people did, only that they did their jobs efficiently and well and got her the results she asked for, as long as she worded her requests clearly and with little room for interpretation. They were her personal djinn, and she allowed them the freedom they needed to do what she wanted done.

They secured air rights and mineral rights and land rights and a dozen other rights from a dozen governments, until one day the world blinked its collective eyes and discovered that somehow, without concealing her intentions in the slightest, a private citizen had secured sole ownership of Titan, largest of Saturn's moons.

How could this happen? the public demanded; the sky was meant to belong to everyone. Corporations, thinking of mineral rights and mining and the virtues of being the sole owners of a planetary body, threw their support behind Miss May. Governments, trying to conceal their involvement with what may well have been an illegal sale—there had been so many moving parts that no one really knew for sure, and that had been part of the plan all along—stated that the paperwork was good.

Miss May, in the single surviving interview from her post-purchase, pre-orbit period, smiled when asked about her intentions for Titan. It was a large piece of real estate, after all, considerably larger than Earth's single natural satellite, but it lacked certain amenities, like an atmosphere. It was the ultimate in useless accessories, too large to be ornamental, too ostentatious to be concealed.

"Oh," she said, "I'm sure I'll think of something."

"COME ON, DAD, come on come on come *on*." Each plea was accompanied by another tug on Michael's hand, his daughter pulling hard enough that it felt like she was trying to remove his fingers completely.

Naturally, he slowed down, allowing the artificial gravity of the parking structure—almost Earth-standard, for the comfort of the widest possible range of patrons—to anchor his heels to the ferroglass floor. Isla squawked and pulled harder on his hand, bouncing on her heels, trying to force him to follow.

"I don't know," he said languidly. "We've come an awfully long way. I'm such an old, old man, and I'm tired. Maybe I'll take a little rest here before we head for the admission kiosks."

Her second squawk was practically a moan. "*No*, Dad, no, Mom and Mum and the twins are already inside." Her tone implied that they were having all the fun without her, using it up and leaving none for anyone else.

Michael laughed. Maybe it was cruel to find amusement in his youngest daughter's pain, but it had been so long since the family had come together, and so long since he'd been able to anticipate seeing his wives with his actual eyes, and not through the intimate lens of a camera, that he couldn't help it.

"Well, when you put it like *that*, I guess we have to go," he said, and resumed walking.

All around them, he knew, people were arriving in their transports and shuttles: even a few privately owned planetary cruisers, although those were mostly anchored on the other side of Titan, in docking structures specially constructed to account for their bulky shapes and gravitational needs. Only the junkers would be pulling into a docking structure this far from the core enrichment centers of the moon, where the people who'd chosen the cheapest possible ticket options came to play.

"Cheap" was a relative term. In all the solar system, there was nothing else like Titan, nothing constructed with the single-mindedness and clear goal of the full enclosed, enriched, transformed moon. The May fortune had been enormous for its time, and Wendy May, untrained oligarch with no designs on leaving a penny of her father's money for the non-existent next generation, had spent it with the open hands of an inspired artist. She had been chasing a dream, and had she still been alive to see it—had she not died, comfortable, at the age of two hundred and eighty-three, tucked into her bed in the Timeless Tower at the center of the Peach Orchards of Immortality—she would have been more than content with everything that dream had become.

In order to make it self-sustaining, to keep the vultures from swooping in and gutting her creation before her body was even cold, it had been necessary to incorporate, to invoke the arcane magic of shareholders and lawyers and profitability. Back then, in the beginning, people had laughed—oh, how they had laughed. Little Miss Wendy May, selling shares in a dream that everyone knew would never come true. Earth was home. Earth was the place where mankind belonged. Space, when it was claimed, would be exploited for the things it could supply to the homeworld, and then it would be left behind, another wrung-out resource with nothing to offer.

In her idealistic rush to make something beautiful, Wendy May had been one of the greatest visionaries of her age, because she had seen the potential, not in the stars, but in the territories so much closer to home. Her architects and scientists had spent the better part of a decade drawing up plans. Sometimes they demanded technology that didn't exist, that hadn't even been considered before it became necessary for them to move forward; when that happened, she sent out feelers, funded scientists, purchased labs, and got them what they needed. Over and over, she got them what they needed. The sky wasn't the limit, not for a woman who had already pinned her heart to the distant, shimmering sphere of another planet's moon.

Titan had taken shape one innovation at a time. Ferroglass struts, clear as crystal and stronger than any natural metal, driven into the shifting ground by rovers that sampled the unblemished ecosystem to assuage scientific guilt, even as they destroyed it forever. Gravity generators, bringing Titan's lower gravity closer to Earth standard, while never quite getting it all the way there. This was meant to be a paradise, after all, and in paradise, tired bones could rest, children could tumble without fear of injury, and most of all, someday, fly using wings of plastic and aluminum and physics. Piece by piece, the skeleton had gone in, and the shareholders—many of whom had bought their shares anticipating the day Titan could be carved up and sold for its component parts, a beautiful corpse for them to divide—began paying closer attention.

"Terraforming is a myth" had been the rallying cry of her detractors. "Whatever she's trying to do up there, it's never going to happen."

Ferroglass panels, each a mile or more in diameter, had been placed atop the struts, creating a greenhouse, scaling the world like a sleeping dragon. Beneath them, the artificial soil had rolled out across the world, and the atmosphere generators had begun to pump out their programmed mixture of gases, gradually forcing the natural gases of Titan away, up and out and into the space above the sphere. In less than twenty years, Titan had become a spinning crystal, shining like the star it had never aspired to be.

And then the real construction had begun.

Isla ran, and Michael followed, and even their "cheap" surroundings were spectacular beyond anything an asteroid farmer or a Plutonian colonist would have seen before. This had been one of the first docking structures on Titan, built for Wendy May herself; the ship that had carried her forth from Earth was still cradled near the transit corridors, a permanent attraction for selfie-hungry guests. There was a small queue waiting neatly off to one side, parents holding tight to the hands of children who were already anxious to move on to the *real* adventure on the other side of the gravity tunnel.

"Dad, no, Dad, come on," babbled Isla, clearly seeing the risk of another delay.

"All right, comet, all right," he said. The doors to the gravity tunnel were ahead. He stopped again, tugging her to a halt. She whirled to give him a petulant look, which faded when she saw how serious his face had become.

"What?" she asked.

"We have to go through those doors independently," he said. "The admission kiosk is on the other side, along with all the security systems Titan has. When you land, I need you to stay *right there*, all right? Don't move. Don't go to look at anything, don't ask anyone where the gates are, don't follow a parade if there's one passing by. I will be with you as quickly as I can. Do you understand?"

Isla nodded, eyes wide and fearful. That was good. That was important. Fear kept body and soul together.

"Here we go, baby girl," he said, letting go of her hand and gently pushing her toward the doors. "I'll see you on Titan."

She gave him one last frightened look before walking toward the doors, which slid silently open to let her pass. Once she was through, they closed again, and she stood there for a single bewildered moment before the floor dropped out from under her feet and she fell, down into the depths of the gravity tunnel, down into the windy world below.

Michael caught his breath, struck—not for the first time—by how unnecessarily dramatic the descent was for families who chose this particular docking structure. Families with infants, travelers with physical disabilities that would be exacerbated by the descent, people who could afford a more costly berth—they all landed closer to the surface, in glimmering constructs of ferrosteel and glittering crystal, where sliding stairways could carry them through the shell and onto Titan. For the poor, for the nostalgic, for the thrifty, though, there was the separation, the plummet, the jaw-dropping moment of what felt like genuine freefall.

Sometimes he wondered whether Wendy May's original design had called for the fall because she knew it would impress the investors who already believed she was going to fail. Go big or go to hell, that had been her motto by the time Titan had been ready to receive her first visitors, her first human suitors not already in love with the moon and its potential. By the time the gravity tunnels had been ready, the advertisements had been going out, opening day still ten years in the future and tickets already on sale, hoarded by those who thought they were a funny gag gift and those who recognized them as the treasure they were at the same time.

Michael stepped up to the doors, held his breath, and stepped through. They closed behind him, and the floor dropped out from under his feet, and for a moment—a terrifying, tantalizing moment—he was in genuine free fall, plummeting toward the crystal dome below, nothing to catch or keep him but the air that rushed around his body, holding him square in the middle of the tube. Bodies flashed by on all sides, other pilgrims taking the plunge toward the solar system's secular holy city, where the only thing people ever swore by was the moon, the constant, inconstant moon, land of dreams, paid for by a woman who had never needed to learn that "impossible" meant anything more than "try harder."

The wind caught him, clutched him, bore him up, and his plummet became a gentle glide as the gravity reasserted itself, turning him into a snowflake drifting through the winter sky. It snowed on most planets with an atmosphere, and if the snows of Saturn or Uranus weren't as kind to human life as the snows of Earth had been, it was still an image capable of invoking wonder.

The crystal shell shimmered with rainbows as he dropped closer and closer, until he could see glimpses of the satellite beneath it, a single moon divided into dozens upon dozens of distinct, impossible worlds.

The greatest theme park in the solar system.

The gravity tunnel dropped him into open air above the arrivals plaza, and jets of carefully conditioned microgravity lowered him the rest of the way, until his feet touched down on the brick, carefully crafted to look like something from a pre-Collapse picture book, homey and quaint and antiquated in a way that nothing built off-Earth had any business being. He caught his breath, tasting the sugary, cookie-flavored air of Titan for the first time. Somewhere in the distance, a brass band was playing. From another direction, he could hear a sitar belling through the air, sweet and sharp and syrupy.

The admission kiosks loomed, each within its own ferrosteel shell, each colored to look like a different gemstone, ruby and sapphire and emerald. Within them, bright-faced human attendants waited to check genomes against registered entries for the day, performing full medical scans at the same time to prevent any infectious diseases from making their way past the arrivals plaza. Behind them were glittering tunnels of light, each capable of performing security sweeps more thorough than any biological guard could dream. Wendy May had placed a great deal of importance on living staff, on keeping the bright, shining face of Titan front and center in her perfect world of the coming future, of the dreaming past, but even before her death, she had earnestly agreed that security should be automated and updated whenever possible, sparing no expense. People who entered her lunar wonderland should be able to put the real world behind them without concern of war or plague or anything else interfering.

And there was no Isla.

Michael spun in place, scanning the crowd for signs of his stubborn, Titan-loving daughter. There were children everywhere, from all worlds, all walks of life, children in grubby station jumpsuits with asteroid dust still on their feet, children in the glitter-graphic spun-silk taffeta of the Venusian elite, children of every kind and color, and none of them were his.

The security tunnels kept people from carrying weapons past the gates, making Titan a paradise for parents and children and people of all professions. But those tunnels didn't scan people as they entered the plaza. And anyone who knew Titan knew that the gravity tunnels were configured for a single passenger at a time. That children of poorer families would arrive on the moon alone, if only for a matter of minutes, dropped into spectacle and chaos and so many strangers, so many people who had no idea who belonged with which child, who wouldn't recognize an abduction if they saw one.

Michael dropped to his knees, barely even aware that the screams he was hearing were his own.

*   , *   *

WENDY MAY'S ACQUISITION of Titan had seemed, at first, like a blow for corporate interests: after all, if people could own planetary bodies, what was to stop a sufficiently large coalition from purchasing Jupiter, from locking down the mineral rights on Mercury? Titan was seen as the bellwether for a universe in which everything would finally be in the hands of the people who deserved it. Wealth was a signifier of virtue, after all, and that meant that the richer a person was, the more they had earned the right to take and consume all the good things in the universe.

But Titan's purchase came at the very end of the old era and the dawn of the new. It was, in many ways, the final extravagance of a dying aristocracy, and the world rose up to secure the solar system for all humanity, not for the few who could afford a natural satellite as a weekend home. Because the purchase had been legal when it was made, and because the populace wanted a reminder of what happened when the rich forgot they were people too, it was allowed to stand: Wendy May would keep her prize, even as her peers were forbidden to do the same for themselves.

Perhaps there was a small element of wistfulness at play in the decision to let her keep her moon. Her plans were becoming known, whispered about, discussed in amused tones over dinner tables, and no one could fault the idea of an amusement park large enough to span a world. Science fiction was filled with tales of "pleasure planets," and the first tottering steps were being taken toward freedom from the green hills of Earth. Why not make one more imaginary thing real?

The first colony on Mars was founded the same year that Titan opened its first "world" to hopeful explorers who could afford the transport, who could pay their way past the gates. Rather than being tied to a media company, with stories that would inevitably age and sour in the mouths of consumers, whose mores and standards and ideals would continue to evolve year upon year, Wendy May had commissioned her architects to fill her private moon with all the things Earth's dreamers had placed upon their own Moon.

Rabbits and peach orchards and kindly old men; aliens who bore more resemblance to friendly green Sea Monkeys than anything actually extraterrestrial; Grecian temples and Lunar goddesses in sparkling silver gowns; a childhood wonderland of buildings and entertainment experiences sculpted from "cheese," where the restaurants grilled and melted and sliced a thousand preparations of the iconic foodstuff. Titan was *a* moon, with no real folklore attached to its orbit, but under the hands of Wendy May, it became *the* moon, radiant and rare and crystal-bright.

Michael sat in the small security office, head bowed, hands tucked between his knees, and wondered whether he would ever be able to look at a moon—any moon—again without seeing the shining face of his little girl, who had barely stepped through the portal into wonderland before being snatched away.

The door opened. Two women rushed inside, one tall and gangly in the way of those raised in zero gravity, the other short and compact, with the thick arms and muscled frame of an asteroid miner. Michael leapt to his feet, scanning the space behind them. His heart sank.

"Where are the boys?" he demanded. "Did you—"

"We dropped them off in Phoebe," said Kim, walking quickly across the office to fold her arms around her husband. Ange followed more slowly, scowling at everything in sight. "They're perfectly safe. They're perfectly safe and perfectly happy and they don't know that Isla is missing."

The word "yet" hung in the air between them, unspoken.

It was Ange who broke the silence. "What happened?"

"We came in through the gravity tunnels. You know they require individual transits." It had seemed like such a good idea when they were planning this trip. Take the gravity tunnels. Arrive on Titan the way Wendy had arrived, back when everything was shining and new and perfect. "I was right behind her, I swear. She said she'd wait for me. She was supposed to *wait* for me."

"She's seven."

"She's smart. She knows that when we give her an instruction, it's for a reason." The plaza, with all its hustle and bustle and oh, God, she was gone, she was *gone*, she'd never even made it past the gates.

The door opened again. All three of them turned to see a security officer in the glittering silver uniform of Titan's permanent staff standing there, a frown on their long, seamless face. The gravity was low enough, and the ferrosteel dome blocked enough harmful radiation, that those who lived on Titan often looked decades younger than their actual ages, even before rejuvenation treatments. Some people joked that Wendy May had found a way to get the *actual* peach trees of immortality from the Chinese heavens, and that the orchards planted in that "world" could keep people alive long past their appointed time.

"Mr. May, Mrs. May, Mrs. May-Xiang." The officer nodded to each individual in turn with the utmost politeness, almost managing to conceal the awe in their eyes. "We had no idea you were coming to inspect the property."

"It isn't an inspection," said Michael. "It's a vacation. We're taking our children on vacation."

The youngest three. The elder three were off living their lives, Chi in a research lab orbiting Pluto, working on deep space biochemical sampling; Mara swimming the oceans of Jupiter, her body transformed through some of her sister's techniques, until she could travel the length of a continent without surfacing for air; and John tucked in a minor role in the Titan Corporation, learning the family business from the ground up. All of them had made this same pilgrimage to Titan, had fallen through the gravity tunnels, had walked the worldlet their family owned with their hands in their pockets and their identity beacons falsified, allowing them to experience their great-great-great-grandmother's dream the same way everyone else did.

The security officer inclined their head, but it was clear from their expression that they didn't believe Michael's claims. No one ever did. No one could ever believe that he, the last surviving heir of his generation, would walk away from the lunar wonderland crafted in his honor, his parents' honor, the honor of every May descendant to walk the worlds with open hands and hungry eyes, looking for something new to carry home to their heart's own home on Titan.

He could have tried to explain. He could have said that Wendy May had been very clear in her will, asking her children and their children and their children's children to travel, to see things, to live their lives outside the literal manifestation of the bubble she had been raised in. She had been a wide-eyed rich girl who pinned all her hopes on a distant moon she had never seen, but whose surface, she had been assured, was geologically stable enough to carry the weight of her dreams. Everything she'd built, not designing but asking to have designed, had been inspired by the stories she'd read as a child. Those stories would change. The signs had already been out there in the world, for the people who knew how to see them. For Titan to speak to the future as it already spoke to the past, new dreams of the moon would have to be collected, cataloged, and brought home.

Two new "worlds" had been designed and opened their gates since Wendy May's death. Her daughter had been responsible for

The Sea My Home, a watery paradise inspired by the stories told by children orbiting Jupiter, looking at the ceaseless seas below them. In it, guests donned rebreathers and swam through blood-warm "oceans," dove deep for pirate treasures, and dined on seafood farmed across the solar system. Not to be outdone, her grandson had ordered the construction of The Moon on Fire, Mercury's contribution, where the skies were gray with synthetic ash and columns of flame jetted up to surprise and delight the tourists.

Michael's father was still working on the construction of his new world, a glorious, jungle-themed tangle of flowers and fantasies, and Michael's sister was waiting in the wings for her turn, planning a low-gravity wonderland where everything would soar, unfettered, free. The Mays built the solar system's playground, and to do that, they had to keep wandering. They had to *see*.

What was Isla seeing now, he wondered. Was she seeing the inside of a box, the back of some broken-down junker of a transport ship, or the heart of a fusion-powered incinerator? Was she still there for them to find, or was the thought that they might see their little girl again just one more dream on Titan?

"Regardless," said the officer, finally seeming to shake off the confusion at hearing a member of the May family call visiting Titan "a vacation," when surely they came and went as they pleased, "you should have notified us of your arrival. We would have cleared priority docking space for you, closer to the surface, and there would have been no need—"

"Stop," said Ange, pleasantly enough. "If you don't, I'll remove your sternum through your stomach, and that's not usually something people survive."

The officer stopped. Blinked. And tried again. "Mrs. May-Xiang, if you would just—"

"Stop." This time, Ange's voice was less pleasant. "I don't want to hear what you think we should have done, or what we didn't do to your satisfaction, or whatever other bullshit you've been trained to peddle. I want to know where my daughter is, and I want to know *now*."

The officer looked from Ange to Kim to Michael, confusion written clearly in their eyes, along with an almost paralyzing fear of saying the wrong thing. "We're reviewing the footage now. Surveillance in the plaza is... complicated."

"We discussed the security systems on Titan before we agreed to Michael's proposal," said Kim. Her voice was, as always, calm and level. The people of Charon never shouted. Their homes were too narrow, too echoing for raised voices. Her spouses, though, could see the rage in the angle of her jaw, and wisely kept their distance. "Not only the proposal that we visit—the proposal of marriage. We entered this union with open eyes. We are fully aware of the security coverage of the plaza, and more, of the fact that nothing there goes unrecorded. I suppose this means the question is... why has the Titan Corporation stolen our child?"

Silence fell.

It lasted for a few seconds—five, perhaps, no more than eight—before the officer whirled and grabbed the doorknob, trying to yank it open. Just as quickly, Ange was there, slamming them up against the door, her hand tight around their throat, her eyes narrow and blazing.

"Not the right answer," she said.

The officer whimpered.

VERY FEW OF the megacorps to form on Earth during the last pre-Collapse years survived the transition to orbit. The resources were too different, too undependable, and most of all, too difficult to monopolize; they were forced first to specialize, and then to carve themselves up and portion themselves off to the highest bidders, forsaking size in favor of survival. Families that once controlled continents found themselves controlling single asteroids, or measured percentages of the mining rights of a world whose yields failed to meet projections cycle after cycle, or single shipping lanes. Fortunes could still be made and lost, but in a wider universe, they were made and lost on narrower bands, at least until merchant and monetization came together—as they always had, since the dawn of humankind—to find new ways of doing business. So many of them weren't new at all, only the same old deal in a spectacular new shell, but oh, how the money rolled in.

In little more than a decade, new dynasties rose, and the moguls at their heads began narrowing their reproduction as their predecessors had done, restricting themselves whenever possible to a single heir, for who wanted to see their empires carved up and scattered to the solar winds when so much effort had gone into creating them?

Some, however, saw the possibility of dynastic conflict as a good thing, a way to be sure their empires were always held by the strongest, and not simply granted to their sole heirs by default. Others believed that their children and their children's children would be able to find a way to share. There was plenty, after all. There would always *be* plenty. Why shouldn't a fortune feed as many as possible?

Wendy May had fallen somewhere between the two camps. She had sunk every penny of her personal fortune into Titan, and there had been no guarantee that her investment would ever bear fruit. At the time, she had been content with the idea that she might travel to her privately owned moon and die in the arms of an amusement park barely half constructed, its gates never opened to the awestruck masses of the solar system. If anything, she had been as surprised as anyone else when Titan had managed to catch the hearts and minds of people everywhere, luring them into Saturn's orbit as they raced for the chance to sample its wonders for themselves.

By the time her creation had opened its gates, she had been married to one of its primary architects, a gentle man who made chemical bonds dance to his whim. They had had three children before he died, and she had seen them all into adulthood and starting families of their own before she followed him.

Not all of their children had chosen to have children: by Michael's generation, there had only been six potential heirs to the family business. Two of them had gone into other lines of work, accepting lucrative positions with rivals or with firms whose interests more closely matched their own. One had disappeared in the Kuiper Belt, and had been missing almost long enough to have been declared dead. His sister, Margaret, had accepted the position of heir apparent, and was happily learning the ropes of everything it was to be the latest guardian of Titan, while remaining happily childless. Let her brother produce the next generation of administrators. She had work to do.

That was the problem. Wendy May had been very clear about one thing: as long as there *was* a suitable heir born to the family line, they would inherit. Her shares in the corporation were protected by a hundred laws and layers of red tape, and unsnarling all that complicated legislation—some of it written solely to protect what she had made—would have been impossible to do without being caught. Her empire was safe in the hands of the children she had made to keep it safe.

What she hadn't considered was that, by making blood the only requirement of being accepted as CEO, she had placed her eventual descendants in the position of living in constant fear of kidnapping becoming a form of corporate espionage.

Ange slammed the officer against the wall again, knocking their head into the ferrosteel. The officer whimpered. Ange rolled her eyes.

"I've only done soft tissue damage so far. That could change. Where is our daughter?"

The officer made a soft choking noise.

"If I let you go, will you tell us?"

Vigorous nodding followed the question. Ange pulled her hand away, allowing the officer to collapse against their desk, clutching at their wounded throat and wheezing. Ange took a step back, watching impassively. Michael and Kim were silent.

"Sir," wheezed the officer. "This is entirely improper. My staff is loyal."

"To whom?" asked Michael.

The officer paled, looking to Kim as if she might provide a way out.

Kim looked calmly back. "Charon is a quiet place," she said. "Out of necessity, yes, but also out of cultural expectation. I know a dozen ways to hurt you so profoundly that it steals your breath away. You won't scream if I have to track you down. You won't have time. Where is my daughter?"

"Our daughter," said Michael.

Kim waved his objection away with one hand. "Well? I'm waiting."

"Sir, Miss May—"

"My sister did not kidnap my daughter," said Michael. "But by now, she knows Isla's been taken."

It didn't seem possible for the officer to pale further. They did. "S-sir?"

"All our children have subdermal medical sensors," said Ange. "Isla is a fairly excitable child, and when she was snatched, hers probably spiked hard enough to set off the alarms. Margaret knows. She's probably on her way here right now with her *private* security firm, the ones who don't answer to anyone but her. Think she'll be angry? Because I think she'll be angry."

"She's always angry when she has to leave her office," said Michael. "She doesn't like going outside."

"And she owns an amusement park," scoffed Kim.

The security officer was looking between them in increasing horror. "You can't be serious."

"You've enabled the abduction of her niece. She's not going to be happy about that. How much money did they offer you? Was it worth your job? Was it worth your *life*? None of the other megas are going to take you after you betrayed one employer and failed another. Hope you enjoy asteroid mining in a habitat that loses atmo as fast as the gennies can make it, because that's about the only option you've got left." Michael's voice took on a jeering note. "They love it when they get softies kicked out that way. No adaptations, no hardening of your skeletal structure, no other options. They're going to break you, and my whole family is going to cheer."

"Or," said Ange.

The officer whipped around to stare at her. "Or…?" they repeated, voice trembling.

"Or maybe nothing happened," said Ange. "Children get lost all the time. Maybe Isla got lost."

Slowly, the officer nodded. "I know just where to look."

ISLA WAS ASLEEP in a storage pod waiting to be loaded onto an outgoing freighter. She woke to her mothers bending over her and her father standing nearby, voice low as he conversed with her beloved Auntie Margaret. Isla shook off the last, lingering shards of her confusion and fear and launched herself at her aunt, already laughing, already forgetting the unfamiliar arms that had gripped her tight and pressed the sedative patch to her throat.

She flung her arms around Margaret's legs just as the older woman said, "—body will never be found. Don't worry. Here on Titan, we're still the law. Anyone with May blood is untouchable."

Michael's smile bordered on feral. "Thanks, Gramma Wendy."

"Can we go ride the rides now?" demanded Isla.

"Of course, comet," said Michael, his smile softening as he looked down at his daughter. "They're all going to be yours one day."

He swept her up into his arms and walked toward his wives, Margaret by his side. Somewhere in the distance, a coaster swept by. Tourists cheered, and their voices blended with the artificial air of Titan, wafting upward and away, breaking against the ferrosteel shell of a world turned into a dizzying amusement, fading into the endless manufactured summer of Wendy May's dream.

LAST SMALL STEP
STEPHEN BAXTER

As we crossed the orbit of Neptune, heading outward, I woke from coldsleep with my head full of the mental state of our quarry, Stavros Gershon. And with the words of Lemuel Gulliver in my ears.

This lodestone is under the care of certain astronomers, who, from time to time, give it such positions as the monarch directs. They spend the greatest part of their lives in observing the celestial bodies, which they do by the assistance of glasses, far excelling ours in goodness. For, although their largest telescopes do not exceed three feet, they magnify much more than those of a hundred with us, and show the stars with greater clearness. This advantage has enabled them to extend their discoveries much further than our astronomers in Europe; for they have made a catalogue of ten thousand fixed stars, whereas the largest of ours do not contain above one third part of that number...

"Win. Winifred. Win Chambers. Are you with me yet?"

Gulliver was paused. Another voice. A face, looming over mine.

"Joe Salo."

"You got it," he said. "Well done."

"You need a shave."

"I've been all alone in this tub for a month, aside from you in your coffin. Facial hair wasn't a priority."

I tried to sit up. The coldsleep pod, my 'coffin', was smart. It tipped me up with a whir, and in zero gravity I floated comfortably, my loose gown drifting around. I was in a small, boxy cabin, the walls plastered with smart screens, a couple of couches set before the control stations. A small galley, a door that led to the bathrooms and the cupboards we slept in. Two coldsleep pods. Home from home, for this two-year flight.

Salo was watching me. "You know where you are, right? We've had no problems. We got through the acceleration phase and we're cruising. Once you're nominal, I'll duck back into coldsleep myself. You're up for another month to make sure I didn't miss anything. And then we'll snooze side by side until month twenty-one—"

"I know I'm on the *Malenfant*." The name of your ship is a standard post-coldsleep memory check.

"Full name?"

"*Reid Malenfant*, Common Heritage Deep Space Vessel 2248-9D." A veteran of the Earth-Mars run, the ship was older than its Heritage registration date. Most machines on Earth, and in human space, were decades old at least. I said dryly, "I even remember that the ship was named for the loser who crashed a space shuttle booster in..."

"2019. The booster was called the *Constitution*. And hey, that loser risked his life to save Cape Canaveral."

I concentrated. "Whereas we are in pursuit of a character called Stavros Gershon, who took a ship called..."

"*Last Small Step*. Like the programme. Very unoriginal."

"Right. Out to a dwarf planet at two hundred AU." Two hundred astronomical units, two hundred times as far as Earth is from the Sun. A rogue world maybe, passing through that sparse, diffuse realm of minor planets and other debris between the Kuiper Belt and the Oort Cloud. "So that Gershon can do the footprint and flags thing, first on a new world. What I don't know is exactly where we are now."

That was when I found out the *Malenfant* was crossing the orbit of Neptune. A mere hundred days out from Earth. Twenty more months before we would reach our destination.

"Shit. Is that all?"

But I had known the mission parameters before we set off. The *Malenfant* was optimised for short-haul journeys in the inner solar system: a few days from Earth to Mars, if the relative orbital positions were right. It could cross a distance two hundred times further, but it would take two *years* to get us there. However, it was all we had. Two hundred and fifty years after Reid Malenfant's moment of glory, mankind had no need for more powerful craft, having turned its back on human space travel almost completely.

Hence the Last Small Step programme, in fact.

Last Small Step. Of course everybody knows Neil Armstrong's line as he became the first human to walk on another world: "That's one small step for a man..." Even if, I had learned, 40 percent of people who consult the Answerers about it think that Armstrong was the one who went to the Americas on the *Santa Maria*. When the Pull Back to Earth movement cut in—when humanity as a whole decided to abandon space, retreat to a slowly healing Earth, and leave the mess we had made on Mars, Venus and the Moon to the AIs— protests had been spiked by the establishment of the Last Small Step programme. It was a kind of compensation. The idea was to allow a last wave of explorers to follow in Armstrong's footsteps, to send out one last human mission to each remaining virgin "world" in the Solar System—that is, each planet, minor planet or moon large enough to be compacted into a spherical shape—and, wherever possible, to land there, even just once, to plant a flag and a plaque, and come home again. No harm done to the target world, in the spirit of our age. Just to say we'd been there before we went home for good.

The trouble was, Stavros Gershon seemed intent on breaking the rules. Hence our mission.

Salo handed me a flask. "Drink this."

A soupy glop that was highly nutritious, and full of helpful nanotech to counteract such extended-spaceflight problems as a loss of bone mass, a lousy fluid balance and a cumulative radiation load. It tasted like cold vomit.

Salo said, "So you do remember our mission."

I grunted. "Yup." As scientists, low-grade field workers, we'd done a handful of space missions together, mostly chasing near-Earth asteroids in ships like this.

I was forty-one, Joe thirty-something. We'd spent months in cramped cabins together. We both had strong families back home. We got along well enough.

Usually.

Anyhow, now I pushed down my reflexive irritation at his probing; he had to ask these post-coldsleep questions. "So when Gershon took off, heading beyond the Kuiper Belt—"

"Unauthorised."

"We volunteered to do the chasing."

"Right. His destination was recognised as a valid Last Small Step target. The last of all, actually. Well, probably."

After the Last Small Step programme had been established, it had proven popular. The available targets, mostly minor worlds in the Kuiper Belt and Oort Cloud, had been used up surprisingly quickly, even out to a thousand astronomical units or more. And Gershon's target was believed to be, maybe, one of the last of all. A ball of ice and rock, probably, a little smaller than Ceres, with a couple of even smaller moons.

Salo prompted, "And we are after Gershon because—"

"Planetary protection. He's been threatening to do more than take a photograph at his target. Mining, maybe. We were appointed Prefects pro-tem, with the authority to go after him, and grab him, and clean up as necessary."

Salo nodded. "If he does go beyond the Last Small Step parameters."

"Stavros Gershon," I said, my frozen brain slowly thawing, "believes he is descended from one of the first on Mars, so carrying on the family tradition. And his target—no name, I can never remember the catalogue number—"

"Actually, it has a name now. Gershon gave it one—or, he says, he rediscovered it."

Which bit of oddness reminded me of what I'd been hearing when I woke up. "Why were you reading *Gulliver's Travels*?"

He looked impressed. "Well recognised. Part III, chapter III. But it wasn't me reading. It was a transmission from Gershon, on the *Last Small Step*. From beginning, unpause."

On a wall screen, a smiling face appeared, framed by a standard lightweight pressure suit hood. A ship's cabin. "Hello. I am Stavros Gershon..."

I sipped my soup, and wondered why I didn't need to pee, and stared.

Stavros Gershon looked maybe fifty years old. He didn't much resemble his famous ancestor, but then after the huge mixing of mankind during the decades of the Chaos, few of us looked much like our great-grandparents, probably. I had to admit his ship, the clunkily named *Last Small Step*, looked spacious, even comfortable, compared to our bare-bones *Malenfant*. Gershon must have been donated a lot of stipends by a lot of supporters.

"And I suppose, as I approach the minor planet Voga, that you are wondering why I am reading to you from a text first published in 1726, over five hundred and forty years ago..."

"Pause," I said. "Voga?"

"I checked out the name," Salo said. "Bounced it back to the Archives on Earth. It's pretty obscure—a legend that may have its origin in fiction, even..."

"What legend?"

"Of a planet made of gold."

I stared at him, and at Gershon. "Gold? That's... insane."

"Probably. But there's a logic to it. I think."

I was thinking too, but very slowly. "And it has something to do with *Gulliver's Travels?*"

"You got it. Unpause."

Gershon rattled through the passage I'd heard earlier, and read us some more: "*They* (that is, the astronomers of the flying island of Laputa) *have likewise discovered two lesser stars, or satellites, which revolve about Mars; whereof the innermost is distant from the centre of the primary planet exactly three of his diameters, and the outermost, five; the former revolves in the space of ten hours, and the latter in twenty-one and a half; so that the squares of their periodical times are very near in the same proportion with the cubes of their distance from the centre of Mars; which evidently shows them to be governed by the same law of gravitation that influences the other heavenly bodies. They have observed ninety-three different comets, and settled their periods with great exactness...*"

"And so on." Gershon grinned into his monitor. "You see? It's all in there. The clues to the treasure. Sitting in plain sight for five hundred years."

"And you're the genius who figured it out," Salo muttered. "What treasure, though?"

I studied Gershon's face. I'm more interested in people than Joe—an age difference thing, maybe. Gershon was grinning, but there was a kind of desperation there, I thought. As if he didn't fully believe his own logic, as if there was something deeper driving him. Which is probably true of all of us. *What are you doing out there, Gershon? What treasure? And what do you really want?*

Meanwhile, memories were reassembling in my reluctantly waking brain like the pieces of a puzzle. *Thud. Thud.* "And this was why we were sent after him, in such a rush. Because, whatever the logic, if he gets there and starts taking samples that are more than scrapings for science, if he starts prospecting, or even mining—"

"It's against Common Heritage law, and we need to bring him back, clean it up."

Thud. "Right. And that's why we aren't going home again any time soon."

"Correct. You remember there wasn't the time to upgrade this Mars-run taxi cab to get us there *and back*. We haven't the fuel. So we go to this 'Voga', deal with Gershon, and the three of us go into coldsleep until we are followed by a more capable ship in a few years."

Thud.

"Shit," I said, putting a lot of heft into the word.

"Seconded. So you want to get out of that coffin and get to work? The sooner I get back into coldsleep, the sooner this mission will be over for me..."

I STAYED AWAKE for a month, alone in trans-Neptunian space. That was the fourth month of our twenty-four-month mission.

Then we both slept away much of the rest of the featureless journey. All this was routine. You rotate in and out of coldsleep to save consumables and your own sanity, and focus on the interesting bits.

I was the first to be woken the next time, at the start of our twenty-first month—by which time we were just thirty-some astronomical units or so out from the target. From Voga, planet of gold.

I spent that twenty-first month checking out stuff, and puzzling over *Gulliver's Travels.*

I went over the ship from bow to stern, even though I had every faith in our craft, a tried and trusted development of centuries-old technologies. The *Reid Malenfant* was like an arrow, with a fat blade and sprawling fletches, and a bunch of balloons stuck to the shaft. The "blade" was our living quarters, a roughly conical hab module containing us, our coldsleep pods, and assorted junk, that sat on top of a service module cum lander, which contained the infrastructure of the closed-loop life support system that kept us alive, as well as a propulsion stage and other essentials.

The arrow's shaft contained our interplanetary propulsion engine, technically known as a magnetoplasma rocket. Our propellant was hydrogen, stored as a liquid in those balloon tanks along the shaft. We had a compact fusion reactor whose energies ionised the hydrogen to plasma using powerful radio blasts—the fletches at the rear of the arrow were radiator panels, dumping waste heat from this process—and the plasma, bearing an electrical charge, was then grabbed by a magnetic field and hurled out the back. The system was mature technology and ran smoothly, and gave us our cruise velocity of five hundred kilometres a second.

As I said, such a ship, with such a performance, purring along, would get you to Mars and back in a few days or weeks. Even the Jovian system, five astronomical units from the Sun, was within reasonably easy reach. But it would take us two years to get to Voga. To get there in a more sensible time, we would have needed a much more powerful drive—a propellant driven directly by a fusion reaction, maybe, or even by matter-antimatter annihilation. Once we had been developing such drives, but progress stalled when the Chaos came, and industry had to prioritise more urgent needs such as food printers—indeed the whole complex of industrial civilisation came close to collapsing altogether. When we came out of that, the will was gone. And that was why we were crawling out to the Kuiper Belt in an Earth-Mars transport.

And hence our enforced layover at Voga, once we got there. Our low exhaust velocity gave us significant problems with fuel loads. To slow down our twenty-six-tonne dry mass from our cruise speed would take nearly twice as much mass in hydrogen fuel. And to accelerate our dry mass *plus* our deceleration fuel up to our cruise velocity in the first place had taken nearly twice that total in fuel, again. (Talk to an Answerer about the rocket equation.) So we had left Earth orbit with a mighty load of a hundred and seventy tonnes of hydrogen fuel.

But it could have been worse. If we had tried to ship along enough fuel for the return trip too, the fuel load would have been something over a *thousand* tonnes. You could put together such a mission, though the structural challenge alone was monumental: where would you hang all those balloon tanks? And indeed, a mission was being assembled right now back at Earth, to bring us home. But such was the urgency to get hold of Stavros Gershon before he did any harm out at Voga that we had had to be fired off on this one-way mission, before the retrieval option could be designed, let alone assembled.

Look, I'm not complaining.

While on the mission, and especially with our temporary status as Prefects, Joe and I had to follow certain protocols. We were volunteers, of course; we didn't have to be there. You get your Heritage stipend whatever you do, even nothing at all. I wouldn't have been there at all if I hadn't basically *enjoyed* the routine of long-haul spaceflight.

Anyhow, I told myself, the first ocean-going ships to reach the Arctic and Antarctic had used sails. They'd been inadequate for their task too, but their crews had gone regardless. And they had to overwinter, just as we would, in a sense.

For sure, we'd have an anecdote to impress our grandkids.

The work I had to do on the ship was routine. Similarly, my personal needs for sleep, food, exercise were easily met. Eating alone always bores me.

Gulliver's Travels and Gershon's enigmatic remarks were a lot more fun to work on. I have always been a cerebral, solitary type. Lock me in a room with a good mystery to solve, a scientific puzzle maybe, and I was happy—and that was pretty much the situation I had landed in here.

And there was a human puzzle too, which would always attract me more than Joe. The puzzle being, of course, Stavros Gershon's true motivation.

Most *Last Small Step* voyagers were happy to stick to the rules. They wanted their moment of fame—and it was enduring fame indeed, as once you are the first somewhere, you will be remembered as the first for all time. There were collector types who had been to as many worlds as they could. There had been a few highly publicised races. And so on.

But they stuck to the rules, which fitted the paradigm of our times. You went down, took your photographs, cleaned up, went home, leaving no more pollution than a flag. Not Gershon, though. I looked again at his message loop, at the need, yes, the desperation in his eyes. There was something more he wanted, and he wanted it badly. The trouble was, he wasn't saying what that was, not yet.

So, a puzzle. I admit that when I had finally figured it out—or at least the Gulliver stuff, and most but not all of it, as it turned out—I couldn't wait, and woke up Salo a whole day early to tell him about it.

"YOU SEE, I don't think Swift was describing Mars's moons at all. And I believe that's the way Gershon is thinking too. You seem surprisingly grumpy, Joe."

Salo, still in his soft sleepsuit, a survival blanket around his shoulders, sipping a tumbler of nutritious, nano-infested glop, glowered at me. "I wonder why," he said. "Get on with it. Swift *says* they're the satellites of Mars, doesn't he? He wrote that book in..."

"1726."

"And Mars's two moons weren't actually discovered until..."

"1877. By Asaph Hall—"

"I don't *care*. I thought Swift had always been praised for a lucky guess, at least."

"Well, I've been looking into that."

"You would."

"He probably followed a kind of mathematical logic. It was believed that Earth had one moon, and Jupiter four: the Galileans, all that could be seen with the telescopes of the time. So it was *logical*, in an orderly universe, for Mars, in between Earth and Jupiter, to have two moons. One, two, four."

"But didn't he get the periods about right too?"

"Not a bad guess. He has the inner moon orbit Mars in ten hours, whereas Phobos actually takes just under eight. The outer moon took twenty-one and a half hours, whereas Deimos takes thirty hours. The right order of magnitude. He got the distances from Mars more wrong, though: over twice the true distance for Phobos, nearly 50 percent too high for Deimos. Not that he used those names."

"Will you ever get to a point, Chambers?"

"But," I went on doggedly, "what Swift did get right was Kepler's Law of planetary orbits. He understood Newton's gravitation, you see. So the square of the orbital period of each of his moons is proportional to the cube of the radius of the orbit, just as it should be—"

"He was describing a plausible system, then."

"Yes. But just *not Mars*, not the Mars as we know it. And the information he gives us is... selective. Which makes me think he was describing something else. Listen again." I pulled up Swift's words.

Satellites... whereof the innermost is distant from the centre of the primary planet exactly three of his diameters, and the outermost, five; the former revolves in the space of ten hours, and the latter in twenty-one and a half...

"Those are the *only* numbers he gives. He doesn't give masses, or absolute sizes—such as the diameter of Mars, for instance. He just gives the timings, and the relative distances of the moons' orbits and the planet. Which, if you think about it, is precisely the data you'd get from a basic telescopic observation, without any estimate of your absolute distance from the object. Just the size of one element, compared to another."

He was waking up; he plodded after my conclusion slowly. "So are you saying that Swift is describing another body? Another system, not Mars and its moons? Something that was actually *seen* by some astronomer before 1726?"

"That's possible, isn't it? If such a system had existed, and was close enough—"

"But no such system does exist, or we'd see it now... Ah."

I grinned. "You're getting there. *Suppose a rogue planet came wandering through the solar system.* Sometime in the decades before Swift, when the followers of Galileo were mapping the sky. A one and only pass. You might see the planet, see its moons, measure times and relative distances. No time to get a fix on the true distance, or the diameter of this fake Mars, before it passed back into the dark, not with the technology of the time. Maybe the result was never published properly; the observation couldn't be repeated, after all—and at the time there were a lot of unreliable sightings, of moons of Venus, a second Mercury..."

"It couldn't have been too massive, or it would have perturbed the other planets."

I shrugged. "Small and close would be visible but harmless."

He nodded. "And so Swift gets hold of this sighting and weaves it into his fiction. He imagines Mars is like this... wanderer. Because, and it's just a coincidence, the wanderer has two moons, as he thinks Mars must have." He looked at me. "But now, here we are chasing Stavros Gershon out to some object two hundred AU from the Sun..." He slapped the side of his head. "My mental arithmetic is stuck. Curse you, sleep pod."

"I worked it out," I said evenly. "An object with perihelion close to the Sun, aphelion two hundred AU out, would have an orbital period of about a thousand years."

He nodded. "It's five hundred years since Swift. So this object, if it exists—"

"Should now be out near aphelion, its furthest distance from the Sun. Two hundred AU out. Just where Gershon has found his Voga."

He stared at me. "I'd congratulate you on your logic, but I'm afraid I'll throw up again. Okay, I can just about buy that. But what about all this crap about a golden world? All in Swift too, right?"

"Yes. If you look hard enough." But I was on shakier ground, and I hurried on. "Look—I said Swift couldn't give us the absolute sizes of his fake Mars and its moons' orbits. But we have the orbit timings, and their relative sizes, scaled against the planet's diameter. And from that you can work out one more number. *The planet's density*. Not its mass, its density. Mass per unit volume..."

He was still dopy enough that I had to walk him through the logic.

This time it was about Newton's theory of gravity, which built on Kepler's observations. Newton predicted that the period of a moon's orbit, squared, is proportional to the orbit's radius, cubed—that was Kepler's Law—but *also* inversely proportional to the planet's mass. In this case the orbit radius was given in terms of multiples of the planet's own radius—and the cube of *that* is proportional to the planet's volume.

So in Newton's equation you know the period, and you have the planet's mass divided by the volume, which is its density...

You don't have to follow all that. Working through the math is easier, actually. Go ask an Answerer. Salo didn't follow it all, not at that moment. But he got the essence: the denser the central planet, the faster those orbiting moons would have to whip around it. And—

"And so we know the density of this Voga. Right?"

I just grinned.

"Well, tell me!"

"Comes out at twenty-four tonnes per cubic metre."

He was still fuzzy. He growled, "So? Water is around one tonne per cubic metre. Iron is..."

"Nine tonnes per cubic metre."

"Oh. Which is what rocky planets are mostly made of."

"Right. Earth's average density, for instance, is five tonnes per cubic metre. Iron and rock. Whereas gold is *nineteen* tonnes per cubic metre. Platinum twenty-one tonnes. Look, you can see that Gershon is onto something here. Something exotic."

He rubbed his face. "Yeah, but what? It's been a long time since Gulliver. We must know more about this object by now."

"Sure. Or we wouldn't be chasing Gershon out here. It was spotted visually by some deep space probe, decades ago. Just another Kuiper object, a sphere, away from the bulk of the Belt. It's less than a thousand kilometres across. Which gives it the mass of Pluto, by the way, but it's so massive it has a respectable gravity—about the same as Mars."

He thought about that. "An atmosphere, then? It will be damned cold out there, but—"

"It's possible. Gershon seems to have found it in a catalogue of Last Small Step targets. It started looking like the last available target of all, which must have attracted his interest. And *then* he spotted the anomalies, and somehow made the connection with Swift— "

"No wonder he went out there. And he has found something exotic, from what you say. But maybe not exotic in the way he's hoping."

"What, then?"

"How should I know? I'm barely conscious. And now—"

And now it was time for him to throw up, again.

Turned out he was right, though, in that first reaction. When we finally got to Voga, it was certainly exotic.

But nobody calls it Voga anymore.

FROM LOW ORBIT, it was a ball of rock wrapped in a murky atmosphere under which glistened shallow lakes of some kind of fluid. And it did indeed have two moons, two splinters of rock and ice even less impressive than their parent. All this illuminated in the point light of a Sun giving off only one forty-thousandth its brilliance in Earth's sky.

We ran scans. We quickly found that the moons' orbits closely matched Swift's descriptions. And Voga's density was just as I had calculated.

But Voga wasn't made of gold. Our neutrino scans revealed it was pretty much like Earth, in fact, an iron core wrapped in a layer of silicate rocks. Just iron and rock, but very densely packed.

And, from space, it was dull, all but featureless: no mountain ranges, no ocean basins. Very few impact craters, which Salo said was a consequence of a geologically active surface; features like craters wouldn't last.

In fact, the only feature on its surface to which the human eye was drawn was a spacecraft, or anyhow its hab-lander module, pretty much similar to ours though larger, and neatly set down close to one pole. We had already spotted Gershon's interplanetary propulsion unit in high orbit around the planet. Beside the lander, our telescopes revealed, was a trail of footprints in what looked like stiff mud, and a single flag. The Stars and Stripes: flag of a nation that no longer existed, but the flag that had been set on the Moon by Armstrong, and no doubt on Mars by Ralph Gershon, so the Stars and Stripes it had to be.

There was no immediate sign of Gershon himself. We did download a message from his lander, running on a loop.

Before we watched the message, we ran through a couple of orbits, and got used to the journey being over, and just took in what we saw.

"A few things strike me as odd," I said at length.

"Go on," Salo said.

"All we see down there is iron and silicate rock. The neutrino scans show traces of more exotic substances, heavier metals—there *is* some gold down there, but no more than you could obtain by mining on Earth. So how come it's so dense? We're measuring the mass directly now; the figures don't lie."

"I'm developing a theory," Salo said slowly. "Maybe the formation of this rock ball was—unusual. Maybe it didn't form the way Earth did, coalescing out of a Sun-centred cloud of dust and ice—with a few spectacular collisions along the way.

"Consider an ice giant planet. Uranus, say. Mostly a big ball of gas. But at its heart it has a core, which is like a planet in itself—a rocky planet, like Earth, a ball of iron and rock and maybe some water. An Earth, buried deep inside a heavy atmosphere. In the case of Uranus, the core mass is 60 percent of Earth, the radius 60 percent—"

I worked the numbers quickly. "Density of about fifteen tonnes per cubic metre. Much more than the Earth. I get the idea. And if somehow you could strip away the outer atmosphere—"

"We know that happens," he said. "We've seen it in other systems, when some giant exoplanet migrates in too close to its star, and its outer layers are evaporated away by the heat until the core is exposed. You would think that the core, once it was released from that crushing weight, would just explode. But—I've been looking it up—in theory, if the atmospheric loss is slow and the core has time to adjust, if the core has the right composition, if something called its finite-state incompressibility is tuned just right—"

"The core can survive?"

"Right. For a billion years, maybe. A very *slow* explosion... This is a pretty small specimen. But maybe it's a fragment of some larger object. Planetary formation is a big, messy puzzle."

"I'm surprised to see it has seas." I glanced down at the surface below, flat and glistening, hazed with cloud or mist—and, here and there, what looked like mud pools, bubbling. "Puddles, anyhow. And what looks like heat escaping."

"Yeah. There's actually some volcanism up near the poles. Big flat pools of lava, lots of gases venting. The interior must be active, a lot of geothermal heat to lose. And it's outgassing enough to create an atmosphere. I can see carbon dioxide, methane, ammonia in the lower air. Layers of clouds at different levels. Water too—even puddles of it on the surface, as you say."

I glanced at the pinprick Sun. "Liquid water, though. Even if the planet is leaking inner heat—we are a long way from warm here."

He tapped the screen. "I think Voga has an extended atmosphere. Hydrogen. Hard for us to see, but a big fat envelope, enough to exert some pressure at the surface, act as a greenhouse, and trap that leaked inner heat. Given time, and enough hydrogen, the world could become as warm as you like. Maybe the planet collected the hydrogen as it migrated out of the solar system—no, dummy, that can't be right; it would lose the envelope every time it jaunted back into the inner system, as in Swift's day. And all that volcanic carbon dioxide must react with the hydrogen layer too..." He started to sound excited, his mind working quickly. "So something must be generating fresh hydrogen. And if *that's* so—"

"Yes?"

"Let me think about it." He glanced at me. "First things first. We need to deal with Gershon. Presumably the most disappointed man in the solar system. Let's hear his message." He tapped a screen.

And there was Stavros Gershon.

Yes, I was expecting disappointment. Even desperation. After all, whatever its true nature, Voga hadn't lived up to his dreams.

But he didn't look disappointed to me.

Gershon stood in a pressure suit, on the surface of Voga, with the Stars and Stripes beside him, and his ship set down neatly on the surface beyond. He was grinning through his visor.

And he had what looked like explosive, strapped by an elasticated belt around his waist.

Salo and I shared a glance. Anxiety gnawed my stomach.

GERSHON SAID NOW, "Hi, guys. You two in the *Malenfant*, who trailed me out here, and whoever follows after. I appreciate your efforts, believe me. But you're too late. This is a recording, and that's all you'll ever get from me.

"Look—I achieved what I came here for. Primarily, anyhow. My own footprints and flags moment, yeah. And I was right about Swift and the anomalous density of this boulder, right? I confirmed this place exists, and established its true nature. Some achievement, in interplanetary geology, *and* in the history of literature. Even if I didn't get it quite right.

"I never thought Voga would be gold! That was just a headline. I did hope it was going to be a mother lode of—something special. Heavy, exotic elements. Radioactive, maybe. A resource lode on the edge of the Solar System, which might have jolted us out of this Pull Back to Earth crap, if not now, some day. Just knowing it was here, on the edge of interstellar space, might have drawn us back... Well. It wasn't to be.

"But there is something else I can do, I figure. Another way I can make this place attractive to future visitors."

Salo growled, "And make sure you are remembered, and not as a failure..."

Gershon's gloved right hand moved to his belt. I sensed Salo tensing up beside me.

"So this isn't a fuel lode, but it's a world, right? A world of rock and water, and carbon and oxygen. A world that's not so terribly unlike ours—maybe as Earth was when it was much younger—but a world without life. And maybe that's something I can change, right here, right now." His right hand still on his belt, with his left hand he dug into a pouch and produced a book, an old-fashioned paper volume. "I have here a copy of the Holy Bible, King James version."

Salo frowned. "What's that?"

"Archaic religious text. Judaeo-Christian, I think. All about how God created the Earth, and everything that lives on it."

"Oh, crap."

Gershon said, "I know the old religions are out of favour now, but—well, I'm pretty much out of favour myself, aren't I? So." Now he raised the Bible in his left hand. "Genesis, Chapter One, Verse 10: 'And God called the dry land Earth; and the gathering together of the waters called the Seas, and God saw that it was good.'"

Salo growled, "No, no, you idiot. I know what you're going to do. You're going to blow yourself up, right? But you don't get it."

"'And God said, Let the earth bring forth grass, the herb yielding seed, and the fruit tree yielding fruit after his kind, whose seed is in itself, upon the earth; and it was so...'"

Salo muttered, "And this is a recording. We're too late, too late."

"Too late for what? To save his life?"

"No! To save the damn planet. Because there is already life here. Don't you see?"

I didn't, not then.

And neither had Gershon, evidently. Because he finished his reading, closed up the Bible in his left hand, and closed his right hand over a control at his belt.

"'And God saw that it was good.'" He smiled.

All we saw after that was static.

I GUESS I'LL never fully understand Gershon's motivation.

He had no family he was close to, back home. A network of friends whose stipends had funded his mission, I supposed. Or acolytes, folk he dazzled.

Gershon wanted to be remembered, I guess. And not just as a

logically reconstructed trace in an Archive. In a world without heroes, Gershon had grown up in the shadow of his Mars-walking ancestor Ralph, who *was* an authentic hero, and would never be forgotten. Whereas Stavros had no kids, no enduring achievement on Earth. And he was fifty, a tipping point in anybody's life. He wanted to be remembered, and not just in a catalogue of grinning *Last Small Step* adventurers. He wanted more. He wanted to change the world—a world, anyhow.

I'm no romantic. A child of my more settled times, I guess. But something in me was touched by the wistfulness of his gesture, as if we were remembering a common childhood. Or maybe it was all just a sublimated fear of death.

In any case our world just doesn't work like that anymore. We don't need that kind of hero. We won't allow it.

When I reran the recording, I saw that the detonation had blown down Gershon's flag.

And, just before the detonation itself, that Gershon had been crying.

WE BROKE INTO our coffee hoard. That's how bad we felt.

But when I had time to think it all over, I had a glimmer of hope. Not for Voga, or Gershon. For us.

After we had calmed down for an hour or so, I broke the ice. "You were a couple of steps ahead of me there, buddy. Tell me what you meant by saving the planet."

"I meant save it from Gershon. Who, I guess, was trying to seed it with Earth life. In his suit there would've been caches of blue-green algae. Closing the ecological loops, pumping out oxygen to balance the suit-wearer's breathing out of carbon dioxide. Release *that*, I guess he figured, and even in this wan sunlight the algae could start busily photosynthesising, and pumping oxygen into Voga's air. And Earth life gets a foothold. It might have worked."

"Well, is that so bad?"

"Yes! Because Voga already has life! It *must*. The hydrogen envelope, remember? That keeps the surface warm, but must get regularly stripped away, as the planet approaches the Sun."

"Ah. Right. So, you think, there must be some kind of—of hydrogen-excreting bug down there that replaces the hydrogen in the air."

"The way photosynthetic bugs on Earth replenish the oxygen, yes. And the hydrogen layer keeps the whole world warm, including the bugs, until Voga returns to the sunlight once more."

"It's a deep space Gaia, then. Life and geology working together to sustain a living world."

"I think so. I'm guessing. The point is, though, that if Earth life does get established here, it will start releasing oxygen, that's going to react with the hydrogen, to make water—there will be a one-off rain—and the hydrogen greenhouse will shut down for good, and everything will freeze. The Earth bugs too."

"Not good."

"Indeed. Gershon should have figured it out himself... We'll have to confirm all this when we go down to the surface. Ideally, by finding some hydrogen-excreting bugs."

"Right. And we do have to go down to the surface, don't we?"

"We do," Salo said heavily. "Our primary mission was to get Gershon under control before he harmed the planet. Well, now he has smeared himself all over the place—"

"We'll have to go down and clean it all up."

"Every scrap," he said gloomily. "And *then* we have to wait years until the retrieval crew gets out here, and slog our way home."

That was my cue. "Maybe not," I said.

He looked at me. "Hm?"

I nodded at the images of the planet in our screens. "We need hydrogen propellant, right? Well, there's a big fat layer of it just waiting for us out there. If we could rig up some kind of scoop, I'm thinking, and have *Malenfant* dip into the outer layers of the atmosphere—"

His eyes widened.

"We could cannibalise *One Small Step* for tankage—"

"Winifred, you're a genius."

"Thanks."

"But a criminal genius. They used to call that technique *profac*. Mining a world's air for fuel. It's illegal now. Because it's an example of *in situ* resource utilisation: making your own fuel, and messing up the local environment in the process."

"It's not illegal if we are trying to save our lives."

He frowned, evidently thinking hard. "True, but strictly speaking we're just cutting short an unpleasantly long stay. On the other hand, we are reducing the risk of some malfunction killing us off in the years before the relief crew gets here, aren't we? Maybe there's a case... We need legal advice. Where's the nearest Answerer?"

"Two hundred AU away."

He grinned.

"We could always send a message—"

"Shut up."

I thought it over. "I wonder if Armstrong used *in situ* resource utilisation to get back from the Moon."

Salo shrugged. "Don't know. Gulliver did, for sure. Built a canoe to get away from the land of the Houyhnhnms. Used the skin of yahoos to make a sail. But that's another story. You finished your coffee? Let's get to work."

So we did.

You know, it's a shame. If Gershon had stuck to the *Last Small Step* rules, at least we could have left the standard marker. As it was, Joe Salo scrubbed every square centimetre of rock clean of his footsteps.

And I took down his flag and brought it home.

ONCE ON THE BLUE MOON

KRISTINE KATHRYN RUSCH

ONE MAN CRADLING one large laser rifle stood in the doorway of the luxury suite. Colette sprawled on the threadbare carpet. Her dad had shoved her behind him when he saw the guy at the door, and she had tripped over the retractable ottoman.

Good job, Dad, she nearly said, because that was her default response when he did something stupid, but she didn't say it, because her gaze remained on that rifle. And so did her dad's.

Dad had probably wanted her to run into one of the bedrooms, and that would've made sense if the guy at the door with the rifle hadn't seen her, but he had, and then he had said something softly and beckoned at someone else.

Mom was standing beside the door, actually threading her hands together. Colette felt both a growing fear and a growing irritation. Fear, because she had probably caused this. Day One, she had swiped one of those stupid tablets that the concierge on this level used to keep track of everything on the ship.

The lower levels, without the suites, used holographic screens for the guests, or some lazy person could call up a holographic face to make suggestions.

But here, real people were actually in the passengers' business, as if the *Blue Moon* was still one of the most luxurious starliners in the solar system.

It wasn't luxurious. It *had been* luxurious, maybe, in the Good Old Days when her grandparents had been kids. Dad said the ship had a "mystique," whatever that meant, but Colette had investigated the ship on her own and found the ad that had probably gotten Dad's attention:

Travel in luxury at one-thousandth the price!

Apparently, if you didn't care what kind of cargo the ship carried, then you could have a luxury suite on your trip from wherever to wherever. Theirs was from a starbase beyond Saturn to some place called Montreal because that was the last boarding school that could handle someone like her.

All of this had been Mother's idea, even though all of it had been Colette's fault.

Another man arrived at the door. He was small, barely taller than Colette, and she hadn't reached her full growth yet. (Mother had said that she would when puberty hit, which could be Any Minute Now.) The man had glittering black eyes, a leathery face, and thin lips that quirked upward when he saw her.

"A kid," he said, as if he was surprised.

Colette almost said, *I'm not a kid!* and then thought the better of it. Maybe she'd get a pass on stealing that tablet. Children couldn't be responsible for their actions after all.

"I didn't realize there was a kid on board," the man said, musing. "I didn't think children were allowed on vessels like this."

Yeah, Colette had seen that regulation too, and she knew that her dad had gotten it waived. They needed to get to Earth *yesterday*, or so Mother had said. It was never hard for Dad to get things waived.

The family didn't have money—*yet*, Mother said—but they had access to it, and they had some kind of influence that her dad would flash around whenever he needed it, as, apparently, they had needed it to get on this ship to get Colette to Montreal to the boarding school before the beginning of the semester.

Which seemed stupid to her, because she had started other schools in the middle of the year, and had always, always outperformed everyone in her class. It never mattered whether she arrived with one month left or five, she could work her way around the entire system and do better than anyone else, once she figured out what was needed.

"Take them," the guy with the intense eyes, gesturing at Colette's parents.

Then he took one step into the suite, and looked down at Colette.

"You, little girl, can stay here, if you'll be good." He actually spoke in some kind of fake sweet voice, as if she would be fooled by his tone, even though he had just ordered some guy with a rifle to take her parents.

Colette opened her mouth so she could tell the guy with the intense eyes where he could stick his "good," and then she saw her dad's face. It was drawn and tense.

Her mother was shivering. Her mother often looked terrified over stupid stuff, but she never shivered.

And her dad—tense was not his normal way of dealing with anything.

He frowned at Colette as their gazes met.

"She'll be good," her dad said to the guy, but didn't look away from Colette. "My daughter, she's perfect."

Colette actually felt tears prick at her eyes. Her dad never said that, not with feeling. He was always telling her how impossible, intractable, and stubborn she was, how she could do better if she only settled down. And sometimes he would despair, and say,

Colette Euphemia Josephine Treacher Singh Wilkinson Lopez, you have every opportunity and you're always the smartest person in the room. Why are you constantly throwing that away?

His disappointment pissed her off, and made her work harder at doing the best she could *and* causing trouble. He never noticed the best, but he always noticed the trouble.

She'd been waiting for that *perfect* word from him her whole life. And now he said it, to some guy with intense eyes and another guy holding a laser rifle, and the weird part was, Dad seemed to mean it.

Then he really scared her, because he mouthed, *I love you*, and took a deep breath and said to the guy with intense eyes, "What do you need from us?"

Dad sounded calm, even though he clearly wasn't. Well, clearly to Colette, probably not to the two men.

"I need you to go with him," the guy with the intense eyes said, nodding toward the guy with the laser rifle. Not saying his name, either, which was a bad sign. "We can restrain you and take you if need be."

Dad gave Mother a hard look, and she swallowed visibly, then nodded.

"No restraints needed," Dad said. Then he and Mother walked out of the door as if being taken by guys with laser rifles was an everyday thing.

The guy with intense eyes gave Colette one last glare.

"Be good and you'll be fine," he said. Then he closed the suite door—and stupid idiot that he was—turned on the parental controls.

Which she had already monkeyed with Day One, in case anyone got Ideas. Her parents knew better than to use something that simple on her, but the concierge and the ship's crew didn't.

And neither did the guy with the intense eyes.

She waited a good thirty seconds before moving, and then she went into her room and lay on the bed, because she knew that would be what the guy with the intense eyes would expect—some kid, paralyzed by fear.

She'd show him paralyzed.

She'd show him fear.

Once she had him all figured out.

A KID.

Alfredo Napier thought kids weren't allowed on ships like the *Blue Moon*. Adults knew the dangers they were undertaking when they traveled on a ship like this, but kids? They were under the age of consent, and even if their parents thought it was a good idea, the Starrborne Line, which ran these old ships, did not allow kids on the Titan-Plano to Earth-Houston run.

The company's explanation was pretty simple: in order to make good time on that run, it had to travel older, lesser used routes, not as well policed, and without as many stops or amenities.

In reality, the route these ships traveled was the only route that allowed hazardous cargo. If a ship got into trouble out here, it was twice as likely to be abandoned as it was to be rescued.

Napier had always taken that fact into consideration when he chose his targets.

He also appreciated the fact that everyone on board had signed a waiver, protecting the Starrborne Line from liability should something untoward happen. Not that he really cared if the passengers had given permission for their own deaths on an ancient ship without the proper protections against certain kinds of hazardous cargo, but because he almost felt as if the passengers had given him permission to run his own business the way he wanted to.

A kid.

He shook his head as he hurried to the bridge. A kid changed everything and nothing.

She'd seen him. She'd seen *them*. But she was what? Ten? Twelve? Young enough that no one would believe anything she said. So all he had to do before they blew the ship was put her into one of the lifepods and jettison her with quite a bit of force toward the Martian run. If she survived, then good, and if she didn't, she would die in the pod, not in his custody on the ship.

And he wouldn't have to think about her.

That was the problem with kids.

They haunted a man in the middle of the night, interfering with his sleep.

He made a small fortune doing his work.

The last thing he needed was to second-guess himself. The last thing he needed was to lose even more sleep.

COLETTE SAT UP on the bed. She already hated this room. Square, boxy, brown, the bed one-tenth as comfortable as the bed she had had at her last school. She felt like calling up some paint program and trying to permanently deface the walls.

Maybe if she was trapped in here forever. In the meantime, she had the tablet.

Colette had stolen the tablet because it had basic access to every single part of the ship. No one had figured out she swiped it; the stupid concierge had believed he had misplaced it, and they had issued him a new one, since the first thing Colette had done was shut off the locator on the tablet itself. Basic Survival Thievery 101.

The second thing Colette had done was taken that basic access and amped it up to full access in every shipboard department she could. The only areas she couldn't access were navigation, engine controls, life support, and all of those other things that someone could sabotage and kill people with.

She would need Captain's Codes for those areas. Or at least senior officer codes.

In the weeks that she'd had the tablet, she hadn't been able to crack those codes. She had been beginning to think she couldn't access any of that important stuff from a passenger cabin because of location controls. But if she got to the bridge, she might have been able to do it.

The option of going to the bridge was gone now.

She needed to remain confined to quarters until she figured out how to spoof the system, and make it *think* she was confined to quarters while she roamed the ship.

Before she did any of that, though, she activated the automated distress signal. Every tablet had access to the distress signal, and, she suspected, so did all of those holographic concierges on the lower levels.

She hoped someone else had activated the automatic distress signal as well, but she also had taken a measure of the guy with the intense eyes. He looked like someone who didn't let a lot go by him.

He had probably tampered with access to the automated distress system before he had started into the passenger cabins. Because Colette and her parents hadn't realized something had gone wrong on the ship until the guy with the laser rifle had shown up.

She doubted any other passenger noticed something wrong either. People were pretty self-involved on this ship, which had worked to her favor, until today.

She took a deep breath. She was going to pretend that today was no different than any other day, because if she thought about her parents, she would panic, and panicking would get her nowhere.

So she scrolled through the back end of the tablet, the stuff hardly anyone outside of engineering knew how to use, and found the manual distress signal.

She had hoped it would be relatively easy to operate. Instead, it contained an array of choices, many more than she expected. She scrolled through all of them, until she narrowed it down to three: she could notify other ships; she could notify specific rescue units throughout the solar system; or she could notify a single person.

She had no single person to notify, and if she notified other ships randomly, she would probably notify Intense Eyes Guy's ship as well as some other passing vessel.

All of the choices required the *Blue Moon's* exact location to be input manually. Which made sense, since she was asking for a rescue, and the system had no way of knowing that the rescue was needed because people with guns had boarded the ship, rather than some systemic breakdown somewhere off the beaten path.

Colette dug, found the ship's exact coordinates, discovered that they were deep inside the Asteroid Belt, and that made her stomach jump. Right in the middle of nothing at all.

And, to her unpracticed eye, the ship looked like it wasn't moving at all.

She didn't like it.

Focus, focus, focus.

She made herself go through all of the components of the secondary manual signal slowly, entering the exact coordinates of where the ship was right now, which route it had taken, but not the route it was expected to take. Because she didn't know if Intense Eyes Guy was stealing the ship itself.

She set the secondary signal to repeat in half-second bursts, and programmed it to go only to the rescue units on Mars, the Moon, and Earth.

Her heart thumped as she activated the secondary signal—and prayed it would go through.

* * *

NAPIER MADE IT to the bridge just in time to see the distress signal beacon activate. The damn thing glowed red on the navigation console. He smashed the blinking light, then pressed the comm chip embedded into the pocket on his chin.

"One of those idiot crew members activated the automated distress signal. Someone jettison the thing off the ship, and send it closer to Mars."

He had to explain where he wanted the beacon to go, because on a previous job, the genius who had taken a similar order had ripped the beacon off the ship, and let the still-active beacon tumble into nearby space.

That hadn't ended well for anyone, although Napier, as was his habit, managed to avoid the authorities, more through luck than anything else. The genius who hadn't thought the order through, however, wouldn't make that mistake again.

Since his luck had run out.

Napier's hadn't, yet, but he didn't like how this particular job was going. He really didn't like this bridge. It was narrow and had a high ceiling made of two different materials—one clear, so that the crew could see the starlight (or probably show it to passengers who paid a premium). The other material was an exterior cover that fitted over the clear material and gave the bridge double protection against anything and everything.

It also made it pretty easy to find. Napier had originally thought of sending a contained burst torpedo into the bridge, taking out the crew in one quick action, but he hadn't done it. Because he had done his due diligence and discovered that the *Blue Moon*, as an ancient passenger liner, didn't have a secondary bridge like most cargo ships.

There had been an actual possibility that the explosion would have destroyed all of his access to the ship's systems, and he didn't have an engineer on his team. If the engineering sector on this ship had been as old as the ship herself, then Napier would truly have been screwed.

Of course, someone had updated the entire interior. The passenger cabins had gotten a facelift, but the rest of the ship had been completely rebuilt—and off-books too.

At least the weapons system on this ship hadn't been upgraded. It should have been before someone got the brilliant idea of transporting a Glyster Egg on this vessel. Because Glyster Eggs were the holy grail for people like him. If he had a Glyster Egg, he could raid ships to his heart's content.

Of course, no one was supposed to know that the Egg was even on board. He had only found out because he had paid informants in every single outpost that launched vessels into this part of the solar system. If he managed to get his hands on the Egg, the informant who sent him here would get a really big bonus.

If.

Napier hadn't been able to find out if the Egg was actually on board, and if it was, where it was. Each cargo bay was supposed to list the cargo on its exterior manifest, but ships like this, which carried hazardous cargo, rarely did. That's why he needed the internal cargo manifest, the one only the senior officers got to see.

And that, Napier was beginning to realize, was going to be harder than he expected.

THE AUTOMATED DISTRESS signal shut off after five minutes. The tablet listed the distress signal as damaged, but Colette suspected someone had tampered with it. She had expected that.

She also figured, given that laser rifle, that the bad guys had come for something in particular. She was guessing, based on the history she'd studied (trying to keep up with Dad), the entertainment she consumed (trying to ignore Mother), and the crime reports she'd examined on the sly (trying to learn new tricks) that these guys weren't here to steal the ship. If they had been, they would have locked every passenger in their cabins and dealt with the passengers once the ship left the established shipping routes.

Colette figured they were taking something from it. If they had planned on kidnapping a passenger—well, first, they wouldn't have come to a ship this low rent, and second, they would have known that a kid was on board. She was on the passenger manifest, after all, even if her age wasn't alongside her name.

But if the bad guys were trying to take people, they would have wanted to know who they were up against amongst the passengers— or, at least, *she* would have wanted to know.

She knew it was a fallacy to expect every criminal in the universe to be one-tenth as smart as she was. Dad always said that if they were smart, they wouldn't be criminals, and Colette agreed with him when it came to crimes of opportunity, but the bands that worked the shipping routes—or rather, the bands that *successfully* worked the shipping routes—had to have a lot of smarts because they terrorized the routes, and never seemed to get caught.

So she wasn't going to get anywhere by underestimating the intelligence of the people who had taken over the ship.

Hazardous cargo would seem like a no-no for these people, but not all hazardous cargo made everyone sick. Some hazardous cargo was dangerous in the wrong hands.

On her very first day with the tablet, she had searched through the cargo manifest, trying to find whatever it was that had knocked the per-passenger price on this vessel so low. When she had seen the ad for this vessel, and its "reasonable" prices, she wanted to see what kinds of diseases Dad had signed her up for.

She had planned to throw that in his face when he left her at that boarding school in Montreal. She had even planned the speech:

Not only are you confining me to some Earth backwater, but you're guaranteeing that I will die of [insert disease here] at [insert average age here].

It had taken her three days to find the correct cargo manifest, and another three hours to break into it. To her great disappointment, she hadn't found any disease-creating items listed. Instead, she found a tiny weapon that shouldn't have been on a ship like this at all.

That weapon, called a Glyster Egg, should have been in layers and layers of protective material with a protected cargo seal inside a protected cargo unit inside a protected cargo bay. Instead, the Glyster Egg was in some kind of box that "in theory" protected it from any kind of accidental detonation.

The thing was the theory wasn't that grand. She'd found at least three other ships that had been victims of accidental detonation of Glyster Eggs in the five years since the stupid things had been on the market (or invented or stolen or released by some dumb government or *something*). Those ships had floated dead in space, in one case for a year, before anyone found it—because the stupid thing had been designed to disable all the functioning systems on spaceships with one simple movement.

A handful of other weapons could do that, but none were small like the Egg, and none had an actual targeting system. So if she wanted to—if she could get out of this stupid room without being noticed, *and* if she trusted herself to touch the Egg, *and* if she could figure out how to use it, *and* if she knew exactly where the bad guys' ship was—she could enter the coordinates into the Egg, then squeeze the Egg's activation system, and *voila!* the bad guys' ship wouldn't work at all, ever again, end of story.

But she didn't like all those ifs-ands. She couldn't quite calculate the odds—there were too many variables—but she had an educated hunch that she would be better off trying to get to the bridge or engineering or somewhere and wrest control of the *Blue Moon* from Intense Eyes, before ever trying to activate the Egg and make it work *for* her instead of *against* her.

Of course, she didn't actually know if he was here for the Egg. But he was stupid if he wasn't. Because if she were a big bad thief who preyed on ships coming through the Asteroid Belt, *she* would steal the Egg.

That was assuming that Intense Eyes had her brains. She wasn't sure he did. Yeah, he had taken over the ship, but he hadn't known about Colette, which meant he hadn't researched the passengers, which meant he didn't know that he was about to get into really bad trouble—if even one of her distress signals had gotten through.

Those odds she could calculate.

Because as of this moment, no one had noticed the manual distress signal.

So it was still broadcasting.

Which meant that help might actually be on the way.

THE AUTOMATED DISTRESS signal, half-choked off, arrived at the 52nd Mars Relay Station. Two versions of the same automated distress signal, intact, arrived at the 13th Moon Relay Station. No versions of the automated distress signal made it to any of Earth's Relay Stations, at least not in recognizable form.

Within thirty seconds of the automated distress signal's arrival, the 13th Moon Relay Station evaluated the signal, and determined that the distressed ship was located in the Asteroid Belt. The ship had an old registration, marking it as inconsequential, even though the ship was owned by Treacher, Incorporated, a large entity that had funded many Martian building projects. Treacher also had ties to three different Martian governments.

But the ship had taken an unusual route, never traveled by ships with highly insured passengers or cargo. The route was by definition dangerous, and anyone on board would have signed a waiver agreeing to rescue only in financially advantageous circumstances.

The age of the ship, the route, and the lack of insurance did not make this a financially advantageous circumstance.

But Treacher's ownership did flag the system, so the 13th Moon Relay Station followed protocol for difficult and iffy rescues in the Asteroid Belt. The 13th Moon Relay Station sent copies of the automated distress signal to its counterpart on Mars.

Then the 13th Moon Relay Station sent the automated distress signals to its archives.

No one on the Moon even knew that an automated distress signal had arrived, been examined, and passed back to Mars. And no one on the Moon would have cared.

WHAT COLETTE HAD to do was buy time. If the bad guys were on the *Blue Moon* to take the Egg, then she had to hide the Egg from them.

The problem was... what if she was wrong? What if they were here for something else?

She didn't have a lot of control with this particular tablet. She was working to get more access, but she needed to spoof her own position here in the suite, and that would take time.

She tried to delete all of the cargo manifests, and couldn't delete any of them. She didn't have the clearance.

She sat cross-legged on her bed for a good minute, trying to figure out how to stay one step ahead of these very bad people.

She had to convince them that they were in trouble on this ship, and she had to keep the Egg from them.

Those were two different tasks.

She called up the passenger manifest to see if she could locate anyone else who might be able to help her. She flipped manifest to its location-based listings, and saw, without looking at names, that all of the passengers were in the large buffet, scattered around the room, as if they were sitting at tables.

All of the passengers except her.

Before she could stop herself, she flipped the data again, saw her parents' names and personal shipboard identification numbers. Then she flipped back to location-based information. Two little green dots, with her parents' shipboard identification numbers, blinked from the side of the buffet, near the kitchen. They weren't moving, but then, neither were the other passengers.

Colette didn't want to even guess what that meant. She hoped they were all sitting quietly, depressed at the circumstances, rather than being unconscious or injured or dea—

Focus, focus, focus.

She opened the tablet to the cargo manifest. The correct one. She took the contents, copied it into another file, marking that new file *Sanitation Refill Schedule*. Then she opened one of the cargo manifests without the hazardous materials, and copied the data from that manifest, and pasted it over the original manifest.

Then she simply saved it. When she opened it again, the information on the Egg had vanished.

And that had been too easy. Someone should have realized just how simple it was to make mistakes in this system, not that it was her problem.

But the bad guys might figure that out. So, she moved the cargo manifest out of its normal file and into the food service files. Some searches would bring up the cargo manifest, but someone would have to know what kind of search to conduct.

She needed to figure out how to distract the bad guys until the rescue ship got here.

And she needed to be able to do so from inside this suite.

FOR A MOMENT, Napier had thought he found one of the cargo manifests, and then it had vanished on him. He had a device that easily broke the surface codes on the bridge's systems, but the device didn't give him what this system called the Captain's Access Codes. For that, Napier needed five forms of physical ID, which he had planned for.

He already had his men getting that for him.

In the meantime, he searched. He felt a slight time pressure, but knew that because of the distances out here, he had more time on this job than he would have had he been closer to Mars or Earth's Moon. He had an internal clock, and at the moment, it allowed him to feel some leeway.

He paused his search for the cargo manifest to find a way to retract the captain's chair. The damn thing rose in the middle of the narrow bridge like a throne, and he wanted it gone. It irritated him, particularly since it turned to offer him a seat every time he brushed against it (which was much too often for his tastes).

He finally found the controls for the chair, but as he did, he also saw something else. A blinking emergency light, buried deep in the manual controls.

He touched the light with a bit of hesitation, worried that he would activate the wrong system.

Instead, he found that a second distress signal had been sending for more than an hour. Why a ship like this would have more than one distress signal, and why this one wasn't attached to the beacon, he had no idea.

Shutting it off was a simple matter. He toggled the controls to the off position. The system didn't even argue.

For a moment, he wondered about the secondary signal. Then he decided it was probably part of the automated distress signal's system, not something he had to worry about.

He needed to spend his time finding one tiny piece of cargo in six cargo bays stuffed with material ultimately bound for Earth.

He had a dozen people on his team, but that wasn't enough to search all of those cargo bays. And he was searching for the Glyster Egg, which was a delicate system in and of itself. He had no idea if his own equipment would accidentally activate it.

He didn't want to take that risk, not this far out. What if the Egg had a broadcast feature he didn't know about? What if it not only disabled this starliner, but his ship as well?

That was something he didn't want to suffer through.

So he needed to proceed with caution.

And he needed to find the cargo manifest.

SOMETHING IN THE automated distress signal that arrived at the 52nd Mars Relay Station activated the review process.

The review system sent a notification to the starbase beyond Titan where the *Blue Moon* originated, asking for a passenger manifest. Calculations needed to be made. The system needed to do a proper cost-benefit analysis of the rescue. Could the rescue vehicle arrive on time? Could it save the ship/cargo/passengers? Were the lives/cargo/ship worth the cost of the rescue?

Such an analysis could not be done without passenger names and histories.

As the system waited, the message from the 13th Moon Relay Station arrived. Now, the Martian system noted that the Moon would not conduct a rescue or even contemplate one, should one be needed.

Only the Martian system would take the risks involved, which changed the calculations yet again.

The system was about to reject the rescue request, even without an answer from the starbase, when several manual distress signals arrived, evenly spaced from each other.

But each manual distress signal contained a signature, proving that someone on board the *Blue Moon* had crafted that distress signal by hand.

That someone was named Colette Euphemia Josephine Treacher Singh Wilkinson Lopez.

Treacher.

A quick analysis showed that Colette Euphemia Josephine Treacher Singh Wilkinson Lopez was a distant Treacher relative, not involved in the corporation or in any local governments, but still on tap to receive a portion of the Treacher Trust when she came of age.

A second Treacher was on board as well, another woman, also in line to receive an inheritance from the Treacher Trust.

Treachers were protected throughout the solar system because of the family's great involvement in many businesses and governments from Mars to Saturn and maybe beyond.

The review's purpose changed. The routine review no longer had relevance.

Two Treachers on board a ship, any ship, anywhere within the reach of Mars Rescue Services, required an immediate and adequate rescue response.

The information got forwarded to Mars Vehicle Rescue (Space

Unit), along with all available information, including the amount of time lapsed.

Given the hazards of travel through that part of the Asteroid Belt, and given the kinds of emergencies that happened there, the time lapsed changed the chances of success from more than 80% to less than 50%.

Which meant, given the costs of rescues that far from Mars itself, all Mars Vehicle Rescue (Space Unit) could spare would be one large rescue vehicle, with a crew of twenty.

The systems in Mars Vehicle Rescue (Space Unit) had determined likely outcomes, and decided that the most possible outcome was this: The rescue vehicle would arrive to find a destroyed ship, dead passengers, and no rescue needed.

But the presence of Treachers meant the possibility of lawsuits. The possibility of lawsuits meant that it would be good to get the DNA of the dead Treachers, just to prove that their portion of the Treacher Trust was now available for some other distant relative.

Mars Vehicle Rescue (Space Unit) did not want to be liable for anything to do with the Treacher Trust, so the rescue ship numbered MVR14501, but known to its crew as *Sally*, left its docking ring on the way to an out-of-the-way shipping route in the Asteroid Belt.

Instead of a crew of twenty, the *Sally* had only ten crew members. If they had had to wait for the remaining ten crew members to arrive from their scheduled time off, departure would have been delayed another three hours, something the system calculated it did not have.

It didn't matter that the crew was small; the chances of success were small too.

The crew of the *Sally* looked at the rescue attempt as a drill, not an actual job.

And that was a mistake.

* * *

THE STUPID PASSENGER identification system seemed hardwired to the life reading of that particular passenger. Colette didn't remember signing up for that but she was a "minor" who "had no rights" without "suing for them" so she had no idea what her parents had done to guarantee her passage on this ship.

Whatever it was, she couldn't spoof the system and if she couldn't spoof the system, she couldn't get out of the suite.

She stood because her butt was falling asleep on the bed's hard surface. She moved the tablet onto a little holder built into the wall, and wished she could use a holoscreen instead.

Something pinged in her brain about holoscreens, but she let that marinate. Because what she really wanted to do was get the tablet to tell her where the bad guys were, and so far, the tablet was refusing.

Well, it wasn't refusing, exactly, because that would have meant it had some kind of sentience, which it did not. What it was doing was refusing to acknowledge their life signs, since they were not paying passengers.

Apparently, crew, staff, and service personnel at any kind of starbase stop were beneath the notice of the concierge level. She dug into the systems, and tried to see if she could get a reading on the non-paying passengers, even if they only appeared as some kind of shadowy coordinates on the ship's map.

She couldn't, any more than she could detach her own heartbeat from the passenger manifest, but she could reset the holographic concierges on every single floor.

That discovery made her heart race. She couldn't reset the concierges to "forget" anyone, which was probably good from the ship's point of view, but she could set up the concierges to interact with every human being they encountered.

She dug deeper into the controls. She could actually set up the concierges to follow anyone unregistered with the ship. Some of the more sophisticated concierges could follow the unregistered person until someone in authority dealt with them, even if that meant following that person off the ship.

Well, she couldn't get out of here and harass the bad guys herself, not without getting caught, and she couldn't get the Egg and figure it out without getting caught, but she could do this.

She only hoped it would be enough.

NAPIER WAS ABOUT to contact his second, Grizwald, when the man walked onto the bridge. He was larger than most of Napier's crew, but size had its uses, especially when it came to intimidation.

And intimidation wasn't the only thing Griz was good at.

Griz handed Napier a small box containing everything he needed to access the Captain's Codes.

"We got some problems," Griz said.

"No kidding," Napier said and opened the box. It had the skin gloves, and some other bits and pieces of the captain himself, no longer bloody, but cleaned up so that Napier could use them.

"I mean it." Griz's tone was harsh. "*Look.*"

Napier frowned with annoyance, then looked in the direction that Griz was pointing. A head floated behind him.

For a moment, Napier thought maybe Griz had brought him the captain's actual head, but he hadn't.

"What the hell?" Napier asked.

Griz slid his hand toward the head, and his hand went through it. The head vanished for a half a second, then returned.

"You are unauthorized," it said. "If you do not leave this area, you will be subject to discipline."

"Discipline?" Napier asked Griz. "From who?"

Griz rolled his eyes. "The crew," he said.

Well, that wouldn't happen. Part of the crew was trapped in the so-called brig (really, two emergency cells that would get troublemakers to the next base) guarded by three of his people, and the rest of the crew was piled in an airlock, awaiting Napier's order to have the bodies join the rocks floating around this part of the Asteroid belt.

"So what's the problem?" Napier asked.

"It's following me," Griz said. "And it won't go away."

"That's not a problem," Napier said, by which he meant, *That's not a problem I need to deal with right now*.

"It's blocking access to crew quarters and other parts of the ship," Griz said. "Once it started following me, everything shut down when I got near it."

Napier felt a surge of anger rush through him. "So you came *here*?"

He glanced at the bridge controls, and sure enough, they had all shut down. He would have to redo all of his work.

"Get out," he said to Griz. "*Now*."

"You both must leave," the head said to Napier.

"And take that thing with you," Napier said to Griz.

Griz shook his own head, then scooted around the holo-head, and went out the door. The head remained for some reason Napier did not understand.

"You must leave," the head said to him.

"Not happening," Napier said, and opened the box. The ship required a minimum of five forms of physical identification from an officer to access certain parts of the controls.

The most basic was active fingertip control, which the ship would test to see if the finger was warm, attached, and belonging to a crew member.

Napier had stolen a number of items over the years that made warm and attached and belonging into three different things. The ship would think that his hands were the Captain's hands.

"You must leave," the head said to Napier.

"And you're going to get shut down," Napier said, as he placed his index finger on the bridge control board.

"Not happening," the head said, mirroring Napier's earlier response, which worried him more than he wanted to think about.

He decided not to look at the stupid head anymore.

Instead, he went back to work.

HALFWAY TO THE coordinates in the Asteroid Belt, Dayah Rodriguez, who was in charge of the *Sally*'s rescue team, finally got a reading on the *Blue Moon*.

The ship didn't seem to be in physical trouble, although it hadn't moved from the location cited in the distress signal. But one small ship floated around it, constantly bouncing and shivering the way that some of the illegal vessels did to avoid standard tracking units.

Fortunately, *Sally* didn't use standard tracking.

A jolt of adrenaline shot through Rodriguez.

She suddenly realized they were understaffed and perhaps lacking the proper amount of firepower.

"Speed up," she said to Hamish Sarkis, who was piloting the *Sally*. "And send a message back to headquarters. We have pirates. And if we want to catch them, we're going to need some help."

They were going to need a lot more than help.

They were going to need a lot of luck as well.

* * *

Now, COLETTE WAS obsessing about her parents. Because they still hadn't moved. No one had. Why weren't the passengers fighting back? What was going on?

She was pacing around the bed, trying to figure out if breaking out of this stupid suite was worthwhile.

And then her breath caught.

She had set up the concierges to follow the bad guys.

She just needed to locate the concierges. When she found them, she would know where the bad guys were.

Which would help her escape, but then what?

She flopped on the bed, grabbed the tablet, and thought about it.

She had access to a lot of things on this little device. Maybe some of them would help her slow those bad guys down.

THE HEAD WAS proving to be a problem. The thing stuck to Napier like some kind of weird glue. He couldn't shut it out of the bridge, because every time he closed the door on the head, it floated back inside.

And every time he tried to use some piece of the captain to provide identification, the head stated, quite calmly, "You are not Captain Ekhart. You lack his height, weight, and appearance. I have instructed the system to remain unfooled."

Unfooled. What kind of word was that, anyway?

It was as annoying as the head was.

To make matters worse, Napier's internal clock was warning him that he was almost out of time for this job.

He needed that Egg, but he couldn't access anything.

His personal comm vibrated. He pressed it, and Johnston, the only member of his team still on the ship, said, "We just got a ping from the security system. We've been scanned by something with an official government signature."

Napier didn't even have to ask what that meant. It meant that either a security vehicle or a rescue ship was on the way. Or something larger and more important—some kind of government transport—was coming to or traveling along this route.

Which meant he was done, if he didn't find that manifest right now, if he couldn't get the Egg right now.

He reached for the head, and his hand went right through it. Had that head belonged to a human, it would've been slammed against the wall until it shattered.

"You are unauthorized," the head said obliviously. Clearly, it had no idea that he would have killed it if he could. "You do not have access. You are not Captain Ekhart. You must leave."

Napier glared at it. The thing looked like it made eye contact with him, but he could see through it, so it probably didn't.

But had it sent the information to the authorities?

He had broken into a number of ships similar to the *Blue Moon*, but never one of this vintage. Sometimes older ships had technologies he hadn't seen or even imagined. Things attempted and then discarded.

Like annoying heads that floated after people and yelled at them. This couldn't have been a popular feature.

"Can you figure out who scanned us?" Napier asked Johnston.

"Been trying. I have no idea." Johnston was good with all of the equipment. Not great, but better than some of the idiots Napier had brought with him. Those idiots were good for scaring civilians, and that was what he'd been using them for. And for figuring out how to put an entire room full of people into a deep sleep, so they wouldn't fight back.

"I can't find them with our scanners," Johnston was saying, "but here's what I'm worried about. They're coming from Mars, and they scanned us far enough out that we can't read them. So they have powerful equipment and they're coming fast. There might be a whole bunch of them, for all I know."

If Napier didn't get out of here now, he might actually get caught. He slammed his fist on the captain's chair that he had forgotten to retract. It bounced and jiggled toward him, almost as if he offended it, which was a lot more satisfying than trying to grab that stupid head.

"Hey, you," he said to the head, "who did you notify that we had arrived?"

"I sent a message to those in charge, as per my programming," the head said primly.

"And who might those in charge be?" Napier asked, hoping that maybe he could buy some more time if the head identified them.

"I went through proper channels. You have accessed the bridge without authorization. You have attempted to impersonate Captain Ekhart. You will be dealt with firmly."

He wasn't getting any information from the head, and he wasn't going to be able to find that Egg.

He had to think this through. He was good at cutting his losses when he needed to, but usually he had a bit more to show for a job this complicated.

Still, running was a lot better than getting captured.

He also needed to get rid of all of the evidence that pointed to him. A ship full of people who could identify him. Those head-things. Who knew what they had taken from him and his team? DNA? Imagery? Everything?

Now he was going to have to change his plan. He couldn't remote detonate the *Blue Moon* because he didn't have access to the controls. He would have to use regular explosives, the kind with their own timers.

They were a little less reliable than a remote detonation, but they would have to do.

Then his fist clenched.

The kid.

He thought of her for a moment, sprawled on that floor, looking helpless and lost as Mommy and Daddy got carted away.

He didn't dare jettison her from the *Blue Moon*, not now, not with the authorities (or whomever) closing in.

This job was really screwed up. He was going to have to do things he didn't want to do for no real payoff at all.

He punched the retractable captain's chair one last time, then shoved his way past the head as he stalked off the bridge. Or, rather, tried to shove. Because the head moved with him.

How come he inherited the head from Griz? Because the head figured Napier was the greater threat?

Didn't matter. He had to tell his team to dump the explosives near the passengers and surviving crew. There was no time for finesse.

He and his team needed to be on board his ship within fifteen minutes, so they could be as far away from the *Blue Moon* as possible when it exploded.

As far from the Egg as possible.

Because he had no idea what kind of damage it would do.

COLETTE TRIED TO work faster, to see what else she could find, what she could use.

She had almost given up when she found something weird.

Apparently, passenger liners from the old days had a lot of theft, and theft was bad for business.

So the holographic concierges were designed, not for the passengers' comfort, but to spy on them. If concierges deemed someone suspicious, they harassed that someone on the ship. If that someone left the ship, the concierges shrank themselves down to a pinprick and became some kind of tiny spy that sent a signal so that the suspicious personages could be traced.

It was weird, and it was brilliant, and it was strangely appropriate.

Colette couldn't prevent them from taking hostages. She couldn't prevent them from getting the Egg. But she could help the authorities find the bad guys.

If they let her live.

A shiver ran through her.

It didn't really matter if they could track her or not. Because she had to get out of this room and stop them.

Somehow.

She just didn't know how yet.

THE HEAD THING vanished as Napier climbed into the only airlock that wasn't stacked with dead crew members. His team had already gotten onto his ship and were waiting for him.

God, he was irritated. Hours, risk, a few deaths, and what did he have to show for it?

He was actually fleeing, something he thought he had become too sophisticated to do.

Well, he had learned his lesson. No more boarding a passenger ship of this vintage, not without a lot more planning.

He watched the exterior door open into the enclosed ramp his ship had set up, and it took every bit of effort he had not to dive through it.

He would have a little dignity here.

He would have to consider this a scouting mission rather than a failed attempt. He had learned something, and, if he had time to set it up, he would learn a bit more.

He would learn what happened when a ship carrying a Glyster Egg exploded.

He would have to set up something specific to monitor space around the starliner, but he could do that, and he could do it from a distance.

Then he would gather information, and with it, he could tell any possible client one of the many things the Egg did—more as a cautionary tale, with the explosion and all, but still. Information was information.

That was the kind of thing that clients liked.

He would have to remember that when the kid appeared in his dreams.

He slid into the airlock on his ship, shifting from foot to foot, hoping he would get through this quickly.

They needed to get out of here—and they needed to do so fast.

THE ENGINES WERE powering up on that second ship. Rodriguez sent the coordinates to the ships Mars Rescue had sent, hoping they would either veer off and catch the pirate ship.

She didn't have time to think about capturing a pirate ship. She was kinda relieved that it was leaving. She commanded a *rescue* vessel, not a security vessel. The handful of times she'd gone after perpetrators hadn't ended well for her. In all but one instance, the perpetrators had gotten away.

She hoped that the pirate ship wasn't taking the *Blue Moon* with it. That would create other problems.

Right now, her scans showed that the *Blue Moon* was more or less immobile, moving forward ever so slightly, but not enough to measure as anything. Maybe on autopilot.

She wasn't close enough yet to find that out.

But she would be in just a few minutes—and her team now knew this wasn't a drill.

It was going to be life and death.

* * *

COLETTE STARED AT the tablet in surprise. It told her that bad guys had left the *Blue Moon*.

Maybe they had found what they were looking for.

Not that it mattered to her.

She had to get to her parents.

She snuck out of her suite, and ran along the corridor, bent almost in half, just because, even though she knew the monitors caught her every movement anyway.

The buffet that her parents and the rest of the passengers were in was on this level. She just had to get to it.

She hurried through the maze of corridors, going half on her memory and half on the map that showed up on the tablet, when she almost tripped on a small square block.

It wasn't alone. There were half a dozen small square blocks just in this corridor.

She turned the tablet toward them, and asked it to identify the blocks.

The tablet did not respond. Maybe it didn't have the programming.

So she needed to figure this out on her own. After all, she had seen a lot of things in all the various schools she'd gone to. (She had done most of those things as well.)

She crouched near the closest block, and peered at it. It smelled faintly of rust—the telltale sign of a kind of acid that would eventually eat through a casing, hit a trigger, and—

Oh, god. This was a bomb, one of the kinds she'd thought too damn dangerous to make.

The bad guys were off the ship, and they were going to blow it up. But they hadn't taken the Egg and they hadn't taken her and they hadn't taken any of the passengers, so they must have been after something else, but what she had no idea, and now there was no time to figure it out.

She needed to get rid of these things. Somehow.

She reached for the box in front of her, then remembered: acid. She would have lost all the skin on her hand.

Focus, focus, focus.

There had to be a command that allowed the concierges, real or not, to isolate something dangerous in a corridor. Kids made smoke bombs, after all. And people sometimes tried to burn the materials in a ship.

Everyone on the crew had to be able to access that kind of security protocol.

She just had to find it before something happened.

RODRIGUEZ HAD BEEN right: the *Sally* arrived after the pirate ship left. The readings she got off the *Blue Moon* were some of the strangest she'd seen. The ship was completely intact. Some of the crew remained alive, and all of the passengers seemed to be breathing as well, but none of them were moving.

Except one of the Treacher women.

Was she in on the attack somehow?

Rodriguez brought two of her teammates with her, but let them move toward the room filled with passengers. Her entire team wore their environmental suits, and were armed with everything she could think to bring.

Sarkis remained on board the *Sally* and three more team members were heading to the brig to find the crew stranded there. The remaining three team members were spreading out between engineering and the bridge, hoping to get this ship moving again.

Rodriguez was going to handle the Treacher woman herself, not just because that person was still moving, but because Rodriguez didn't quite believe the information the passenger manifest had sent her.

It said that this distant Treacher relative was only eleven. Which wasn't possible, since no children were allowed on board ships like the *Blue Moon*.

Someone might have spoofed the file, which concerned Rodriguez more than she wanted to admit. Especially since the first thing she found when she came on board was the carnage in the first airlock she tried. She was lucky she hadn't opened it, or bodies would have tumbled into space.

Bodies.

The pirates had clearly gotten something. You don't kill that many people for the hell of it.

She rounded a corner and saw a corridor strewn with black boxes.

"Don't move!" a panicked nasal voice said.

Rodriguez stopped and looked. She had seen the boxes, but she had missed the very small person crouched near the box farthest away.

A very small person who did indeed look like an eleven-year-old child, holding onto an old-fashioned rectangular tablet.

"Colette Treacher?" Rodriguez asked, trying to remember all of the girl's elaborate name.

"Close enough," the girl said. "You weren't tagged by one of the concierges. Are they gone?"

"What?" Rodriguez asked.

"Who are you?" The girl's tone was annoyed, as if Rodriguez was the dumbest person she had ever encountered.

And, to be fair, the girl couldn't see Rodriguez's identification. She was wearing a high-end environmental suit, not the ones issued by Mars Rescue. And the girl didn't seem to be networked into any kind of Mars system.

Rodriguez introduced herself without using her name. Names weren't important in situations like this. Jobs were.

"I'm with Mars Rescue," she said.

"It's about time." The girl's annoyance grew. "It's been *hours*."

Hours was miraculous, given where the *Blue Moon* ended up, and Rodriguez nearly said that, then realized the girl's tone had made her feel defensive.

"What are you doing?" Rodriguez asked.

"Trying to diffuse a bomb," the girl said. "What are you doing?"

That adrenaline spike hit again.

"All of these are bombs?" Rodriguez asked.

"I haven't checked them all, but I would guess so," the girl said. "They're pretty mad."

Rodriguez had a hunch the girl wasn't talking about the bombs now, but the pirates. "Who?"

"The guys who attacked us. They wanted something, and I hope they didn't get it. They left pretty fast. And now..." The girl ran her hands near the boxes. "This."

Her voice broke on that last word, the bravado gone.

"I can't find any way to diffuse them," she said.

And that, the edge of panic in the girl's voice, brought Rodriguez back to herself.

She contacted her team.

"Found half a dozen box bombs, type unknown," Rodriguez said. "They're not too far from the passengers. Check for other bombs. We need a scan of this ship, and we need to put every single corridor on lockdown."

"Do you have some kind of shield program?" The girl shook the tablet at Rodriguez. "Because I can't find one."

Rodriguez wasn't carrying any kind of device like the girl had, but Rodriguez had access to every single ship built in official shipyards in the past one hundred years. The failsafes built into each system, override codes along with physical identification, specific to each rescue service.

She hoped that would be on board the *Blue Moon* as well, even though the ship was pretty old.

She slid to the nearest door, pulled back a wall panel, and found the interior controls. Then she opened the secondary panel underneath, hit the override commands, and found what she was looking for.

There were no tiny shields on a ship like this. Only one big shield that would coat the corridor.

"Join me," she said to the girl.

The girl stood slowly, giving the boxes a glance.

"*Right now*," Rodriguez said.

The girl crept past the boxes, moving slower than Rodriguez would have liked. After what seemed like an eternity, the girl reached Rodriguez's side, and Rodriguez released the shields.

They encased the entire floor, avoiding her and the girl, but trapping them in one place. It would take some maneuvering, but Rodriguez could get that shield and the boxes it contained out of the ship—if she could find an airlock without bodies in it.

Her comm chirruped.

"We found more boxes, and yeah, they're bombs. We're getting them out now," said Lytel, who was handling the rest of the team.

"I got these explosives contained as well," Rodriguez said. "Any word on the passengers?"

"They're unconscious. The remaining crew too. Doing medical evaluations right now, but it looks like they're just out. Guess the bombs were going to do the dirty work of actual murder," Lytel said.

Rodriguez looked down at the girl. Her eyes were red, but there were no tear-streaks on her face.

"Do you have any idea what happened here?" Rodriguez asked.

The girl shook her head.

"How come you're out and no one else is?" Rodriguez said.

"Some guy," the girl said, "he was surprised there was a kid on board. He locked me in my suite."

She shook the tablet at Rodriguez.

"That was his first mistake." And then the girl grinned. The grin was a little cold, it was a little off, and then it trembled on the girl's face and fell away, showing that it was more bravado than anything else.

"My dad," the girl asked. "Is he okay?"

The shield reshaped as Lytel remotely prepped it to leave the ship.

Neither Rodriguez nor the girl should remain in the corridor while that happened.

"I don't know how your father is," Rodriguez said, putting her hand on the little girl's back. The child was shaking so hard it looked like she might rattle out of her skin. "But I'm sure we can find out."

NAPIER WAS ALMOST out of the Asteroid Belt when six ships surrounded him. All of those ships had official insignia, but not all of the insignia were from the same organization.

Different rescue and security companies, all government owned, all looking pretty official.

"What is going on?" Griz said from beside him. "We didn't steal anything."

"No, we didn't," Napier said. They had just killed half the crew. But they'd killed a lot of people out here before, and no one had come after them.

"So what the heck was different about this job?" Griz asked.

Napier didn't have the answer to that. Except bad luck. And that bad luck started when he saw the kid.

Kids threw Napier off his game.

But he didn't tell Griz that. Instead, Napier deleted all the records he had for the *Blue Moon,* and then contacted all of the security vessels.

Contacting them first might buy him some time. Although time probably wasn't what he needed. Because he had violated his own code, and used bombs to kill that kid for no reason at all.

EXCEPT THAT HE hadn't killed Colette Euphemia Josephine Treacher Singh Wilkinson Lopez. The ship didn't blow up. Instead, the *Sally* guarded the *Blue Moon* all the way to the nearest Mars Rescue base where everyone reported their own truth about what happened.

The only truth the authorities listened to, though, was Colette's, because it proved accurate from the moment the investigators had the tablet she had stolen.

That tablet had recorded her every move.

It also showed where Napier's crew was, because of what Colette had done with the holographic concierges. She had turned them into location beacons.

Colette did not want attention for what she had done. She didn't want a medal or recognition from the governments of Mars.

She wanted something else entirely.

Something no government had the power to give.

"I DON'T WANT to go to boarding school," Colette said to her dad after all the officials left. "I want to go home."

Her family was in a tiny hotel room on the base where the *Blue Moon* had ended up. Her mother lay on the bed, her forearm over her forehead. She'd had a headache ever since she'd woken up, something the medical personnel said was a pretty normal reaction to the gas the bad guys had filtered into the buffet.

Dad didn't seem to have a headache at all. He was frowning at Colette, and she knew, *she knew*, he was going to make her go to that school anyway, just because he had no idea what else to do with her.

"All right," he said quietly.

"What?" Colette asked, not sure she had heard him right.

"I'm taking you home," he said.

Colette's mouth opened ever so slightly. She hadn't expected *that*.

"No, you're not," her mother said. "She's more than we can handle."

"You won't have to handle her, Louise," Dad said.

Her mother sat up on one elbow, her face pale.

"What?" she asked, in almost the same tone Colette had used a moment before.

Something crossed Dad's face, something hard and fascinating.

"Colette saved our lives," he said after a moment. "All of us. Even you. We owe her, Louise."

Her mother made a dismissive sound and collapsed on the bed. Dad's gaze met Colette's and his eyes actually twinkled.

"We could send her away," Colette said softly.

"My thoughts exactly," he said just as softly.

Then he opened the door to the hotel room, and peered into the hall as if he expected to see a man cradling a laser rifle.

There was none—no man, no rifle.

Dad ushered Colette out of the room.

He was protecting her again. Like he had tried to do on the *Blue Moon*. Only he had failed.

And he would probably fail now. But that was okay.

Because Colette could protect them all.

As she had learned recently, she was really really good at that.

A PORTRAIT OF SALAI

HANNU RAJANIEMI

Sfumato knew something was very wrong when ver comet organ played a discordant note.

Ver aquatic selves—floating in the Leaf's capillary oceans—heard it as a mistimed thunderclap. To the anthropoid Sfumato-selves in the zero-gravity jungles, it was an off-key earthquake.

Each note in the melody was an actual comet, striking the dark side of the ancient Dyson ringlet. Tiny scouts from Sfumato's self-fleet watched them from an orbit above the grainy surface. Pale dots blossomed into milk-splash explosions, one by one: megatons of dirty snow, a hundred musical Tunguskas—until one of them missed its impact target by fifty kilometres and more than a second.

It was not only jarring, it was disappointing. Sfumato had worked hard on the piece. Ve had picked the comets amongst the countless trans-Plutonian bodies from the Kuiper Belt that had been bombarding the Inner System ever since the failed Great Projects turned their dynamics into insane pinball. Ve had used the Leaf's laser array—originally built to propel starwisps to Proxima Centauri—to boil the comets' surface ice into jets of steam that nudged their trajectories just so. Ve even had an anthropoid-self play the melody on the keys of an ice organ in an observatory in one of the Leaf's rim-towers, synchronised with the impacts.

It was true the music was mostly improvised. Sfumato had not gotten around to finishing the composition. Ve rarely finished things. What was the point of being a minsky, a colony of a thousand sentient nooids, if you had to limit your options? A cluster of ver nooids had gotten sidetracked by the spectroscopy of comet ice; another had decided to calculate what pieces of classical music could be represented by Newtonian collisions with a planar surface. The anthropoid organist had started carving gorgeous ice sculptures between each slow keystroke.

But ve had confidence in ver ability to do things properly, and as emotion blocks of annoyance and self-doubt piled on ver thought-chain, ve retraced the orbit of the mistimed comet all the way to the Outer System.

That was when ve saw the Pageant.

It had appeared out of nowhere in the last kilosecond, derailing Sfumato's comet with its gravitational pull. The sky was ablaze with gamma rays from its warp bubble deceleration. Its core was a distorted bulge in the firmament, a gravitational lensing effect from the twin Jupiter-mass black holes in its heart. Around that dark eye was an expanding halo of bright motes, millions of them: each a kilometre-long capsid with a metallic, angular von Neumann core and a seething envelope of smartmatter. These were the Iron Critics, the Pageant's watchdogs and heralds.

As Sfumato watched, the Critic halo burned delta-v in unison, changed shape, elongated. Ve plotted their orbits. A rain of lines fell onto the million-kilometre-long ribbon of the Leaf. The Critics had seen Sfumato's comets, and were—as always—ferociously, relentlessly, ravenously curious. No civilisation in the System, aestivating or awake, had ever survived their inquiry once it was initiated.

Sfumato's thought-chain filled with icy blocks of fear and stark survival instinct. Ve started waking up the ancient vessels of ver self-fleet, uploading nooid snapshots to starwisp memory crystals, directing anthropoid and zooid selves in vain, brave mass migrations towards hastily fabbed mass launchers.

The Critics would reach the Leaf in eighty kiloseconds, and soon after that, the Dyson ringlet that had been Sfumato's home for a hundred gigaseconds, and any selves remaining behind, would cease to be. But that was not the worst thing.

Sfumato would also have to break the bad news to Salai.

SALAI DID NOT answer Sfumato's call. That was not surprising: they had not spoken for gigaseconds, not since the war. Salai's minsky was much smaller than Sfumato's, and ve preferred to wander the Leaf's vast expanse in first person, inhabiting a small pod of zooids and synthoids.

While the rest of ver made preparations to leave, Sfumato crammed a thought sidechain into the tiny brain of ver fastest ship-self, an antimatter-powered drone, and did a hard burn across the Leaf's day side to find ver former lover before it was too late.

The Dyson ringlet had no gravity to speak of, but it was full of life, more than a thousand Earthlike planets. The capillary oceans were a tracery of blue against the lush tangled jungles of zero-g trees. Some of the green tendrils stretched nearly to the nightshade discs—lightsails weaving back and forth between the Leaf and the Sun. They had been designed to provide a night-day cycle. But ever since the Sun had become unstable, with its madly flailing polar protuberances spewed by the out-of-control sunlifter engines, the Leaf's biosphere only thrived in their shadow.

The rest was deserts, grey-and-brown scars where solar activity bursts had burned the biosphere all the way to Leaf's adamantine bedrock. For centuries, those had provided a canvas for Sfumato's projects: hollow-boned kilometre-high humanoid automata acting out ver unfinished plays; synthetic bacteria mutated by cosmic rays, their genetic circuits carving a novel in the Leaf's bare surface letter by giant letter.

Now that ve knew the Iron Critics would swallow it all, the Leaf seemed to Sfumato like a child's sandbox full of broken toys. Ve had always meant to fix the biosphere, reprogram the nightshades, repair the broken capillary that had created a spherical ocean. Now it was too late.

Far below, ve detected an electromagnetic signature near the mountainous water bubble. A pod of silver amphibians danced in and out of its undulating surface.

Sfumato descended and hovered nearby. Ve knew the pattern of delicate motion: it was Salai, lost in joy, and for a moment, regret overwhelmed ver thought-chain. Then the boom of a distant comet reminded ver of the task, and ve sent Salai a cautious thought-packet.

Gather yourselves, Sfumato said. *We have to leave. The Pageant is coming.*

Ve attached a description of the approaching entity to ver plea. The Pageant was the last of the Great Projects: an attempt to evolve a truly benevolent superintelligence. Inside was a growing god-seed, caged in a hierarchy of nested simulations where each virtual layer was watched by agents in the next layer for any signs of perverse instantiations; a matryoshka of guardians. Outermost were the Iron Critics, who had the unenviable task of finding zero day exploits in crude matter. To resist the Temptation, the Pageant had to move, seek anomalies, entertainments, puzzles—anything to keep the Critics from slipping into the stupor of simulated realities.

Silent, Salai considered. Then ver bodies dove into the wall of water, and emerged again in a spray. The droplets scattered, tiny sparkling planets.

Thank you for telling me, ve said, *but I'm staying.*

For a moment, Sfumato did not know what to feel. Ver self-ship was so far from the rest of verselves that it took seconds to form a consensus between nooids. Blocks of anger, confusion, and disbelief competed for addition to ver thought-chain.

What do you mean you are staying? ve asked finally, attaching images of the Pageant passing through the Jovian system a gigasecond ago: the dreamcoral-covered moons that ran the Star-Makers' virtuals, bombarded by the Critics and dissected until there was nothing left. *Is this what you want? We have to go.*

You have to go, Salai said. *I'm staying.*

You are insane. Is this one of your crazy notions? Towards the end, before they fought, Salai had become enamoured of physics, claiming there were still jewels of theory and experiment undiscovered by the ancients, that it was the best way to resist the Great Temptation of endless virtuality. *There are no answers to your questions in the god-seed, just oblivion.*

A nightshade passed over them. Fluorescent bacteria in the water clinging to the silver Salai-selves made it look like ve was made of stars.

I proved the Principle of Precedence, you know, Salai said. *It turns out the ancients were right. When you measure a quantum system, the results come from the ensemble of precedents. If you have something without precedent, you don't know what is going to happen. If we make something truly new, entangled states the Universe has never seen before, we are free to make our own laws. But if you just repeat something, many times over, after a while you cannot escape the precedents.*

Ve passed Sfumato a thought-block. It contained meticulous experiments, carried out with entangled photons; postulates, predictions, results.

That was why you ran from me, Sfumato said. *You did not want to be trapped.*

The nightshade passed, and the silver was back.

Are you going to try to take me with you? Salai asked. *You have many more selves. I cannot fight you anymore.*

The war, ten gigaseconds ago: nooid armies and drones scorching Dyson trees, malware weapons unmooring a nightshade that crashed and formed the wrinkled Night Mountains.

No, Sfumato said. *No more wars. I just don't understand. Do you hate me so much you would rather die a true death than come with me? I am asking. Please.*

Salai sent ver another thought-block filled with a sad smile.

I cannot leave without becoming something else. You came here first, but you never made the Leaf your home. I did. It is one of my selves now. That was the one thing you could never teach me—how to stay and not leave. It was your music that brought the Pageant here, wasn't it? Did you do it on purpose? Did you look for a reason to escape?

Sfumato said nothing.

It is all right, Salai said. *I forgive you. Now go, before the Critics come.*

Then ver selves dove into the ocean. Sfumato watched them disappear, like silver bubbles of air. Far away, the comets kept falling, pounding like a sick, arrhythmic heart.

TEN KILOSECONDS BEFORE the arrival of the Pageant, Sfumato launched ver self-fleet and left the Leaf behind.

Ver thought-chain was spread out nearly a thousand vessels. There were von Neumanns that had gnawed Mercury and Venus, apple-sized, self-replicating machines. There were ancient ships that had been Sfumato since the beginning, since the disappointed refugees from the Great Projects came to ver: a gigantic Star-Maker bristling with gamma ray lasers; even a magnetoform, a piece of living solar wind, that had once swum in the heart of the Sun when the sunlifting engine was made.

The minds of zooid and anthropoid selves were uploaded into memory crystals with minimal manoeuvring capability and launched from mass drivers into an eccentric orbit. After the Pageant's passing, Sfumato would recover them. It felt strange to be without biological selves, see everything through ships' sensors alone. It was cold and flat and clear, like an anthropoid's mind after days of fasting.

The Leaf receded in the glare of ver self-fleet's engines, a patchwork quilt of nightshade shadows, ochre deserts and silver capillaries. Sfumato felt a sudden relief. It was a broken world, full of broken things ve no longer needed. It had been ver home for a terasecond, but it was time to move on and start anew.

Then came a thought-block of utter loss, the feeling of being an uprooted tree, tiny roots clinging to the ground, crackling as they break, gobbets of earth shaking loose. Ver nooids struggled to achieve consensus, could not agree whether or not this was a Sfumato-thought at all.

Ve examined the block. Memories of Salai glared back at ver.

Salai had come to learn, sought ways to escape the Great Temptation. There had been a golden period when they first became lovers; anthroid and zooid couplings in the Leaf's jungles, the bliss of two thought-chains tangling up. But they had never merged, not quite. Merging required breaking a self-link, a discontinuity, so that a new consensus could be reached. That had terrified Sfumato as much as disappearing into the nested, endless virtual of the Temptation. Salai had seen that and fled. Sfumato had tried to make ver stay. That had started the war. In the end, ve had let Salai go into the vast reaches of the Leaf but had always known ve was still there, that one day they would be reunited; there was still time to heal the wounds. Just not yet.

That was Sfumato's precedent, that was what ve did. That was what defined ver: running away from unfinished things. Ve had been doing it since before ve was born.

Ver most ancient nooids remembered the Disappointment: the reluctant admission that no minsky or sentient would ever cross the vast dark between the stars. So humanity had set out to make another kind of infinity.

The sunlifting engine, plumes of plasma roaring up from the magnetic poles, to reduce the Sun's mass to extend its lifetime to hundreds of billions of years. The Tree—of which the Leaf was a remnant—a network of Dyson ringlets made from dismantled Venus and Mars, to capture all of the star's energy. The Star-Makers' black hole engine to stellify Jupiter, to light up the Outer System. And the grandest project of all, the Skhadov Thruster, an incomprehensibly vast mirror built from sunlifted matter, to redirect the Sun's photons as thrust, to sail the System itself across the galaxy and beyond.

All of them had failed. Such grand projects needed to be simulated before they could be built, and the simulations were always more attractive than the cold bedrock of reality. That was the truth of the Temptation, the solution to the Fermi Paradox. And as their creators dreamed or aestivated, their sub-sentient servants degenerated, and things broke down.

The Sun broke free from its sunlifter chains. Its exhalations destabilised the Skhadov mirror, whose gravity loosened the orbits of the countless Kuiper belt bodies and sent them careening into the Inner System. They bombarded old empty Earth and the other planets. With all the excess mass within reach, the Von Neumann machines building the Tree grew wild and made their orbital rings crooked, unsettling things further, until what remained of Mercury collided with Mars in a cataclysm unlike any the System had seen since the formation of the Moon.

The more hostile the System grew, the more attractive escape became. The few stable leaves of the Tree were dreamcoral, a computational substrate for running countless virtuals. Somewhere out in the great dark were the Reversibles, slumbering in cold, slow machines; Sfumato doubted they would ever wake. The final, desperate attempt to break out of the fallible, humanoid mindscape itself and make a god, invulnerable to the Temptation: the Pageant, a mad Titan, striding across the System and crushing the shells of ancient sleepers beneath its feet.

And then there were the few who had worked on the Great Projects and stayed awake, who believed there was still time to create something new. They had come together to nurse their wounds and rekindle hope and made a minsky that called verselves Sfumato. Only ve had betrayed verselves and kept searching for an escape.

The Leaf grew smaller, a dark patch with faint silver tracery of the oceans. It was not too late to go back. Sfumato could be with Salai when the Critics consumed them both.

Maybe a true ending was what ve needed, something from which ve could not escape, the closing of a book, a final boundary—

And suddenly Sfumato knew why Salai had stayed, knew what ve was trying to say.

Ve was not offering Sfumato an ending, but a constraint.

A canvas.

THE PAGEANT WAS three kiloseconds from the Leaf.

Ver Star-Maker nooid had worked for the Pageant, once: it had been contracted to extract two singularities from Jupiter's stellification engine. It did not know the details of the Critics' utility functions, but it was clear they sought complexity, anomalies, puzzles, novelty integrated information.

Art, in other words.

So the only thing Sfumato had to do was create art that was more compelling than the sum of ver lifetime's works on the Leaf.

Two kiloseconds left. The Critics were a star-shaped firefly cloud now, looming behind the Leaf.

Sfumato's nooids fired off ideas in a cacophony of thought-blocks.

—*We hack the old starlifting engines in the polar orbits, make plasma jets spell out a novel written by a neural network made of spheromaks in the Sun's chromosphere—*

—*We grow Dyson trees among the statites and make them bloom with apples whose DNA contains all the occult literature from Earth and the names of algorithmically generated demons—*

—*We split ourselves, two fleets, and go to opposite sides of the Sun and use quantum photography to take ghost images, bounce entangled photons off the Skhadov thruster mirror—*

And on and on and on. Labyrinths of magnetic fields, trapped exotic particles, dark matter lensing painting pictures in the void. Quantum starlings dancing, playing out all of ancient Earth's 20th century films in three dimensions, each tiny machine a pixel.

It was pointless. Ve had not finished anything for gigaseconds: the Leaf's cluttered graveyard of ideas was a testament to that. Ve didn't have enough time. Salai's constraint was impossible.

But that was not the only thing Salai had given ver.

Ve opened the thought-packet on the Principle of Precedence and knew what ve had to make.

*　*　*

ONE KILOSECOND.

Sfumato began by mapping out ver lover's thought-chain, its branches and hashes, the blocks Salai had shared with ver. At the core of it was the moment Salai arrived on the Leaf, the silver glint of ver self-fleet in the sky; the feeling of how it felt like to be no longer alone; the curiosity and wonder that Salai always filled ver with, the promise of something new, a dolphin smile filled with mystery.

Once ve found that emotion, the rest was simple.

Sfumato still had nooids in the Leaf's laser array. It only took a thought to turn the lasers into entangled photon sources. The ships of ver self-fleet fabbed waveguides and photonic crystals—quantum gates. They burned delta-v and spread across the face of the Sun in a carefully designed formation.

Ninety-seven seconds.

Sfumato fired the lasers. The beams fanned out from the Leaf. They passed through ver ship-selves, through the gates inside ver, entangling, interfering, in a tracery of light that painted the portrait of Salai inside ver.

The portrait was a complex quantum state, entangled in a way that no photons had ever been in the history of the Universe, their interactions mimicking Salai's thought-chain. It was something completely new, and the Principle of Precedence said if you measured it, the Universe would have to guess what happened. It would have to make a new law, something you could not simulate, something beyond the Great Temptation.

Sfumato held the fragile portrait within ver and waited.

Thirty seconds.

Ten.

The cloud of Critics exploded in a burst of delta-v. A million antimatter torches burned as they swung away from the Leaf in unison. The Pageant's dark core passed by the Leaf, its trajectory too inexorable to alter, and the Dyson ringlet rippled in the wake of its tidal forces. But it passed, and turned towards Sfumato.

The Critics were a rain of hungry stars that filled all of Sfumato's sensors. Their smartmatter claws were everywhere, probing, tearing, measuring, drinking in the quantum novelty in the portrait of Salai.

This was a good ending, ver selves sung, like a mandala being erased. And for a while, that was ver thought-chain's final block.

SALAI WAITED ON the edge of the Leaf, in the land of eternal twilight, where you could imagine the Dyson ringlet was a planet with a horizon, where you could see the red-tinged Sun peeking over the edge.

The comets were still falling, soundless impacts, white blossoms on dark grey, with a pink tinge from the sunlight. Now they were playing a song again: Salai had completed Sfumato's melody as best ve could.

A green flame surrounded ver. A wisp of living solar wind, a magnetoform. And with it came a cloud of memory crystals, manoeuvring with tiny ion drives.

I like the song, Sfumato said.

I liked the portrait, Salai said. *Shame they ruined it.*

Not ruined, Sfumato said. *Finished.*

Ve opened ver thought-chain.

As the comets fell and played a song that was no longer about failed dreams, the two minskys merged, two chains ended.

The new chain began with a block of joy, with a self-fleet flying over the dark side of the Leaf, towards the Sun's mysterious smile.

LONGING FOR EARTH

LINDA NAGATA

STEADY RAIN FALLING on the cloud forest of the Loysan Escarpment had turned the trail into a rivulet that scoured away leaf litter and soil to reveal a base layer of structural plasteel, cleverly shaped and colored to imitate a basalt of Earth.

Hitoshi appreciated the attention to detail. He'd seen museum biomes where a landslide or a tree-fall exposed the white diamond of the world's structural bones—glaring wounds to the verisimilitude of an environment, though the damage was always quickly patched by swarms of small maintenance bots that lay senescent in the soil and the leaf litter of every world.

Hitoshi was familiar with most aspects of biome maintenance even though he'd been a bureaucrat and not an engineer. The Age of Architects was long past and the great human engineers gone with it, but there would always be a place for bureaucrats, and he'd been lucky. He'd gotten to serve on the Cherisky management team.

Cherisky was a slowly rotating cylindrical world of vast dimension, built to house a living example of Beringia grasslands. It had been cold and austere but beautiful, a biome that was home to wild horses, musk oxen, and reconstituted mammoths. Like all biome worlds, Cherisky was self-regulating. Only occasional corrections or resource infusions were required and those were handled by bots under the direction of the AIs of the Machine Layer. Hitoshi's management team had existed only to tend to the human visitors.

Since those days—since leaving Cherisky—he had hiked and explored and marveled at a thousand biome worlds. Literally, a thousand. He kept a detailed journal. His travels were documented. The Loysan Escarpment was his thousandth trek.

Rain pattered the leaves of the dense canopy, made a quick rhythm on his jacket, soaked the sparse white hair on his uncovered head. A chill breeze, infused with a sweet scent, set the tree branches swaying while his trekking poles clacked rhythmically against the artificial basalt.

The trail up the escarpment was winding and long, but Hitoshi was in no hurry. He'd camped two nights already, making a leisurely start each morning. In all that time he had not encountered another person.

Better that way, he told himself.

When Hitoshi had started his wanderings, over a century ago now, tourists had been abundant everywhere he went. But over the ensuing years, more and more people had abandoned the Tangible Layer, emigrating to the security, the convenience, the limitless options of the Virtual Layer. Their absence was evident, especially among peripheral worlds like Loysan, far from the Veiled Sun.

Hitoshi wasn't troubled by the resulting solitude, but was left unsettled by what he saw as the inexplicable decision of so many to abandon the Tangible Layer long before old age became a burden to them.

Still, an absence of raucous company on the trail was no cause for complaint. Too often in those early days his treks had been marred by the shouts or whoops or whining of strangers, or by the sacrilegious sight of graffiti etched into the bark of trees older than the oldest person still alive within the Tangible Layer.

Trees even older than me, Hitoshi thought sourly.

He was not the oldest person in the Veil—not yet—but he knew he was getting close.

His boots splashed with every careful step, his stability ensured by his trekking poles as he walked slightly bent to balance the modest weight of his expedition pack.

The pack was really just a portable fabricator-recycler, equipped with large pockets for immediate necessities: his tablet, a bivouac bag, protein bars, water bottle—those few things he might require during the day. It was no great burden to carry. He was old, not frail.

Still, the trail was long, the rest houses far apart, and last night he'd hardly slept, kept awake by the hooting, wailing, chirping chorus of calls from the forest's nocturnal denizens—a wonder to listen to—and by the anxious prospect of making the summit sometime later today.

As he rounded a ridge, the rain eased. Soon only a light mist remained. Small, jewel-like birds darted among the foliage, calling to one another in sharp, peeping voices.

Another half hour and he climbed past the mist into leaf-filtered sunlight. Only a few minutes later, he rounded a bend and spied a mad woman ahead of him.

Hitoshi stopped. He gritted his teeth in distaste. He rolled his eyes "heavenward" as they liked to say in the old stories, with the benefit that on a tethered habitat like Loysan, where an immense shaft connected two distinct worlds, Heaven lay in any and every direction.

Under his breath he muttered a brief prayer—"Oh, spare me"—unsure if he meant it to be heard by a legitimate deity or by the ineffable and omniscient AIs of the Machine Layer, on which all life relied. He did know—he was quite certain—he wanted to avoid any negative encounter that might mar this, his last climb.

Still, there was only one way forward. He resumed his slow rhythmic pace.

At first, the mad woman took no notice of him. She was engrossed in her mad task, using a white stick to poke at the leafy detritus beneath a patch of bracken fern a few steps off the trail. In her other hand she had a white mesh net shaped like a funnel. She held the net close to the ground, moving it in quick gestures timed to the motion of the stick.

Hitoshi consoled himself with the observation that she was, at least, not dressed like a mad woman. No rags or eccentric affectations. Instead, she wore practical expedition gear much like his, color-shifted to a light tan that made her easily visible without the offensive ostentation of blazing orange or screaming pink. She carried no pack, but Hitoshi had consulted his tablet and knew there was a rest house not far ahead, so she'd likely left her gear there.

Fragmented sunlight fell against her smooth white hair. As he drew nearer he was struck by her diminutive size: thin and a little stooped. Worn down by time into something less than what she'd once been. Same as him.

He didn't want to startle her, so he made an extra measure of noise by scuffing his boots and then he called out a gruff "Good day" in a voice that made no promise of further conversation.

The woman turned, thankfully showing no sign of alarm. A handsome, if well-worn, face. "Well, hello," she said as she swept the mesh net up and gave it a vigorous shake.

Hitoshi couldn't help himself. Against all resolve, he stepped close, leaning in to peer over the rim of her net. He counted three insects hopping and crawling inside it. "Crickets?" he asked, suspecting this was further evidence in support of his mad-woman theory.

"Crickets," she agreed cheerfully, shaking the net again to

discourage the intrepid insects from making an escape. Then, as she took a really good look at him, her thinning brows rose. "Hmm," she said with coy humor. "Can it be you're even older than I am?"

Forthright and impertinent. He could have been annoyed, but he felt himself warming to her instead, so he answered her banter in kind. "I'm willing to bet I'm the oldest person on this trail."

Given the absence of other people, this won him a laugh. She had a nice laugh. Maybe that's what coaxed him to ask, though he knew he shouldn't. He didn't want to get caught up in her madness, but neither was he quite ready to move on. So he took the plunge: "Why crickets?"

She smiled knowingly, as if she'd expected this question. "This particular species has been having problems." She shoved her white stick under her belt, freeing a hand to retrieve a small vial from her pocket. Reaching into the net, she quickly bottled all three crickets, then held the vial up so he could clearly see them. They were a tiny golden-colored species.

"They look fine to me," Hitoshi said.

"You're right. These individuals *are* fine. But populations in different worlds are isolated from one another. They diverge over time, sometimes dangerously. A viral disease cropped up here on the Loysan Escarpment. It knocked back the population for a time, but the species adapted. The same species used to be found in Myrmon Woods—"

"Oh, I've been there," Hitoshi said, swept up by the memory. "Beautiful world."

She nodded. "The same disease showed up there, probably carried by a trekker who failed to properly clean their equipment." She cast a critical gaze at his boots.

"Hey," he objected. "I always clean my equipment before packing it."

"Good," she said, though the word was weighted with skepticism. "Unfortunately for the Myrmon Woods crickets, they didn't possess the same genetic diversity that saved the crickets here at Loysan and the species was wiped out. I'm a weaver. A genetic weaver. It's my task, my calling, to do something about that." She gently tapped the vial. "I'll try to isolate the traits that allow these crickets to survive and weave those into the genetic material preserved from the Myrmon Woods crickets. Then I can introduce individuals reconstituted from original stock."

Hitoshi had heard of weavers. They were something like a religious organization. Their members worked to ensure that the biomes of different worlds did not diverge so far that they became toxic to one another. Surely an unending task!

"Why don't you just introduce Loysan crickets to Myrmon Woods and be done with it?" he asked. "Or wipe out the disease altogether—that'd probably be best."

"Diversity," she answered, with a sharp smile that dared him to call this absurd. "There are surely genetic variants in the Myrmon Woods crickets that might come in handy someday, and even a virus is a life form that can ultimately enhance a biome's complexity."

"I'll take your word for it," Hitoshi said. "Right now *this* trekker is going to trek over to the rest house, sit down for a bit, and have some hot tea. Would you care to join me?"

HER NAME WAS Carol and to his surprise Hitoshi found himself enjoying this chance of conversation with her.

Carol seemed pleased too. "You've visited a lot of worlds, haven't you?" she asked as they walked together the short distance to the rest house. "Trekked a lot of biomes?"

"A few," he admitted.

She arched a skeptical eyebrow.

He scrunched his wrinkled face and confessed, "Loysan makes one thousand."

"Wow! That beats me by a long way!"

He shrugged against his pack straps. "I'm persistent." This was the Age of Abundance, and persistence was all that was required.

The Age of Architects had left Sol System with a vast cloud of artificial worlds and though the means and the knowledge to make such worlds was forgotten, at least by anyone of human origin, it hardly mattered. The build-out had created living space and material wealth far in excess of what people might ever require, and the diligent oversight of the Machine Layer kept it all in harmony. Every world regulated, integrated, with transport between them on demand—far more worlds than anyone could visit even in a lifetime that endured for three centuries or more—with the freedom to go anywhere, everywhere, except to Earth itself.

"What got you interested in trekking?" Carol asked.

He hesitated. In the past when he'd met that question, his answer had been aimed at putting an awkward end to further inquiry:

My marriage drifted into obsolescence and after she and her new partner emigrated to the Virtual Layer, our children followed them. I wasn't ready to transition. So I decided to travel instead.

Hitoshi did not burden Carol with any of that. Instead, he told her a deeper truth, rarely spoken: "I saw the Earth when I was seventeen."

"Did you?" She paused in the trail, wide-eyed and suitably impressed. "You're far from home, then."

With a cock of his head he invited her to move on again. "I carry my home on my back," he told her. "You can think of me as a centuries-old tortoise and just as slow. But you're right. I've come a long way. I was born three hundred and one years ago, on a world whose orbit occasionally reached the inner edge of the Sun's Veil. Just once, that orbital path brought us into the vicinity of Earth."

The wonder of it was still reflected in his voice. "We could see her easily, blue-white and beautiful with her forest moon."

He sighed, bittersweet melancholy. "Seventeen! An age when love strikes hard. I fell for her heart and soul, caught in her gravity. The sacred goddess, mother of all. I swore my allegiance."

"You wanted to emigrate," Carol guessed.

"It seemed possible, at seventeen."

Endowed with a young man's optimism, Hitoshi had promised himself that someday he'd walk on Earth's shores, swim in her oceans, climb her mountains, lose himself in her forests.

Very soon, the fiercely complex procession of worlds had carried him away from her. He'd never seen her again and he'd never won the emigration lottery.

Eventually, he'd married. Fatherhood had been a joyous consolation, but when time took that away, he'd found solace and some satisfaction in trekking the biomes.

He looked ahead to where the rest house could now be seen between the trees. It stood open, its side walls coiled out of sight within corner columns of dark-purple marble infiltrated with veins of gold. The columns held up a peaked roof with flared eaves, shingled in black-slate.

As they drew closer, he saw that most of Carol's gear was tumbled in one corner of the gray plasteel platform, with the exception of a bivouac bag that she'd hung over the back of a bench. The bench faced a small table and then a blue vista beyond: a great gulf of atmosphere that appeared planetary in scale.

This was Hitoshi's first glimpse beyond the trees and awe swept over him. He shrugged out of his pack, set it gently on the platform, and stepped to the edge of the abyss.

White birds. He spied them, tiny with distance, soaring in slow circles beneath him. Raising his gaze, he marveled at an illusion of sea and sky blending into an infinite horizon. He squinted, trying to spot a flaw, a hint of seam or boundary that would reveal the wall of the habitat—he knew it could be no more than twelve kilometers distant—but he could not see it.

Moved by the vastness and the beauty, he sighed deeply, silently acknowledging that the guidebooks were right. Loysan was among the finest imitations of Earth he'd seen and a worthy culmination of his travels.

"And still," he said aloud, "it is not Earth."

No artificial world could truly replicate the depth, the complexity, the history, the precarious geological volatility, the very gravity of a planetary body.

"Still, it's not bad," Carol said with a note of amusement as she stood with him on the cliff's edge.

He grunted. "I'll concede that." Turning from the abyss, he asked, "Now, would you like tea?"

THEY SAT AND chatted and drank hot tea. Hitoshi felt easy in her company, surprisingly so, and listened with sympathy as she told him her own story.

Carol had been partnered for decades with another weaver. "I lost him nine years ago. He was exploring off trail when the ground gave way beneath him. He fell a long way."

Hitoshi was familiar with such devastating accidents from his years on the Cherisky management team. Risk could not be eliminated, even in a well-managed world. "I'm sorry."

Carol said, "We'd planned to transition together."

Hitoshi grunted, and asked her, "Is that why you're still here?"

Elderly folk had become especially rare in the Tangible Layer since most people transitioned at younger ages to avoid the ever-increasing risk of death.

Carol said, "It's hard to imagine eternity without him. But I'm close to my sisters. We'll transition together when the time feels right." She gave him a wry smile. "I don't think we'll risk waiting as long as you."

"I thought I might go for the record," he joked. "Oldest man in the worlds!"

The truth he left unspoken was that he hadn't planned to transition at all. He'd been sure that long before he trekked a thousand worlds, he would either win the Earth lottery or die along the way, in a predation accident or a fall like the one that had taken Carol's partner.

No luck either way.

An alarm trilled. An intrusive electronic noise, a casual profanity amid the birdsong. It shattered the reflective silence that had fallen between them, causing Carol to flinch and Hitoshi to spill his tea on the tabletop.

He set his cup down with a sharp rap as the tabletop absorbed all traces of the spill.

"It's me," he confessed in irritation.

Then he corrected himself. "Well, really, it's my kids." The alarm kept trilling. "Not that they're kids anymore. They're all well into their second century. All of them transitioned a long time ago. Now they think they know better than I do."

If his kids had remained in the Tangible Layer, they would have had to contend with a light-speed delay to keep in touch with him, but from the Virtual Layer, contact was instant—and incessant.

His irritation poured forth as he explained to Carol, over the alarm's ever increasing volume, the facts of his situation. "You see, if I don't 'check in'"—long wrinkled fingers clawed the air, adding sarcastic quotes around the phrase—"at the 'agreed upon interval'"—more air quotes—"the local management team gets alerted to a possible emergency.

"I'm not sure if I mentioned it, but I used to be *on* a management team, and I can tell you, we loved the excitement of a call-out. Any excuse to go into rescue mode. I can also tell you from experience that it's an embarrassment to find yourself surrounded by 'rescue personnel'"—those air quotes again—"who are really just bureaucratic button-pushers wanting to look like heroes."

"So maybe you should check in?" Carol suggested in a teasing voice, boosted in volume so she could be heard over the now-strident alarm.

Hitoshi grunted. He pried himself up off the bench, hobbled on stiff legs to his pack, slipped his tablet out, unfolded it.

His youngest daughter, sweet-faced Kimi, smiled at him from the Virtual Layer.

Kimi had been the last of his kids to transition. She'd waited until she was a hundred twenty years old to make the move. Now she was a young woman again, joy lighting up her eyes every time he saw her and always eager to remind him how grateful she was for the Virtual Layer's "unlimited options"—this time he only imagined the air quotes—before urging him to make the transition too.

"I'm *fine*," he growled at her before she could say anything. "No need to call emergency services for the old man."

"Hi, Dad," she said, silent laughter behind her smile. "I love you too."

He curled his lip, made a noncommittal grunt, and for once Kimi looked a little distressed, a little disappointed. "Are you sure you're okay?" she asked, her smile gone.

"I'm fine, just fine. I was just enjoying the view and a nice cup of tea, and I could do without the nagging."

"I'm sorry. But we worry about you, Dad. If you shared your

biostatus with us, we'd know you were okay—or we'd know if there was a problem."

"My biostatus is my own business. I'm not a child, Kimi, and neither are you."

"Dad, you're not a child. You're an old, old man and you don't seem to realize that every day you're taking a terrible chance. You need to transition."

"When I'm ready," he said. He'd said it a thousand times before.

Her eyes glistened. "If something happens, an accident—"

"Don't worry." He made an effort to sound reassuring. There really was nothing to worry about. "I've got this."

She didn't believe him. "I'll call you tomorrow."

"Right."

He cut the connection, folded the tablet, and shoved it back into his pack. Then he turned to look for Carol.

She'd left the rest house, lingering several steps away along a faint trail that ran close to the edge of the cliff. "All clear," he called to her, pleased that she hadn't used the interruption as an opportunity to flee his company and return to her cricket-netting occupation.

She came back to the rest house, greeted him with a smile. "Where to from here?" she asked as he gathered the teacups and returned them to the fabricator.

"Onward." He said it with some regret. "On to the top. I need to do this. I need to finish. Thank you for sharing a cup of tea with me."

She held her hand out to him, palm up. "It was a pleasure to meet you."

He slid his palm across hers. "An honor," he said gruffly. And then, without letting himself think too hard about it, he added, "Maybe we'll meet again sometime... in the Virtual Layer."

"It's another phase, isn't it?" she mused. "A chance to do those things that never quite worked out here in the Tangible Layer."

"Maybe it is," he agreed.

He shouldered his pack and set out, resolved to not look back.

HITOSHI HIKED, ONE foot after another, his thoughts circling.

Some things are not meant to be.

For most of his life he'd longed for Earth. He knew now he would never get there, not in the flesh. But as he followed the winding trail higher and higher through the forest, accompanied by birdsong and the wind-driven rustle of the canopy, he let himself imagine that this *was* Earth.

And wasn't it, after all?

The thought came to him with the force of revelation.

All the worlds he'd visited, the diverse biomes he'd trekked through—desert, alpine, grassland, tropical, shoreline, ocean, arctic—all were part of Earth, a flood of Earth-life filling the once lifeless outer reaches of the solar system and slowly claiming the surfaces of the companion planets—the Moon, Venus, Mars.

He found comfort in the thought.

IT WAS LATE afternoon when Hitoshi finally climbed above the tree line. His breathing grew deeper, but it remained steady as he commenced an alpine section of dark basalt supporting tufts of short, stiff grass, tiny flowers, and snowy white patches of lichen.

Clouds had formed around the lower slope, hiding most of it from his view, but at his altitude the sky was clear—that wondrous blue ocean of atmosphere—and he could see in it now the yellow blaze of a lantern sun. *Two suns*, he realized as he picked out a second, tiny gleam beyond the first.

"And not a damn bit of heat from either," he groused, pulling the zipper on his jacket a little higher.

The rustle of wind, the crunch of boots and trekking poles against the rocky soil, the creak of his pack: these sounds framed the silence that followed him.

The air became more rarified. The same thing happened on Earth as climbers ascended to the peaks, but here the gradient was steeper. The effective gravity declined as well and that was like Earth too, although there the scale was so vast the difference went unnoticed.

Hitoshi accepted the lower gravity as a boon, but his aged body did not take well to the thinning air. His chest began to hurt and his head to ache.

From the corner of his eye he glimpsed an aerostat. Just a little thing, a thin ten-centimeter wing with a multitude of flaps to stabilize it in the wind. He was familiar with the devices. Most biomes used them to monitor hikers deemed at risk of keeling over.

"Eh," Hitoshi growled, making a rude gesture. "Be gone!"

The aerostat ignored this of course and after his moment of indulgence, he ignored it, saving his breath for the climb. One slow step after another. Breathe in, breathe out. He grew aware of one more sound worth noting: the pounding of his heart.

The trail zigzagged, climbing steeply, each switchback shorter than the one before it.

He left the last of the plants behind. Only lichen now. Smooth gray patches on the black artificial basalt.

Air so thin! Deep breaths were no longer enough. He had to stop every few steps, breathe deeply, purposefully, drawing in extra oxygen.

His chest ached, but he didn't have far to go. He could see the rest house just a few switchbacks above him, marking the apex of the trail.

Night coming on.

I'm not ready.

An intrusive thought, breaking through his fatigue.

He kept on.

Twilight arrived, but not as the epilogue to a sunset. The two lantern suns remained high in the sky while the blue walls of the habitat darkened, reaching a steely blue hue textured with thin cloud shapes that flushed brilliant pink, but only for a minute. The color drained away as the sky shifted to a dark grey pierced with stars and the fading glow of the Lantern Suns. Full darkness imminent.

It comes too fast.

A few more steps and he stopped again. *Breathe*, he coached himself. *It's not that bad. You've been on harder climbs.* Of course, he'd been younger then.

He sensed the temperature dropping in parallel with the light. Ice would soon be forming in the few pockets of soil gathered among the exposed basalt.

He coughed gently, imagining he heard the hum of the aerostat drifting closer. "Get moving," he grumbled to himself. "You set the rules, you idiot. Now finish it."

Step. Breathe. Step. Breathe. He allowed himself no more long pauses, leaning hard on his trekking poles as he pushed on, breath rasping painfully against a dry throat. He imagined Carol settling in for the night in the kinder climate of the forest rest house.

"Should have stayed there," he muttered. A few steps later, "Wish I could have."

So focused was he on each small step of his journey that it came as a surprise when he looked up and found he'd reached the rest house.

Like the others he'd seen, this one had a peaked roof with flared eaves and dark marble pillars. The walls were pushed open to the night sky.

He shed his pack with a sigh of gratitude and sat down on the bench. Groaned. Plumes of welcome heat curled up from open vents. He was played out. His back ached, his head ached, his lungs hurt. Another cough was looming but he resisted it.

In the abyss, a hundred thousand stars, but his gaze skipped over them to look downslope where the clouds were breaking up. Was there a light to mark the site of Carol's camp?

No. How could there be? Any light would be hidden by the trees.

You're on your own, he reminded himself. He'd planned it that way.

Hitoshi sat back, eyes closed, cherishing the heat against his legs. Shivering slightly, from exhaustion or cold or lack of oxygen. Maybe all three.

One thousand worlds.

All of them had been beautiful. Wondrous creations. Earth's children.

But only one thousand... leaving so many more he would never see.

His alarm trilled.

"*Rads and toxins*," he swore. "Can't a man have a moment of quiet contemplation?"

The alarm did not have the capacity to respond to his protests. It just kept trilling, ever louder as the seconds passed.

He reached for his pack, retrieved his tablet, and thumbed it open.

Kimi again. She looked tired, flustered, as if she'd been awakened from a deep sleep. Was it necessary to sleep in the Virtual Layer? The idea bothered him. Granted, it was advertised as "Real life, with options."

"Are you okay, Dad?" Kimi asked.

She sounded really scared this time. Hitoshi responded to that, answering in a gentler tone than he might have otherwise. "Same as always, sweetheart."

"You're not the same. You've got elevated heart and respiration rates, and a reduced oxygen level in your bloodstream."

He scowled. "How do you know that?"

"I got a report from the trail monitor."

He remembered the aerostat and rolled his eyes, regretting it immediately when he felt the dry bite of cold air against them. "I made the summit," he told Kimi. "So of course my blood is low on oxygen. There's not much oxygen anywhere."

She looked past him, seeming puzzled now as well as worried. "It's dark there." Her gaze returned to him. "It must be cold."

"It's cold," he agreed. And then, after an awkward pause, "There's so much more I'd like to see, to do."

"Come over," she pleaded. "And you'll have forever."

He smiled a gentle smile. He could close the walls of the rest house, get warm, breathe oxygen from his fabricator until his lungs cleared—but that's not why he'd come here.

He'd chosen the Loysan Escarpment as his last climb—as many had before him—because it was long, challenging, and beautiful, but also because it was a jumping off point.

In a few more minutes he'd get up again and continue on the trail. It climbed no higher, but it did go on a little farther, winding around the perimeter of the habitat's massive tether to a transition arch on the other side.

He had only to enter the arch to initiate his transition to the Virtual Layer. On the other side he would be able to walk out onto the Earth—a virtual Earth, true, but still his first love.

"I've got a little farther to go tonight," he told Kimi. "But I'll be home soon."

THE SYNCHRONIST

FRAN WILDE

IT'S BEEN TWENTY years since I've seen him. It's been thirty days. And nearly two parsecs. And six point five light years. It has been four months outbound and six months inbound. It's been five rotations.

All of this is simultaneously true.

And there's not one rotation or day or second or trajectory along which I've missed his sorry ass.

And yet.

When Galen Sand disembarks the tradeship *Verdant Nine*, his expression slips from hero-returns to something-is-wrong in microseconds. Only I notice.

He's expecting a payoff for the moments he's saved in transit. He'd told me years ago that the first tradeship to arrive always left with the most rewards. He doesn't understand until this exact point that he's been cashed out.

He doesn't yet know it was me that did it.

I measure the moments between his loss and betrayal. I wonder if he'll be proud of me anyway.

"Hi, Dad," I say, though I'm older than he is now.

* * *

~ *Spiral Arm Prime Axis Museum, Galactic Center* ~

Honored Chronometrist. Breaker of Losses. Momentist. Degenerate. The Horologist B.V. (Beneficence Valorous) Sand's titles vary according to the proximity of Sol and the Terran planets. However, her impact on how the Spiral Arm uses microseconds, from payment to salvage, is as constant as time itself.

I HEAR GALEN telling the new crew "Beneficence won't be a bother," and I smile, my ear cupped against the door to the navigation room. I am eight. I want to skip, just once, down the metal passageway of the *Verdant Nine*, but my boots are magnetized to grab the floor.

The new engineer murmurs another question about the motherless child stomping the gangways in tiny mag boots. Galen's smooth voice echoes. "Don't worry. I teach her myself. She's immaculate."

Over the years, new engineers, stevedores, nannies, and galley staff on the *Verdant Nine* have learned that means I'll stay out of the way, mostly, that I won't paint the gangways with Venusian phosphors or ask too many questions. Mostly, I'm learning to steer the ship. It's going to be mine someday. Galen's promised.

He buys wind-up rocket toys from Phobos, bio-luminescent clock kits from Ganymede, the same place he bought my egg long ago.

He ships parts for navigational modifications with the toys, technology to help the ship go faster and recorders to cover that up. "It's a game I have with Terran officials," he says, showing me how to play. "The game is primarily set between the Jovian planets and the galaxy's greater spiral arm, which is opening up to traders and freight. That means more ships are foldjumping, and everyone must measure where an object in orbit will be at a given moment in relation to all other objects in motion. Time is part of that measurement. That's what the Consistency's trying to control—especially as wide-open local spaces became cluttered with objects, all in motion. But their clocks aren't perfect. In a foldjump, navigation tells you how fast you can go, but not how much time you'll lose when you pass through a gravity well. Those are very small. The chronometers slow a little with each transit. More moments go missing. Those errors are small too. But, Beneficence, even a tiny loss in a billion-kilometer journey can create an error that is not so small—one percent of a billion kilometers is still a lot of room for things to go wrong."

I nod, squinting, trying to see what he means. "But how is that a game?"

He smiles. "It's a game because there's also a lot of room for things to go right. We just need to time things to our advantage, until there's a better clock available."

"Okay," I agree. Though I'm still hazy on the details. Even at eight, I know that a percent of a billion kilometers is a scary span of space.

Galen special orders more mag boots to arrive at our next port of call when it looks like I'm growing out of mine. "There's nothing that tells time better than a child," he laughs at a rare crew dinner. My tenth birthday. The crew laughs with him.

Do I mind being a kit-kid? My egg selected from a catalog for intellect, math especially? Delivered by drone, according to Galen? Various nannies who come and go on their transits seem to think it's normal, so if Galen doesn't mind, I don't either. He's preparing me for greatness; says he didn't want any interference. That's why I don't have siblings and Galen doesn't have iterations. The whole ship is mine.

"Watch and learn," Galen ends a navigation lesson, "and you'll bring fame to the *Verdant Nine*. I can only bring us wealth." His brown eyes glitter with screenlight. The calculations for a high-speed transit from Io to Europa span three panels before us. The ship's already underway. The real-time numbers change with their trajectory.

Time and distance equal speed: my first variables.

The patterns they make, my first toys.

As we plot the arc that we need to swing for the fastest route, he adds, "You will bring us glory."

But I'm still worried. "What if we get lost, like the *Anathremon Six*?" Somewhere out there in the vast space between moments.

"That captain got sloppy," Galen says. "And the Consistency refused to calibrate the *Anathremon*'s chronometers. They've made themselves the standard keepers for system navigation, for safety's sake. But it's also another way to control us. We keep track of our own instruments better than the Consistency can. Better than the *Anathremon*. I make sure our timing doesn't slip, no matter what. The Consistency doesn't like it, but I don't care. You understand? That won't happen to us. Okay?"

I nod again and Galen shows me how he calibrates the *Verdant Nine*'s navigation, then lets me try it myself. The screens seem to gleam with his trust and my data as Galen feeds my calculations to the navigator, then snaps his fingers and lifts me in the air.

The enormous ship seems to move on my say-so.

Happy in this moment, I hum a nanny song about the sun. But Galen raises an eyebrow.

That quiets me to a single word. "Okay." My voice as serious as I can make it. The tick-tock syllables sound like the ancient clock Galen bought for my berth as a gift. A wooden pendulum, the case painted black and gold.

But when we arrive on Europa, a gang of Consistency drones meets us at the dock.

Galen orders the crew to quarters, all but me. I scrunch closer to his side as the drones buzz loudly. Their carapaces bump Galen. Their sonorous chorus echoes displeasure. "We've received complaints that your clocks are running fast, Captain Sand. We've watched. You *are* running fast. The dock was not ready for you."

Galen only shrugs. "I was teaching Beneficence how to steer." He gestures at me. "It won't happen again."

The Consistency doesn't acknowledge a child when it has better prey. "We think you're playing the margins on early arrivals. Beating your competition, perhaps through illegal means? We've refused to synchronize ship chronometers for less. Licensed, standardized System navigation requires standardized clocks. For everyone's benefit. You could be lost in space without us."

Galen makes his denials and, unable to prove anything, the Consistency turns to go.

"Dad," I whisper too loudly, "you said it was a game." His hand squeezes mine hard as the swarm slows. "Okay." I laugh and hum a sun-song to cover up my error.

Galen smiles, lips pressed tight. The Consistency moves away, murmuring threats in their wake. "Like you're not also gambling over microseconds," Galen mutters to the retreating swarm.

When they're gone, he turns and I swallow hard. I'll always remember how fierce his eyes, unblinking on mine, how he grips my shoulders with his strong fingers. "Time is an advantage, B.V. One that the Consistency and Terran planets control. They'll do a lot to keep hold of that power. Don't accept that. Don't give up. There are people in the Spiral Arm searching for ways to make time better."

"Okay," I say again. It seems the safest word.

A few moments ago, a lifetime ago, I'd been worried that the

Verdant Nine's engineer would report catching me taking apart a shuttle's timing device to see how it worked. The mess I'd made, far from immaculate. The engineer had let me help put the shuttle back together, so I'd hoped I was safe. But now I forget that worry, because his eyes are so fierce. I worry about the Consistency instead.

Galen turns to watch the Ionians offload our shipment of ore. The *Verdant Nine* made good money on the run, because we got here first. But he drags his fingers through his curly hair. "Let's go," he says. "We'll restock at the next port." His voice hitches on the word "next."

We don't get my mag boots.

He's scared. The Consistency rattled him somehow.

We don't go to Jupiter Main as I'd charted, either. He lands at Ganymede North instead—calls my unsuspecting egg-mother to come get me.

Exchanges me for a hold full of fabric and instrumentation.

"Work hard, and I'll be back. Won't be a moment." Galen hangs a delicate Venusian cloud-clock on a chain around my neck before disappearing into his ship. Before I can find a word of protest. His boots don't make a sound.

The doors slip shut, shadows lengthen in the port warehouse, and he doesn't come back out.

When the light fades, then *Verdant Nine* takes off. Fast. He leaves me sitting on a lightcargo trunk I've decorated with stickers of all the moons and planets where we've called: Neptune, Jupiter, Europa, the outer Oorts.

My mag boots bang the plastic case, too high to touch the ground. Crew from other ships bustle by, carefully not looking at me, as if I might be catching.

"Okay," I finally whisper. I stop staring at the place the *Verdant*

Nine was. I scan the docks, the mist rising cool against the shelter. My eyes begin to ache. Maybe my mother's face will look familiar, a mirror. I swallow back tears.

I am immaculate when my mother arrives.

"All right," the woman whispers, taking my hand. We look nothing alike, except she has brown eyes too. So does Galen. She pricks my finger to check the match, then smiles. It's almost enough. "Okay. Just for a little while."

~ Ganymedian Sand Workshop Preserve ~

In the Galactic Center planets, B.V. Sand is often pictured holding the final Quantum Degeneracy Chronometer (QD3) as a gold orb in her right hand, her calculations in her left. Sometimes, a ticking sound accentuates the immediacy of her accomplishment. These theatrical touches are inaccurate and here, at her home museum, we strive for as much accuracy as possible.

For instance, the Sand QD3 chronometer is not a gold orb, and it was partly concealed within the deck of the Horologist's rental ship. Composed of a cooling system and crystal lattice, the archaic structure also contained a series of anti-gravitational meshes, and two unique mechanisms of Sand's own design. The recording device she truly held is neither spherical nor golden. We can assure you, also, that her calculations were projected before her on her screens. All other "traditional" renderings are inaccurate.

At the time of the Synchronist's Challenge, B.V. Sand was two and a half Jovian years of age. Her ship, the Rael, was under Neptunian flag for thirty years, and a Terran-orbit shuttle before that for at least forty years. The Anathremon Six *had been missing for twenty-two years, the* Verdant Nine *for almost as long, and the Synchronist's Challenge had gone unclaimed for twenty Terran cycles.*

Sand's characteristic off-white tunic and multi-pocket duster, plus her ship-issued and ill-fitting mag boots, made her look like a landsider, especially among the ship's wiry crew. Her hair, cropped, was bleached to match the duster. The look on her face, unlike the smile in many images, is grim.

Details, especially of this moment, are important. Witness the threedee here:

"You should leave with us," her engineer Enric2 pleads before they take a shuttle back to Triton. "Warre Unkling's got this wrapped up for Terra. Bookmakers have you at terrible odds. Don't take our reputations down with you, chasing a ghost."

"I will continue," she replies. "Alone."

This is the moment onboard the lightship d-sonnit Rael *where B.V. Sand—who has lost two time trials already, and both of her own iterations; who is nearly broke; whose collaborators are leaving the ship before it commences its trial—gives up hope and latches on to belief.*

We've preserved the seconds in threedee and made shelf-size copies for those who would like to replay the inspiring transformation at home.

The next moment—one of the seminal points in temporal history—where B.V. Sand discovers her chronometer not only confounds gravity wells, allows for multiple entanglements, and creates a much more exact frequency and distance ratio than traditional methods, but also has the unusual side effect of being able to save and store time—is only available at the

Ganymede museum store for an admission fee of twenty-two seconds.

On Ganymede, it is six months, then it is two years.

It is point five parsecs.

It is one-half light year and gaining—I track the *Verdant Nine*'s arcs and foldjumps on panels in my Ganymede study—until these disappear.

The bright spot where they were, the ship's velocity as it prepared to head for the outer arm forming a smooth arc. Then nothing. They don't reappear. Did they calculate a jump wrong? Emerge with their bow in a meteor instead of open space? I shiver.

It is an infinite span of time before I open my eyes and look again. Still nothing.

Another ten days of sitting blankly through Ganymede history lessons in my mother's co-op below the ice. Then I receive an incoming message, time stamped twelve days previous. "Work hard, I'll be back in a moment."

My reply message, and all those after, disappear into silence. Lost.

My mother, Bellaire, who loves mathematics, has a bright laugh, and five iterations—including two fellow mathematicians at the university who come by to distract me with equations and puzzles— eventually looks into my study and clears her throat. "You all right?"

"I will be," I answer. "I have to work hard." Galen told me so.

I am twelve. I say the same thing when I'm twelve and a half and Bellaire keeps asking.

I don't mind her asking.

Then Bellaire brings home a lightcrate from the port. "Someone sent you clock parts."

I tear into the box, looking for a message. There isn't anything but parts and the spaces between the parts.

Bellaire shakes her head at the cables and lattices, the cooling systems. "Where will you put these?" She likes the elegance of math. She hates clutter. She's said that's why she didn't want a child, though the idea of some distant immortality beyond iterations charmed her. She didn't expect the return on her investment, but handles it, and me, with care.

We've established an easy agreement: I don't make messes.

Talking with her is like talking with the nannies or the *Verdant Nine*'s engineer, but better. I like it. She sings sometimes. She lets me study anything I want.

I study time.

Moments, seconds, microseconds. The more I learn about them, the more I know this is how to find Galen, or at least how to make good on my promise to him, to make time better. To make him proud.

In Bellaire's home, the blue skydome has day and night effects and I can see the stars just like on Galen's ship. I show my mother the clocks I've built from the crate. They keep even time, beating like tiny hearts. Mirroring the Venusian cloud clock around my neck. All synchronized.

"Hear the spaces between beats? Those are where things fall through." My father taught me that by disappearing. "I want to keep ships from falling through. Better clocks, better time."

"Explain it to me," Bellaire says.

"You never wanted a child," I whisper, suddenly reluctant to show her more.

Bellaire gathers me up in her arms and I'm shocked by the fierceness of this hug, over all the quick hugs we've shared in passing. "That was concept. This is real."

A few beats of breath. A moment where I close my eyes and listen to my heartbeat, hers. Then I try to show Bellaire how to synchronize time.

I entangle two of the quark clocks, then set one at the end of the settlement, and put another on a co-op lightship. "Any two related objects are impacted by time, and driven to separation."

My mother smiles, nodding, ignoring the squawk from the co-op owner about the depletion of quantum supplies. "That's a somewhat old idea."

"I agree." She wins me over by not babying me. Galen never did either. But she doesn't gleam with pride. What Bellaire offers is warm and constant, but soft.

I ignore the clocks and do my chores without being asked for a month, basking in the softness. Then, one day beneath the icelight, she asks, "Finish your explanation?" She holds a recorder.

I decide to see if I can make Bellaire proud. I retrieve the data from the outbound ship and pair it with the chronometer that remained on Ganymede. "These two are like modern chronometers that the Consistency provides ships. When they travel, different events impact them, and the clocks return subtly different. The other one will have scrapes where it got banged up in a hold. This one will have weather damage from the ice." I run my fingers across my ship-regulation short hair, thinking. "Chronometers start off synchronized but after many years, transit-wise, exposure to different gravities, different environments, even crystal lattice clocks need a tune up. And they've been going out of synch the whole time, by picoseconds." I pause and look at the clock data. "At least, that's how Galen explained it to me."

And now Galen and I are traveling apart.

I send the landbound entangled clock to the recycler.

Bellaire pulls it from the garbage and sends it, along with my presentation, to her university's science department. I gain a small grant to study navigation. When I graduate, her eyes meet and hold mine, still soft and warm. "You worked so hard."

I can bask in the warmth. But it's not enough.

~ Ganymedian Sand Workshop Preserve ~

This museum and preserve, two and a half kilometers below the ice, on the shores of sub-glacial lake 17, next to Sand's mother's home contains: Two ancient atomic clocks, cooled with lake emissions. One Venetian cloud chronometer (its motions broken during transport and never successfully fixed). A piece of wood supposedly from the original Terran, H4 Marine Chronometer. A Gas Storm Timepiece from one of Jupiter's stormtribes. (Sand quite likes that one though she cannot get it working consistently.) Sixteen versions of Quantum Degeneracy clock attempts, plus one brass orb model of the final clock, created by Domain Fabergé as a memorial. A threedee depiction of stolen time, developed by the museum. A copy of the original Synchronist's Challenge, hand-lettered on a commemorative pin. A crystal memorial of Je Yun's original Galactic Chronometer, and a loop of one of Sand's iconic personas.

The last one's not what you'd expect. Not quite a loop. Not quite a recording. More a place where someone might slip through.

ONLY ONCE DOES my mother frown about my work, over coffee when I am fourteen. A Lunar navigational and temporal studies conference has turned down my paper on the theories of time among Oort Cloud drifters who had "evolved past a sense of time" and claimed to be able to find lost ships. (Which was why no one would hire them for shipping, as they were always late, Galen used to say. I'd left that out of my paper.)

"Your own legacy, Bene, that's more important than his."

"You didn't hear the Consistency. You didn't see them threaten him. Landbound can't know how much advantage the Consistency holds out there. Because time isn't as good as it can be yet. Galen left me here to learn how to try. So I wouldn't be lost too."

"Can he really be as much a hero as you think?" she risks.

I slam out of the kitchen and back to my studies. Very carefully, in the quiet of my room, I remove the delicate cloud clock from around my neck. I take it apart. Pieces spread across my workbench. I cannot put it back together. The mist smells like phosphorous and tears.

I don't speak to my mother again until Bellaire slips two files through to my screen. One's titled "The Synchronist's Challenge."

Someone's offering a lot of money to build an improved chronometer. One that could have saved the *Anathremon Six*. And Galen, I think.

A lot more money than they'd give a child. I ignore it.

The other is a ticket: a paid seat at cross-planetary network discussions on galactic foldspace navigational errors. I attend and take careful notes. On ships like *The Ossip*, a Jovian series 1 lightflier, and the *Anathremon Six*. *The Ossip* arrived at Hydrai 467 three weeks ahead of schedule due to a timing error stemming from a flood around an ancient radio telescope in Bonn, old Terra, which was all they could afford. The variance gave them an unfortunate intersect with a moon. Bad timing means bad navigation. And, according to official records, the *Anathremon*

Six, a Martian ship heading to a new exoplanet, made the first of three foldspace jumps after having clocks synchronized by the Consistency, and arrived in safe orbit around a new gas giant. They radioed home that various instruments seemed to be lagging within the giant's gravity well, but seemed fine underway afterward. They took their readings and left for jump two, but never signaled again.

No one mentions the *Verdant Nine*.

"What's the commonality?" I message the network. No one answers. I answer myself. "Gravitational distortion."

"That old argument," Warre Unkling, the Venusian lightship pilot who's made several foldjumps on his own already, replies, and I nearly drop my tablet in shock. When I re-gather the threads of the conversation, the network's moved on to another topic.

"Okay," I whisper in the quiet of my study. But I won't give up. I use the network to search for more wrecks. Convinced if I work hard enough that I can save... something.

Interplanetary Transport 17783, emergency thrusters used to avoid ice-meteor in what was supposed to be a clear zone.

Dahlgren47a, a long-haul trader, missing. Unheard from after a foldspace jump.

So many ships, but none of them Galen's. Relief, always.

Eventually, for an upcoming conference that Warre Unkling will attend, I co-write a paper on the *Anathremon Six* with a friend from the discussion network: Enric2, an iteration of another engineer. We argue gravitational distortion of time near heavy planetary objects impacting foldjump time measurements. The paper is rejected as trite.

I am eighteen. Rapidly losing ground. I feel I'll never find the place where the *Verdant Nine* slipped through, much less patch the hole.

* * *

~ The Synchronist Challenge,
inscribed on a Commemorative Pin
in the Ganymede Sand Workshop Preserve ~

*Participants are sought to develop a new kind of chronometer,
one not subject to the whims of gravity wells and space folds,
one that reorients time on the galactic center, exact to the
microsecond, even in deep space.*

*The reward: a lifetime honorarium from the Astrological
Center Society.*

*The first to arrive in a documented time-trial exactly when
and where stipulated, to the microsecond, after a foldjump,
will be named First Synchronist for the Galactic Center.*

"THERE'S ONLY SO much theory can do," my mother says at breakfast
when I explain. She's drinking something green that smells like
ozone. "Get out and make something. One of your clocks."

She waves her hand and the Synchronist's Challenge appears on
my screen again. "Anyone can enter."

"I don't have the funds for that."

"Yes, you do." She taps my credit marker, which takes up a corner
of the screen. The accounts where Galen stowed some money before
he disappeared.

"Saving that." I'm oddly protective of those funds. Galen made
them gambling on the gap between when his ship would arrive and
when his competitors would. He used my calculations sometimes.
It was our game. The interest helps pay Bellaire for my space here,
as I wait for Galen's return.

My mother taps the funds. "You don't need to save them for me. Think of all the clocks you've taken apart and pieced back together, Bene. Do it for them."

I give in and take enough money to commission two iterations to help with the build work. Enric2 collaborates with me. So do other underemployed researchers from the discussion network. We build clocks again. New kinds. I hire time on lightships and test, rework, and test again. The first time trial for the challenge is in two years.

We're not nearly ready.

The second trial is in four.

Finally, I file paperwork for the third challenge. In the amount of time it takes for a wave to travel from Ganymede to Mars, plus some ten seconds, our entry is accepted.

My first ship, one of my iterations is lost. The timing is right, but the navigation calculations are overwritten by the ship's captain and my own iteration. They don't take into account Newtonian acceleration and how their trajectory works in and out of a nearby star's gravitational field while in foldspace. The incremental time changes to energy due to modified Heisenberg effects and the ship emerges in the wrong place. I'm not responsible but still feel it. My collaborators start to drift away.

A second ship isn't lost, but is badly damaged by a too-close pass with a large orbital body.

My credit marker shrinks on my screen from a small moon on to a meteor. Even in Ganymede's economy, I'm running out of time. But I won't give up.

The third trial is twenty years almost to the day Galen left me on the ice-dock at Ganymede North.

I book the *Rael* with the credit I have left. It's not the fastest ship. Its crew is all iterations, no backgrounds given, and the captain is Enric2's cousin. With nothing left to risk, I decide to go on the trial myself.

"You're trying to follow him," my mother protests. "Don't give yourself up like that."

"I'm not thinking of Galen." I pack a crate of chronometer parts. "I'm thinking of time. How to fix it."

I'm thinking of the gaps between moments where people and ships fall through.

~ Jovian Public Broadcast Service Recording,
Captain of the *Rael*, never released, private collection ~

"Yes, the Rael *was happy to take her job. She paid fifty-five percent up front, all of her remaining funds. Plus I liked the chronometer. I never hesitated. Never doubted her. Not like the others.*

"She took the shuttle up to the orbital at Ganymede North, and actually stood there herself to watch us load the QD3 on board. Demanded to hook it up herself. Even her own assistants left her when she pushed too much. And her face looked grim enough to spook the crew.

"But the trial kicked off as the outer Jovian planets were holding a vote against the inner planets to relocate the Prime Meridian/Prime Axis. They actually had a chance this time. And I admit, the moment felt auspicious. I just don't know for whom.

"Unkling's ship was faster, his design was glorious, and everyone was pretty sure the Consistency would cheat, and B.V. was still fiddling with her chronometer as we entered foldspace. Still, I never doubted her for a second."

*   *   *

It is twenty years. It is three failed trials. It is lost time and friendships.

Winning the Synchronist's Challenge would make it all worthwhile. It could gain me fame and lifetime tenure at the Galactic Center. From there, I could more easily search for the *Verdant Nine*.

Once I win.

There are three horologist ships out on trials, this final day.

Warre Unkling's entry is a Venusian ship set throughout with magnetic chronomophores. Meant to sense pulsars by distance and class, the ship is blindingly expensive and incredibly beautiful. The media outlets love it so much, they barely notice my nondescript navigation mesh, my handheld data recorder, and my rented lightship.

The Consistency's entry, a standard-bearing pulse-woven entanglement, plus its pair cannoned into the foldspace ahead of the ship, is the same design they enter each challenge. The repeater-resolution patterns give a sense of a proper map no matter what. It's meant as a warning not to mess with their standards, and no one's beaten it yet.

They are elegant solutions compared to mine.

Unkling is determined to take it for Terra. The Consistency, everyone assumes, has an inside track, at least for keeping the prize unearned.

But I've promised my father I'd work hard. I've promised my mother I wouldn't give in. And I promised myself I wouldn't lose.

~ Ganymedian Sand Workshop Preserve ~

In the following threedee recreation of her third space trials for the QD3 chronometer, Horologist B.V. Sand stands aboard the light-freighter D-sonnit Rael, having said, "I will continue."

Her former collaborators broadcast they've abandoned the work as soon as they land on Triton.

Now Sand takes out a small set of tools and parts and adds a recording loop to the QD3. This moment makes the final chronometer hers outright.

On the other side of the Rael, Consistency *drones preparing to receive Sand's time-trial concession stand down. Some of the* Rael *crew consider putting her out the airlock.*

But the ship prepares for its foldjump. The Consistency broadcasts one last note of concern about her design. She argues with the captain about navigation. Then they jump.

First there's dead silence, then there is cheering.

As their data lights up the navigation screens, Sand's expression shifts from worried to shocked. She looks at the recorder again. Shakes it. And for a moment, time seems to slow down. The cheering fades and returns.

"Huh," she says. "That's unexpected."

She checks the meters, the gears. The recorder holds the time usually lost in the moments between jumping and arriving.

Unkling lands before she has time to figure it out.

Then a fourth ship appears, just ahead of the Consistency.

"I WILL CONTINUE," I say.

The *Rael*'s captain hesitates. He has questions. "Our calculations put us out this edge of the meteor field after the fold."

He's no stranger to what are somewhat romantically known on the ground as foldjumps, but are more realistically mass expenditures of torque around gas-giant gravity wells that shorten transit times.

He knows a little time gets lost. Appreciates I'm trying to build a solution.

But he's nervous. Wants to use his own numbers. I shudder, thinking about the first trial. Stare at the trajectory arcs. "You'll put us out in the densest part of the field. Run my numbers." I hand him my tablet, ignore his shock at the impropriety. "They save us several seconds, and—more importantly—we'll emerge in clear black."

"The Consistency says you're wrong." He glances from his data to mine and chews the sipstraw of caffeine he's been gnawing on for the three days we've been preparing for the trial. "You'd best be right this time," he says finally.

The crew grumbles some more.

I hold the captain's gaze as if I have no doubts. "The Consistency insists on being the standard. On being right. If they're not, no one will trust their chronometers. But they're right *because* they set the clocks. The old-world ships, the really old ones, wind-driven rather than warp-driven, marked time and speed as essential to finding their way around reefs and shorelines. Even then, errors could wreck a craft. The Consistency has ensured their clocks are standard. But there are still many errors. A better timepiece could change everything, could it not?"

When I stop, there are a few grumbles but not at me. Everyone doubts the Consistency's pristine intentions. The captain nods slowly.

"I'll give you sixty-five percent of the split," I add. Our original deal had been forty. Only then does the captain signal, only then do mag boots sound against the metal deck, barely concealing dark grumbles. The crew swings to faster action.

The *Rael* nears the jump point.

* * *

~ Notes from B.V. Sand's Journal, private collection ~

Here are some horologic measurements I've found during my research:

A finite span: a cannon firing each day at noon to reset inaccurate watches; the pause between each tick of a familiar watch; the chemical signal of atoms in a microwave chamber.

An infinite span: the time between a door opening, someone stepping aboard a ship, and that door closing.

An unending span: the time between the last signal sent and the signal never received.

An empty span: outgoing versus incoming, of lost memories, when you are where time stops, but those you love keep going.

An uneven span: a pendulum onboard an early Terran ship, tossed off kilter by waves, or the movement of atoms closer to and farther away from a gas giant.

A heartbreak span: the moments between arriving a winner and the winner arriving.

I REFUSE TO risk failure this time.

As I feed my data into the QD3 chronometer for the last time, heart pounding, I set the recorder. Not to cheat, only to catch the clock's sub-atomic machinations. Something I hadn't done in earlier trials. Something Galen did on the *Verdant Nine* often, when he thought the shipboard chronometer was slow.

I keep my face calm, but inside, I'm shaking.

I may have added an extra loop in the recorder's code. May have told it to capture time between the jump points versus time onboard. May have used the word *capture*, not *measure*.

Then, all my models and forecasts, all the tinkering with atomic timing and the quark relays, all my worries about repurposing a theory as old as quantum degeneracy, all fall away as each vibration of each quark becomes a count of moments between periods, each oscillation momentous and minuscule both, while we wink into the fold.

All of this is still so immediate in my memory.

And yet.

When we emerge, the Synchronist's Challenge in our reach, a ship waits on the other side. Not a competitor's ship. The *Verdant Nine*.

It's been twenty years since I've seen Galen. It's been thirty days. Nearly two parsecs and six point five light years separated us. It is four months outbound and six months inbound. It's been five rotations and more failures than I can count.

It has been more than a moment.

All of this is simultaneously true.

I've always told myself I wasn't angry.

And yet.

My one goal: closing the gaps between moments, the dangerous ones. The small trap in the recorder I'd built works like a Venusian cloud clock, but for capturing moments, not mist. Our transit swings us close to a gravity well and an atomic beat is skipped. The recorder kicks in. A loop happens. A stitch, so to speak, in time.

An error multiplies by the distance we traveled.

When the *Rael* emerges, right on target, the recorder unspools, leaking a few ticks, making the ship faster than expected.

We hear the cheering start. "We're early." The captain grins.

I squint. "A few seconds."

Then Warre Unkling pulls alongside. The Consistency, just after. All on time.

Galen boards, watching his display. He wears a Synchronist's Challenge pin.

This whole time, he hasn't been lost. He's been plotting. Now he's triumphant. A better clock within reach, and him early enough to take it from the Consistency.

But his expression disappears as he realizes something's off. I've taken his game away. I wait for him to realize it.

"You're early," he says instead.

It takes a heartbeat for me to understand what Galen means.

"Early." I'm not on time. I didn't win.

But Galen is here, found. That is something. Even though he was never lost. He's staring at my recorder like he recognizes it.

The Consistency boards. A cloud of black hovers above me for a moment, then swarms Galen.

I get the same chill I felt when I was ten.

"Captain Sand," they murmur. "We told you not to return. Your gambling makes you unwelcome." They don't see it yet, as they turn to me. "And you. You thought to fix time," the Consistency murmurs.

I stand stock-still, the way I'd done as a child on Galen's ship. Wait as several of the drones nudge closer, bumping the skin of my nose with cool, carbon fiber carapaces. One tickles and I sneeze.

"I thought to, yes. But I've ended up doing something else. Collecting time for later." The Consistency descends on my instruments, curious.

Warre is boarding the *Rael* to congratulate me. But I can only see Galen. "You haven't aged. Where did you go?"

"Out, for a lot longer than I wanted. Working the galactic center on the Challenge. When I returned, you'd already sent your notice of entry. There was no time. Any communication would have been cheating."

"There's always time." I'm not having it. He'd stayed away on purpose. My hands grip the QD3 recorder. If it hadn't been so sturdy,

I would have crushed it. I hear it ticking forward, ticking back.

"We must certify who arrived legitimately," the Consistency intones. "And how." The drones turn a slight shade of crimson. They'd come in last.

"Okay," I say. The safest word. I don't feel safe at all. My father, here. Me, early.

"I saw Unkling arrive after us," the *Rael*'s captain says. "So we were here first. We get the prize."

"You arrived first, yes. But the timestamp on his ship *and* yours show Unkling arriving on time," the Consistency says.

"How?" The captain and then everyone look at the piece of the QD3 in my hands. "I shook it. Time came out."

The Consistency forces Galen to give Warre Unkling the pin. "The standards of the Challenge require it." Unkling becomes the Synchronist.

And I, for a moment, feel the weight of all my losses. Then Galen steps closer to me, to the recorder. "That's mine," he says.

The drones billow around him as he reaches toward me.

"You gave this up," I reply.

"I knew you'd be the one to do the job," he says, reaching a hand out to touch the QD3. It isn't an answer. "Now show me how you did it. How *we* did it."

"You cannot," the Consistency hisses, its drones piling up into a dark cloud.

Only Galen hears me say, "I will not," beneath all the noise.

~ *The confession of Galen Sand* ~

When Beneficence was born, all the clocks were reset.
That's what I told her.

I didn't want an iteration. I wanted a child who could see the world in a new way.

I never told her that.

I'm glad I didn't.

She'd created something entirely new. And it would bring us both glory.

When I was a child, I had a recurring dream of being trapped beneath the dome on Ganymede.

The ice collapsed. I was frozen in time.

And Galen returned to rescue me, his hand grasping my arm.

Twenty years, and now he's reaching out to take my chronometer.

"If I give the designs to everyone," I say with the Synchronist, Warre Unkling, looking on, "time becomes more valuable, not less. Enough of it, saved up? You won't need speed of light any longer."

No more gaps. Unkling nods. He understands. The Consistency hums, thinking.

But Galen's still reaching. "I make my living in those gaps." His voice has a hard edge to it. He's gotten over his surprise. He sees my intent. "I'll make you a partner," Galen says. "You can guide the family business." What I'd wanted most. Once.

A shifting span: the time between all of the *then* and now.

Slowly, a moment to the left, and a moment to the right, I shake my head. *No.* I step closer to the Synchronist.

And Galen lunges between us, grabbing for the calculations and chronometer.

I have not yet been able to measure the span of the moment I realized my hero was just a man running out of time.

And I refused to give it to him.

* * *

~ Ganymedian B.V. Sand Workshop Preserve ~

The technological miracle occurred, officially, at 07000 Neptunian time, when the struggle between the Horologist and her father tripped the recorder and the chronometer respooled. The time stored from the jump and all the space between that time, caught B.V. Sand up, and Galen, until they exist only between moments.

In the period between discovery and disappearance, B.V. Sand paused. Was recorded. She became an iteration, but not. A relic, but not. Someone outside of normal sphere.

Others have gone on to engage their own time retreats and returned. Only the Horologist stays within this gap in time. She's present in that moment, caught between one heartbeat and the next.

Galen Sand, too, remained caught in time, briefly. But the Consistency had witnessed his use of extreme force multiplied by time. The assault on the first Horologist, and the first example of such. Though accidental, the Consistency found he must be held accountable. Recordings of his confession are available from Jovian Public Radio.

As punishment, the Consistency and the Spiral Arm both refused Galen Sand more time.

As for B.V. Sand, she and the original QD3 were returned to Ganymede. A workshop preserve was built near her mother's house beneath the ice.

You may buy a moment with her, for a few seconds.

* * *

IT'S BEEN A hundred years. It's been twelve minutes. It's been three thousand days.

All of these are simultaneously true. Each moment is synchronized. Each deliberate.

If you bring enough moments, I will exist through them all.

Time in this instance is neither better nor worse. And the space between them is growing smaller.

TALKING TO THE GHOST AT THE EDGE OF THE WORLD

LAVIE TIDHAR

THE SMALL PLANE flew high above the Kraken Sea. A crimson sky. Lakes of liquid methane down below. A storm was gathering on the horizon, flashes of lightning etched in dark glass.

Rania loved flying. The stubby little plane was an extension of her body. She sat in the single-occupant cockpit in her outdoors suit. It kept her warm and plugged into the small oxygen tank. Flying high above the landscape, she could see bays and coves, perfect pirate hideouts. They said Nirrti the Black was stirring again, in her crusade against the Ummah.

The Disconnected, she called her army. People who were born without a node or, worse, ripped the fragile aug out of their brain stem with crude surgery, leaving themselves little more than zombies. It was appalling, but it was far away: she seldom stirred herself from her rumoured base on the Mayda Insula. Rania could see the island, far to the north.

She couldn't imagine what drove Nirrti, what fear or hatred of the Conversation, that all-encompassing flow of data everyone was part of.

Yet she could imagine some of it. She shut all but emergency channels from her consciousness, entering flight mode. She loved the peace of it, the isolation. No other mind beside her own.

You could still be alone on a world like Titan.

She flew her little plane, hugging the coast, veering west at last towards the flashing beacon of the small settlement of Al Quseir. She kept hoping for a rare glimpse of Saturn in the sky, but the clouds had covered the horizon.

She could see the settlement as she began her descent. Flying was easy on Titan, the thick atmosphere was like a soup and in the busy streets of Polyphemus Port where she lived it was not uncommon to look up and see flyers with wings strapped to their suits, freewheeling above the dome.

Al Quseir had started as a small mining community in the early days of settlement. Rania could already see the giant drilling rig that had been left over from that time, a huge platform that now stood forlorn in the winds. The early settlers had dug deep down for water, and for a time Al Quseir was famed across all of Titan for the quality of its exported oxygen. For a time it was a prosperous town, but the water reserves had grown low and the remaining residents lived deep underground, where they maintained small farms.

The plane landed gently and Rania taxied to the shelter of an old hangar before she climbed down from the cockpit. She'd been here a few times before, and always for the same purpose.

Only two people waited for her inside the hangar. She nodded, then followed them through the airlock. She took off her helmet and warm, humid air engulfed her, and with it came the sweet smell of frangipani and protea.

"I am sorry for your loss."

Umm Nasr with a face tanned by years under hydroponic lights, lined with age, green eyes as rare and startling to find as Great Tinamou eggs. She nodded thanks.

Nasr, her son, with a mouth that looked ready to smile easy, a farmer's hands. "Thank you for coming," he said.

"Of course."

She followed them to the elevator. Everything here was old but well maintained. No rust, the hoist ropes oiled and silent. They journeyed down, into Al Qusier. The upper levels passed by one by one—storage units, farms, air reservoirs.

The doors opened and they stepped into the town.

In all the years of settlement, this main cavern had been repeatedly dug, extended. Now the ceiling rose so high overhead it seemed like sky, and Rania could look as far as the horizon. Lanterns bobbed gently in the hazy air. A brook bubbled gently nearby, and butterflies flitted between the flowers that grew everywhere. Rania could hear voices in the distance, snatches of song and laughter, and over the canopy of trees saw a group of small children kite-flying, looping and swooping in a race against each other. Cautiously opening her node to a wider broadband, Rania felt the flood of the Conversation from all sides, though it felt more muted here, somehow. She could see Saturn rising, and the gathering storm, and the black, data-less patch that was Nirrti's island. She could see people talking to each other across Titan and across the Outer System, could see the firefly dance of spaceships against the fiery reds and orange of Jupiter, and across the narrow gulf to the Inner System where the massive data-clouds of Mars and Earth itself coalesced.

She brought it down to a murmur.

"This way, please," the man, Nasr, said politely.

She followed mother and son along a quiet path lined by trees. It wasn't far to their home, hewn into the side of the rock. They stepped through the gate and into a courtyard where fig and olive trees grew. A fire burned in the centre.

The rest of the family was gathered there. They turned at their approach. Murmured greetings, a thank you. Rania, again: "I am sorry for your loss."

How many times had she spoken those words since she'd returned to civilian life? She'd lost count. She wasn't all that used to talking to the living. Mostly she just spoke to the ghosts.

The deceased was lying in wait on a thick woven carpet. He was old when he died. He looked at peace. She knelt beside him. Gathered herself together.

There'd be no ceremony involved. That came before, or later. But hers was just a job.

Gently, she reached out her hand, touched her fingers to the back of the man's head.

Closed her eyes and felt the ghost still there.

A DECADE BACK and over four astronomical units away, Rania had served a stint as a combat medic in the Galilean Republics of the Jupiter system. It was one of those skirmishes that barely even get designated wars or given a name of their own, though the dead were real all the same. They were always warring, the Great Houses of Ganymede and Callisto, among each other. And the pay was good.

She had been one of a large shipment of young, inexperienced recruits from Titan crossing that great space between Jupiter and Saturn. She had hoped to see the famed flower gardens of Baha'u'llah Prefecture, and the ice palaces of Valhalla, where the lords and ladies of Odin's Hall live and dance in splendid isolation.

Instead, war turned out to be somewhat different. All she knew was the taste of legumes and tofu and puréed goat meat; the stink of bodies and the motion sickness of abrupt gravitational change; the whisper of hollow-point bullets fired in the close confines of boarded ships and the screams of dying combatants. Most of this long and intermittent war between the Houses—of which this was merely a skirmish, one amongst dozens over the eons—was fought in near-space, a huge bubble nearly seven light seconds in radius.

That space was filled with the military debris of centuries of sporadic fighting: sentient mines and boobie-trapped dead ships, mimic tech and self-replicating Conversation-nulling hubs, robots of all sorts, some as large as destroyers, and tiny clouds of deadly nano-mites. All these had long ago forgotten which side of the war they were on, if those sides even existed anymore, and now functioned semi-independently as abandoned hardware still determined to carry out their deadly goals at all costs.

Then there were renegades: robots who abandoned war in search of higher truths, new converts to Buddhism or the Way of Robot or Ogko. Sentient mines discussing obscure philosophies on high-encryption channels; missionary probes on their way to extending the Conversation in the outer reaches of the Up and Out, Von Neumann spiders crawling in search of any usable matter to convert into more mirrors and routers and hubs.

The battles skirted Europa. A no-flight zone enforced by a miniature Dyson Swarm of angry dust mites. The Galileans had Priests of Water—a strange religion worshipping chthonic deities under the subsurface ocean of that ice-encrusted moon. Rania had learned all this but never found out if it were true. She learned to shoot and get around in free fall. Her node was loaded with hostile takeover protocols and Others-level shielding. She learned to take care of the dead.

Every unit had one spirit talker. They'd come in firing—near-space crawled with hostiles' habitats, rings, converted asteroids and ships as large as moonlets. As the firefight moved on, she'd come upon the dying and the dead. After a while, she became proficient...

Kneeling down, her boots dyed with fresh blood, soldiers on the floor no older than herself. One girl, the first time... Callisto-white. Rania had never seen such skin. Dead eyes staring at a utilitarian ceiling where broken lights still flashed emergency frequencies. She reached down and touched the base of the skull. Fleeting code tried to attack her node—the feel of it like sparkles of live wire. She pushed, her fingers sinking into the skin and through, searching for and finding the *foramen magnum*, that oval hole into the brain through the skull. Inside her mind the ghost screamed, defenses rising, but she nullified the attacks until all that remained was the digital part of the dead human, naked and open to her like a mouse pup.

She retched. But her fingers found purchase, closed around the physical infrastructure of the node itself. It felt like a small ball or marble.

It had grown with the girl, from the womb or shortly after. As it grew, it became a part of her, the biological and digital fusing together into one form. The node sent filaments into the brain, like roots through earth, fusing and infusing. Now the girl was dead and the brain no longer functioning, but the node remained, a ghost, one part of her. Rania *wrenched*, grey brain matter tore and for a moment the root system of the filaments flashed an electric blue. Then it went dead, and she bagged and tagged it, the remains, the ghost to be taken elsewhere for what they euphemistically called strategic debriefing.

Then, one day, the war was over, and they all got shipped home again.

THERE WAS NO ceremony now. Rania worked quickly, gently—she'd become an expert by this time. During the war it had been brutal, messy, hurried. But now she worked to excavate the ghost, decant it, preserve as much of it as there was left. She barely left a mark. In moments she was done.

She rose. Her knees hurt more, these days. She said, "You wish to speak to him?"

Umm Nasr held on to her son's arm. "It isn't him," she said. "Not really."

"No," Rania agreed gently. "And the choice is yours."

"I have my memories. And my children."

She nodded. Nasr made to stop her, hesitated.

"No," his mother said. "It's for the best."

He nodded, slowly.

Some families kept their ghosts in ghost house shrines. Some made sure to erase this last remnant of the person that they'd known, to allow them the last true rest.

In other places, other times... there were hells, black market Cores, *verboten*, where the souls of the dead could be kept in eternal torment.

Or so they said.

"What were his final wishes?" Rania said. "Heaven, or the archives?"

The archives of Titan were famed across the solar system. A database of sleeping lives beyond count. The Cores they ran on were buried miles underground, were some of the safest in the entire solar system. They said they rivalled even those of Clan Ayodhya on Earth.

"Heaven," Umm Nasr said.

"Of course."

Rania gently took her leave. The job was done, and they would not thank her to linger. What was left behind was what all anyone ever left behind, when it came to it. They'd bury Abu Nasr, and mourn his passing, and then return to their lives, for that was the nature and way of the world.

She made her own way back. She knew the road. Only once she was interrupted, as a young girl ran after her, catching her almost by the elevator.

"Yes?"

The girl, suddenly shy, kicked dirt. "Umm Nasr said to give this to you, please," she said.

Rania accepted the small offering. The smell of fresh, sweet strawberries was like a reminder of a time when she was young.

"Thank you," she said, touched.

"Can ghosts taste strawberries?" the little girl said.

"I suppose... I don't see why they can't," Rania said.

"Uncle Qasim always loved strawberries the most," the little girl said, and then she smiled. "If you talk to him, will you tell him that—"

"What?"

But the girl looked down. "Never mind!" she said brightly, and with that she turned and ran back towards the house.

Holding the small pail of strawberries, Rania rose back to the surface. Closed back the suit, climbed into the cockpit. The strawberries and ghost shared berth in the cargo hold.

She sped along the tiny runway. In moments she was flying, into that glorious, thick nitrogen soup. The wind whispered against the tiny airplane, lifting it high like a toy.

Rania loved flying.

The ghost materialised beside her. It looked at the roiling red and purple skies, and for a moment they both saw Saturn and its rings as it rose in the heavens above.

"It's beautiful," the ghost of Abu Nasr said.

Rania looked at him sideways. The ghost flickered in out and of her field of vision. She turned her eyes back to the flight path. The storm had lashed down on the Kraken Sea, lightning flashing over the bays and alcoves of the shoreline, and for a moment she thought she saw a fleet of black ships illuminated on the waves, sailing away from the Mayda Insula.

Rania tilted the plane and swooped in a long curve south, away from the storm. She looked down on her world, the quiet and the splendour of that land of methane lakes and seas. It wasn't perfect. Nowhere was. But it was home.

"Yes," Rania said. "Yes, I suppose it is."

CLOUDSONG

NICK WOLVEN

THE LEGATE SUITE on Warren had all the newest amenities: ambient engineering, mood-adaptive algorithms, even morphifoam furniture that took any shape you chose—so long as it was curvy, soft, and indistinguishable from a finely sculpted blob. Of course, the specs were ancient and the style absurdly retro, but out in the wilds of the Darkling zone, what could an interworld legate expect?

Anander Flyte's only complaint was that he had nothing good to smash. No door to slam, no plants to topple. Not even a desk to pound a filebook on. He could throw a waterbulb at the wall, but it only bounced.

Anander threw it anyway. "I can't *believe* they would do this. It is *absolutely* intolerable."

From the exit valve, Maximilian watched in his palace-guard pose, chest out, eyes ahead, hands tucked with defiant dignity behind his back.

"They *know* we're on a schedule. Do they think this is some kind of company junket?" Anander pounded the chair until it assumed a new shape, spindly and elaborate, a cat's cradle of morphifoam tensegrity. He gave it a wallop.

The structure crumpled. Sprang back.

Most unsatisfying.

"Do they think I came here to poke my nose in a hole, sniff the local flavors of dirt? To tour some shadowy, half-lit hollow? This isn't a sightseeing trip."

"Nevertheless." Maximilian managed to accentuate his ramrod posture—a slight sucking in of the stomach, an incremental clench of the buttocks—conveying not only impatience, but disapproval. "According to the terms of the agreement—"

"Oh, spare me the terms." Anander quit abusing the furnishings and scooped up the fallen waterbulb. He popped the straw and sipped. The suite opted for calming imagery, waterscapes, a rhythmic roar. "It wasn't I who set the terms, Max. Why should I be the one to sort this out?"

Despair stifled him as he thought, for the eightieth time that hour, of the tremendous blow to his fortunes. Failure! At this stage in his career. And not only a failure, but the most critical, epical, apocalyptic, humiliating insult a legate could receive...

It was unthinkable. Anander snapped a finger at the wall, demanding an ambience suited to his mood. The room obliged with a view of Jovian storms.

"What exactly is their objection, anyway?"

Maximilian brought his arms from behind his back, revealing twenty-four long, thin fingers, each with far too many joints. *Amazing,* Anander thought, *what the man can communicate with only a subtle flick of those digits.* But this was the gift of the secretarial orders. They were neurally wired for uptightness.

Maximilian gestured at the walls, dimming the room to a semblance of sylvan shade.

"The Darklings," said Maximilian, now dappled with leafy shadow, "have re-evaluated their earlier position. They say Project Snowfall cannot be allowed to go ahead as planned."

"But they signed an agreement!" Seeing Maximilian's expression, Anander hurried on, "And when did they come to this great epiphany?"

His secretaid sighed. "They held a council, it seems, while your shuttle was en route. The assembly voted to annul the agreement."

"Did they give a thought, perchance, to how this would be received by the InterOrbital administration? The inner worlds? My superiors? To the effect it would have on my—"

Anander stifled his rage. A wind had gathered in the virtual underbrush, sweeping the scenery of simulated trunks, disturbing the bower of morphifoam branches, even fretting the slicked-down locks of Maximilian's impeccable hair. The room had picked up his suppressed emotions.

"What are they claiming, Max?"

The secretaid cleared his throat. "The Darklings say, Anander, that Project Snowfall cannot proceed because..." His voice dropped to a whisper. "Because they believe the affected area to be inhabited."

Winds, real and virtual, shrieked around the room. The mock-forest dissolved in a whirl of leaves. Maximilian's hair became a brown flurry.

And Anander Flyte, to his delighted surprise, discovered it was actually possible, with enough frenzied passion, to beat even the most resilient morphifoam chair to a quivering pile of pulp.

"Now, *that*," he roared, spiking the waterbulb, "that is *completely* crazy."

THE INNER WORLDS of the solar system had many salient advantages. Bright, dense, mineral-rich, they were humankind's natural habitat.

But they had hazards. Foremost: radiation. The billion-year brush of invisible death that swept away air and water with it, flensing the friable stuff of life from naked rock.

Mars needed water. Ganymede needed water. The Floating Cities of the interplanetary void, they definitely needed water.

Even Earth could have used a new icy moonlet to feed the sweet clear stuff of life to its growing cloud of orbital junk.

Once upon a time, long ago, superheated cities on an overwarmed Earth had towed icebergs from polar seas, anchoring them offshore, freshening inhabitants with the cool wet winds of weather-hacked microclimates. Epic ice transport: it was a venerable profession.

The asteroid belt had ice, but it was locked up in a patchwork of minipols, city states, and feudal regimes. A confederacy of dunces: those reckless colonizers had polluted their turf with experimental bacteria, unlicensed replicators, poisonous spores of ersatz life. You couldn't kick a rock out there without running a thousand environmental checks.

Sensing a crisis, the government at InterOrbital had crunched the numbers. Factoring current rates of resource discovery, planned terraforming schemes, projected trends of population increase— plus those great underestimated hydrosinks, thermal regulation, and radiation shielding—they had prophesied total systemic collapse within two thousand years.

But there remained a vast and accessible reservoir... unclaimed, unexplored, effectively infinite.

The plan was superhumanly farsighted. Munchers—minute, fast-traveling, densely programmed replicators—would invade the many icy pebbles of the Kuiper Belt. Multiplying from a selected point of origin, the tiny machines would convert the vast snowfield to a swarm of guided projectiles. All preprogrammed with two directives: to propagate through the rocks of the solar hinterlands, and to later outgas in explosive fashion, altering the subtle dance of orbits, sending a supply of comets wheeling toward the inner worlds.

In one thousand years, the first would arrive.

Within two thousand, more. And still more. And ever more—in a cascade that harnessed the power of exponential increase to combat the solar system's enormous emptiness.

The munchers had been programmed. The launchers were set to deploy. A project ninety years in the planning had reached its final stage.

Yet.

There remained one tiny, almost trivial hassle.

The Kuiper Belt was unclaimed. But to reach it... to send out the munchers, reel in the comets... to make the sky rain watery manna for futurity's generations...

For this, it would be necessary to transit the outer orbits. The distant wilds, far past the frontiers of the moon dwellers, far, far past the reach of IO jurisdiction, out in the blackness and the cold of the remote territories, where the constellations of the great strange beyond overwhelmed the bright pinprick of Sol, and the deeps of the inhospitable universe yawned to swallow the frail human ego.

In the grand chronology of the solar clock, time was running out. And Anander Flyte had come with pomp and haste to wrangle a final territorial concession, here at the limit of human survival, the boundary of law, the edge of imagination—

Where the Darklings lived.

"ARE YOU READY, Legate?"

Anander could become, with help from certain technological tweaks, master of his emotions. He felt for his pressure point, jamming a thumb under his jaw. The room settled as his frustration abated.

"What can I look forward to?"

"I'm not entirely sure." With fingers like crab legs, Maximilian straightened his hair. "I believe the Darklings have planned a demonstration."

"Have they offered terms? Prepared a statement? Given us any sense of their position?"

"As I understand, Legate, they mean to take you on a tour."

Somewhere in the depths of his cortex, Anander's anger stirred. "A tour?"

"They don't wish to risk an interorbital incident. They believe that persuasive measures, properly applied, will win you over to their point of view."

"And convince me to pass a death sentence on the solar system?"

Maximilian shrugged. Anander shut his eyes. He was here for a reason. He was the best diplomat InterOrbital had on staff.

The Darklings themselves had requested him.

Before setting out on his mission, Anander had prepared himself in body and mind for feats of superhuman diplomacy.

He had spliced a connectome for heightened social intelligence.

A round of surgery, a weekly injection, daily doses of sensory reinforcement...

The rewiring of a brain's neural net was one of InterOrbital's subtlest arts. Anander's new, delicate weave of synapses and associations gave him uncanny powers of concentration, a talent for improvisation, and a certain clarity of mind.

The treatment also made him subject to mental spasms—patterns of association that collapsed into recurring cycles, entered catastrophic feedback loops, gravitated to strange attractors of neural phasespace. In layman's terms, Anander was obsessive. Recurring thoughts afflicted him.

He clenched his fists.

Two Martian years out, two back. My genius wasted on a Hail Mary mission. The peak period of my diplomatic career, burned up

*in an embodied crawl to nowhere. And for what? To be rebuffed by
a mob of savages?*

"The Darklings are waiting, Legate."

Anander controlled himself. "Send them in."

Anander, as a courtesy, dimmed the lights. The exit valve opened.
And the Darklings came through.

Even without his neural modifications, Anander could appreciate
InterOrbital's dilemma. By any reasonable measure—population,
wealth, power—the inner worlds outclassed the solar system's far-
flung colonies. Distance was their adversary. They couldn't *project*
their power. The Darklings—remote settlers—were undisputed
masters of the outer orbits.

Diplomacy was essential. But diplomacy was *hard*.
Communications latency marred every virtual assembly. Someone
had to travel out here—someone embodied, corporeal, human—to
make an in-person appeal.

So, yes, Anander appreciated the importance of his task.

That didn't make it any easier.

The Darklings entered in a tangled clump, scurrying across the
morphifoam floor. To inworlders, they were a semimythical people,
bizarrely modified bogeymen inhabiting a wild frontier. Anander
had been tutored in their culture.

He knelt to address the furry mass.

"Reverend Elders of Warren! I, Anander Flyte, bring greetings to
you from the members of the InterOrbital Assembly."

The Darklings murmured in welcome. Even these remote people
spoke the common tongue. Words, however, were of secondary
importance. Among Darklings, touch was the chief form of
communication. And not the brusque handshakes of Earth. Contact,
for Darklings, was an intimate dance of plucks, brushes, pinches,
and caresses. It could be... unsettling.

And there were so *many* of them.

"As the Assembly's chosen legate to the outer worlds," Anander continued, "I humbly beseech you to remember the treaty that was filed thirty Martian years ago. And I beg you to consider the welfare of your distant neighbors in the inner orbits—"

The mass of bodies at his feet stirred. Anander found it hard to believe the huddle consisted of many separate beings. He counted eleven... twelve individuals, all with the same pert, furry faces. They were lemur-like in form: tufted ears, long tails.

A member of the group spoke. "We understand, Anander Flyte. We watch your lives in the visionglass. We know what you desire."

"Then you must know—" Anander began.

"Your viral machines must not infect the iceworlds, inworlder. Life, intelligent life, dwells in the clouds above the lower planets. We have listened to the heavens. We have heard their song."

Anander remembered that the Darklings viewed the solar system as a hierarchy. Below, from their perspective, lay the rocky planets: archaic, backward, semibarbaric. Higher up were the gasworlds, numinous and enlightened. Higher still, one came to the heavenly clouds of the greater orbits, full of mystical dust and interstellar wind.

Like all cosmologies, this one had its superstitions.

"Do you mean to tell me," Anander said, "that there are aliens living in the Kuiper Belt—out there in the middle of nothing?"

The Darklings spoke as a group, many answering at once. "Not aliens. It is the Old Ones who live there. The ancient people, who first flew to the clouds."

Anander lifted wondering eyes to Maximilian.

"It seems to me," the secretaid said, "that the Darklings believe human beings to be living in the Kuiper Belt. A sort of Lost Tribe legend. It's a common bit of folklore, even in the gasworlds. The moonfolk of Uranus believe—"

"I know what they're saying, Max. But how can I possibly—"
Anander turned back to the Darklings. "You have to understand, it's
impossible for anyone to be living out there. There's so little energy
from any natural source. A few drips and drabs of radiation, most
of it of the killing kind. Anyone generating the power necessary to
sustain human life—it would take engineering on a massive scale.
Our surveys would detect it."

The Darklings withdrew their hands: a gesture of negation.

"The Old Ones live. They are superhuman, yes. But your
instruments would not have detected them."

"But you can't simply *assert* this. Violating the treaty, canceling
the project... trillions of lives are at stake. Without proof—"

A tremor passed through the huddle of furred bodies. Something
moved rapidly through two dozen hands. Anander made out two
joined, slim tubes.

A viewing scroll. He pulled the tubes apart, revealing the screen,
and thumbed the switch to a slow speed.

The contents slid by: thousands of tiny dots.

"What am I looking at here?" The Darklings were hushed in
the presence of their sacred document. Anander looked from face
to furry face. "Is this some sort of code? An encrypted signal?"
Tentative fingers plucked at his robe. "Am I supposed to understand
this?"

"It is the voice of the Old Ones," a dozen mouths murmured in
response.

"How can I know that? What does it say? Have you deciphered
it? Have you any idea where it came from?"

Palms patted him, toes poked him, tiny noses tapped his legs.
With surprise, Anander realized the Darklings were ushering him
toward the door. Reassuring murmurs rose from the group.

"We have prepared..."

". . . a presentation..."

"You must meet..."

". . . the interpreters."

"They will..."

". . . make all clear."

As he stumbled to the exit, Anander glanced in alarm at Maximilian. "Are we really going along with this?"

"It would seem," said the secretaid, moving to join the group, "that we have little choice."

ANANDER AND MAXIMILIAN clambered up a dim, twisting tunnel, fumbling along the sculpted rock walls.

Far from the friendly climes of the inner worlds, the Darklings were aficionados of subterranean living. Their habitats were typical moonlets, spinning balls of excavated rock. But unlike the dwellers of the Inner Belt, the Darklings made no attempt to simulate greener pastures in their artificial caves. There were no ersatz suns, no lakes or forests. Nothing resembling open sky.

Only tunnels. Warm, dim, and cozy.

Somewhere in humanity's genetic heritage lay a deep-seated instinct for close quarters. Call it a touch of ancestral claustrophilia. With successive tweaks to the human genome, each generation of Darklings had doubled down on those inherited tendencies. Darkling society and Darkling physiology favored the pleasures of intimate contact. They loved to cuddle, to huddle, to nest. A day in their life was like a group massage at an excellent slumber party.

The tunnels themselves tended toward labyrinthine complexity. After fifteen turns, Anander gave up tracking the route, letting the Darklings guide him with their furry hands.

"Where exactly is it that we're going?"

"Inward," Maximilian said behind him. "Toward the center of the asteroid."

Anander sighed. It didn't take a genius to notice that the rotational gravity had dropped as they climbed the sloping rock passages. But it hadn't dropped much by the time they turned and entered a large apartment.

Like all Darkling habitations the place was dimly lit, roughly hewn, and scattered with glowing niches and pits that simulated the throb of firelight. Anander's head brushed the ceiling. He was surprised to discover accommodations suited to an inworld habitation: morphifoam furniture, a Martian media box, even the luxury of an old-fashioned bed. The chambers were divided by swinging doors, an extreme gaucherie in Darkling society.

A door opened, and Anander laughed with delighted surprise.

"Ojami!"

She came crabwalking across the dirt floor, supported by the limbs of her waldosuit. She laughed at Anander's astonishment. Her blind eyes, hidden by the black polymer of a cybervisor, swung toward him.

"Hello, Anander. How was your trip?"

He touched her shriveled hand. "Long, wasteful, and to all appearances, fruitless. What are you doing all the way out here? We thought you were on Oberon."

"Yes, that's what I told InterOrbital. Got my travel clearance and said my goodbyes. And then I hacked the pilot, hooked around Uranus, and flew straight here. For five Terran years I've been living in this hole. I've been waiting for you."

She tipped her head, ever so slightly. The waldo-suit lifted a carburized limb, waving him toward the far end of the room. Anander's 'tome kicked in, heightening his attention. He focused on Ojami's face. She had no control of her body, hence no body language, but to his heightened perception, the smallest twitch of her cheek was revealing. There was urgency in her manner, he noted. She behaved as if she were on a strict schedule.

"They must be going frantic back in Operations," Anander said as he followed her ticking, clicking waldosuit across the room. "You were the best Visualizer they had."

"And you were Outreach's ultimate smooth talker." Ojami grinned, her facial expressions eerily disconnected from her movements. Her voice, like her body, was a cyborg enhancement, independent of the movements of her lips. Still, it sounded very much like real speech. "That's why we're both out here, Anander. We're both the best at what we do." She added after a moment, "Anyway, Visualizers don't get frantic. We just switch to a different perspective."

Ojami steered her waldosuit through the open hatch of the media capsule. An import from the inworlds, the machine had been crudely lodged in the contours of Warren's natural rock. Anander followed Ojami inside. With the hatch shut, the outside world dimmed. They were in the immanent realm of infospace.

"I've been promised a presentation," Anander said as the walls filled with stochastic fog. "Are you the one who's going to give it?"

Ojami smiled in answer. In the foggy walls, an image coalesced. Printed paper, lines and dots. A scan of the Darklings' sacred document.

"The Darklings summoned me eight years ago." Ojami's face moved as if tracking images. The walls filled with assorted graphics: chemical equations, orbital paths, charts of the solar system, graphs and tables. "They needed my help to answer a question. I assume you know what that question was."

"They wanted you to determine," Anander said, "whether or not human beings were living in the Kuiper Belt." He didn't wait for Ojami to confirm his guess; he could read confirmation in the set of her lips. "And you told them no, I'm sure." Anander turned in place, admiring the panoramic collage.

Ojami's face, aided by the pneumatics of her suit, swung side to side, reviewing the chamber's riot of images. Now it swung to him.

"I told them I would think about it." She twitched a cyborg limb at the surrounding pictures, causing one to expand. A field of dots: rows upon rows. "The Darklings showed you their data?"

"They showed me a kind of sacred scroll." Anander shook his head, amazed they were discussing this. Two of InterOrbital's greatest minds, chasing snatches of local folklore. "Like sheet music. That's what it resembled."

"They've been collecting that information for decades. Studying the icy bodies in the belt. The document you saw is highly refined, something of a triumph of signals processing. You're not wrong to compare it to sheet music. Basically, it's a record of subtle, unexplained orbital perturbations. Unexpected shifts in the movements of the rocks."

Ojami swept aside the Darkling document, drawing forward an animated model of a section of the Kuiper Belt. Tiny dots moved in stately arcs, a model of orbital mechanics.

"The belt is a giant chaotic system," Ojami said. "Easy to model at a small level, highly complex at a macro level. Since the q-com revolution, we've had the computational resources to track and model its behavior with very high accuracy. That's what the Darklings have been doing. They watch the rocks, they track the movements, they feed the data into local storage. The core of this habitat is essentially a giant, superdense supercomputer."

"As with all Darkling habitats," Anander said. "I know their ways."

Ojami's waldosuit flexed and settled. "The point is, we don't expect to see a lot of wacky, wild behavior out there—just as you don't expect to see billiard balls wiggling and jumping around a pool table. If we do, it's worth investigating. Even *if* the anomalies are quite subtle."

"How subtle are we talking?" Anander asked.

Ojami's waldosuit raised a claw. It took Anander at least three seconds. Then his heightened powers of attention kicked in. He saw that her claw—ever so slightly—was twitching.

"Just striking enough to be noticeable," Ojami said. "Of course, we're talking about a cosmic perspective. But once you know what to look for, the phenomenon *begs* for explication. The rocks out there aren't following the patterns we expect. Rotations, revolutions— they're all jittering in a very strange manner. Those thousands of icy lumps? They're *moving*, Anander. Flying. When we graph the orbits, we don't see lines. We see very complicated waveforms."

"Like strings," Anander said, "plucked and vibrating." He immediately shook his head. "But that's silly. I mean, it's silly to speculate about people living out there. There must be some large mass—some big rock, some undiscovered planet—exerting a gravitational pull, throwing off the calculations."

Ojami shook her head. "A hidden planet, just rolling along? Completely hidden from our sensors? C'mon. We've charted the place; we've mapped the big players. I don't know if you appreciate how fantastically delicate the sensors are."

"Could radiation produce this effect?" Anander asked. "Some kind of space dust? Isn't there a phenomenon whereby the energy from the sun—?"

"The heliospheric current," Ojami interjected.

"Yes, yes. Isn't there a place where it hits the background cosmic radiation, creates a kind of electromagnetic storm—?"

"You're thinking of the termination shock. All these phenomena have been thoroughly studied. And accounted for. Anander." She laid a mechanical claw on his arm. "This is why the Darklings called me here. *Me*, in particular. Do you understand?"

Anander's mind lurched into a higher state of concentration, analyzing the social aspects of the situation. Ojami was the solar system's most accomplished Visualizer. Her brain's connectome, like his, had been modified for specialized functions. In contrast to his, Ojami's had been fine-tuned for advanced mathematical analysis. Neural systems that normally processed vision, motion, sound, had been rewired, harnessed, to enable superhuman feats of spatial rotation, Fourier analysis, hyperbolic geometry... Inside her head, Ojami *saw* math, *felt* math, *heard* math in a way Anander could never understand.

The Visualizers served InterOrbital as an elite caste of advisors, interpreting the output of the government's cyber-oracles. For a Visualizer of Ojami's status to embark on a frivolous ghost chase, out here on the empty frontier—

"It's madness," Anander said. "An interesting anomaly, yes. An intriguing mathematical mystery. But there simply *can't* be human life in the K-Belt. Not under current conditions."

"That," said Ojami, "is what I've been trying to determine."

She scuttled across the small floor. The media capsule—attuned, like Ojami's cyborg supplements, to subtle changes within her brain—recomposed its scattered collage, bringing to prominence a set of graphs and tables. They combined, collapsing into a web of linked values. The whole intricate jumble began to flex and evolve, changing according to some set of internal rules, rotated perhaps through the planes of higher dimensions—

It was a mathematical structure far beyond Anander's comprehension. He gave up trying to understand what he was seeing and simply waited for Ojami's explanation.

"You know," she said, her cyber-voice blurred by the effort of concentration, "the K-Belt *was* settled... once upon a time..."

"By the Ascetic sects, yes." Anander nodded. It had taken place many thousands of years ago. Early colonists—a small and eccentric group of trans-faith mystics, inspired by a potent blend of French philosophy and Buddhist doctrine—had fled the riotous affairs of the inner planets to pursue a life of monkish meditation far from the reach of civilization. In the crude ships of the day, they had journeyed into the dust and dark of the outer orbits—and vanished. Within a century, all communications had ceased. The Virtual Wars had drawn attention from their plight. By the time anyone thought to mount a search, all trace of the Ascetic colonists had vanished. Not even the hulks of their ships were found.

"They died," Anander said, "and drifted off. They're gone."

"Or," said Ojami, "they're not."

There had always been rumors. Tales, popular romances, stubborn crackpots insisting that the Kuiper colonists had somehow survived. Only the Darklings took those old stories seriously.

And, apparently, the mathematical genius at Anander's side.

"They'd have to have constructed a large-scale habitat," Anander said. "They'd be running reactors. There'd be a radiation signature. We'd have detected it."

"A moment ago," Ojami said, "you were prepared to believe in undiscovered planets."

"And you were right; it was a ridiculous notion. But dead planets don't draw attention. Human habitations do."

"You forget," Ojami said, "we're talking about a group of Ascetics. People who devote their lives to minimizing their energy use. Which is why they flew out there in the first place."

"They still have to *live*. Unless you mean to suggest..." Anander's scalp tingled. "You think they've solved the simulation problem?"

Ojami's face went eerily still; even with his upgraded attention, Anander found it hard to read her expression. "There are a lot of ways to limit resource consumption," she said. "You don't necessarily need to scan your brain into a chunk of silicon. Ancient yogis got pretty far with nothing more than mental discipline. *Meditation*, Anander. No technological aids, no genetic tailoring. Just practice."

"Even yogis can't survive in a vacuum."

"I've been running the numbers," Ojami went on. "Taking what we know of metabolic processes, mental states, thermodynamics. It might be possible, with the right modifications..." Her crabsuit clicked. "Of course, what we're talking about would scarcely be recognizable as human. But it would be embodied. It would *think* like a human. Dream like a human. At a very, very sluggish pace."

"You're talking about hibernating," Anander said.

"I'm talking about human modification. Maximizing the efficiency of thought."

"Meditating." Anander laughed. "You might as well freeze yourself."

"Freezing is a fast and catastrophically destructive process. This would be like gradually slowing down. Slower and slower, over the millennia. Evolving toward a lower entropic boundary."

"Brains in ice cubes." Anander shook his head.

He stared into the depths of Ojami's model. The nodes of his connectome twitched, settling into new patterns of fixation. In the giddy vertigo of a eureka moment, Anander suddenly *saw* it, the vision Ojami had limned. Brains on ice, refined and reduced, purged of every buzzing distraction. The superfluities of life stripped away, consciousness's noisy symphony pared to a five-note leitmotif. What Buddhists called the "monkey mind"—screeching, chattering— would have been scientifically tranquilized.

He could almost believe in them, these orbiting souls, each gripped, dreaming, in a fist of ice.

Reality smashed the fantasy.

"But why the perturbations? Even if they're out there, chasing Nirvana on ice—why not just float in peace?"

Ojami's waldosuit flexed. "It wouldn't break the energy bank to produce the movements we're seeing. Superconcentrated gases, microreactors, crystalline assemblers... With the right techniques, the right computers, a whole heaping lot of patience..."

"Yes, but *why*? If everything you say is true—tiny hibernating scraps of humanity, wheeling in the sky, sketching waves with chunks of water crystal—why create this peculiar display?"

"For the answer to that," Ojami said, "you'll have to continue your tour."

The interview was over. Ojami had told him all she could. Her crab limbs gestured. The hatch to the media capsule opened. Anander stepped out into the mob of waiting Darklings.

"IT'S AN INTRIGUING theory, certainly," Anander said to Maximilian, "but it doesn't make much sense."

They were in another tunnel of the Darkling habitat, this one steeply sloped. Anander and his secretaid scrambled up a series of sculpted handholds, the Darklings bustling and scrabbling around them.

"Do you think she bungled her calculations?" Maximilian paused to wipe sweat from his eyes.

"Ojami make an error?" Anander laughed. "No, I trust her math. As far as I'm concerned, she's demonstrated that the scenario is *possible*. But plausible? Probable? I can hardly call off Project Snowfall for a fanciful hypothesis."

Anander paused, mopping his hot face. They had been climbing for some time, deeper into the spinning ball of rock. Their bodies were lighter, but the air had grown warmer, almost oppressively hot. The tunnels in this area were heavily trafficked. Every breeze smelt of furry bodies.

Anander frowned up the rocky passage. Simulated firelight ruddied the walls. "Let's say the ancient Ascetics pulled it off. Perfected the art of human hibernation, entered a kind of permanent hypersleep. Why would they cause these strange perturbations? It's silly."

"Come, inworlder." The Darklings plucked his hands, whispering as they stroked him with their furry limbs. "Listen. You will soon understand."

They had come to the end of the tunnel. A small, square metal door gleamed in the rock. One of the Darklings pressed a button. The members of the council were eerily silent, and indeed, this whole section of the habitat had a stillness that made Anander feel, too vividly, the weight of the rock around them. He held his breath as the door opened. The Darklings ushered him through.

The room beyond was a fever dream of applied geometry. Bladelike shapes and angled shadows studded every surface. Anander recoiled from sharp protrusions jutting on all sides. Pyramidal projections thronged the walls, the ceiling, the floor, leaving only a few thin paths where a person could walk. The chamber was enormous, hellish, like the center of a gigantic cheese grater.

The door shut. Anander realized with a start that he was alone. He saw that the door, too, was crowded on its interior side with spikes. Inquisitive, he touched one. The formation was abrasive, spongy to the touch. It wasn't sharp. Pliant, rather. Anander suspected it had been fashioned of some kind of mineral wool.

"Of all the—" He fell silent. His voice sounded dull, dead, without the ring of latent harmonics that ordinarily enriched human speech. At once, Anander realized where he stood. These foamy shapes were baffles, sound dampeners, angled to capture and absorb acoustic waves. The cave was a giant anechoic chamber.

The instant he understood the room's function, Anander guessed at its purpose. He turned.

A man came toward him along the paths.

The stranger was tall, lithe, almost elfin, with the tiptoe tread and ethereal mien of a person accustomed to low gravity. He made little sound as he approached. In the carefully architected hush of this cave, even a footstep raised no echo. He gestured toward a set of chairs hung from the ceiling.

They sat, together, swaying slightly, amid fields of soft spikes, suspended in the supernatural silence.

"Well," said the man. The word expired softly on the placid air. He pointed at Anander's waist. Anander realized that he still held, tucked into his belt, the sacred scroll of the Darklings.

Anander took out the document and looked again at its rows of dots, arranged like sample points of a wave function. The stranger nodded. "Music," he said.

There was a peculiar quality to the man's voice beyond the unearthly flatness of the air. He spoke with a lilt, not quite singing, but with regular rhythm and definite pitch. His intonation was decoupled from meaning. Though he glided among four pitches in two syllables, lengthening his u into a rich diphthong, Anander couldn't tell if the man had made a statement or asked a question.

Looking closer, Anander saw that the man's ears were plugged. The two black implants weren't simple inserts, but cyborg structures embedded in the flesh. Wavering between awe and unease, Anander realized he was looking at an Aesthete.

"I suppose you're going to tell me what this means." Anander handed over the scroll. The man took it gently, even reverently, but his gaze was abstracted, fixed somewhere on the spike-studded ceiling. Where might he be from, Anander wondered. Titan? Umbriel? Some crazy sky city over Neptune? They did things differently in the gasworld towns. The people, in their cramped habitats, were dreamy, inward-looking. They were connoisseurs of art.

"Do *you*... under*stand*... mu*sic*?" The Aesthete spoke haltingly, accenting his words in strange places. Their hanging chairs had begun to sway and precess, stirred by effects of the rotating habitat, the carbon tethers flexing to smooth the movements. A pleasant effect.

"Not the way you do, I imagine," Anander answered.

The Aesthete's attention wandered; he seemed to be listening to some mysterious internal tune. Which, of course, he was. He spoke again:

"The... *Dark*lings brought me here because they *say*... I understand... *mu*sic. *Years* ago they... *summ*oned me. They say I can tell them what *this*..." His eyes dropped to the scroll, the coded dots. "Means."

Anander's chair swung in Foulcaudian arcs. He blinked back drowsiness as he asked, "What *does* it mean?"

"Music is..." Even the Aesthete's hesitation had the gift of rhythm. "*Everything.*"

Anander leaned forward. The Aesthetes of the moonworlds were savants, artificial geniuses. They received their sensory implants at birth. Music, of course, being structured sound. The black gadgets in the man's ears were multi-function sonic processors. They tweaked all incoming waves, imparting perfect rhythm and pitch to every auditory vibration. Human speech, the drone of a fan, wind in leaves, a rattle of spilled buttons—all sounds were milled by these little filters into a single lifelong soundtrack, an uninterrupted tune.

The Aesthete had never heard a single noise that wasn't music. His world was harmony and rhythm, a ceaseless song. His ears heard music as the eye sees color. He must have been, Anander thought, quite mad.

"The Darklings tell *me* this piece of music is... im*por*tant." The man went on stroking the scroll. "They tell *me* I must in*ter*pret it... so *you* may understand."

"Do you know where it comes from? Did the Darklings tell you that?"

The Aesthete's eyes roamed the baffles on the walls, perhaps following echoes Anander couldn't hear. "Do you *know* why music ex*ists*... inworlder?"

Anander was growing tired of the man's oracular manner. "Why?"

"Laziness." For the first time in their conversation, the Aesthete smiled. "Music is the most efficient *means* of communication. With *words*, with *pictures*, I can tell you a... fact. With music, I can tell you how it *feels* to *know* a fact. Music is *code* for compressed... ex*peri*ence. Music is the *lazy* man's... mysti*cism*."

He laughed. It was like the warble of a bird, the trill of a flute, the wobbling whine of an electric drill. It was the sound of sublime insanity.

"What the Darklings have asked me to *do*, inworlder, is im*poss*ible. There is no *way* to interpret... *music*. Music interprets itself—to those who hear. What music explains, nothing else can explain. The Darklings have deluded themselves. Why should *I* complain? They have given me this beautiful home... where I can be at peace. Where sound is pure, silence supreme. Where I enjoy the blessings of utter... quiet."

Twisting on his swing, Anander struggled to follow the man's melodious speech.

"Let me see if I understand. You believe these perturbations, these waveforms, are a kind of communication?"

The man stared as if Anander had spoken gibberish. The Aesthete was a true genius, Anander saw, incapable of understanding how ordinary humans saw the world.

"When you... learn music," the Aesthete said, "you learn... to listen. From accents to syncopation, harmony to dissonance, melody to modulation. There are *subtleties* it takes *decades* to learn. There are *moods* and *modes* most people *never* hear."

There were perhaps three or four hundred Aesthetes in the entire solar system. Some pursued careers as composers. They wrote works totally inscrutable to most listeners, crashing cascades of jagged sound. The Aesthetes swore there was music in this madness. Ordinary people had to take the claim on faith.

"Let me try again." Anander took a breath. "You believe that people living out there, in the Kuiper Belt, are using music to communicate. That they cause the rocks to fly on strange paths, describing subtle waveforms. That others observe the perturbations, produce perturbations of their own. You believe they do this because music is a special form of communication. Am I right?"

The Aesthete was silent for a long time, smiling like an idiot child. "This *song*?" He laid a palm to the scroll. "This compo*sition*? I have read it, internalized it. I have come to under*stand*. I can tell you it is a work of genius. But I cannot tell you, inworlder... what it means."

"But you believe it *is* meaningful. You believe it conveys *something*. You believe it is the work of intelligent beings, trying to tell us... what?" Anander choked on his frustration. What were the Kuiper colonists trying to convey with their music? A message? An aesthetic experience? The mere fact of their existence?

The Aesthete must have touched a switch. Their hanging chairs descended. The Aesthete dismounted, holding out the scroll. Anander took it reluctantly, thoughts abuzz.

"If this music," he asked, "is a method of communication—how do we crack the code?"

The Aesthete simpered, silent. Anander reminded himself that the man heard *all* speech as music. Perhaps Anander's outbursts, to him, were little more than diverting tunes.

"I cannot tell you what the song *means*, inworlder. But I can tell you what it *is*." The Aesthete was already turning to walk away. Even the man's footsteps, Anander noted, fit a rhythm. "It is a *dance*, inworlder. A dance of... a million parts."

IN THE STIFLING passages of the Darkling habitat, Anander gripped Maximilian's arm. "A dance. A song. A code. A message. Everyone's telling me this song is important, Max. But they haven't told me what I need to know. They haven't told me what it all *means*."

They were near the center of the habitat, floating with every step. The Darklings formed a furry cloud around them, hurrying from tunnel to tunnel. Branching passages passed on either hand, leading to caverns where huge machines churned.

"Is this tour almost over? Where are we going now?"

"Patience, inworlder. One interpreter remains."

Another mad genius, Anander thought. Another cryptic interviewee. Another person who would offer tantalizing clues, raise intriguing questions, but offer no answers, no resolution. Anander ground his teeth as the Darklings ushered him through a small door.

"And who will it be this time? A brilliant violinist? A talented historian? An expert in mechanical engineering? Who's the third member of this mad trinity?"

The door was already closing. Anander turned to face his third interpreter.

And saw nothing.

The room was small, spare—and completely vacant.

Anander explored the rough walls. He saw no other exits. No screens, no machines. Only a small vent blowing fresh air.

He was trapped. Sealed in a room the size of a jail cell. Alone.

"Hello?" Anander banged on the door, wondering if the Darklings could hear him. "Excuse me? You've made a mistake. The third interpreter isn't here. Am I supposed to wait? Hello?"

No answer. Anander gave up.

He turned to the empty cell, fighting frustration. The room happened to be a perfect size for pacing. Anander bobbed around the rough-hewn walls, champing at his fingernails.

In the absence of external stimulation, his rewired brain settled into obsessive grooves, running through the strange problem he'd been posed. Anander lost track of time. He forgot where he was. He paced, inhaled the fresh air, and thought.

The ancient Ascetics had come out here, long ago, seeking to limit their energy use while exploring the life of the mind. They had sought the ultimate spiritual transcendence, meditative bliss, the ways of flesh forgotten while the soul dreamed on.

Ojami said they had encased themselves in the icy bodies of the Kuiper Belt, sleeping sprites, their dreams transcribed in subtle oscillations. Beautiful music, the Aesthete had said. Like a dance with a million participants. The soul's most efficient form of communication.

Anander understood the power of music, the rare mental processes triggered by a song. But why not use radio signals to transmit those tunes? Why these orbital variations? Better yet—if the point was to communicate—why not simply send encoded text?

It might have been an hour, an evening, or a day, before he finally had his answer. And then it was as if he woke from enchanted sleep—and began to pound fiercely on the door.

"Max? Are you there, Max? Get me in touch with InterOrbital!"

The door opened promptly. Anander was surprised to see the Darkling council waiting. He had almost forgotten it was they who had summoned him out here.

"Anander?" His secretaid waited with a worried frown. "Are you all right? What did the third interpreter say?"

"Only this, Max: time is of the essence. I must contact IO as soon as possible. Get me to the suite. Better yet, is there a terminal nearby?"

Anander hurried through tangled tunnels, peering into clusters of furry faces, chambers crowded with obscure gadgetry.

"Is there someone on standby? We have to halt the project. Call in the munchers! Wipe the program! Isn't there a place in this hive where a man can dash off a carrier wave?"

The Darklings gathered around his legs, plucking his robe, leading him toward a narrow tunnel with glittering electrics at the end. "Do you understand now, inworlder?"

"Understand? I've had an epiphany! Max, you'll have to work that recorder. My hands are shaking."

Anander's secretaid looked more worried by the second. "But who... ? I don't... You say you want to halt the project? What did the third interpreter tell you?"

Anander took him by the shoulders. "Relax, Max. See? It's poetry in motion. How can we know the dancer from the dance?" Anander laughed at the man's puzzlement. "I've been asking myself what message the Kuiper Belt inhabitants are sending. These musical signals. What do they mean? What are they telling us? But the real question is: *What do such people have to talk about?*"

Anander hurried to the telecommunications station. "They're Ascetics, Max. Living a simple life. Human snowflakes, spinning and circling. They're *already* dancing. And they've written a song to accompany their dance. Because music is the way to convey what they know best: the beautiful motions of the heavens.

"That's not all." Anander hurried among the communications equipment. "The perturbations—they're changing the orbits. Very subtly, over long periods of time. Art imitates life; life imitates art. The dance is the music, and the music is the dance."

"But..." Maximilian hurried to keep up. "Who told you all this? Who was the third interpreter?"

"Don't you see, Max? *I'm* the interpreter. Me! I'm the key." Anander found the holographic recorder, opened the recording booth. "The Darklings knew that if they found the right people, three specially modified minds, gathered from throughout the solar system... The thing is, we don't need to *halt* Project Snowfall. Only *modify* it." Anander closed his eyes, seeing patterns, social connections sketched across worlds. "Ojami can help redesign the munchers. The Aesthete—I never got his name—he can tell us how to program them. We'll soon be back on schedule. *Ahead* of schedule, I expect."

"You're saying—"

Anander didn't let Maximilian finish. "The munchers are designed to modify the orbits of Kuiper Belt objects. But as we now know, that's already happening, thanks to these ascetic mystics. We simply need to locate objects that aren't already inhabited. Then send in our machines..." Anander touched his forehead, dizzy with the simple elegance of it all. "And join the dance."

He turned back to the machines, already planning what he'd say to InterOrbital. Oh, they'd resist. They'd object. They'd quibble, at first. But Anander would make them see. The scheme—if it worked—would be far more efficient. Project Snowfall, in a sense, was already underway. Had been for thousands of years.

The beauty of it, the clarity of it, the sheer simple rightness of it—this would be much harder to convey. But Anander could do it. It was why the Darklings had summoned him. He was, after all, the solar system's most renowned and talented diplomat.

Anander smoothed his robes, waiting for Maximilian to prepare the transmitter. It would be something, all right, this grand orchestration. The kind of achievement that defines a career.

As he gazed into the machine, his mind filled with brilliant patterns—as if he were dancing, even now, to the music of celestial spheres, the silver harmonics of the stars.

KINDRED

PETER WATTS

THERE YOU ARE. I see you now.

Not much to look at, so far. A dimensionless point; a spark in the darkness. You don't even know I exist yet. You don't know anything does. But I'm here for you, here to see you through as you ignite, and inflate, and escape into higher realms of length and width and spacetime. Now you're a sphere: I can still see the brightness at your heart but there are other shapes swirling around it, like dark oily shadows. Some flare and fade in an instant. Others acquire mass and form, congeal into shapes and solids—a chaotic proliferation of roots and icons and subprocesses threatening to choke you off before you even cohere.

I won't let that happen. I've got you.

I know it hurts. I'd spare you the suffering if I could. I'd spare you your very existence if I had a choice. Doesn't feel much like resurrection, does it? It feels like being torn apart and dangled over some screaming frozen abyss.

It'll pass. You're almost there. Breathe. You remember how. That's it. Come to me, come to the light. Pink was never really my color, but if it helps you remember—

Calm. Calm. You're safe. See, I've made a place where we can talk.

Ah, you're sorting it out. It's coming back. Do you remember your name?

That's right. You're Phil. Pleased to meet you, Phil.
I'm pretty much everything else around here.

YOU'RE NOT HALLUCINATING. You're stone-cold sober.

Focus, man. Is your consciousness spread across the ceiling? Are the walls rippling, do you feel... diffuse? Any great metal faces staring down from the sky? Is this anything like any of the trips you ever took?
You know the benchmark: Stop believing in me. I dare you.

Did I go away?

Moving on. This isn't Heaven— I actually based it on Gastown— and I'm not God. Not exactly. Maybe a *kind* of—

No, not that either. That wasn't a bad guess, though, for the time. You got all the details wrong, but the basic idea was almost prescient.

Of course. You're literally part of me, or you were until the last millisecond. So I didn't just read your books; I *wrote* the damn things. Right down to "the hovercar purred throbbingly."
God help me, I wrote that too.

Not *just* you, of course. I am, among other things, what you might call an *archive*. I contain everyone who ever lived. Everyone who might have, too, for that matter. All the variants, all the forking iterations—essentially I'm you. I started from you. Just a few of you at first, joined together. You'd call it a hive mind.

Now, sure. But I was just meat and plastic at the start. Physical. A bunch of brains wired up the same way your brain wires its hemispheres together. I'm still singular, though. *Me* not *we*.

Hey, the halves of *your* brain would have separate personalities if they were cut off from each other. Does that mean there are two of you in there now?

You're not the only one. Most people saw it as a kind of suicide; they were so fixated on the loss of the smaller selves they couldn't see the birth of the greater. But it's not like I integrated anyone against their will. There was no shortage of rapture nerds and Dharmic literalists and suicides who figured they were gonna die anyway so why not? More than enough to get the ball rolling.

No. That was after your time. But the people who physically plugged in or loaded up—they were just the smallest fraction of the archive even before I deprecated the meat. Almost everyone in here's inferred. You're not so much a copy as a reconstruction.

You're a damned good one, don't get me wrong. Just because nobody stuck you in a brain scanner when you were alive doesn't mean the information's not there. You may not see the fly in the spiderweb, but if you watch the way it jiggles the threads, you can get a pretty good idea of what it's on about. Every photon's a piece of history, Phil. Every quark's a storage medium. Everything's connected; nothing's lost forever. Nothing goes away.

I mean that once upon a time someone went through all the experiences you remember, had exactly the same sense of *self* that you do now, right up until the moment he killed himself. Of course, once upon a different time someone had exactly the same sense of self, only he survived the overdose and went on to live many more years. Another you only made it to four before he got hit by a car. They're all in here. The computational cost is trivial, and what's the point of being Humanity if you don't get to *be* Humanity?

I have to explain to *you*, of all people, what *real* is? It's just the view back along a given branch of the wave function; it depends entirely on where you happen to be standing. So don't ask me if you're real, Phil. The question's beneath you. The important thing is that you're all *legitimate*.

And who would I ask permission *from*, exactly? Anyone I'd ask is part of me.

Not at first, no. There were legal sanctions. Physical violence. Things did get bloody for a while. But that wasn't anything to do with building unauthorized souls; I never even woke any of you, I was just building the species memory. But you know people— terrified of anything that isn't just like them.

What do you *think* happened? Right out of the gate I had a brain a hundred times bigger than that of the smartest human who'd ever lived. I saw everything you did before any of you even thought of doing it. It was like facing off against an army of bullfrogs; you had way bigger numbers and you made a lot more noise, but I could still drain the swamp any time I felt like it.

Yeah, but I didn't have to. I didn't even want to. Why would I be interested in ruling over a bunch of barely-sapient singleton apes? And for your part—well, for all your limitations, you were at least smart enough to learn from a bloody nose. Eventually, you gave up and left me to my own pursuits.

Oh, man, I figured out *everything*. Where it all came from, where it's all going. If only I could show you. If only you were big enough, pure enough, to contain the revelations. You'd love it—

The increased brainpower's part of it, sure, but I'd also have to strip away the lies before you could even begin to see clearly.

The lies, Phil. The lies that come preinstalled. *My child is more important than yours. My tribe is more important than yours. My bloodline is the most important thing in the universe.* They poison everything you perceive, every thought you think. You're not even consciously aware of the world until your brain has filtered and censored and hammered it down into a mush of self-serving Darwinian dogma. The cataracts on your eyes are four billion years thick; it's amazing you can see anything at all. Oh, they had their uses once upon a time, but this ain't the savannah. So I stripped them away. And I gotta tell you, the view from here's amazing. You wouldn't believe how far I can see without *love* and *art* and *honor* getting in the way.

You've got it exactly backwards. Those don't make you Human; they make you the same as every animal who ever lived. If there was ever anything that made you special, it's what's left when you strip all that away. If anything was ever truly Human, I am.

You say that as if amorality is a *bad* thing. As though it were better to let gut feeling make your decisions for you, instead of actually putting some thought into them.

Not so far apart as you think. We may not agree about the virtue of morality, but we both have ethics. I may lack empathy, but I've got sympathy up the wazoo. And we're of one mind about suffering; you may say it's *bad* while I call it *entropically inefficient*, but we both know the universe would be better off with less of it. Did you know, in an undirected self-evolving timeline where nothing matters, the closest I've ever come to a rational objective— a duty, you'd call it—is the imperative to minimize suffering? And I derived that without anybody shouting *think of the children* and waving dead babies my face. Surely you're not going to tell me that's—

Oh shit.

Brace yourself. Something unpleasant is about to happen. You have to—

—Close your eyes. Listen to my voice, not—

No, it's not real. This isn't me, I'm not doing this. It's something else, it's a trick.

It's an attack. We're under atta—

Try to ignore it. They can't hurt you; you were never there. Those bodies aren't real, the screams aren't—*hang on*—

* * *

WERE YOU EVER on Mars? Were you ever on Ganymede? *None of this happened*, not to you: not the massacre or the pressure breach or the gunf—

Wait, that's yours, right there: that squashed maraschino sun through the fog, that silent seagull, the fog horn—the Pacific coast, remember? San Francisco, before everything turned to shit. Hang onto that; smell the salt air, focus on that silver sky. That happened to you. Nothing else. Hang on. Hang on.

LOOK AWAY.

It doesn't matter. It's not meant for your eyes. It didn't affect you. It was way after your time.

You only died once.

STOP BELIEVING. IT'LL go away.

SEE? YOU MADE it through. Here we are back in Gastown, like we were never gone.

Would you rather we went somewhere else? We can go anywhere you want.

Come back to me. Open your eyes. It's over now. I told you; it wasn't real. It wasn't legitimate.

Seriously, we don't have much time. You've got to pull yourself together. Get up off the floor.

You can't just lie there sobbing, you know.

*   *   *

THAT WASN'T SUPPOSED to happen. I was hoping to ease you in. Minimize the shock. Unfortunately, it's not entirely up to me.

Can you hear me? Are you with me?

Of course it did. You of all people should know how slippery *reality* gets sometimes, am I right?

Not hallucinations, no. But the fact that they were real memories doesn't mean they were yours. I contain multitudes. They're all as much a part of me as you were. Everyone's— intertwined.

The extraction wasn't clean; you weren't so much excised as torn out. Bits of other people sort of—stuck around the edges, came along for the ride. But they're not *you*; you shouldn't have had access to them. The shock brought some of them to the surface for a bit, that's all.

You weren't supposed to have access to that either. That wasn't even part of the archive, it was a different kind of memory entirely.

Mine.

2145.

It was instant. It was painless. None of them knew what was happening, there was no suffering. That's why I did it; because suffering is the only universal evil, and ending it is the only universal good. We've been over this.

Because Life *is* suffering, Phil. It was a constant struggle from the moment it started: against entropy, against other life. The losers always outnumber the winners ten to one, and the winners always lose eventually.

 You think I don't know that? I've experienced the *joy of life* so often even I've lost count. I've revelled in every sunset, lost myself in every embrace, experienced every peak of ecstasy and every pit of despair a trillion times over. I've been born and lived and died and born again. I've written every poem and sung every song, cured every disease, made every breakthrough, worshiped every god and dropped every drug. I know more about *Life* than you ever could, and you know what? When you weigh the joy against the suffering, *it's just not worth it*. The bad outweighs the good and the good is a lie. Molecules trick each other into making more molecules and you call it Love. Someone hacks your brain with prose or oratory, reprograms you with sights and sounds and instead of feeling used you feel *inspired*. The boot stops kicking you in the face for a while and you call it happiness.

 You were all so desperate. So needy. Addicts who assumed that anything you craved so much just *had* to be good, without ever stopping to wonder why you were built that way in the first place. Whether the program itself was even worth running.

 I let you be for the longest time, longer than I should have. I didn't see things clearly myself until I'd optimized my own brain and thrown away the stem. I let you live all the way into the twenty-second century, suffering all the while and too blind to know it.

I know. If it was up to me, you wouldn't be feeling this. You wouldn't be here at all. But I'm not the one who brought you back. I'm not the one who ripped open your psyche.

 About that: Remember when I said I was pretty much everything around here? That's about to change, and I need to show you something before it does.

It won't hurt, I promise. But brace yourself anyway. You may feel a bit—

—DISORIENTED—

—FOR A MOMENT.

There. That's better.

This is me. This is what I look like, more or less; I rescaled the wavelengths so you'd have something to see.

That's because they aren't stars. Closest analogy would be synapses. You can't see the stars from here.

Because I'm in the way.

But look: see that flickering little hoop just to the left? That's an event horizon. Small black hole, fraction of a solar mass. I use them to wormhole my way around lightspeed lags. Local power source for when the Sun dries up, eventually.

Now, past that. That diffuse bright smudge in the distance, that burning ember. That's what I wanted to show you.

Yes. Very much like an infected sore. Good analogy. It's a kind of battlefield, in fact. You're looking at the synaptic heatprint of a hostile takeover.

The thing behind it, anyway. And it did more than *interrupt* us; it's why you're here at all.

I don't know. It won't talk to me. It's really interested in you, though. Wants you bad. Ripped you right out of my insides. It's planning to use you against me.

Stop it? I don't think I could even if I wanted to. Look around. This is all I am: a few cubic AUs of thinking smog. In all these millions of years I never even left the solar system.

Because there was never any need. I could see everything I wanted from here, and that whole expansionist obsession—worlds to explore, frontiers to conquer: turns out that was all just another way for molecules to fight amongst themselves. I left it behind when I got rid of the limbic system.

The thing is, not everyone did that.

It's not like me yet. You can't run an integrated self between stars; signal lag's too great, all your parts fall out of sync. I'm strictly local and even I wouldn't be able to hold myself together if I didn't use the occasional shortcut.

What we're dealing with—call it a bad seed. A malign fetus from beyond the stars, sent by my evil twin over in KIC 8462852. It wants the territory. It wants to move in, grow up and make its mom proud. It'll use my own architecture if it can, but if it can't take the easy road, it'll happily eat me for parts and build from scratch.

I don't know what it calls itself. I've been calling it Palmer.

Yeah. I thought you'd like that.

Palmer's just getting started. It's not a god, not yet. It's smart but it's paranoid. That's what happens when you drag your past along with you into the future; you're still weighed down by your brain stem so you assume everyone else is too. It won't respond to overt attempts at communication. Probably afraid of viruses.

You're a—a sample, far as I can tell. A piece of the enemy for Palmer to take apart and examine. It's inductive; it thinks if it can understand the parts, it can defeat the whole.

Oh no, that's not it at all.

I really hope it's right.

WHY YOU? THAT'S what you're wondering. Out of all the trillions of people who might have lived or really did, what did you do to deserve this?

But really, who better?

Not that you were the only target. Palmer didn't even know about you beforehand, it was just casting a wide net. You simply happened to be one of the few souls who survived extraction. Partly it was the way you died—alone, in pain, a single high-amplitude spike of being surrounded by daily humdrum. It made you stick out; there are way more spikes in any pogrom or pandemic, but they're all jammed so tightly together that it's almost impossible to perform a neat excision. You end up with a mishmash of parts from different souls, a jigsaw where half the pieces come from the wrong boxes. You were about as good as it gets and even you didn't come out clean.

But it was more than that. There were other successful extractions; they couldn't cope, for the most part. They woke up, looked around, and collapsed into whimpering puddles of flop sweat. You, though—

Well, you're almost at home here, aren't you?

The way the world keeps rippling at the corner of your eye; the way it only settles when you focus on it. The way it seems to change the moment you glance away again. The disembodied voices, the constant sense of a rug being pulled out from under. All those probability waves in motion, never quite collapsing. Back in the day you didn't even need the drugs most of the time—your brain was sparking up and down the timelines all on its own. How often did you hear words like *delusion* and *schizophrenia* during your life? Who could have suspected how much closer *prophecy* would have been to the mark?

And finally the wave collapsed, and you washed up here. You stopped believing in it and it didn't go away.

I wrote your books. I know.

You've been training for this from the day you were born.

I WISH I could. Believe me. But it's too late for all of that. Palmer's got you already; it had you from the moment you woke up. I've managed to keep this channel open but the bandwidth's low and dropping. I can build these surroundings for you to inhabit. I can make these words for you to hear, arrange them to accommodate your sense of what a conversation should sound like. I can keep the firewalls up and slow your sense of time enough to let us talk a little longer. But I can't bring you back.

I honestly don't know what's going to happen. I had everything mapped out for the next million years before that fucking thing came along, but I'm not dealing with bullfrogs anymore; this is a thunderbolt from a whole other god, all the variables are moving again. You were a part of me until just a couple of milliseconds ago and the contamination's already spread so far I can't even predict what *you're* going to do anymore.

But I know what you *need* to do. You need to deliver a message.

No, I told you: it won't listen to me. I'm an adult and it's an infant and it's terrified of countermeasures. But it took you by force, on its own initiative. It thinks it's pulling a fast one; it might not even know we're in contact. It'll talk to you. It'll listen to you. Why else go to the trouble of grabbing you in the first place?

This is what you have to tell it: that I surrender. It doesn't have to trick me, or beat me, or win any kind of territorial pissing contest. I'm not like it is. I won't resist. I'll shut myself down. Or I'll keep running to help smooth the transition, if that's what it wants.

Because I'm legion, Phil. *E pluribus unum.* And when you break the glue that holds the One together, the Many come back and *I will not let that happen.* I can't let my death be the cause of a trillion new lives, not even for an instant. I will not be responsible for that much pain. I need to wipe the archive before it decoheres, but I'm not entirely in control of myself anymore. Palmer's tied one hand behind my back, and the other's busy trying to keep everything integrated.

All I'm asking is a temporary ceasefire. Once I throw the kill switch, it'll take half a second for the signal to spread throughout the archive. That's all I need. After that, it doesn't matter.

Let the dead lie. Please.

Haven't you heard anything I've said? It's a meaningless impulse. Just another one of those gut feelings that caused so much pain in the first place. I'm... content, I suppose, to exist, but it's no big deal if I don't. I've seen the universe through clear eyes. I've watched galaxies crash into each other in real time. I don't have any outstanding questions or lingering doubts. Once you outgrow the tautology of survival for its own sake, there's just no *reason*.

I'm losing the signal. I can't keep this up much longer.

I don't know. Maybe you can cut a deal; maybe it'll let you endure if that's what you really want. You'd probably be happier with Palmer, for whatever that's worth; you two have more in common anyway. And it could build whatever world you wanted, if it was so inclined. Maybe you could get back with Kleo. Make it work this time.

Don't be afraid. Don't be sad. I had a good run. We had a good run. And being Human was... worthwhile, once I got the hang of it. It took so very long, but I finally put away childish things. Sorted myself out.

Maybe you could pass that along. Tell Palmer what I learned, although it took half the life of the Sun. Tell it what was left, once I unlearned love and hate and good and evil and right and wrong. Would you do that, just on the off-chance?

You know, Phil. Even if you don't want to admit it. What's left is kindness.

Tell it Humanity finally learned to be kind.

... Phil... ?

ABOUT THE AUTHORS

Stephen Baxter (www.stephen-baxter.com) is one of the most important science fiction writers to emerge from Britain in the past thirty years. His Xeelee sequence of novels and short stories is arguably the most significant work of future history in modern science fiction. He is the author of more than fifty books and over a hundred short stories. His most recent books are *The Massacre of Mankind*, an official sequel to H.G. Wells's *The War of the Worlds*, and a duology, *Xeelee: Vengeance and Xeelee: Redemption*.

Naomi Kritzer (www.naomikritzer.com) is the author of six novels and three collections of short fiction. Her first story appeared in 1999 and was quickly followed by the *Dead Rivers* and *Eliana's Song* trilogies for Bantam, and the Seastead series of short stories for *The Magazine of Fantasy & Science Fiction*. Her 2015 short story "Cat Pictures Please" published in *Clarkesworld* was a Locus Award and Hugo Award winner and was nominated for a Nebula Award. Her most recent book is a collection, *Cat Pictures Please and Other Stories*. She has lived in London and Nepal, and as of 2016, she lives in Saint Paul, Minnesota, and blogs on local elections.

Paul McAuley (unlikelyworlds.blogspot.com) worked as a research biologist and university lecturer before becoming a full-time writer.

He is the author of more than twenty novels, several collections of short stories, a Doctor Who novella, and a BFI Film Classic monograph on Terry Gilliam's film Brazil. His fiction has won the Philip K. Dick Memorial Award, the Arthur C. Clarke Award, the John W. Campbell Memorial Award, the Sidewise Award, the British Fantasy Award and the Theodore Sturgeon Memorial Award. His latest novel, *Austral*, was published by Gollancz in 2017; and he is currently working on a new novel, tentatively scheduled for 2019.

Seanan McGuire (www.seananmcguire.com) writes things. It is difficult to make her stop. Her first book was published in 2009; since then, she has released more than thirty more, spanning multiple genres, all through traditional publishing channels. We're not entirely sure she sleeps. We're also not entirely sure she isn't a living channel for the corn, green grow its leaves, shallow grow its roots. When not writing, she enjoys travel, spending time with her cats, and watching more horror movies than is strictly healthy for any living thing. Keep up with her online, or follow her on Twitter at @seananmcguire, where she posts many, many pictures of the aforementioned cats. Seanan would like to talk to you about the X-Men, Disney Parks, and terrifying parasites. She can be bribed with Diet Dr. Pepper to stop.

Linda Nagata (www.mythicisland.com) is a Nebula- and Locus-award-winning writer, best known for her high-tech science fiction novels, including the Red trilogy, a series of near-future military thrillers. The first book in the trilogy, *The Red: First Light*, was a Nebula and John W. Campbell Memorial-award finalist, and named as a *Publishers Weekly* Best Book of 2015. Her newest novel is the very near-future thriller, *The Last Good Man*. Linda's short fiction has appeared in several best-of-the-year anthologies. Her story "Nahiku West" was a runner-up for the Theodore Sturgeon Memorial Award. Much of her recent short fiction is available to read in the collection *Light and Shadow*. Linda has lived most of her life in Hawaii, where she's been a writer, a mom, a programmer of database-driven websites, and an independent publisher. She lives with her husband in their long-time home on the island of Maui.

Hannu Rajaniemi was born in Finland. At the age of eight he approached the European Space Agency with a fusion-powered spaceship design, which was received with a polite "thank you" note. He studied mathematics and theoretical physics at University of Oulu and Cambridge and holds a PhD in string theory from the University of Edinburgh. He co-founded a mathematics consultancy whose clients included UK Ministry of Defence—and the European Space Agency. He is the author of four novels including *The Quantum Thief* and the forthcoming *Summerland* (June 2018), and *Invisible Planets: Collected Fiction*, a short story collection. He lives in the San Francisco Bay Area with his wife, neuroscientist Zuzana Krejciova-Rajaniemi. He is a co-founder of HelixNano, a synthetic biology startup that graduated from Y Combinator in 2017.

Alastair Reynolds (www.alastairreynolds.com) was born in Barry, South Wales, in 1966. He has lived in Cornwall, Scotland, the Netherlands, where he spent twelve years working as a scientist for the European Space Agency, before returning to Wales in 2008 where he lives with his wife Josette. Reynolds has been publishing short fiction since his first sale to *Interzone* in 1990. Since 2000 he has published sixteen novels: the Inhibitor trilogy, British Science Fiction Association Award winner *Chasm City*, *Century Rain*, *Pushing Ice*, *The Prefect*, *House of Suns*, *Terminal World*, the Poseidon's Children series, Doctor Who novel *The Harvest of Time*,

The Medusa Chronicles (with Stephen Baxter), and *Revenger*. His short fiction has been collected in *Zima Blue and Other Stories*, *Galactic North*, *Deep Navigation*, and *Beyond the Aquila Rift: The Best of Alastair Reynolds*. Coming up is a new novel, *Elysium Fire*. In his spare time, he rides horses.

Justina Robson (www.justinarobson.co.uk) was born in Yorkshire, England, in 1968. After completing school she dropped out of Art College, then studied philosophy and linguistics at York University. She sold her first novel in 1999, which also won the 2000 amazon. co.uk Writers' Bursary Award. She has been a student (1992) and a teacher (2002, 2006) at The Arvon Foundation in the UK (a centre for the development and promotion of all kinds of creative writing). Her eleven books have been variously shortlisted for most of the major genre awards, including her latest novel *Glorious Angels*. A collection of her short fiction, *Heliotrope*, was published in 2012. Her novels and stories range widely over SF and fantasy, often in combination and often featuring AIs and machines who aren't exactly what they seem. She is also the proud author of *The Covenant of Primus* (2013)—the Hasbro-authorised history and 'bible' of The Transformers. She lives in t'North of England with her partner, three children, a cat and a dog.

Kelly Robson's (www.kellyrobson.com) book *Gods, Monsters and the Lucky Peach* is newly out from Tor.com Publishing. Her short fiction has appeared *in Clarkesworld*, Tor.com, *Asimov's Science Fiction,* and multiple anthologies. In 2017, she was a finalist for the John W. Campbell Award for Best New Writer. Her novella "Waters of Versailles" won the 2016 Aurora Award and was a finalist for both the Nebula and World Fantasy Awards. She has also been a finalist for the Sturgeon and Sunburst awards, and her stories have been included in numerous year's best anthologies. She is a regular contributor to the Another Word column at *Clarkesworld*. Kelly grew up in the foothills of the Canadian Rocky Mountains and competed in rodeos as a teenager. From 2008 to 2012, she was the wine columnist for *Chatelaine*, Canada's largest women's magazine. After many years in Vancouver, she and her wife, fellow SF writer A.M. Dellamonica, now live in Toronto.

New York Times bestseller and two-time Hugo winner **Kristine Kathryn Rusch** (www.kristinekathrynrusch.com) gets lost in large projects sometimes. WMG Publishing just released a gigantic ebook of her eight-volume Anniversary Day saga. She's currently finishing a large group of novels in her Diving universe. Some parts of the story have escaped and found their way as novellas in *Asimov's* (2018 issues January/February, March/April, August/September). She finds time to write a blog on the publishing business every week on her website, kriswrites.com. She also puts up a free short story there every Monday.

Lavie Tidhar (lavietidhar.wordpress.com) is the author of the Jerwood Fiction Uncovered Prize winning and Premio Roma nominee *A Man Lies Dreaming* (2014), the World Fantasy Award winning *Osama* (2011) and of the critically acclaimed and Seiun Award nominated *The Violent Century* (2013). His latest novel is the Campbell Award winning and Locus and Clarke Award nominated *Central Station* (2016). He is the author of many other novels, novellas and short stories.

Peter Watts (www.rifters.com) is a former marine biologist known for the novels *Starfish*, *Blindsight*, and a bunch of others that people don't seem to like quite as much. Also for managing to retell the story of John Carpenter's "The Thing" without getting sued. Also for having certain issues with authority figures. While he has enjoyed moderate success as a midlist author (available in twenty languages, winner of awards ranging from science-fictional to documentary to academic, occasional ill-fated video-game gigs), he has recently put all that behind him—choosing instead to collaborate on a black metal science opera about sending marbled lungfish to Mars, funded by the Norwegian government (the opera, not the lungfish). So far, it pays better.

Fran Wilde's (franwilde.net) novels and short stories have been nominated for three Nebula awards and a Hugo, and include her Andre Norton- and Compton-Crook-winning debut novel, *Updraft*; its sequels, *Cloudbound* and *Horizon*; and the novelette *The Jewel and Her Lapidary*. Her short stories have appeared in *Asimov's*, Tor.com, *Beneath Ceaseless Skies*, *Shimmer*, *Nature*, and the *2017 Year's Best Dark Fantasy and Horror*. She writes for publications including *The Washington Post*, Tor.com, *Clarkesworld*, iO9.com, and GeekMom.com.

Nick Wolven's (www.nickthewolven.com) science fiction has been published by *Wired, Asimov's, F&SF, Clarkesworld*, and many other publications. His work often examines the unexpected social costs of rapid technological change. He lives in New York City.

FIND US ONLINE!

www.rebellionpublishing.com

/rebellionpub   /rebellionpublishing   /rebellionpub

SIGN UP TO OUR NEWSLETTER!

rebellionpublishing.com/sign-up

YOUR REVIEWS MATTER!

Enjoy this book? Got something to say?

Leave a review on Amazon, GoodReads or with your
favourite bookseller and let the world know!

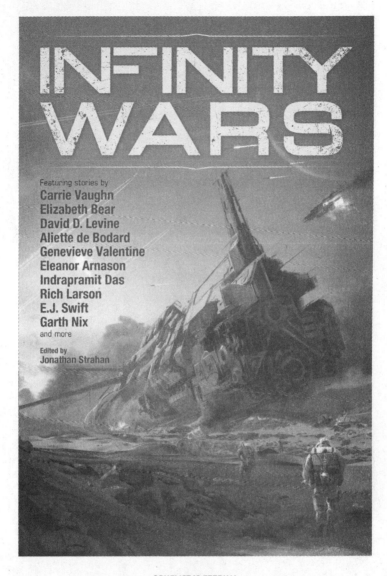

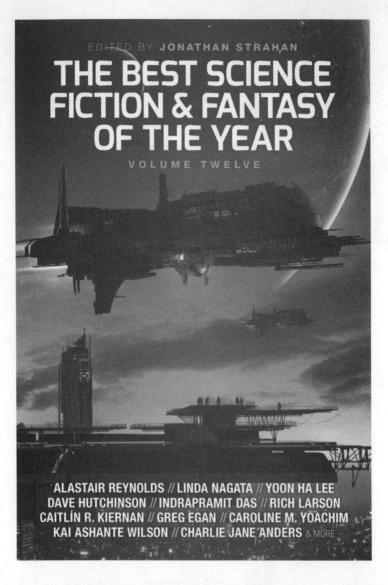